A Christmas Gift

A Christmas Gift

THELMA ALEXANDER   BETTY COTHRAN

STACEY DENNIS   PHOEBE GALLANT

DIANE E. LOCK   LINDA SWIFT

ZEBRA BOOKS
KENSINGTON PUBLISHING CORP.

ZEBRA BOOKS are published by

Kensington Publishing Corp.
850 Third Avenue
New York, NY 10022

First Printing: November, 1995

Printed in the United States of America

CONTENTS

The Perfect Gift

Thelma Alexander

To Lindsey

"Only eleven more days till Chanukah."

Jean Wexler watched with amusement as Carrie, her six-year-old granddaughter, laboriously counted on her fingers, then grabbed her twin sister, Cathy's hand, for the eleventh finger.

"Yes, and I have a lot more shopping to do," their cousin, seven-year-old Ashley, said. "Last week at Sunday school the rabbi told us we should think of gifts that fit the person we're giving them to. So," she added in a self-important tone, "I've spent a lot of time on my list. I want the presents I give to be perfect."

Jean leaned back on the couch. She always enjoyed the monthly Saturday night visit from her three grandchildren. Ashley, her daughter's child, had slept over since she was an infant. Then, when her daughter-in-law had the twins, they, too, joined Jean's once-a-month slumber parties. "What are you getting your mom, Ashley?" Jean inquired.

"I asked Daddy to get an extra set of car keys made for her because she always forgets where she puts them. Once she even locked them in the car."

"What shall we get our mommy?" Carrie asked her twin.

"I know the perfect gift," Ashley offered. "Vitamins. She told my mom you need a lot of energy when you have twins."

Jean smothered a laugh. Trust Ashley to have an idea on anything and everything. But this time the twins didn't go along with her. Cathy shook her head. "Pantyhose," she suggested. "Mommy's always getting runs in them."

Carrie agreed. "Grandma, would you write that down?"

Jean did, then listened as Ashley, always the leader, continued to conduct the discussion. Jean was amazed that the children were so focused on what they were getting for others rather than on what *they* wanted.

"And guess what I'm getting for Grandpa Jonathan," Ashley said.

"What, dear?"

"An electric razor. It's the perfect gift."

"Why is that?" Jean asked.

"Well, he's getting so old, I bet his hands are starting to be shaky, and he might cut himself with that old razor he uses."

Jean smiled. She'd only met Jonathan Klein once, at the wedding of her daughter Sue to his son eight years ago. She remembered a handsome man with laughing brown eyes and a dashing smile. But she supposed, to Ashley, anyone over twelve was ancient.

"Maybe you should get him a pet," Carrie said. "He might be lonesome without your Grandma Ellen."

That was sweet, Jean thought. Jonathan's wife had died eighteen months ago. Jean supposed he must just be getting over the worst of the loneliness and despair. It had taken her that long when Allan had died four years ago, and there were still times when . . . She swallowed the lump in her throat and listened to the girls' conversation.

Ashley shook her head. "I can't get him a dog. He'd have to take it outside. Minnesota's too cold for that. I'm buying him the razor."

End of discussion, Jean thought. Once Ashley had made up her mind, there was no changing it. She wondered if Ashley thought her grandfather was too old to venture out in the snow with a dog.

"Guess what," Ashley said. "Grandpa Jonathan is coming for Chanukah."

"How nice."

"Do they let old people get on the plane first, like children traveling alone?" Ashley asked. She had made a short flight to Dallas to visit a cousin and had been impressed by the attention the airlines paid an unaccompanied child.

"I imagine he can handle the trip without help," Jean said. "Your grandpa isn't that old."

"Oh, yes he is. He's even older than you are."

Jean pulled Ashley into her lap and tickled her. "And what makes you think I'm old?"

"Just teasing," Ashley giggled.

"You're not old, Grandma," Cathy, the family peacemaker, said softly.

Jean let Ashley go and hugged Cathy, then opened her arms to include Carrie in her embrace. She glanced at the clock. "It's getting late. If you girls want a snack before bedtime, I have some milk and chocolate chip cookies."

With eager squeals, they followed her to the breakfast room and helped her set out the snack. "You make the best chocolate chip cookies in the whole wide world," Carrie said.

"Thank you. I have to, because I have the best granddaughters in the whole wide world."

"What will you do, Grandma, when we're teenagers and start having dates? Then we won't be able to have our Saturday night slumber parties," Carrie remarked. "Won't you be lonely?"

"I guess I'll have to adopt some new grandchildren." Jean made her tone light, but Carrie had touched a nerve. One day the girls would be too busy for her. That was as it should be, but she *would* miss the weekends with her beloved granddaughters. She pushed the thought aside. Their adolescence was still a long way off. "We'll have lots of Saturdays together in the meantime," she added.

"We haven't thought of Grandma Jean's gift," Cathy said suddenly.

"That's right," Carrie said. "What do you want?"

"No, don't ask," Ashley said sternly. "We'll think of it ourselves."

"Couldn't she give us a hint?"

"No hints. We'll decide when we're in bed."

"And since you mentioned bed," Jean said, "it's that time."

The girls kissed her good night and trotted off with very little argument. Jean heard them giggling—about her gift, no doubt. She wondered if they thought she needed something for an old person, too, maybe a heating pad. At fifty-three, she certainly didn't feel old. She could still cut a rug with the best of them. Whoops, "cut a rug" had probably been out of fashion for thirty years. Okay, she could boogie with the best of them.

She remembered Sue and Mark's wedding. She'd danced with Jonathan Klein then, and he'd been no slouch on the dance floor either. What would the man say if he knew his granddaughter thought he might need help getting on and off an airplane? Jean chuckled to herself and went to get ready for bed. As she passed the girls' room, she heard another round of giggles and called, "Go to sleep, young ladies."

"We will," Ashley called back. "We've almost decided on your present."

Carrie's laugh turned into a hiccup. "You're gonna love it."

"I'm sure I will. Now, quiet down." She heard a few whispered comments, more titters, then silence.

The next morning at breakfast Carrie piped up. "We picked your gift, Grandma Jean."

"Yeah, it's perfect," Cathy said.

"Shall I guess?"

"You can try," Ashley said, "but you'll never get it."

"Cookie ingredients."

"No."

"A cookbook."

"No way. You already know how to cook."

"A new hat."

Cathy's eyes widened. "You don't have any hats."

"All the more reason to get me a new one."

The little girl considered for a moment, then chuckled. "Oh, Grandma."

"No more guessing. You'll just have to wait and see." Ashley's eyes sparkled. She looked at her cousins and the three of them collapsed into gales of laughter. By the time they stopped, Carrie had the hiccups again.

Jean shook her head as she went into the kitchen to get her granddaughter a glass of water. Whatever gift those three little monkeys had in mind, it was certain to be clever and she was bound to love it.

Jean stood before her mirror, fastening an earring. She was due at Sue and Mark's house in twenty minutes to celebrate the first night of Chanukah, and she was running late. When the telephone rang, she was tempted to ignore it, but even though she kept the answering machine on, she'd never been able to ignore a ringing phone. She picked it up. "Hello."

"Grandma," Ashley sounded breathless, "are you ready to come over?"

"I'll be on my way in a minute. Does Mom need me to bring something?"

"No, I just called to—" She giggled, then she must have put her hand over the receiver because Jean heard muffled words and more giggles. "—to see what you're wearing."

Jean glanced down at her outfit and wondered why in the world Ashley wanted to know. "My rust-colored pantsuit and a cream-colored blouse. Why?"

"Oh, Grandma, this is a holiday. Why don't you wear that pretty blue dress with the gold buttons?"

"I'm already dressed. If I change, I'll be late."

"No, you won't. Daddy called a minute ago and said he was just leaving his office, so you have time."

"Sweetie, the blue is too dressy. This is a family get-together—"

"Puh-lease," Ashley wheedled.

How could she resist? "Okay."

"Yeah! See you. Oh, and be sure and wear those dangly gold earrings." Before Ashley hung up, Jean heard an excited whisper of, "She's doing it. She's wearing the dress and the earrings, too." Then, in the background, she heard a man's voice that sounded suspiciously like Mark, Ashley's father. But Ashley had said he was going to be late. What did that little imp have up her sleeve?

Jean put down the phone and opened her closet. Maybe the kids had gotten her a scarf to go with the dress. She quickly changed her outfit, earrings included. She was becoming a pushover in her old age, she told herself. On the other hand, Ashley could probably talk a macho little boy into buying a Barbie doll. She'd be working for the State Department someday. Most likely, she'd be running the State Department.

Jean checked herself in the mirror, then put on her coat and gloves. Outside, she shivered. An Arctic cold front had moved into Houston earlier in the afternoon, and the temperature was dropping rapidly. Of course, to Grandpa Jonathan, this thirty-degree weather must seem like spring. Thinking of Jonathan Klein made Jean glad she'd worn the blue dress. He was an attractive man, and though she wasn't looking for someone to fill Allan's shoes, she liked to look her best.

"Jean. Oh, Jean." Jean turned at the sound of her name. Trudy Meyers, her next door neighbor, stood in her doorway, bundled up in a hooded jacket, waving.

"Hi, Trudy."

"The delivery service tried to drop a package off for you this afternoon. I told them I'd keep it for you. Come in a minute, and I'll get it."

"Thanks." Jean crossed the yard and followed her neighbor inside.

"I have it in the kitchen. It's from Los Angeles. Isn't that where your sister lives?"

Jean nodded. She sat down to wait for

Trudy. In a moment, the woman reappeared with the box. She squinted at Jean as she handed it over. "I see you're all dressed up. Are you going to your daughter's for Chanukah or your son's?"

"To Sue's."

"Well, that's nice. That little daughter of hers is going to be a beauty. I noticed the last time she came over."

Jean smiled. Trudy noticed everything. Keeping up with the comings and goings in the neighborhood was her occupation. Jean often thought if the CIA needed a seventy-two-year-old busybody, they couldn't do any better than Trudy Meyers. Jean thanked Trudy and left, wondering if Trudy had figured out a way to sneak a look inside the package

Ten minutes later, she pulled up in front of Sue and Mark's house and gathered the spinach casserole and the bag of Chanukah presents she'd brought. She hurried up the sidewalk, her breath frosting in the chilly air. Through the lighted living room windows she could see one of the twins jumping up and down. Jean rang the bell and her son-in-law answered the door.

"Mom," he said, taking the casserole from her, "you're late. We were getting worried. Is everything okay?"

Before she could tell Mark that Ashley had told her *he* was running late, the imp herself appeared at the door. "Daddy, Mommy says for you to come in the kitchen. I'll help Grandma with those gifts."

Jean decided not to say anything yet to Ashley about her obvious fib. She followed her granddaughter into the living room.

The living room was decorated with blue and white crepe paper streamers and a banner that read Happy Chanukah. The silver menorah already held the first candle as well as the *shamash,* the helper candle, that would be used to light it. Mouthwatering aromas floated in from the kitchen. Turkey, Jean noted, and *latkes.* It wouldn't be Chanukah without the traditional potato pancakes.

Jean greeted her family, then turned as Jonathan Klein rose from his chair. He certainly didn't look like someone who needed help on an airplane. He appeared handsome, fit, and amazingly youthful for a man who had to be in his mid-fifties. When Jean gazed closely at him though, she saw lines of sadness around his mouth and eyes. Only someone who'd also grieved for a spouse would recognize them.

"Jean, it's good to see you." He enveloped her hand with his.

Grip still firm registered in Jean's brain. Ashley didn't have to worry about her grandfather. The man looked as if he could handle a razor or anything else. "I'm sorry about your loss," she told him quietly and saw his eyes cloud with pain.

"Thank you. I appreciated your letter." Then he smiled and the sorrowful expression disappeared.

She sat next to him on the couch, and Ashley, who had been arranging Jean's presents on the corner table, scooted in between them. "Grandpa's going to teach me to play Parchesi," she said, patting Jonathan's knee. "And poker."

"Watch out for her," Jean warned him. "I taught her Go Fish when she was three, and she never loses a game. By the way, Ashley," she added, "your daddy seems to have made it here before me."

Ashley's cheeks reddened for a moment, then she tossed her head. "I told you a white lie, but I had a reason. You'll see later, when you get your present."

"I hope so. I don't approve of lies, even white ones."

Ashley nodded, her hazel eyes wide and guileless. Then she reached up to toy with Jean's earring. "I'm glad you wore the dangly earrings. They're so pretty. And so's your dress. Don't you think so, Grandpa?"

Jean blushed as Jonathan's brown eyes made a leisurely journey from her throat to her knees. "Very pretty," he murmured.

"See? You'll be glad you changed," Ashley said.

The rascal had managed to divert Jean's attention and her grandfather's, too, from the "white lie." Jonathan's eyes were still focused on Jean's legs. She resisted the urge to smooth her dress down over her knees.

She was relieved when Sue appeared in the doorway. "Dinner's just about ready. Shall we light the Chanukah candles?"

They all gathered around the menorah. "Dad, will you do the honors?" Mark asked, offering the *shamash* to Jonathan.

Everyone was quiet as he said the three blessings for the first night of the eight-day holiday in a deep, melodious voice. When he recited the third prayer, "Blessed art Thou, Oh, Lord our God, King of the Universe, Who has kept us in life and sustained us and enabled us to reach this season," Jean saw again the glint of sadness in his eyes. Again, it disappeared quickly as they all joined in hugs and good wishes.

"Can we open our presents?" Carrie asked.

"After dinner."

They adjourned to the dining room, where a feast awaited them—turkey, dressing, salad, Jean's spinach casserole, which had been part of their holiday tradition since her kids were small, and of course, crisp potato *latkes* accompanied by sour cream and applesauce.

Jean sat between Jonathan and Alicia, her

son Neil's wife and the mother of the twins. Surreptitiously, she glanced at Jonathan Klein. He was an exceptionally handsome man. His hair was thick and slightly wavy, and his hairline hadn't receded a millimeter. His cheek showed a hint of five o'clock shadow, which Jean had always thought was sexy. He had strong features and long, dark eyelashes a woman would kill for. Nice hands, too—

"Grandma." Cathy's voice held unaccustomed annoyance.

"Yes, honey."

"Pass the applesauce, please." From Cathy's tone, Jean guessed she'd asked several times.

"Sorry. Here you are." Inwardly, she admonished herself for staring dreamily at Jonathan and paying no attention to the conversation. Nevertheless, she had to admit she found him attractive. When his shoulder brushed against hers, she felt a pleasant tingling.

He turned to her. "What are you doing these days? I remember when we met before, you were thinking of opening a shop. Handmade items, wasn't it?"

She nodded, surprised he'd remembered. "But those plans were put on hold when Allan got sick. After he died, I was pretty exhausted. I wasn't ready to undertake a full-scale business, so I began freelancing.

I make sweaters and other knitted goods and sell them through several stores. I also fill special orders."

He smiled at her. "Maybe while I'm here, I'll stop by and order a sweater."

She imagined measuring the width of his shoulders and, to her embarrassment, blushed again. She seldom reacted this way. She enjoyed the company of men but no relationship had gone past friendship in the four years she'd been alone. Why did this man make her go all shivery inside? Had that happened when she met him at the wedding? He must have made an impression, because she remembered so many details about him. She'd liked him and found him easy to talk to, but she hadn't experienced this rush of awareness. Well, of course not. They were both married then. Now, things were different.

She realized she was daydreaming again and pulled herself back to attention. "How long will you be in town?" she asked Jonathan.

"I may stay a few days after Chanukah is over," he said. "I've rented a car and I may drive out west. Arizona is great this time of year, and not much goes on in the home-building business in Minnesota."

They continued talking through the meal and dessert, a flaky apple pie. Sue brought coffee, but the children became increasingly restless, their eyes straying toward the living room and the waiting presents. At last Mark pushed his chair back. "Anyone want to open presents?"

Three shouts of "Me, me!" gave him his answer, and they went back into the living room. The two small candles in the menorah had burned down, leaving the odors of candle wax and smoke, smells that Jean forever associated with Chanukah.

Mark began passing out packages. Jean watched with amusement as the girls' gifts were bestowed on their parents. The twins had indeed bought pantyhose for their mother and a spelling dictionary for their father, a notoriously bad speller. Sue received the extra set of car keys, and Mark several pairs of socks, each with an extra, "Because he's always losing one sock," Ashley explained.

"I am not. The washing machine eats them."

"Oh, Daddy," she said, rolling her eyes.

Mark reached for a thin package wrapped in blue Chanukah wrap and decorated with a lop-sided silver bow. "Here's one for you, Moth—"

"Oh, that's from us," Ashley interrupted. "Save it till last. You can give Grandpa his."

Jonathan was suitably impressed with the new razor. Fortunately, Ashley didn't mention her reasons for choosing it.

Gradually the pile of presents grew smaller until only one was left. "Mom," Mark said and handed Jean the gift.

She turned it over in her hands. There was no box, just something flat, like a piece of paper.

"Hurry and open it," Cathy begged.

"I'm trying to figure out what it is," Jean said. "Hmm." Not a scarf. Not pantyhose, though she ran hers often, too. Maybe a gift certificate. She glanced at Jonathan and hoped it wouldn't be for something embarrassing like a girdle or one of those new push-up bras.

Carrie jumped up and down. "Come on, Grandma."

Jean gave in. "Okay." She tore off the wrap and found an envelope with her name printed on the front in careful second-grade script. She opened it and pulled out a sheet of paper.

She glanced at it. It wasn't a gift certificate. It was . . .

She pulled her glasses out of her purse, put them on, and read it over. Then she looked up. "I . . ." Her voice came out in a squeak. She cleared her throat and tried again. "Girls, what is this?"

Ashley grinned broadly. "It's the perfect gift. See? We signed you up with Select Seniors Dating Service. We're going to find you a husband."

Dead silence.

Jean's cheeks flamed. All the adults stared at her, their expressions running the gamut from shock to amusement. She glanced through her lashes at Jonathan, who sat across from her. Immediately, he looked down and began studiously examining the new razor.

"A . . . a husband?" she asked with another squeak. "What gave you that idea?"

"The other night when we talked 'bout when we'd get to be teenagers and wouldn't spend our Saturday nights with you, you looked awfully sad," Cathy explained in her soft voice. "We don't want you to be lonesome, so we're getting you someone to keep you company."

"Besides," Carrie put in, "we want a new grandpa." She glanced at Jonathan, realized she'd committed a *faux pas,* and quickly added, "I mean, Cathy and me want a new one. Ashley has you, Grandpa Jonathan, but both of *our* grandpas died and . . ."

"It's okay," Ashley said. "I want two of them."

Jean stared at the paper in her hand. The girls were cute, and she was touched that they'd been sensitive to her emotions the other night. Of course, she didn't want to hurt their feelings. She'd tell them a white lie, the kind she'd warned Ashley never to tell. She'd bury the paper, say she'd met a few men, and everyone would be happy. She slipped the membership certificate into her purse.

"Wait," Ashley said. "There's more."

"Lots more," Carrie said, pirouetting in excitement.

"Lots more?" Jean gulped. Somehow she had a feeling she wasn't going to like this.

"Let me explain it to her." Ashley, as usual, took over. "You've been all alone for a long time, Grandma Jean, and we didn't want you to have to wait for years to find the right husband. So we got you some to choose from."

"To choose from," Jean muttered. She seemed unable to come up with a statement of her own. So they had a pre-selected assortment for her. Were they going to stage their own version of *The Dating Game*? *Suitor number one, what's your favorite way to end a date?* "You have a list?" she finally managed. If they did, she'd lose it along with the certificate.

Ashley shook her head. "We thought four would be a good number to start with, so we made four dates for you—"

"One every night, starting tonight," Carrie interjected.

"Uh-huh. Mr. Rose, your first date, should be here any minute," Ashley finished.

Jonathan Klein put his hand over his mouth and began to cough. If she could have reached that far, Jean would have ground her heel into his instep. She knew a disguised laugh when she heard one. The rat probably thought she couldn't get a date on her own. She certainly could; she just didn't want one. At least not from a computer dating service. She glanced at the stunned faces around her, and telegraphed an urgent message to her children: *Help me out, one of you.*

"Just a minute, Ashley," Mark said sternly. "How did you arrange all this?"

"Norene helped us. We looked over the pictures together and Norene called in the ones we picked."

"Norene helped you?" Sue choked. "You mean Norene, your babysitter? That nice teenager I *trusted* until this very minute? How . . . how . . . ?"

"How did you get her to do it?" Alicia said.

Ashley batted her lashes. "Sweet-talked her."

"I always knew you were a con-artist," Sue muttered. "But wait till I get my hands on Norene. I'll fix her good."

Not if I get my hands on her first, Jean thought. *There won't be anything left of her!*

"Look, girls—"

The doorbell rang.

Jean jumped.

"I bet that's Mr. Rose," Ashley said with

a broad smile. Then she lowered her voice. "Listen, Grandma, if you don't like the first four dates, we have four more picked out."

"More," Jean croaked as the bell chimed again.

Everyone seemed frozen in place. Finally Jonathan asked, "Is anyone going to answer the door?"

Not me, Jean thought. Her legs had turned to stone.

"I'll get it," Mark said, then paused. "Mom? What shall I say to him?"

"Tell him I'll be right with him." She couldn't embarrass a man who'd gone to the trouble of planning an evening with her. She pulled herself to her feet. "Sue, may I see you a minute before I leave?" She headed for the coat closet with Sue trailing along behind her.

"Honestly, Mother, I had no idea—"

"Of course, you didn't. But you'd better think of a way to get me out of this without disappointing the children. Tell them the other dates were abducted by aliens, tell them *I* was abducted by aliens, tell them anything, but rescue me."

"I'll take care of it. I'll ask Neil to drive your car home. Um, have a good time."

Jean shot her a lethal look and turned toward the entry hall where her fate, in the person of Mr. Rose, awaited. One glance at him convinced her that Fate was not kind.

One glance almost had her spinning around and making a break for it.

Her escort was a good two inches shorter than she . . . and Jean was only five-four. He was completely bald, his head shining like a flesh-colored bowling ball beneath the entry light. Jean knew it was silly and shallow of her to find baldness so unattractive, but that was one of her quirks, obviously one unknown to her granddaughters.

Mr. Rose wore a suit and tie that had been in style, perhaps ten years ago. Maybe he hadn't been on a date in that long. Jean found herself softening toward him as his cheeks turned scarlet and he lifted his hand to fiddle with the end of his tie. She'd have to make the evening bearable for both of them.

"Mom, this is Sidney Rose," Mark said.

"Hello, it's nice to meet you," Jean said in her most cheerful voice. She sounded like a kindergarten teacher, she realized. *Hi there. We're going to have fun. Want to come in and play with the nice blocks?*

"How do you do." Sidney offered a hand. *Limp as a dead fish.* She shook his hand quickly, then dropped it.

"Mr. Rose, would you like to come in for a drink first?" Mark invited, obviously trying to come to Jean's aid.

"No thank you," Sidney said quickly, then gulped and looked uneasily at Jean, his fingers clutching convulsively at his tie. "Un . . . unless you'd rather . . ."

She coughed. Maybe if she feigned a cold, she could get the evening over with as quickly as possible. "No, I don't want to spread any more germs to the children." Another white lie, but who was counting? She wiggled her fingers at Mark in a good-bye wave and reached for the door.

"Oh, let me," Sidney said, almost stumbling in his haste to hold it for her.

Jean took a deep breath as they walked silently toward Sidney's car. She hadn't had a blind date since she was fifteen and now she knew why. Come to think of it, the only difference between Sidney and her last blind date was that Sidney didn't have adolescent acne. And, unless Sue saved her from a fate worse than death, she had three more nights of this. No, that was impossible, she decided as Sidney opened the car door and she got in. Even a city the size of Houston couldn't have three more Sidneys. She'd already hit rock bottom. The only way to go, if she had to go any way at all, was up.

"Where would you like to go?" Sidney inquired.

Home. "How about a movie?" That would keep them occupied for most of the evening as well as providing a topic for conversation afterward.

He turned to her with an eager smile. *"Galaxy Raiders, Four* is at the Meyer Park theater."

Yuck! Sci-fi wasn't Jean's thing. She'd never seen a *Galaxy Raiders* film, nor had she ever intended, too, but, *Whatever turns you on, Sid.* "That sounds great," she said, forcing enthusiasm.

Once they had settled on the movie, Sidney lapsed into silence. Jean resorted to questions, one after another in rapid-fire interview fashion. Where was he from, where did he live, how long had he been in Houston—all of which he answered in monosyllables. She was grateful when they pulled into the movie theater's parking lot. She would soon be asking him the name of his dentist, his favorite color, and what he ate for breakfast.

Galaxy Raiders was absurd. Jean didn't know the characters, missed the inside jokes, and had trouble following the senseless plot line. Several times she caught herself nodding off to sleep.

Afterward, Sidney suggested a cup of coffee. To her surprise, he took her to Cafe Bueno, a charming coffee house with a selection of delicious gourmet coffees. On the way, however, they exhausted the topic of the movie.

Desperate for something else to talk

about while they sipped their coffee, Jean asked, "What sort of work do you do?"

Sidney's eyes lit up. "I write Unix software."

For a change Sidney's nervous hands were still. She'd hit on something, Jean decided. "Really?" She tried to sound interested. "What is Unix?"

"It's a multi-user operating system."

"What does that mean?"

"It means that a CPU can handle multiple users and multiple tasks."

"Ah."

She didn't have to ask any more questions. Sidney took over the conversation, expounding on the advantages of Unix over DOS, whatever that meant. He then spoke at length about his passion for computers, his eyes glittering, his gestures now so broad he almost knocked over his coffee cup. His conversation was incomprehensible to her, but she didn't try to stop him, just injected an "Uh-huh" or "Is that so?" every now and then. He enthused for nearly an hour while Jean's eyelids grew heavy and her mind grew mushy.

At last the waitress appeared at their table. "We're closing, sir."

Sidney flushed. "Oh, I'm sorry. The time got away from me." He handed her some bills, and they left.

Jean smothered yawns during the ten-

minute drive to her house while Sidney continued his discourse on the uses of Unix on
the Internet. At her door, he took her hand
and pressed it warmly. "This was a . . . a
wonderful evening. I . . . I feel so fortunate
that we share the same interests. May I call
you?"

"Well, ah, yes, but I'm . . . out of town
a lot and when I'm here I . . . um, babysit
my grandchildren." Another white lie.
Added together, did they constitute a black
one?

Sidney seemed to take her evasion as a
yes. "Next week," he said, smiling at her.
Then he squeezed her hand. "Wonderful,"
he breathed and scurried off.

Jean dragged herself into the living room
and sank down on the couch. She'd have no
trouble relying on her answering machine to
deal with Sidney's calls. Because she was sure
he was going to call. She'd unleashed a sil-
ver-tongued monster with that question
about his work, and she was afraid it wasn't
going to disappear.

"Oh, Lord," she murmured. First thing
tomorrow, she would call Sue and make
sure the rest of the dates were canceled.

The doorbell rang, and Jonathan strolled
into the living room to answer it. Jean, bundled up in a winter coat, her cheeks rosy

from the cold, stood on the porch. He broke into a smile. He'd been thinking about her ever since she'd left last night. "Come in."

"Thanks," she said, pulling off her gloves and tossing her coat on the couch. "Is Sue around? I called earlier, but no one answered."

"Sue took Ashley to a mother-daughter holiday party for her Brownie troop, and I went out for a jog," he said, sitting across from her.

"Do you know if she got in touch with the dating service?"

Jean wasn't going to like this. "I'm afraid not," he said, keeping his expression serious though he longed to grin at her dilemma. "Their line was out of order."

"Oh, no." She dropped her head into her hands. "I hope Ashley has the name of tonight's date so I can call him and cancel."

He chuckled. "Last night wasn't the date of your dreams, huh?"

She shook her head. "Among other things, we had a communication problem. I speak English; he speaks computerese."

Jonathan threw back his head and laughed. "You have my sympathy. The computer brotherhood is a fraternity I've never aspired to join. I know enough to run my business efficiently, nothing more."

"Good. Then we can talk to each other."

"I hope so," he said, holding her gaze

until a blush rose in her cheeks and she looked away. He'd seen her blush several times, and he found it charming. He found *her* charming. Pretty, too. She had honey-blond hair, a shade darker than Ashley's, deep blue eyes and a wide smile. For the first time since Ellen had died, he felt his blood stir.

His thoughts were interrupted by the sound of the door opening. Ashley bounded in, threw her arms around him, and gave him a smacking kiss on the cheek. Then she noticed Jean and turned to her expectantly. "Grandma, how was your date? Did you fall in love with Mr. Rose?"

Jean caught Jonathan's eye, and they exchanged an amused glance, then she said, "No, honey. He's, um, nice, but I'm afraid Mr. Rose isn't grandfather material."

For a moment, Ashley looked disappointed, then her face brightened. "You'll have another chance tonight and tomorrow. There's always tomorrow." She giggled and burst into the song from *Annie*.

"Ashley," Jean said, then raised her voice. "Ashley! Would you stop dancing a minute. Tonight's date—what's his name?"

"Mr. Berger. Gary Berger."

"Thanks. I want to call him."

The idea crossed Jonathan's mind that if she canceled her date for the evening, *he* could take her somewhere.

The back door opened and shut, and Sue came into the living room. "Hi, Mom. I tried to call—"

"I know, but don't worry. I'm going to phone Mr. Berger."

"But you can't, Grandma," Ashley said, stopping Jean as she half-rose from her chair.

"Why not?" Jean said, her expression ominous.

"He's out of town on business. He won't be back until tonight."

Jean muttered something Jonathan couldn't hear, then her eyes lit up. "After all that traveling, he'll probably be too tired for an evening out. I'll leave a message on his machine—"

"Oh, don't worry." Ashley fished through the candy dish on the coffee table and came up with a peppermint. "He said he's used to traveling. He'll just come straight from the airport and spend the evening with us at Aunt Alicia's." With a wave over her shoulder, Ashley skipped out of the room.

Jean groaned.

Jonathan leaned forward. "Why don't I take you to lunch, get your mind off your . . . predicament?"

"Thank you. I'd like that. There's a deli a few minutes from here."

When they were on their way, he said,

"You have to appreciate the humor in this dating situation."

Her brows shot up. "Would you?"

He thought about that. Successful and therefore eligible, he'd been accosted by women almost from the day Ellen died. Being in demand socially had provided an alternative to nights when he'd felt overwhelmed by grief and loneliness, but a dating service? He wasn't sure how he'd feel about that. "I might find the idea amusing," he ventured.

"Oh, the idea is cute, but you'd soon see that living it out wouldn't be fun, especially if you met a female Sidney." She chuckled. "There are times when our mutual granddaughter is too smart for her own good and everyone else's. Too bad she didn't sign you up, too. We could have double dated."

"I don't think so." He'd rather take Jean out himself, spend an evening discovering what sort of things put the sparkle in those deep blue eyes, exploring common interests . . . touching her. Her skin looked soft, her hair fine and silky. And that perfume she wore—some exotic, come-hither scent that titillated his senses.

He remembered dancing with her at Mark and Sue's wedding. She'd worn one of those mother-of-the-bride numbers—lacy with a full-length skirt and long sleeves in some kind of rosy color. Though he'd never had a yen for women other than his wife, he remembered studying the curve of Jean's jaw, the way the light played across her honey-colored hair, accentuating the golden highlights.

Suddenly the loneliness that came over him at unexpected times engulfed him, the ache almost too much to bear. He had to restrain himself from pulling to the side of the street and hauling Jean against him. He wanted someone, needed someone to hold, to bury himself in, to make that stunning void disappear. He gripped the steering wheel to keep his hands from trembling.

"The deli's in that shopping center," Jean said in such a normal voice that he stared at her, surprised his emotions hadn't been obvious.

He pulled into the parking lot, and by the time he found a space and come around to open Jean's door, the feeling had passed.

But he still wanted to touch her.

He settled for taking her elbow and guiding her inside. The smell of corned beef met his nostrils, and he realized he was hungry. They slid into a booth near the back and gave their orders.

"Tell me about Minnesota," Jean said. "How do you spend your time?"

"It's beautiful. We . . . *I*" he corrected, "have a home on Whitefish Lake. I don't have much time in the summer because that's the construction season, but I try to get up there for at least *a* week and hang around, fish, take the boat out. In the winter, I go ice fishing." Jean laughed, and he asked, "What's funny?"

"Ashley was worrying the other day if the winters in Minnesota were too cold for someone of . . . ah, our generation, and here you are, out ice fishing."

Jonathan chuckled. "Then she certainly wouldn't believe this: I'm thinking of trying out mushing."

Jean looked puzzled. "Mushing? What's that?"

"Sled dog racing. I forgot you're a Southerner."

"Sounds exciting."

"I'll let you know," he said. "I've taken up painting in the last year, too."

"So you paint scenes of the lake?"

He nodded. "I never thought I'd enjoy painting, but it's . . . satisfying. It's helped me deal with losing Ellen. In the winter," he continued, "I go up to the cabin more often. The lake's frozen, it's quiet and beautiful. You'll have to come up sometime with Sue and Mark," he added, surprised at himself for issuing the invitation.

"I'd like that. Allan and I rented a cottage on Lake Travis near Austin a couple of times. I'm sorry we didn't do more of that." She sipped her coffee. "I'm surprised you didn't spend the holidays at your cabin."

"I wanted to be with family."

Their eyes met, and Jean nodded. "I understand. Being alone is hard at first."

"Does the loneliness ever go away?" he asked, annoyed at himself for the question and for the bleak sound of his voice.

"Not entirely, but keeping busy helps, and you're certainly doing that." She looked up as the waiter arrived with their sandwiches, then said, "What kind of homes do you build?"

"Custom-designed," he said, picking up his sandwich.

"Have any pictures?"

He reached into his wallet and pulled out several. "How'd you guess I'd have pictures?"

"Oh, I imagine homes that you build are sort of like children. You give birth to them, and even when they're off on their own, so to speak, you still feel a kinship."

"You're absolutely right." He grinned at her. "Is that how you feel about your sweaters?"

"Oh, of course. You know," she said with a laugh, "that's really true. On the few occasions when I've run into someone wearing one of my sweaters, I want to check them out to be sure they're giving it a good home."

"How'd you get into the knitting business?" Jonathan asked.

"I started when I was pregnant with Neil. Most of my friends were expecting, too, and everyone was settling in, feeling domestic, so we all took up knitting. I'm the only one who stuck with it."

"Will you ever open that shop?"

"I don't think so. I'm happy with things as they are."

"You look like a happy person," he said, gazing at her thoughtfully. She had a spring to her step, an easy smile. And she was pleasant to be around.

"I am happy . . . most of the time," she said. "I still have low moments, on anniversaries or other special occasions, but mostly I do just fine."

"What do you do for fun?"

"Read, travel when I can, exercise. I go to jazzercise regularly. Last year the kids gave me a wonderful picture of a line of very chubby ladies in leotards. The title was 'Jazzercise Class.' "

"*You* are not a chubby lady."

"Ah, but that's because jazzercise keeps me in shape and allows me the pleasure of an occasional corned beef sandwich."

She'd probably never had a spare ounce of fat, he thought, admiring her slender frame. "What else do you do in your spare time?"

"Go to the theater or the ballet. Oh, that reminds me, Ashley is feeling a bit jealous because Alicia and Neil are taking the twins to Disney World, so I promised her we'd see *The Nutcracker* day after tomorrow. I'd better call for tickets as soon as I get home."

"Do you think Ashley would mind if her grandfather tagged along?"

Jean's lips curved into a charming smile. "I think she'd be delighted."

Jonathan wanted to ask if Ashley's grandmother would be delighted, too, but he held his peace. The question seemed premature.

They continued talking. He told Jean about his involvement in a group dedicated to preserving the ecology of the lakes and wilderness areas in Minnesota and nearby states, his enjoyment of backpacking and camping. "Do you like the outdoors?" he asked her.

"I don't know," she said, surprising him. In his experience, women wanting to impress men, at least in the short run, said yes. He'd met an attractive woman who'd enthused about her love of the great outdoors, then reacted in horror to every insect on a simple picnic. But Jean shrugged her shoulders and continued, "I haven't had much experience with the outdoors in recent years. I loved it when I was a kid though. Some of my happiest memories are of Girl Scout hikes and canoe trips. I've looked into a women's adventure tour for next summer. The idea of river rafting or backpacking in the mountains sounds appealing. On the other hand,

I went skiing once." She shook her head ruefully. "Once too often. I looked like I was playing a role in something like *The Marx Brothers at Sun Valley.*"

"I tried skiing once, too," Jonathan confessed. "I broke my ankle."

Their laughter was interrupted by the waiter with their check, and they soon left the restaurant. On the way back to their car they passed a toy store. Jonathan prevailed upon Jean to help him pick out gifts for the twins. Then they wandered into a bookstore where they browsed and compared notes on books they'd read.

By the time they parted company, the afternoon was half over. Jonathan strolled into the house, whistling. He realized he felt better than he had in nearly two years. He was also aware that he was looking forward to the evening and the chance to see Jean again.

"Damn!" He came to a halt, remembering that Jean's date for the evening—Gary Berger, was that his name?—was supposed to join them. No, that wouldn't be a problem. A fellow who had to resort to a dating service to meet women would probably turn out to be another Sidney.

Gary Berger was gorgeous. Tall, with wavy black hair, classic features, cleft chin, and dark brown eyes that were positively mesmerizing. Jean's heart gave a little leap when she opened the door and saw him. Her first thought was that this must be a mistake; the man was at the wrong house. *She* was expecting a Sidney clone. But the stranger broke into a smile. "You must be Jean." He took her hand and shook it warmly. "I'm Gary Berger."

"We, uh, have a full house tonight," she warned, wondering if he might feel uncomfortable spending a holiday evening with his date's extended family.

But he kept smiling. "Lead me to them," he said with what appeared to be sincere enthusiasm. "I've been looking forward to this evening."

Jean ushered him into the living room and introduced him around. She was surprised that Jonathan, who had seemed so cordial up to now, gave Berger only a brusque nod, but she wasn't inclined to worry about it. She led Gary to the sofa and sat between him and her son Neil. "I understand you've been traveling," Jean said.

He nodded. "Just in from Frankfurt."

"Really? What took you there?"

"I'm an importer," Gary answered. "I do business in Europe and the Far East. I've been traveling through Germany, Bavaria mostly."

"You and my son here have something in

common then," Jean said. "Neil's in international law."

"We'll have to talk sometime," Gary told him.

"I'd like that." Neil beamed as he always did when someone showed an interest in his work.

Ashley, who had been watching Gary intently, sidled closer and said, "What's Bavaria?"

"Well, my dear, it's a part of Germany—full of beautiful forests and castles that look like they belong in a fairy tale," he answered, and for the next half hour he kept the entire group enthralled with descriptions of Munich, the Black Forest, and other places he'd visited.

Alicia appeared in the doorway. "We'll be bringing on the *latkes* in just a minute," she announced.

Jean glanced toward the kitchen. "I should help her," she murmured.

"Go right ahead," Gary said. "I'd like to ask your son his opinion on the World Trade Agreement."

When Jean returned from her stint in the kitchen, Gary and Neil were deep in conversation, but as soon as he saw her, Gary rose, smiling, and escorted her to the dining room where the menorah stood on the buffet. When the candle lighting ceremony was over, he pulled out her chair and seated her. It had been a long time since a man had paid her those little attentions, and Jean felt like a princess.

While they ate, Gary continued to charm the family with more stories of his travels. He even captivated the children. Cathy, normally shy with strangers, listened wide-eyed to his conversation and asked, "Do you have any granddaughters?"

"No, I'm sorry to say I don't," Gary told her. "But I'd like a granddaughter, especially if she looked like you."

Cathy broke into a beatific smile and Ashley nodded her approval.

Only Jonathan looked displeased. From the other end of the table, he glowered at Gary throughout the meal. Maybe, Jean thought, Jonathan's mood was the result of loneliness. Holidays were always difficult when you'd lost a spouse, and he probably felt like odd man out tonight. She resolved to include him in the after-dinner conversation.

After the *latkes*, which Gary pronounced superb, the children received their gifts for the second night of the holiday, then Gary suggested that he and Jean take over kitchen duty. "I hope you don't mind," he told her as they cleared the table. "I wanted to have you to myself for awhile."

How could a woman not be enchanted by a remark like that? "I don't mind at all."

"I feel fortunate this evening," Gary went

on. "Computer dating can be . . . disappointing."

No kidding. "I'm surprised you indulge in it," Jean said. Gary certainly looked like a man who didn't need to resort to a dating service.

"It's efficient," he explained. "Since I travel so much, I don't have time for singles groups. The dating service gives me a way to get around that." He began arranging plates in the dishwasher. "I'm surprised you belong," he continued. "An attractive woman like you must have plenty of escorts."

"Well, actually—" Jean told him the story of her Chanukah present.

He chuckled. "Children always surprise you, don't they?"

"Yes, they're a joy to have around."

From the living room came the sound of Carrie's voice whining, "She broke my toy and now she won't share," then Cathy's indignant, "No, I didn't."

"On the other hand," Jean said with a grin, "sometimes I'm glad I'm the grandparent instead of the parent."

"Amen to that," Gary said.

Jonathan scowled at the laughter coming from the kitchen. Far from being another Sidney, Gary Berger was the fiftysomething version of a hunk, entirely *too* good-looking and suave to suit Jonathan's taste. Too smooth, also. And Jean, damn her, was lapping it up. She'd blushed a good twenty times already this evening.

Why was Berger signed up with a dating service anyway? Why wasn't he out in a bar somewhere, picking up chicks? Probably had a hidden agenda. He was probably a con artist who bilked wealthy widows for all they were worth. That'd serve Jean right, he thought nastily and was immediately horrified at his idea. *Jealousy is disgusting, Klein.*

What right did he have to be jealous? Lunch at the deli did not qualify him as Jean's significant other. And he wasn't going to have much chance to remedy that the way Ashley—Damn that cute little meddler!—had every evening of Jean's time scheduled.

She and Berger came back into the living room and sat together on the love seat. Berger stretched his arm across the back and toyed with the ends of Jean's hair.

Trying not to be obvious, Jonathan scrutinized her. She looked happy. Too happy. Her eyes sparkled, her cheeks were flushed. The damn Romeo hadn't kissed her in the kitchen, had he?

Berger's eyes met Jonathan's. "We haven't had a chance to talk. You're Ashley's grandpa, right?"

The way he said "grandpa" made Jonathan feel like he was eighty years old and hobbling about with a cane. "Yes."

"So, where are you from?"

"Minnesota."

"Really." Berger seemed fascinated with that fact. "I've never been there."

Of course not, Jonathan thought crossly. *No castles in Minnesota. No fairy tale.*

"I've always wanted to visit that part of the country," Berger continued. "Tell me, what's it like?"

"Cold."

"Jonathan has a cabin on one of the lakes." Jean was obviously trying to prod him into chatting with Berger.

Jonathan sighed and nodded.

"Wonderful," Berger enthused. "I wish I had the time to relax."

Meaning you're a big businessman.

"Catch anything on your lake?" Berger asked.

"Fish." Jonathan rose. "Excuse me."

He'd had about as much of the smooth-talking Berger as he could stomach. He went out the back door and stood on the patio, gazing into the darkness. The night was chilly and he hadn't brought a jacket out with him, but he didn't want to go back inside. He hugged himself and looked up at the stars.

He wished Jean were beside him. He

wanted to hold her close; he wanted to explore that beautiful mouth, run his hands through the silk of her hair. For the first time since Ellen's death, he was attracted to a woman. And he'd spent the last two hours watching another man cozy up to her. He sighed and leaned against the house. He'd given up smoking years ago, but suddenly he wished he had a cigarette.

God, he hadn't felt this lonely in months. You didn't appreciate love and companionship until they were taken away. He'd always thought he'd cherished Ellen, but he hadn't. Not enough. He should have told her he loved her every day. Too late now.

From behind him, Jonathan heard the door open. "Dad." It was Mark. "Are you okay?"

"Sure. It was stuffy in there."

Mark stood beside him and rested his hand on Jonathan's shoulder. "Missing Mom?"

"A little. The holidays are tough."

"Yeah, I know. I'm glad you came."

"So am I, son." They stood for a few more moments, each lost in thought, then Jonathan suggested they go in.

When they returned to the living room, Jean and Gary were gone. "I think they wanted to be by themselves for a while," Alicia said with a sly smile.

Jonathan was both relieved and annoyed.

He wouldn't have to keep watching Gary Berger ooze charm, but he wasn't pleased with the idea that Berger now had Jean off somewhere, all to himself.

"He seemed nice," Sue said. "Maybe this dating service business wasn't such a bad idea."

"I agree," Neil said.

Jonathan didn't, but he didn't say so. He stared at a picture on the wall.

"You see," Ashley gloated. She twirled across the living room. "I bet Grandma Jean falls in love with Mr. Berger."

God forbid, Jonathan thought.

"Oh, honey. Don't get your hopes up," Sue said. "People don't fall in love in one night."

"Cinderella and Prince Charming did," Carrie said.

"Yes, but that's a fairy tale."

"Mr. Berger said he came from a fairy tale."

"Not exactly," Sue said. "And don't you girls hassle your grandmother about Mr. Berger."

Ashley sniffed, insulted. "Of course not. We'd *never* do that."

"Grandma, are you going to marry Mr. Berger?" Ashley latched onto Jean the moment she arrived the next night. "Can we call him Grandpa Gary?"

Sue clutched her forehead in dismay.

"Sweetheart, give me a little time." But Jean's mouth curved in a secret smile.

Jonathan's eyes fastened on her as she crossed one ankle over the other. Tonight she wore a gray flared skirt with a soft rose-colored sweater that brought out the glow in her cheeks and gave him a tantalizing glimpse of the curve of her breasts. He'd thought of her all last night, imagining himself in Berger's place, then wondering where in the hell Berger had taken her . . . and what he'd done when they got home.

"Are you going to see him again, Mom?" Sue asked.

Jean shrugged. "If he asks me."

That shrug didn't fool Jonathan. She was dying for Berger to call, he thought darkly. Good Lord, he was behaving like a kid with his first crush.

"What's on for tonight, Ashley?" Mark inquired.

"Let's see." She fished a crumpled sheet of paper from her pocket and consulted it. "Mr. Barry Jacobs is coming by at seven." She peered at the new watch she'd gotten for Chanukah. "It's seven-ten."

"Are you sure, Ashley?" Mark said.

"Daddy, you *know* I can tell time."

"I imagine Mr. Jacobs will be here soon," Jean said.

But seven-thirty passed, then seven-forty-five, and Mr. Jacobs didn't appear, nor did he call. At eight Jean said, "Well, folks, looks like I've been stood up."

Jonathan got to his feet. "Why don't *we* go out somewhere?"

"Thank you," Jean said. "That's thoughtful of you, but I don't mind staying home."

"Nonsense," Jonathan said. This was a golden opportunity and he wouldn't be talked out of it. "You're all dressed up, and I haven't seen much of Houston. Let's go out on the town."

She smiled. "Okay."

He drew a relieved breath. "I'll get our jackets."

Mark followed as Jonathan went to the entry closet. "Dad, it was . . . gallant of you to step in. I think Jean was disappointed."

Jonathan grunted in reply. He wasn't being gallant. Selfish was more like it. He'd seized on the chance to have a private evening with Jean.

In the car she asked, "Where would you like to go?"

"Is there a quiet spot where we can have a drink and talk, maybe dance?"

"I know just the place."

They went to The Penthouse, a club on the rooftop of a downtown hotel, with small, intimate tables, dim lighting, and a woman in a slinky dress playing old romantic tunes on a grand piano. Houston spread out below them, its lights twinkling like holiday ornaments. Above them, a sliver of moon and a myriad of stars decorated the night sky.

Over wine, they talked. About their lives, their accomplishments, the dreams they hadn't yet realized. So many of their ideas and experiences were similar, they discovered—involvement in their communities, closeness to their children, even their love of travel. They congratulated each other on Sue and Mark's successful marriage, chuckled over Ashley's antics, speculated about what she'd be like in years to come.

He asked Jean to dance, and to the strains of "Stardust," he held her close, then closer, his arms around her and his cheek against hers. "I remember dancing with you at Sue and Mark's wedding," he murmured.

"Do you? I remember, too."

" 'The Anniversary Waltz.' "

"Yes," she laughed.

"You're wearing the same perfume you did then."

She drew back and stared up at him. "You remember my perfume?"

"Mmm-hmm. And your dress."

"You've seen it every time you looked at the wedding pictures."

"I remember the row of buttons down the back."

"That, too?"

"I remember . . . everything." When her eyes widened, he repeated, "Everything," surprised that was true. He'd liked her then but hadn't been aware of the strong attraction he felt now. Nevertheless, it had to have been there, below the surface.

"I remember, too," she murmured. "You had a mustache then."

"Also in the pictures."

"You lost one of your cufflinks right before the ceremony," she said dreamily, leaning her cheek against his again.

"I was nervous. I dropped it."

"One of the bridesmaids fastened your cuff with a safety pin. You told me while we were dancing."

"Yes." He pulled her closer. She seemed made for his arms. He didn't want to let her go, but the pianist took a break, and they wandered back to their seats. Jonathan reached across the table, captured her hand, and brought it to his lips. "I'm glad Barry Jacobs didn't show."

"Me, too."

"Jean, something's happening here," he said softly.

"I . . . I know, but it's happening too fast. Your . . . your wife just died."

"It's been almost two years."

"Yes, but we . . . we don't know each other very well."

"We can remedy that," he said with a smile. "Can you think of a way to get out of date number four?"

"No, but if we bribe Ashley, she probably can."

He grinned at her. "Consider it done."

He signaled for the check, and they left the club. He kept his arm around her in the elevator and as they walked to the car. On the way home, he held her hand.

At her door, he asked, "May I come in?"

She shook her head. "It's too soon, Jonathan. If you do . . ."

"You're probably right," he agreed. "A goodnight kiss then."

She tilted her head and he put his arms around her and covered her lips with his. So sweet, so soft. He kissed her gently, afraid he wouldn't be able to stop. His head swam, his blood pounded in his ears. Not enough. Not nearly enough. But he let her go.

Her lips were parted, her eyes unfocused. "G-good night, Jonathan," she whispered.

"Good night. I'll call you in the morning."

Jean leaned against the door, listening to the sound of Jonathan's receding footsteps.

She was trembling, she saw with surprise, as she lifted her fingers to her lips. She could still taste him, still feel the pressure of his hands on her back.

Amazed that her legs could function, she went into her bedroom and got ready for bed. She took a nightgown out of the drawer, but instead of putting it on, she stood naked in front of the full-length mirror on her closet door.

Her face was flushed. Her nipples were rigid. She touched one and felt a tingling sensation. She brushed her hand over her breast, and desire curled deep within her, making her breath catch, her muscles go slack. It had been so long, so very long, and now . . .

She glanced at her bed. If Jonathan hadn't let her go when he did, she'd have brought him here, made love with him. How could this be happening so quickly? How could this be happening at all?

She expected to lie awake all night, thinking about the evening, but she slept deeply and dreamlessly. When she woke the next morning, she wondered if she'd imagined the whole thing. The romantic setting last night, the love songs in the background, the wine, could have caused all those crazy feelings. When she saw Jonathan again in the sober light of day, she'd undoubtedly feel nothing at all.

She got out her knitting supplies, flipped on the radio and found her favorite classical station. She worked on her spring line, fashioning a baby-blue short-sleeved sweater sprinkled with pastel flowers. Caught up in her work, she soon convinced herself that the interlude with Jonathan was no more than a figment of her imagination.

The phone rang, and she picked it up. "Hello."

"Good morning."

She'd been fooling herself. The moment she heard his voice, the feelings from last evening returned full force. "Good morning," she managed around the catch in her throat. "H-how are you?"

"Fine, and I'm pleased to report, mission accomplished. I convinced Ashley to break your date for tonight."

"You must be a born diplomat. Few people can talk Ashley into anything. How'd you do it?"

"I appealed to her self-interest. I told her you might have to leave the ballet early if you had to get ready for a date."

"That was good thinking."

"Yeah, but she drives a hard bargain. She agreed to cancel, but since you won't have to hurry home, she wants to go to Hamburger Heaven for dinner."

"That rascal. What did you tell her?"

"What do you think? Yes, of course."

Jean laughed. "I'll see you later."

"I'm looking forward to it," he said, his voice deepening, and Jean felt a flutter in her stomach.

She spent a long time choosing her outfit for the ballet. She wanted to look nice for Jonathan, but not overdressed. She finally picked a light wool dress in soft blue that showed off her figure. She checked herself in the mirror, pleased that she'd retained her youthful slimness. Her cheeks glowed with color, her eyes sparkled with excitement. She looked like . . . like a woman falling in love.

Before that thought could sink in, the doorbell rang. Her heart leapt as she went to answer. Her emotions were as tangled as a new skein of yarn.

Jonathan stood in the doorway for a moment, his eyes sweeping over her, his gaze caressing her. "You look beautiful," he murmured.

Beside him, Ashley rocked back on her heels. She wore a cinnamon-colored coat with a velvet collar. White lacy leotards covered her legs, and sunlight reflected off her black patent Mary Janes. "Get your coat, Grandma. We don't want to be late."

Jonathan took it from her and helped her on with it, his hands lingering on her shoulders. No, Jean thought, she'd imagined nothing last night. Those feelings were deliciously, frighteningly real.

The Wortham Center had been transformed into a child's vision of fairyland for the annual Christmas presentation of "The Nutcracker." On a table in the foyer was a huge gingerbread house decorated with candy canes and cookies, tables held nutcrackers of all sizes for sale, and inside, the curtain displayed a snowy wonderland surrounded by Christmas greens. Ashley exclaimed over it in excitement.

All around them proud parents and grandparents shepherded little girls in velvet and satin, little boys in suits and ties to the plush red seats. Jean and Jonathan sat with Ashley between them.

The wooden soldiers battled the rats, the Sugar Plum Fairy pirouetted. Although Jean was captivated as always by the familiar music, the flawless performance and the magic of the tale, she couldn't help stealing surreptitious looks at Jonathan, couldn't help noticing the curl of his hair, the firmness of his jaw, the curve of his lips. He turned once and met her eyes, and she sat transfixed for a long moment, unable to look away. The rest of the ballet was lost on Jean. Her mind stayed firmly on Jonathan.

"Wasn't it wonderful?" Ashley sighed as they left. "I liked the Snow Queen best, and the Russian dancer."

"I liked everything," Jean told her. She knew, in part, that was due to Jonathan's presence.

Afterward, they slid into a booth at Hamburger Heaven. The juke box blared something by the latest "in" group, children giggled and shouted, and noisy groups of teenagers called to one another. "This place is so cool," Ashley said approvingly.

"Is it?" Jonathan asked with a wry smile.

Ashley studied him over her burger. "Well, you may be a little old to appreciate it."

"I guess you're right," he said. "Maybe your grandmother could recommend—or better yet, maybe she could show me—a place more appropriate for an older person." He glanced at Jean.

"I believe I could."

"Tomorrow night?"

She nodded.

"But, Grandma," Ashley protested, her lips curling into a pout, "what about the other dates? You didn't go out last night or tonight and we still have four more gentlemen for you. How will you find a husband if you don't have the dates?"

Not the dates again, Jean thought. She wanted to spend time with Jonathan, not some boring stranger. "Um, Ashley, your grandfather is a guest, and when we have company, we want to spend time with them,

show them around the city. I won't forget
about the dates. We'll just postpone them,
okay?"

Mollified, Ashley agreed. They finished
their meal and walked back to the car with
Ashley skipping between them, holding
both their hands, chattering about the four
"reserve dates." Jean wondered if any man
on Ashley's list would compare to Jonathan,
then told herself she was foolish to compare. Jonathan was a temporary diversion
after all.

She went back to Sue and Mark's for candle lighting and coffee. Ashley insisted on
riding along when Jonathan took Jean
home, and truthfully, she was relieved. She
wasn't sure what might happen if she were
alone with him.

"There's a Neil Simon play at the Alley
Theater," she told him as he walked her to
the door. "It's gotten great reviews. Would
you like to go after dinner tomorrow?"

"I'd like that very much."

So would she. Too much, Jean thought a
few minutes later as she shut the door and
trudged down the hall to her room. In a couple of days Jonathan would leave, then what?
Unfortunately, she had no answer to that.

They had dinner at Gerard's, a quiet, elegant restaurant that served continental

food. Afterward, Jean couldn't have said what food she'd eaten or what wine she'd drunk. Like a glutton, she'd feasted on the sight and sound of Jonathan, imbibed his every word.

At the theater, they were close enough for her to smell his cologne, feel the texture of his clothing as his arm brushed hers.

At intermission they went out on the balcony and looked at the stars. They didn't talk. There seemed to be no need.

When the play was over, they strolled through the underground garage, laughing over the plot, reprising the funnier lines. He told her about a Neil Simon play he'd seen in Minneapolis, and they talked about their favorite playwrights.

Jonathan parked in front of her house and came around to open her door. He laced his fingers through hers. "May I come in?"

"Yes." She hadn't known beforehand what she would say. This was a dangerous step, she knew, but they had so little time left together. She didn't want to lose a moment of it. They went inside.

"I'll make some coffee," she said briskly.

He followed her to the kitchen and leaned against the counter, watching as she filled the percolator and heated a coffee cake.

They could sit in the kitchen; keeping the

table between them would be safer. But she felt reckless. She got out a tray. "I'll bring this in the den," she said. "There's wood in the fireplace."

"I'll get the fire started."

He'd already done that with his kiss last night. *Slow down*, Jean ordered herself. *Act your age.*

A few minutes later, when she brought the coffee and cake into the room, she found Jonathan kneeling at the hearth. He'd removed his jacket and rolled up his shirt sleeves. He looked at home in her den.

She set the tray down on the coffee table. He turned to her and patted a spot on the floor. "Let's sit in front of the fire."

Jean sat next to him, and handed him a cup. She stared into the flickering flames as she sipped her coffee. "We rarely have weather cold enough for a fire. This is nice."

"Then you'd like Minnesota."

"Tell me about your life there." She wanted to be able to picture him when he was gone, to visualize him in a tangible place, doing something specific. She needed that, she realized, feeling a pang of loneliness even before he left.

"It's a quiet life, but a good one," he said, setting his cup down. "I get up early, jog every morning. Neither sleet nor snow or anything else keeps me from the track."

"You jog when it's snowing? I'm impressed."

"Well, actually my club has an indoor track."

"An honest man," she laughed.

"But I only use it when it's icy out."

As he continued talking, Jean leaned back against the table, hugging her legs. She liked the sound of his voice. They talked about her life, too, about Jonathan's other two children, about Chanukahs past when their children were small. There were endless things to talk about, to laugh about, to learn about one another.

The coffee cooled. The fire burned down, and Jonathan added more wood. They moved to the couch. He put his arm around her, and it seemed natural to lean against him.

They sat in companionable silence and Jean realized she enjoyed the quiet between them as much as the conversation. She felt as if she'd known this man forever.

Then Jonathan turned to her and took her face between his hands. "Jean," he murmured. "Jean."

She closed her eyes and parted her lips, inviting his kiss.

It was tender, achingly sweet. Slow and thorough—a gentle pressure and retreat, a leisurely tracing of her lips with his tongue, then a foray into her mouth to meet her tongue tip, back away, and advance until her own tongue joined his in a rhythmic prelude to the act of love. And all the while, his hands caressing her back, her shoulders, her throat, awakened and aroused her.

He shifted so that he cradled her in his lap. She lay pliant in his arms until he unbuttoned her dress, opened the front clasp of her bra, and kissed her breast.

Heat shot through her, bright as lightning, fierce as thunder. She gave a strangled cry and pulled him closer.

His tongue swept over her, then he drew her nipple into his mouth.

Her hand fisted in his hair, her other hand clutched him to her. "Jonathan," she gasped. "Oh God, please."

"Please, what?" His breath caressed her skin.

"Please, more."

"Yes," he whispered. He took her nipple again, deeper this time.

She couldn't lie still. A wave of energy, wild and erotic, pulsed through her. Her hands raced over him, feeling the stubble of his beard, the silk of his hair, the beat of his heart. She sat up, struggled with his buttons, craving him against her, skin to skin. She tugged his shirt open . . .

The telephone rang.

Jean gasped, disoriented, uncertain what to do. Then the answering machine in the kitchen picked up and she heard Trudy's voice. "Jean. *Jean.*" The next words were indistinct, then, "I'm calling the constable."

"Oh, Lord." Jean struggled out of Jonathan's arms, jumped up and ran to answer. She seized the receiver but it fell from her shaking hand and slammed against the wall. "Damn!" she whispered, dizzy with desire and frustration. She grabbed it again. "H-hello."

"Jean. Thank God."

"What's wrong, Trudy?" she said, trying not to snap. She tucked the receiver under her chin and jerked at her gaping dress, holding it closed as if Trudy could see her through the wire.

"I see a strange car parked in front of your house. It's been there a while. I think you should call the constable. Have you seen any strangers lurking around?"

Half-angry, half-amused, Jean bit her lip. "It's all right, Trudy. I have company."

"Oh?" Trudy waited a beat, undoubtedly hoping to hear who the company was, then when Jean didn't supply the information, she continued. "Well, I didn't see any lights on in your living room . . . ?"

"We're in the den at the back." *Half-undressed and fully aroused, at least we were.*

"Oh, well, thank goodness. I told Harold I always worry about you, all alone. Well, dear, I'll let you get back to your guests."

"Good night, Trudy." With a sigh, Jean replaced the receiver. With trembling hands, she fastened her bra and dress. The spell was broken. What had she been thinking of anyway? She'd been ready to jump into bed with . . . with Sue's father-in-law!

"Everything okay?" Jonathan rose as she entered the den.

Jean sighed. "Just my neighbor checking up."

He went to her and took her arm, urging her toward the couch. "Come here."

She slipped from his grasp. "No, I . . . ."

His brows furrowed. "What's wrong?" he asked softly.

"Nothing." Her voice shook. "I . . . I can't do this."

He took her chin in his hand. "Can't do what? Kiss me?"

Jean jerked away. "It was more than kissing, Jonathan, and you know it."

"And you're upset," he murmured, then glanced around the room, his eyes lighting on a family picture on the bookshelf. "Why, Jean? Because of your husband?"

"No."

"Did your neighbor say something?"

She shook her head, not wanting to speak. Tears were close to the surface.

"Then—"

"Let it go, Jonathan."

"All right." He began buttoning his shirt. "I will, for tonight. I'll call you tomorrow."

Automatically, she followed him to the door. When he'd gone, she went back to the den, picked up the tray with their coffee cups and carried it into the kitchen. She stared out the kitchen window at her neighbors' house.

She didn't know whether to thank Trudy for the phone call or toss a rock through her window. Thank her probably, she decided, as she put the cups in the dishwasher. Trudy had saved her from what could be a very embarrassing situation. A holiday fling with someone she'd never see again was one thing. An affair with Jonathan Klein was something else. Jonathan was not somebody she'd never have to see again. How would she feel, meeting him on future Chanukahs, at Ashley's Bat Mitzvah, at family gatherings, remembering they'd once slept together?

A tear slid down Jean's cheek. She'd gotten involved with the wrong man.

While Jean was having a second cup of coffee the next morning, Sue called, as she usually did. After the usual exchange of pleasantries, she said, "Mother, I want to thank you for being so nice to Jonathan. I know you're busy with your spring orders, and I appreciate your taking the time to show him around the city."

"Nonsense, dear. I was glad to do it." Let Sue think she'd simply been hospitable.

"You know, he's been so lonely since Ellen died."

"Yes, I understand." Jean took a sip of coffee and leaned back.

"I think being here has been good for him," Sue went on. Then she chuckled. "Not that he didn't have some interesting offers for the holidays."

"Oh?"

"Yes, you know how some women are. They throw themselves at any eligible man."

"Yes, I know." A picture of herself writhing in Jonathan's arms, pleading with him for "more, please, more" flashed in Jean's mind. Her face heated.

"One woman invited him on a cruise— her treat—for Chanukah. Isn't that wild?"

"Wild."

"But he said he'd rather spend the time with family than with a love-starved woman. We got a laugh out of that."

"I imagine so." *Please, more.* She put her hand to her burning cheeks. God, she wanted to hide.

Sue continued talking, blithely unaware of Jean's distress. "We're thinking of taking in a movie tonight. Would you like to join us?"

"Um, I don't think so. I'm pretty busy. In fact, I'd better get back to work."

"I'll call you later in case you change your mind."

Jean hung up and dropped her head in her hands. Love-starved! That's probably what Jonathan thought of her now—groping, grabbing, practically begging him to make love to her. Join the family for a movie tonight? Like heck. She wished she'd never have to see Jonathan again. She wished she could disappear.

She imagined Jonathan telling his other son in Minnesota about the love-starved woman in Houston. Would they have a laugh about her? She got up and yanked the dishwasher open, dumped her coffee cup inside, and shoved the rack in so hard that the dishes rattled.

The ring of the phone startled her. *I'll call you tomorrow.* "Don't let it be Jonathan," she muttered, picking up the receiver.

"Jean, good morning."

It wasn't Jonathan, thanks heavens, but who . . . ?

"This is Gary Berger."

"Oh, sorry, I didn't recognize your voice. How are you?"

"Fine. I'm calling from New York. I'll be in Houston in a couple of hours. I know it's short notice, but how would you like to have dinner tonight?"

The perfect alternative to seeing Jonathan. The ideal excuse—she had a date. "I'd love to."

"I'll pick you up at eight. We'll do the town."

"Great." She didn't care if they went to Hamburger Heaven. Any place where Jonathan was not present would be fine.

She took out her knitting and tried to work, but she kept dropping stitches. Finally she gave up and went grocery shopping.

An hour later, as she staggered in from the supermarket with two heavy sacks in her arms, she heard the phone. Monica's Boutique had promised to call today to place their spring order. She set the sacks on the kitchen table and picked up the receiver. "Good morning."

It was Jonathan. She sat down, suddenly breathless. "Um, good morning."

"I want to see you." His voice was soft, intimate, persuasive.

I want to see you, too. But the memory of Sue's conversation made the words stick in her throat. "Ah, I don't think I can today. I . . . uh . . . have deliveries to make."

"What about tonight?"

God, she wanted to see him. She closed her eyes and took a deep breath. "I . . . uh . . . can't."

"Jean," he said, "tell me what's wrong."

She sighed. "The truth is, things got out of hand last night and I think we should . . . uh . . ."

"Slow down?"

"Yes," she agreed.

"I can handle that and still see you," Jonathan said.

"I don't think so."

"Are you saying you can't?"

"Of course not," she snapped. "I'm saying we need to back off. Besides, I have plans tonight."

"The fourth man," he muttered.

"No, the second." The moment the words were out of her mouth, she knew she'd made a mistake.

"Gary Berger." Jonathan's voice was low, angry. His next words were almost inaudible, but they sounded like, "The sleaze."

"Yes. No!" He had no right to call Gary a sleaze. He had no right to be angry. Would he be mad if the love-starved widow invited another man on the cruise?

"Tomorrow, then," he said, leaving the subject of Gary.

"Jona—"

"I'll be leaving in a couple of days. I don't want to go without talking things out. Please."

"All right."

"I'll see you tomorrow," he said. "I'll be over in the morning."

* * *

Ashley held Jonathan's hand, skipping along beside him, as they left the movie. "Wasn't the show great, Grandpa? Didn't you love it?"

"Mmm-hmm." Where were Jean and Gary Berger?

"I'm sorry Grandma Jean couldn't come with us, aren't you?"

"Ashley, your grandmother had a date, remember?" Mark pointed out. "She went out with Mr. Berger."

Jonathan scowled. *Mr. Ham-berger.* That's what the guy was, a ham.

"I think I'm getting a new grandpa," Ashley exulted.

"Don't get ahead of yourself, honey. She just went out with him," Sue said. "Still . . ."

Jonathan's scowl deepened. Had she told Sue she was interested in Berger?

"Mommy, can we get ice cream? It's school vacation, so I can stay up late."

"Why not?" Sue said.

"Grandpa Jonathan, what kind of ice cream do you like?"

"Mmm-hmm." Couldn't Jean see through Berger's slick sophistication? The guy was all flash and no substance.

Ashley's giggle got his attention. "Oh, Grandpa, you silly. 'Mmm-hmm' isn't a flavor." She giggled again. "Didn't you hear me?"

"I guess not. What did you say?"

"What kind of ice cream do you like?"

Jonathan shrugged. "Any kind, I guess."

"You're sure a grumpy grandpa tonight. Grumpy grandpa," she repeated, pleased with the phrase.

He *was* grumpy. "Sorry, honey. I had something on my mind."

Sue looked concerned. "Maybe we should skip the ice cream, Ashley. Your grandfather looks tired."

"No, no," Jonathan said. "We should *not* skip the ice cream." As they drove to the ice cream store of Ashley's choice, he wondered, as he had all day, where things had gone wrong between him and Jean. He'd find out tomorrow, get everything straightened out.

At the ice cream parlor, he forced himself to order a dish of butter pecan, joke with Ashley, and pay attention to Sue and Mark's conversation, but his heart wasn't in it. Jean had taken over his heart *and* his mind. Damn it, he was in love with her.

At the thought, Jonathan choked on his ice cream. He began to cough. For a moment, he couldn't get his breath. *Great, Klein. Keel over before you can tell her how you feel.*

"Dad," Mark said, "are you all right?"

Jonathan nodded and wiped the tears from his eyes. He'd frightened his son. After so recently losing his mother, Mark was understandably nervous about something happening to his father as well. "I'm . . . fine," Jonathan assured him.

But he wasn't. He was in shock. He'd never thought he'd fall in love again, especially not so soon after Ellen's death. But here he was, unmistakably, unremittingly in love. And the woman who'd stolen his heart was out with another man.

Jean glanced around the restaurant and stifled a yawn as she waited for dessert. She was bored.

She'd told herself all day that she was looking forward to her evening with Gary Berger. She'd *insisted* she was looking forward to it. Why not? They'd had an enjoyable time the other night. Gary was an interesting, charming, attractive man. More importantly, he lived in Houston, not Minnesota; therefore, he was available for future evenings.

But she'd been bored from the first. When she'd opened the door and he'd handed her a rose. When he'd complimented her on her outfit. When he'd remarked on the weather. In an effort to be congenial, she'd asked what he'd been doing in New York.

"I was on my way back from London. You know, London at the holiday season beats any other city in the world." He'd proceeded to describe the festivities in detail.

He took her to Le Rendezvous, Houston's current "in" restaurant. This was Jean's first visit. With decor somewhere between flash and opulence, the place reminded her of a high-class bordello.

The maitre d' recognized Gary. So did the wine steward, with whom he had an extended conversation about the merits of the wine he'd selected. He sent it back, chose another, and pronounced it adequate.

During the meal, Gary continued his description of London. Jean began to feel sleepy. She told herself it was the wine. Then he moved on to Paris and Madrid. She'd never cared for travelogues, and Gary seemed to be a walking American Express brochure.

One of the features that made Le Rendezvous popular was its dance floor. "Shall we?" Gary asked when they finished their entrees.

Jean nodded gladly. Maybe the activity would wake her up.

Gary's style on the dance floor was flamboyant—fancy footwork, dips, and twirls. He held her close, too close. Jean usually enjoyed dancing, but not tonight. Gary was hard to follow, and she was half-asleep anyhow. She stumbled, and he frowned.

"Concentrate," he directed. "Give it more . . . *passion.*"

Jean felt she was facing some sort of test and not passing. Struggling to catch her breath, she was tempted to back off and let Gary dance alone. He'd probably never notice. He was the show; she was just a backdrop. She was relieved when the musicians finally took a break.

Back at their table, the waiter hovered with the dessert menu. "Baked Alaska for two," Gary decided without consulting her.

At last two waiters arrived with the dessert. It was a showpiece. Of course. What else would she expect from Gary?

"I think I'd better get home," she said as soon as she finished.

"But the night is young," Gary protested. *What a cliche.* Actually, he was a walking cliche, a parody of every man-about-town in every movie she'd ever seen. "I'm a working woman," she explained.

"Oh, I didn't know."

He should know, she thought. This was the second evening they'd spent together. But Gary Berger was only interested in himself.

He drove her home, expounding on Le Rendezvous and other restaurants he'd visited around the world. She stared out the window and wondered if Gary would kiss her good night. If she was really love-starved, she decided, then his kiss should be as exciting as Jonathan's.

It wasn't.

It was moist and messy, annoying rather than arousing. As soon as Jean closed the door behind Gary, she hurried into the bathroom and grabbed the mouthwash. "Well, what have you learned tonight?" she asked her reflection after gargling vigorously. That Gary Berger won the prize as the most arrogant, self-centered man she'd ever met. No wonder he belonged to a dating service.

She'd also learned she wasn't a love-starved female. Instead, she was . . . Oh, God, she was in love with Jonathan Klein. "And what are you going to do about that?" she asked the face in the mirror.

Her reflection had no answer, but she'd better decide soon because in a few days Jonathan would be gone.

"Jean! Yoo-hoo, Jee-ean!"

"Good morning, Trudy." Jean straightened from picking up her newspaper and turned to greet her neighbor.

Trudy wore a turquoise warm-up suit and tennis shoes. Her gray hair was windblown, her cheeks pink. She'd been out for her daily jog, which Jean suspected was as much an opportunity to check up on the neighbors as it was exercise. Still, it kept Trudy in good shape. For a woman in her seventies, she looked great.

"Your friend Marsha Levy stopped by after you left yesterday," Trudy said, slightly breathless from her jog. "I ran into her as I was putting out the trash for today's pickup. She wanted to drop off some raffle tickets you're supposed to sell for the Jewish Community Center. I told her I'd give them to you today, that I didn't think you'd be home soon because you'd gone out with a very attractive man." She dug in her pants pocket and extracted a book of raffle tickets, handed them over, then stood waiting, with an expectant look on her face. She undoubtedly wanted the scoop on the attractive man.

"Would you like to buy a raffle ticket?" Jean asked.

Trudy's face fell. "Of course. I'll bring you a check later. Will you be home?"

"Yes, I—"

"Oh, you have company," Trudy's voice rose with excitement. "Another handsome man."

Jean swung around. Jonathan!

He got out of the car and strode toward them. Jean's heart began to pound.

"Good morning," he said.

"Hi." Having no choice, she introduced Jonathan and Trudy.

"Klein, Klein," Trudy murmured. "Isn't that . . . ?"

"Jonathan is my son-in-law Mark's father," Jean explained.

"Oh, you're part of the family." Trudy looked disappointed. "Well, I'll be on my way. You two have a nice visit." She headed toward her house.

Jean turned back to Jonathan and took a breath. "Come inside. Would you like some coffee?"

"I'd like to talk," he said, holding the front door open for her.

His words brought forth a flutter of nerves, but she hid her anxiety beneath a veneer of good manners. "Let me take your jacket." She hung it in the entry closet. He went into the den, and when she came in, he was seated on the sofa. "Are you sure I can't get you something to—"

"Jean." He rose and took her arm. "Come and sit down."

She let him lead her to the couch, then pulled her arm away. "Wh-what did you want to talk about?"

"Us."

She raised her eyes to his. "Is there an 'us,' Jonathan? How can there be? You're leaving in two days."

He stared at her intently, his expression serious. "I thought something was happening between us. What went wrong?"

He hadn't answered her question, so she asked another. "What do you mean, 'something was happening?' Do you mean that we almost went to bed together?"

"Ah, Jean," he said, "it was more than that, and we both know it."

"Was it?" The anger and embarrassment she'd felt during her conversation with Sue came flooding back. "Was it?" she repeated. "Or am I just another name to add to your list of love-starved widows?"

His eyes went blank. "What are you talking about?"

"Sue repeated your comment to her about the love-starved women who throw themselves at you, who invite you on cruises." Unable to sit, she jumped up, stalked to the window and stared out. "Well, believe me, I'm not love-starved. I don't fall all over men, you included. The other night was . . . a mistake." Tears suddenly welled in her eyes and she bit her lip. She stared into the back yard, not seeing anything, fighting to control her emotions.

"Jean." He spoke from directly behind her. When she said nothing, he put his hands on her shoulders. "Jean, turn around. Please."

She hesitated, then faced him.

"The other night wasn't a mistake for me."

"Please, Jonathan, don't feel you have to appease me. I—"

He put his finger to her lips. "Shh. Listen to me, Jean. I don't know what Sue told you about the woman who invited me on the cruise. Yes, she's been chasing me, but in no way would I compare her with you. As for calling her 'love-starved,' I never used that phrase. You heard Sue's interpretation. And as for us, if anyone is love-starved in this case, it's me."

Jean stared into his dark brown eyes. What she saw there made her catch her breath. "What do you mean?" she whispered.

"I've fallen in love with you. I never thought I'd say this to another woman, never imagined it could happen. I love you, Jean."

Overwhelmed, she stared at him for a long moment. Then she smiled. "I love you, too."

"Thank God." He pulled her close and kissed her. Tenderly, joyfully.

When they broke apart, Jean said, "Jonathan, what are we going to do about this? You're in Minnesota, I'm in Houston."

His lips curved, his eyes glinted with amusement. "I'd say the obvious solution is to get married."

Jean's mouth dropped open. "You . . . you want to get married?"

"Very much, but only if you're the bride. I know this has happened fast, but I'm very sure of what I want. How do you feel about that?"

She smiled with pure happiness. "I feel wonderful. The answer's yes."

They spent the rest of the day together—laughing, talking, making plans. In the afternoon they drove to Galveston and strolled along the seawall, holding hands, then visited the shops along the Strand. When they returned to Jean's house, Jonathan lit the Chanukah candles. Even though the first night of the holiday was long past, he repeated the special prayer, thanking God for bringing them to this season. Jean fixed dinner, and they sat down together. "The first evening of the rest of our lives," Jonathan said, smiling across the table at her.

Later that evening Jean led him into her bedroom. "Are you sure?" Jonathan asked her.

"We're adults. We know our own minds. We want each other," Jean said and put her arms around him.

She felt as if she were in a dream, as if everything moved in exquisitely slow motion. His lips moved against her mouth, her throat, and he kissed her as if they had forever. His hands were unhurried as he removed her clothes, then his. He urged her down on the bed and lay beside her, kissed her breasts, her body with such leisurely thoroughness, such infinite patience. Passion built by slow degrees until neither of them could hold back. He slipped inside her and filled all the lonely spaces with the warmth of his love. "I love you," he whispered. "Forever."

"Forever."

As always, Jean had the family over for the last night of Chanukah. Alicia, Neil, and the twins had returned from Disney World late the night before, laden with snapshots, anecdotes and Mickey Mouse watches for everyone.

"Grandma," Carrie said, "how were the rest of your dates? Have you fallen in love?"

"I'll tell you after we light the candles," Jean said. "Mark, will you do the honors?"

They crowded around the menorah and Mark said the prayer. Eight candles glowed in the silver holder. "—and may we all be together next year," he finished as he put the *shamash* candle back in place.

"Amen," murmured Jean.

"Will you tell us now about your dates?"

Carrie asked. "Did you fall in love with one of them?"

"Yes."

Cathy's eyes sparkled with excitement. "Are we getting a new grandfather?"

"Yes, you are." Jean grinned, enjoying the look of utter shock on the faces of her children. Her granddaughters, of course, weren't surprised at all. They'd expected nothing less.

"Are you going to marry Mr. Berger?" Ashley squealed.

"No." Jean reached for Jonathan's hand. "I'm going to marry Jonathan."

Surprise, excitement, delight filled the room. The children and grandchildren enveloped them in hugs and good wishes and questions about their plans. Only Ashley stood apart, looking crestfallen.

"Honey, what's wrong?" Jean asked.

"He's already my grandfather," Ashley said, sniffling. "I thought I'd get a new one."

Jonathan, too, had noticed Ashley's disappointment. He crouched in front of her and wiped away a tear with his fingertip. "I will be new in a way. I'll be a double grandfather now."

Ashley cocked her head and stared at him for a moment. "Does that mean you have to give me two presents for Chanukah and my birthday?"

Jonathan laughed. "Absolutely."

Immediately, her face brightened. "That's not so bad then." She gave Jonathan the kind of smile that would someday enchant hordes of teenage boys. "I didn't mean to hurt your feelings. I just expected Grandma Jean to pick one of the men from the dating service." She turned to Jean. "I guess you didn't need them."

"Oh, but your idea for the dates was what got me and your Grandpa Jonathan together," Jean explained. "So, you see, you and the twins were right on target. You did get me the perfect gift."

Magic and Mistletoe
Betty Cothran

Karen Oliver had planned to hibernate through the holidays with a stack of good books and a roaring fire. Why in heaven's name had she agreed to a Christmas cruise in Hawaii? she asked herself for the tenth time since she'd flown out of Atlanta's Hartsfield Airport with her best friend, Vanessa Sutherland.

"Paradise!" Vanessa dropped her two bulging suitcases onto the concrete pier at the end of the gangplank and readjusted the garment bag's strap on her shoulder. She inhaled deeply. "Get a load of that gorgeous ship all lit up with tiny white lights."

"It's something all right." Karen tried to put some enthusiasm in her voice. After a delayed departure from Atlanta, the long flight, and a missed transfer to the dock, she was tired, irritable, and her feet hurt.

"Aloha!" A pretty young woman in a fitted floral muumuu waved to them from the ship's deck. "Don't move. I'll be right down with a porter. *Wikiwiki*. Fast." She disappeared momentarily, then returned with a uniformed man close on her heels.

"Boy, are we glad to finally get here." Vanessa lowered her head when the ship's representative reached out with a fragrant lei of dainty white blossoms.

"Aloha and welcome to Hawaii!" The woman kissed the air next to her friend's cheek, then repeated the whole ritual with Karen.

"Thank you. It's lovely." Karen managed a faint smile, then lifted the soft, aromatic blossoms to her nose. She watched the porter load up with Vanessa's bags, and realized that he wasn't going to be able to take hers, too.

"I can handle my own," she offered, not wanting to leave her bags sitting on a deserted dock at this time of the night.

"American Hawaiian Cruises wouldn't hear of our clients climbing the gangplank with their luggage," the woman told her in a pleasantly insistent tone. "Allow me to take those for you."

"If you insist." Karen handed over her small rolling suitcase and garment bag. "I'm so exhausted from the flight, I'll gladly take the help." She started up the ramp behind Vanessa who seemed to have gotten her second wind.

When they reached the main deck and entered the lavish foyer, Vanessa linked an arm through hers. "I'm so glad you decided to come, Karen. We haven't done anything like this since we were wet behind the ears and barely old enough to drive."

"I know." Karen nodded and laughed. "So you take a woman who swims on average about once a year and drop her on a boat in the middle of the Pacific Ocean?"

"You betcha!" Vanessa squeezed her arm, then fell into single file behind the porter. She barraged the man with questions as they wound their way up the stairs and down a narrow passageway.

Amused, Karen spoke over her shoulder to the woman who'd greeted them. "She just asked me to take this cruise so she'd have a captive audience."

The woman laughed, but didn't say anything.

"Just you wait, sugar," Vanessa called down the hall. "We're gonna gorge ourselves on decadent food and soak up some rays on our poor pale bodies. Heck, I may even drag you out onto the dance floor. . . ."

"Kicking and screaming." Karen rolled her eyes when Vanessa looked back. She loved her longtime pal even though they were complete opposites. Vanessa Jones Mullis Sutherland Armstrong was a short, vivacious woman with flamboyant clothes,

overdone hair and makeup, and fervent
opinions on anything and everything.

Vanessa burst out laughing. "Kicking and
screaming, is that a new dance?"

Karen good-naturedly frowned as Vanessa stopped behind the porter. The man
pushed open the unlocked door with his
foot, then set about putting the luggage into
the storage compartments.

"Look, this is a first for me. Just be happy
that for the first time in my life I'm
here . . . on a cruise." They'd always
shared the important firsts in life—kisses,
crushes, marriages, and babies. And when Vanessa's firsts had turned into seconds, thirds,
and more, Karen had been there for her
friend. She'd even served as bridesmaid for
all three of Vanessa's weddings and had
helped commiserate at their inevitable de-
mise. But between families and children and
grandchildren, the two women hadn't found
the time in years to vacation together.

"Here, Pete." The ship's greeter handed
the porter Karen's luggage before she
turned back to the women. "The room keys
are on the counter," she informed them,
"and copies of the daily schedules are on
your beds. We'll be setting sail as soon as
they crank up the gangplank."

"So soon?" Vanessa asked. She plopped
down on the bed and kicked off her shoes.

The woman nodded and followed the

porter to the door. "Because of your unfortunate travel delays, you ladies were the last passengers to board. But now that you're here, American Hawaiian Cruise line wants your vacation to start with a bang. When you've freshened up, just head up to the deck and join the bon voyage party. By now, it's going pretty strong. Happy cruise and *Mele Kalikimaka*. Merry Christmas."

"I'm probably going to pass, but thanks anyway." Karen sat down on the other single bed. She wondered how comfortable the twin bed would actually be, then figured she was too tired to care tonight.

When they were alone again, Vanessa turned to face her. "Pass?" she demanded in her you've-got-to-be-kidding tone.

Karen crashed onto the bed. "Aren't you tired?" She yanked out a pillow from under the sea foam green bedspread and put it under her head.

"Me tired?" Vanessa placed the back of her hand on her forehead in pretend exasperation, then turned to face Karen. In a somber tone, she added, "It's Christmas Eve and we're on the S.S. Independence in Hawaii. Hawaii, for gosh sakes! I'm personally planning to celebrate my own independence with a vengeance." She stood up and peered into the large mirror over the combination desk-vanity. "Just as soon as I draw on some new lips and eyes, I'm going up on deck and join the bon voyage party."

Karen frowned, but knew arguing with a determined Vanessa was useless. Although Vanessa could pretend, she couldn't fool an old friend. Her happy bravado was unconvincing at best. She knew this last breakup with Herman Armstrong, husband number three and almost husband number four, had been hard on her, even devastating. That was partially why Karen was here; to help her friend get past the latest upheaval Herman Armstrong was putting Vanessa through.

"Well?" Vanessa shot her a forced smile in the mirror. She paused to smack her bright red lips with a tissue. "The way I see it, you've got two choices."

"Which are?" Karen readjusted herself on the bed, while her buddy continued to get ready for the bon voyage party.

Vanessa held up a finger and pointed at her with a long, red nail. "You can go like you are, or—" She held up a second well-manicured finger, then continued, "—shower and change and meet me in half an hour at the poolside bar."

Karen sat up and slid across the bed. When she reached the edge, she leaned across and lifted a third finger on her friend's hand. "Or three. I can crawl into bed and peacefully snooze through the rest of Christmas Eve.''

"We're here to have a good time." Vanessa planted both hands on her full hips. "And I'm determined to make that happen for us both, even if it kills me."

Karen touched her head with a slight salute. "Aye, aye, Captain. But can't we start all this fun tomorrow? I'm bushed."

"But tonight is Christmas Eve . . . what's left of it, anyway." Vanessa's voice was almost stern in its stubbornness. It was a tone Karen recognized. Whenever her companion wanted to put on a little friendly pressure to get her way, she used "the voice." After all these years, it came to her as naturally as breathing.

"What's the big deal?" Karen tried to waylay her, although she knew the effort was still useless. "We'll make up for the time we missed tonight on Christmas Day."

She watched Vanessa's smile turn up a notch. "Oh, good friend, we'll do Christmas Day up right, you can count on that. But that doesn't take the place of Christmas Eve. Where's your holiday spirit?"

Her holiday spirit? Karen hadn't had any since her daughter Nancy had broken the news that she'd agreed to spend Christmas with her husband's relatives in Maine. It was only fair, she knew, but it was still hard to accept being alone for the holidays when it seemed everyone else was surrounded by loved ones. She couldn't be too upset. Nancy had nursed Karen through every major holiday for the past three years since her father had died in an automobile accident.

"Didn't you look forward to Christmas Eve when you were young?" Vanessa gave her a wry smile. "I know you used to put a plate of homemade cookies out for Santa and all that other ritual jazz."

Karen raised up on one elbow to look at her pal. "I also went to bed early so Santa could come with the loot." The thought of Christmas tugged at her emotions a bit. Her four-year-old grandson would have Santa Claus deliver his gifts to his *other* grandparents' house this year. She envisioned him running in on Christmas morning to a strange living room to find out what Santa'd brought him. Karen hated it, but understood.

Vanessa fluffed her hair. "We're both old enough to know that Santa's just a myth."

"You sound like Nancy. Ever since that daughter of mine was eight years old, I've told her that *I* believe in Santa Claus," she teased. "For the record, I'll believe until the day I die."

"You believe in a jolly fat guy in a red velvet suit, but you want to ignore Christmas Eve?" Vanessa asked, shaking her head.

Karen flung her hands over her head.

"Uncle. I give up." She knew Vanessa hated being alone on Christmas Eve. Maybe deep down she wanted to be talked into going to the party. What could it hurt? She stood and glanced at her reflection in the mirror. "I'll take choice number two—the shower and a change."

"Good girl!" Vanessa wrapped her arms around Karen and squeezed. "This is gonna be a holiday you'll never forget. I promise."

Even after Vanessa had released Karen from the big bear hug, she could sense her friend's excitement. Some people thought of Vanessa as pushy, but Karen enjoyed her friend's vivacious attitude.

This cruise is going to be good for both of us, she thought, smiling at her reflection.

Karen waited until Vanessa popped out the door, then headed into the tiny bathroom. A hot shower would do the trick, rejuvenate her. Yessiree, she thought, Christmas was going to be different this year.

Karen followed the rhythmic sounds of the Hawaiian-style music up the stairs to the Upper Deck. A warm Pacific breeze touched her exposed skin as she walked past the crowded Barefoot Bar, and searched the padded stools for Vanessa's familiar face. She continued on around the polished wooden deck when she didn't spot her friend.

A young, white-uniformed waiter stopped her and asked, "May I get you a drink?"

"Well . . . ," she hesitated. "How about something tall and exotic with one of those little umbrellas?"

The waiter flashed her a bright smile. "Might I suggest a Mai Tai or a Piña Colada?"

"Hmm. Decisions, decisions." She lifted her face and deeply inhaled the salty tropical air. "A Mai Tai sounds good."

"Mai Tai it is." The waiter gave her another smile, dazzling against his tanned skin. "Don't worry, I'll find you when your drink is ready. Mix. Mingle. Enjoy yourself."

"Thanks." Karen felt ridiculous hearing such advice from a man young enough to be her son. What did he know about mixing and mingling at her age? It was a good line, but not so easy for a slightly shy water aerobics teacher on a boat full of strangers.

"*Mahalo*," the waiter said with a grin. "That means thank you."

"Then mahalo," she said with a nod. After he left, Karen searched the crowded deck for Vanessa's hot pink pantsuit. Vanessa's got to be here somewhere, she told herself. For a few minutes, she strolled around the fantail and enjoyed the surrounding beauty of the island, the festively decorated ship, even the throngs of passengers happily waiting to set sail. She listened to the laughter intermingled with ukulele music, and allowed herself to relax into vacation mode.

"There you are!" Vanessa grabbed her elbow and steered her to the rail. She held her at arms' length, giving her the once-over. "Ten minutes in the shower and you look marvelous. I'll bet you didn't even put on makeup, did you?"

"I put on some lipstick." Karen glanced self-consciously at her soft lavender chemise and white slip-on sneakers. With only a week's notice to shop for the trip, she'd opted for comfort and versatility over chic style.

"We need to talk. I had a little surprise . . ."

Karen noticed the color had drained from her friend's well-made-up face.

Vanessa nervously wrung her hands. "Uh, Karen, there's no easy way to say this."

"What is it, Van?" Karen continued in an uneasy rush. "Is something wrong? Are you okay?"

"Me? I'm fine . . . until I tell you what I have to tell you." Her laughter had a sharp edge to it.

"Just spit it out Vanessa. How bad can it be?"

Vanessa exhaled loudly. "It's Herman."

"Herman?" Karen blinked in surprise. "What in the world does Herman have to do with anything?"

Herman Armstrong had broken her friend's heart . . . twice. Once when they got divorced after he ran off with the daughter of his lumber supplier nearly three years ago, then again last week, when he broke off their six-month engagement to get remarried. Since their first marriage, Karen had never trusted Herman. She was secretly glad when he'd called things off, figuring it would be better in the long run. This cruise, she'd hoped, would help Vanessa get her life back together again.

"He's here," Vanessa said, her eyes lowered, not meeting Karen's questioning look. "Herman's on the ship."

"What?" Karen blurted out, her voice so loud that people at nearby tables turned to see what was going on. "Sorry," she muttered, slightly embarrassed.

With a shrug, Vanessa tried to explain. "I plopped down at the bar and felt a hand on my shoulder. When I swiveled around to check it out, there he was, smiling like a Cheshire cat, wearing Bermuda shorts and an Atlanta Braves tee-shirt."

Shocked, Karen stood there speechless.

"I'm glad to see him," Vanessa sheepishly admitted.

Karen looked at her friend and nodded, even though she wondered why in the world Vanessa would want to see him after all the hurt he'd caused her.

"There's more." Vanessa's voice was anxious.

Oh great! she thought. "Don't tell me. Let me guess. Herman's a stowaway, and now he wants to share our room. So much for happy vacations." She caught herself searching the area uneasily, expecting any second to see Herman.

Vanessa hesitated. "He brought a friend."

"Another woman?" she cried, immediately angry that the idiotic man could do something so insensitive. "Of all the unmitigated gall!"

"Not another woman," Vanessa corrected. "It's a guy."

Karen took in a quick, sharp breath. "A man? No way!"

Vanessa threw back her head and laughed, a shrill, nervous titter that set Karen's skin on edge. "Not like that. He's just Herman's friend, silly. After all, you and I are here together." She pointed from herself to Karen. "Two women traveling alone."

"That's different." Deep down Karen knew it wasn't different at all, but she didn't trust herself to talk about what was really bothering her. She disliked change, particularly unexpected change, and this qualified as one of the biggest surprises she'd had lately.

"How's it different?" Vanessa asked, her voice slightly curt. "Because they're men, or because it's Herman."

Karen struggled for the right words. "It doesn't seem quite right." Herman had followed Vanessa halfway across the globe and he was the one who'd broken their engagement a few short days ago. What good could come of Herman Armstrong's sudden appearance in Hawaii?

Vanessa grabbed her arm and squeezed. "Trust me, the man is straight as an arrow." She tittered again. "Straighter. And believe you me, I should know."

"Then why?" Karen asked.

"To share the cost." Vanessa shrugged. "Herman's not a very wealthy man, you know. Besides, he's never flown in an airplane before and didn't want to do it alone."

"Okay. Say I buy all that. What's the real reason he's here?" Other than to make Vanessa's life a living hell, she thought, instantly guilty that she begrudged her friend the one man who seemed to make her happy. At least, that's what Vanessa had believed last week. Who knew what was going on tonight?

Vanessa put her hands on her generous hips and frowned. "He said he came to win me back. Is that so hard for you to believe?"

"No, Van, that's not what I meant." Karen regretted the misunderstanding. Vanessa was a wonderful woman and deserved a good, honest, hard-working man who loved every idiosyncrasy and wild notion she possessed. "But why now, here on the cruise? I thought you two were finished. Kaput. Over and done with."

Vanessa chuckled. "I get the message. We were. Are. Hells bells! I don't know what we are anymore, but I sure think I should give him a chance to explain."

"Why, for heaven's sake?" Karen tried to keep the criticism from her voice. She didn't want to send her friend careening into her old lover's arms out of anger at her disapproval.

"He did follow me all the way to Hawaii. That should count for something. Right?" Vanessa looked so hopeful, that Karen couldn't help but want things to be right for her.

"I guess." Karen shook her head. "You never said, why did you two break up?"

A glazed look of despair spread over Vanessa's face as she spoke. "Herman planned to have Christmas in West Virginia with his daughters and their families."

"That doesn't sound like much to break up over," Karen assured her.

"It wasn't just that. He was going there because his ex-wife asked him to. They were gonna have this happy little family get-together, and I was gonna be left at home alone with a TV dinner."

Karen recognized the pain stirring in her friend's features, because she knew what it was like to be left out in the cold. Their personal circumstances might have been different, but the emotions were the same. She reached out to Vanessa with a comforting pat on the arm.

"I gave him an ultimatum." She stared at her with hopeless resignation. "A stupid ultimatum."

"What was that?" she asked, her voice a little louder because of the growing crowd and party noises.

"Me or Doris. Plain and simple." Vanessa shook her head regretfully. "I wanted him to choose."

"But what about the kids?" The look of misery on her friend's face made Karen wish she could bite back the question. It was obvious Vanessa still cared more about Herman Armstrong than Karen had dreamed possible.

"His kids are in their thirties with kids

of their own. They could have come to our
house for Christmas. They knew they were
welcome in our home." Vanessa dropped
her lashes probably to hide her feelings.

Karen swallowed the lump that swelled in
her throat. "Then what was the problem?"

"Doris was making a play for him," she
said in a resigned voice. "I knew what she
was up to right off the bat, but Herman
didn't. I could see right though his ex-wife's
shenanigans."

"Too bad Herman couldn't," Karen
added with a frown.

"Make way," the waiter interrupted. He
maneuvered the drink-laden tray over his
head until he found a spot between the two
women. "One Mai Tai." He gave the drink
to Karen with a cocktail napkin. "I'm sorry,
ma'am, did you order something?"

"No. But I surely could use one."

"Here. Take mine." Karen pushed the
hurricane glass into her hand. "I insist. The
waiter can bring me another one the next
time he comes our way."

Vanessa accepted without argument, then
took a long sip of the drink. "Thanks."

"No problem." At least not with the
drink, she thought. "Where is Herman anyway?"

Vanessa pointed across the deck. "Over
near the other rail at a table behind that

gigantic arrangement of flowers. I told him to wait there until I talked to you."

"And his friend?"

"He's there, too." Vanessa took another swig from the glass "Will you sit down and have a drink, say hello to them?" She gave her a hopeful look.

"I guess." Karen waved toward the exotic arrangement. "After you."

"Shouldn't we wait for your drink?" She lifted the Mai Tai.

Karen shook her head. "Don't worry. The waiter will find me."

"Let's go then," Vanessa said.

Karen followed Vanessa through the milling crowd while strains of "I'm Dreaming of a White Christmas" filled the warm, sultry air. A stab of homesickness hit her as she realized that by this time the family had already put her grandson to bed. She straightened and forced the melancholy thoughts out of her head.

"There's my gal!" Herman jumped up from his seat when they reached the table. "I was about to send out a search party for you two." He leaned across and pecked Vanessa on the cheek in a possessive gesture.

Herman hadn't changed a bit in the looks department. His brown hair was thinning on the top, and his taste in clothes had obviously stagnated a couple of decades ago.

She wondered where his buddy was. "Hello, Herman."

"Karen!" Herman lurched over and planted a kiss on her cheek before she could dodge. Up close, he smelled of spicy cologne and whiskey. "You're looking pretty as ever."

"I'll second that," a deep male voice agreed.

Karen looked up into a pair of dark, almost black eyes, as familiar as the husky voice. Stunned, she tried to focus on the tall man staring down at her.

Luke Wendell.

Of all the men in the world to find in Hawaii . . . Why Luke? He was her one and only blind date since her husband's death—a complete and total disaster. Not only had it been a blind date, but a double date with Herman and Vanessa right around the time they'd started dating again. Stuck on a ship with Luke and Herman! Was this some kind of cruel joke?

"Surprised?" Luke sat down next to her. "I'll bet I'm the last person you expected to see here in Hawaii."

Karen managed a tentative smile and stole a glance at the man she hadn't seen since their disastrous date more than a year ago. He was wearing his thick, silver hair in a shorter, more flattering style. It looked good on him, brought out the strong lines

in his face. Something else was different,
too. He must have been spending a lot of
time outdoors; his face and arms had a nice
bronze hue.

"Tall and exotic," the waiter interrupted,
"just like you ordered."

Karen gave a surprised glance at the
young man who placed her Mai Tai on the
table.

"Excuse me?" Luke asked with a quizzical
look in his eyes.

Karen chuckled. "My Mai Tai," she explained. "Tall and exotic with a tiny paper
umbrella."

Luke leaned closer so she could hear over
the music. "I thought he was talking about
you."

"Tall? Maybe. But you'd have to be blind
to call me exotic." She took a sip of the
drink.

"I don't know," Luke protested. Before
he could finish, the captain announced over
the loud speaker that the S.S. Independence
was setting sail. A loud whistle signaled for
everyone to grab a handful of streamers.

"Let's find a spot," Luke suggested,
pointing to the dockside rail.

Karen nodded. She started toward the
back of the fantail, realizing when she got
there that Vanessa and Herman had disappeared. The drummer struck up a rhythmic
roll and the ship's whistle blew a "salute"

to the S.S. Constitution, the sister ship, as she pulled past them. "We're moving, too," she shouted, feeling the slightest roll as they moved away from the dock.

Luke nodded his agreement and threw a fistful of confetti into the dark night air. A deafening cheer rose from the crowd as the ships took turns signaling back and forth. Streamers blew across the deck and over the sides, giving a festive air to the sail away ceremony.

Seeing the other ship as it moved on a parallel course gave Karen a strange sensation. When the noise died down, she turned to face Luke. "Where's the happy couple?"

He shrugged his shoulders. "I guess they had a few things to talk about."

"I guess," she agreed, then made her way back to the table with him.

"How about a nightcap?" he offered. "My treat."

"I shouldn't," she protested, but he gave her a quiet smile that convinced her to stay a few minutes longer. "But maybe I should, to give Van a few minutes with Herman." She cocked her head toward the far corner where the happy couple was definitely getting re-acquainted.

"Good idea." Luke ordered their drinks. After a few minutes of awkward social chatter, he finally said, "What do you have against Herman?"

"Do you want the truth?" She stared at him directly.

"The truth."

"For my taste, Herman stands a little too close for comfort and laughs a little too loud for polite society." Amusement flickered in the dark eyes that met hers.

"Nobody ever said my buddy Herman was perfect."

"No, but—" she protested.

"Why don't you give the guy half a chance." Luke grinned. "Vanessa obviously has."

Karen drew a deep breath and exhaled. "From the way they're hanging all over each other, that's apparent. I just hate to see her disappointed." She stirred in her chair, uneasy with her own feelings. "I can't explain it, but it would be hard to accept Vanessa and Herman as a couple again." Karen hesitated and measured him for a moment. Finally, she admitted, "I just don't like Herman very much."

"I don't want to hurt your feelings, but it's not about whether *you* like him or not." He pointed to her chest and she stopped breathing for a moment. Karen could almost feel his finger touch her blouse, but not quite. Luke pulled his hand back and chuckled. "Not that it much matters."

"It most certainly does." She stiffened, but forced her mouth into a smile. "Vanessa *is* my best friend and whoever she's with, I'll inevitably see . . . a lot."

With a devilish grin, he crossed his arms. "Then I'd suggest you try to discover something about Herman to like."

She shot him a withering glance that was more playful, than serious. "How do you do it?"

"What?" he teased, his mouth quirked with humor. "How do I find it in my heart to like Herman?"

"Yes." Karen found it impossible not to return his disarming smile. "From what I remember, you and Herman are nothing alike. He's arrogant and loud and . . ." She searched for the right word to describe the man. ". . . just plain Herman."

Luke unfolded his arms, bent his head slightly forward, then rubbed his chin. "Actually, that's what I like about him. He is just plain Herman, so loyal the man would give his best kidney to a friend in need. But that's not all . . ."

She frowned slightly. "I don't understand. What do you mean?"

Luke sat up straight, but avoided her questioning gaze. "Herman does all of the things that I could never do on my own. Some folks see him as loud and obnoxious, but I prefer to think of him as friendly and outgoing." He relaxed his shoulders. "You know what I like most about him?"

"I have no idea." Despite the fact that she didn't care much for Vanessa's choice of male companions, she liked the way Luke was taking up for his buddy.

"Herman never meets a stranger."

Karen pulled her lips in thoughtfully. "Funny, Vanessa's like that, too." She followed Luke's line of vision toward the couple still deep in conversation in the corner.

"That's probably why they get along so well," he said, matter-of-factly.

Karen took another swallow of her drink. "I think I'm going to call it a night," she announced, realizing the long day had finally caught up with her. "I'm not going to disturb the happy couple, but if they come over, tell Van I've turned in." She stood up to make a quick exit. Whatever tomorrow may bring, she'd deal with it, but tonight she only wanted to slip between the sheets and dream of Christmas in paradise.

"Let me walk you back to your cabin," he offered.

She was startled by his suggestion, but managed to object in a steady voice. "You don't need to do that."

"It's no problem," he assured her with a smile. "We arrived on the flight just before yours, so I'm beat, too." He gently guided her by the arm through the mass of people. She was confused by the emotions his mere touch resurrected. Emotions she had long kept hidden.

Right before they reached her room, a waiter bumped into them carrying a tray filled with tiny sprigs of greenery tied with red velvet ribbons. The man picked up a couple of sprigs and pushed them toward Karen and Luke.

"Mistletoe?" she asked.

The young man grinned. "It's a tradition on the Independence. On New Year's Eve we pass out goblets of champagne, but on Christmas Eve, we celebrate with mistletoe." He leaned forward with a conspiratorial wink. "Personally, I find the mistletoe much more . . . entertaining."

"Me, too," Luke agreed as he held the stairwell door for the waiter. When he turned back to Karen, she felt a sudden twinge of anticipation that she couldn't explain. He twirled the mistletoe and smiled, an enchanting smile that warmed her insides.

Why hadn't she noticed his smile before? How could she have missed those crinkles around his eyes that made him seem rugged and so very alive?

"It's the first mistletoe I've seen all year," she rattled on, a little flustered as they made their way down the hall to her door. "Real, too." She couldn't stop herself, the inane words just kept coming. "Not the plastic kind you buy at the mall."

When they stopped, Luke stared at her a long moment. Deep, dark eyes searched hers with a glint of interest and an obvious tenderness. He picked up his sprig and held it gingerly, studying it as if he'd never seen mistletoe before. "We probably shouldn't let this go to waste," he told her in a hushed voice.

Her breath caught in her throat and she couldn't speak. She didn't know if he was teasing or not, so she simply waited for his next move.

Luke lifted the mistletoe above her head and questioned her with a smile.

Tilting her face toward his, she gave him an almost imperceptible nod.

He leaned down and ever-so-gently kissed her cheek. She felt the warmth of his lips on her skin, sensed the heat emanating to every nerve center in her body from that one brief point of contact.

"Merry Christmas," he whispered. "Good night, Karen."

"Merry Christmas." Inside her cabin, she leaned against the door and sighed. This holiday was certainly looking up.

Karen walked downstairs for breakfast in the opulent Palms Dining Room. She'd been asleep when Vanessa had come in last night and again this morning when her friend had slipped out on her own.

"May I show you to your table?" the maitre d' asked with a cordial smile.

"I got in late last night," she explained. "So I didn't have a chance to get my table assignment." She hesitated. "Unless my roommate did it this morning."

"Give me your name," he suggested, "and I'll be happy to check my list."

"Karen Oliver. My roommate's Vanessa Armstrong."

She watched as he slid his finger down the list of names once, then twice, before nodding. "You two were checked in last night and assigned to table fifty-three."

"How is that possible?"

He gave her a wide grin. "Apparently, someone requested you both at their table."

Herman, she thought, dreading the idea of every meal with Herman Armstrong for the duration of the cruise. There wasn't much she could do about it. Look on the bright side, she told herself, that means you'll be sharing meals with Luke.

Luke Wendell.

The maitre d' gave a large menu to one of the waiters clad in a loud Hawaiian shirt and necklace of dark brown kukui nuts strung on a leather strand. "Follow me," he told her. The man threaded his way through a maze of tables to one next to a stained glass window that divided the room into sections. When Karen rounded the glass, she saw him sitting there alone.

Luke glanced up and smiled.

At the sight of his strong, sculpted face, she remembered the kiss he'd given her last night. Remembered the way his lips had felt on her cheek. Karen relived the kiss again, as she had a dozen times in her dreams last night. By morning, the kiss had escalated from a tender peck on the cheek to a toe-curling exploration of her mouth. Seeing him now, she was surprised at her strong reaction to a man who previously hadn't held her interest enough for a second date.

"Good morning," he greeted, a huskiness in his tone. "I'm pleasantly surprised to see you this early. After I found Herman gone when I woke up, I was afraid you'd be sight-seeing with him and Vanessa."

"So that's where they've gone."

"That's my guess," he conceded.

"Great," she muttered sarcastically and wondered what she was going to do with the rest of the day.

You're in Hilo, Hawaii, she chastised herself, one of the most beautiful spots in the world. If you can't find something to do, Karen Oliver, then you don't deserve to be on this gorgeous ship.

"Do I detect a frown on that lovely face?"

he asked after the waiter poured them both
some coffee.

Karen was surprised at his compliment,
but her only acknowledgment was a smile.
"I was hoping to spend the day with Vanessa," she told him with a laugh. "Guess
I take a back seat to the resurrection of Vanessa's romance."

"I'll bet we both came in a close second."
He settled back in his chair and gave a little
sigh. "Friends always do."

"Comes with the territory," she managed
to say, her attention drawn to Luke's white
polo shirt that accentuated his muscular
arms and chest. Karen wished she'd had
more time to get into shape for the trip.
She was no slouch in the looks department,
but held to the adage that one could never
do enough to fight the signs of gravity.

"Listen," Luke interrupted her musings.
"I've reserved a rental car for the day." He
folded his hands together in a comfortable
gesture. "Why don't you join me? We can
see the sights at our own pace, and do what
we please without being crowded onto a van
or bus." He jauntily cocked his head, causing silky strands of silver to fall to one side.
"I'd love to see Volcanoes National Park
with you."

Resisting the urge to push the wispy
strands away from his face, she responded,

"Oh, I couldn't impose." Inside, she was screaming "Yes, I'd love to go."

"Why in the world not?" Luke instinctively ran long, lean fingers through his hair. "Don't you want to see Kilauea Crater?"

Karen hesitated. "Of course I do. Who wouldn't? But . . ." She wanted to go, wanted to spend the day with him, so what was her problem? Where were all these insecure feelings coming from?

"Is it because of our blind date?" The slight lines of tension on his face eased when he chuckled. "Are you going to hold that one strike against me forever?"

"Of course not," she quickly responded. She was surprised at how much she'd missed in Luke on that first date. Hell, she didn't even remember how handsome he was. If she'd bungled something so blatant as that, what else might she have missed?

"Believe me, I've got blind date war stories that would make your skin crawl." He distractedly drummed his fingers on his thigh. "Not that our date was . . . I mean the others were worse."

She smiled, remembering their blind date. "Others plural? You get a medal if you braved more than one. Why don't you tell me about them?"

Luke groaned. "Back then, it seemed like everybody I'd ever known had someone to

fix me up with, my friends, co-workers—"
His expression dulled with an unreadable
emotion. "—even my brother."

"Don't forget Herman," she quickly
added. And Vanessa, she thought. Those
two were the most unlikely cupids in the
world. Their own love lives were nothing to
be emulated. Her mind wandered a moment to what was happening between Vanessa and Herman. Were they getting back
together? She didn't know whether she
should hope for or against their reunion.

"Ah, yes. Herman." Leisurely, he stretched
his legs out in front of him.

Karen noticed his long, muscular legs
and the light hair on his tanned thighs. She
raised her gaze and found that Luke was
staring back at her. A warm blush rose up
her neck and spread across her chest. Unfortunately, the scoop necked shell made it
impossible to cover up anything, so she pretended not to notice.

In a lowered voice, Luke added, "Although, to Herman's credit, the only
woman he ever fixed me up with was . . .
you. He kept trying to get me to . . . well,
to call you again."

There was a tingling in the pit of her
stomach at the thought of another date with
Luke. This Luke was somehow different
than the one she'd gone on a blind date
with over a year ago. She finally managed

to speak. "For months Vanessa kept pushing for *me* to call you."

"But you never did." He gave her a steady,
piercing smile that made her look away.

She was by no means blind to her bud-
ding attraction to him. But was he interested in her? Last time, he hadn't called
her back. Would he call her now? "No, I
guess I didn't. I—"

Luke raised his hand to interrupt.
"Karen, you don't need to explain. As first
dates go, ours wasn't stellar."

She laughed, a low, throaty sound that
helped to alleviate some of the tension that
had been building inside her. "That's quite
an understatement."

In a husky tone, Luke asked, "What do
you think went wrong?"

"Who knows?" She ran her fingers
through her hair, smoothing the windblown
strands into submission. "Maybe we were
just at different places in our lives."

Luke's face brightened. "Aren't all blind
dates doomed from the start? The possibilities for disaster are endless." His voice
raised slightly. "I could have had a bad
week . . . or you could have. One of us
could have been upset about something else
that might have happened that day."

She exhaled after she realized she'd been
holding her breath. "Or one of us could
have hated wrestling—"

He stared, tongue-tied. After a moment, he said in a surprised voice, "You, too?"

"Despised it." She was relieved that she hadn't said the wrong thing. For all she knew he could suffer from wrestling fever. Stranger things had happened.

He stroked his chin and studied her carefully. "Then whose idea was it to go to wrestling anyway?"

"I thought you—," she started.

"No way!" he protested. "Dinner and a movie is more my speed."

Funny, at the time she'd thought Luke loved it, now she realized he was only being polite because he must have thought she was the wrestling fan. "Vanessa told me you were the one who liked it."

"Who the heck really wanted to go see wrestling?" He captured her gaze with his.

"Herman," they agreed in unison, then burst out laughing.

A satisfied light came into her eyes. He wasn't the man she remembered at all. It just proved that until you take the time to get to know a man, you can't really know him. And she never knew Luke Wendell. But she wanted to get to know him now.

As he opened the car door, big blue eyes looked squarely at him from Karen's eager face. Luke was tempted to reach out and smooth the strand of silky hair that framed her delicate features. He resisted and instead offered her his hand. "First stop, Volcanoes National Park," he announced to fill the silence that had fallen between them on the ride from the dock.

Karen took his hand and stepped out onto the sidewalk. "Thanks," she told him with a squeeze, before letting go. "Want to go inside the Kilauea Visitor's Center?"

"Wouldn't miss it," he told her, glad he'd summoned up the courage to invite Karen to come today. She was certainly a pleasant companion, more so than Herman would have been. He liked his old pal, but Herman didn't compare to the beautiful woman beside him. "Want to take a look at the Art Center before or after we go around Crater Rim Drive?"

"Hmm." She went through the Visitor Center's door he held for her, then said, "Why don't we wait until after? I understand it's only eleven miles around the rim of the crater." The excitement was evident in her eyes when she looked at him. "Is that okay with you?"

"Sounds like a plan to me." He tried to level his pulse as he picked up a couple of brochures and a map. Karen Oliver was having a strong effect on him. Being alone with her in a car for nearly an hour had been wonderful and awful, all at the same time.

It occurred to him very quickly that he wanted to make a good impression on this woman. He obviously hadn't made much of one on their first date.

He studied Karen for a moment as she moved from display to display, reading the tiny plaques. She was wearing a pair of dark plum city shorts and a long-sleeved lavender heney with a buttery yellow sweater tied at her waist. Karen was a beautiful woman, more beautiful than he remembered.

"It's good that you brought a sweater. I hear it gets cooler the higher up we go," he said, aiming for dialogue intelligent enough to impress and entertain Karen.

"The guidebook said we're going as high as four-thousand feet above sea level," she informed. A faint light twinkled in the depths of eyes staring back at him, a heavenly blue, so clear he thought he'd see his reflection in them. "You look pretty prepared yourself," she complimented.

"Thanks," he said, a little embarrassed. When she moved on to check out the guidebooks, Luke glanced at his carefully selected attire. The sales clerk had described his shorts as classic bone-colored Bermudas paired up with one of the new red Polartec brand pullovers. Laughing, he remembered from her sales pitch that he was wearing recycled plastic bottles. He wasn't sure about the recycling thing, but the pullover felt great. He'd opted for some sturdy nubuck boots and socks, figuring he'd be climbing over the rocky fissures and craters.

Did Karen go for this rugged look? he wondered, not able to read her face for approval.

Karen stopped in front of a large television monitor where images of recent volcano eruptions were blazing on the screen. "Want to see the movie?"

Luke nervously glanced at his watch. "Whatever you want to do is fine with me." He secretly hoped that they wouldn't waste the time here at the Visitor's Center, when they could be out exploring the real thing.

She turned and flashed him a lively smile. "We'd better decide since it's about to start."

"Your wish is my command," he teased, not wanting to sway her decision.

Her smile grew into a wide grin. "I like the sound of that. Why don't we just head out and see what we can find on our own?"

"A woman after my own heart." He felt a rush of heat slide down his spine as he followed her back to the car, thankful that she hadn't glanced back.

When they got settled, Luke handed Karen the map. "Will you be the navigator?"

"I'd be delighted," she told him. "Navigating is my specialty."

Luke assumed her enthusiasm stemmed from the prospect of seeing the volcano. As Karen directed them along Kilauea's summit caldera, his mind kept wandering. What other specialties did she have besides navigating?

They drove in comfortable silence stopping for all the sights, the Sulphur Banks, Steam Vents, and the breathtaking Kilauea Overlook where they viewed the unforgettable vastness of the lava's destruction, the crooks and crannies burned into the earth's surface by the molten liquid. After a quick tour of the Jaggar Museum, they drove on to the main event, the very active Halemaumau crater.

"Are you ready?" he asked as they started the short hike to the overlook of the enormous, fiery hole in the southwest rift of the caldera.

"I can't wait," she replied, excitement evident in her voice. "Never in my life did I dream I'd be standing in Hawaii, much less smack dab in the middle of an honest-to-goodness volcano."

Before Luke realized what was happening, Karen reached for his arm and tugged him to speed up. He felt her closeness even after she released his elbow, intentionally matching his long strides to hers. With each step, he felt the heat radiating from the barren ground, dark and black and dusty with volcanic ash. Amazed, he asked, "Can you believe how hot the ground is, even though the air is cool?"

Without slowing down, she agreed, "No. It's kind of scary and exciting at the same time. Do you realize that any second this thing could blow and we'd be carried off in a sea of lava?"

"That's reassuring." He laughed. They hiked across black boulders with steam spewing from fissures in the rocks. "It's a little like when I was young and played hooky from school. I'd sneak off to Barney's Pool Hall," he explained with another chuckle. "It was dangerous because any minute I could have gotten caught, but it was worth it for the rush."

"I know what you mean. For me, it was sneaking out of the dorm to go dancing past curfew. Dancing was my downfall," she said with a smile when they stopped in front of a makeshift altar. "I read about these . . . these shrines, but I never believed people were still building them."

Luke studied the pile of molten rock, carefully stacked about three feet high. On the precarious flat top was an empty, pint-sized gin bottle wrapped in large green leaves. "According to legend, this is an offering to the Hawaiian goddess of fire, Pele." He waved his arm at the display. "It's hard to imagine in this day and age that folks are still this superstitious."

Karen shivered. "Makes my skin crawl," she added, vigorously rubbing her arms.

"Mine, too," he admitted. "Here let me help," Luke offered as she untied her light-weight sweater from her waist and slipped both arms into the sleeves. "I noticed back at the Visitor's Center that a lot of people pick up pieces of lava from the park as souvenirs only to send back their booty after long runs of bad luck."

"I saw that display, too, but figured it was something that happened years ago, not . . ." She pointed to the altar. "Not to-day."

Luke nodded. "Now that's really scary." He motioned toward the overlook. "Ready to see the crater?"

"This ground is really hot," she said.

Watching her climb the last few yards to the point, Luke realized he was hot, too, but it wasn't coming from the volcano.

"What a sight!" Her face grew animated as she searched the distance for steam and specks of flowing lava. "I hate that we can get this close, but not close enough to really *see* the lava gushing up."

"You're really getting into this, aren't you?" he asked, surprised at her intense interest. Usually, he traveled alone and discovered these kinds of wonders by himself.

It was terrific sharing it with someone who felt the same way he did.

"How could anyone *not* be thrilled?"

Luke reached for her hand and slipped his fingers through hers. She gave him a startled look, but didn't let go. "Karen, I'm glad you came with me today," he told her in a hushed voice. "I'm having a great time."

"Me, too." She was flattered by his comment. "I'll never forget today."

Wordlessly, they hiked back to the car and started the trip back to the Visitor's Center.

"I'm really sorry we can't drive ahead to Devastation Trail," he said, apologetically.

"It's hard to imagine that only a couple of miles ahead the road's been destroyed by lava to the point that they've closed the area."

"What a sight that must be."

"You know, I'd give anything to see the lava flowing into the sea."

"I'll tell you a secret." He glanced sideways to see her reaction. "I overheard the crew talking this morning and . . ."

"And?" she asked, impatiently. "Tell me. I can't stand the suspense."

"The ship is sailing near enough to the island that at midnight we'll be able to see the lava flowing into the ocean from the deck."

"No way!" She turned to face him with a disbelieving grin on her face.

"Wait and see," he teased.

"You're serious."

"Would I kid about a thing like that?"

She sat back in her seat. "I'll be there front and center."

He paused a minute, then asked quietly, "Would you like a little company?"

"I wouldn't dream of seeing it with anyone else," she assured him in a tone that made him glance her way again.

After a few minutes, they reached the park entrance again. "Here we are," he announced, steering the car into a parking space.

Karen unsnapped the seatbelt, slipped out of her sweater and threw it on the back seat. "I won't take long in the Art Center," she promised.

"Take as long as you need," he assured her as they headed up the sidewalk to the Old Hotel turned gift shop and gallery. "We don't set sail until after dark." Besides, Luke wasn't ready to go back to the ship, back to Vanessa and Herman. He selfishly wanted to have her all to himself for as long as he could.

"Great. I need to pick up a few gifts," she told him as they entered the restored lodge. Strains of Hawaiian music played against a backdrop of water splashing in a pottery fountain near the door.

"Well, you've come to the right place," the sales woman greeted them. "Aloha and welcome."

Karen quickly picked out a hand-carved bowl for her daughter Nancy, a painted Aloha shirt for her son-in-law, and a wooden volcano puzzle for her little grandson. "Could I see that tray of jewelry?" she asked the woman behind the counter.

"Of course. These are all made by an artist from Hilo." She pulled out the tray and added, "They're made with genuine black or pink coral. Will you excuse me?" she asked, leaving to ring up a customer at the register.

Luke joined her from where he'd been talking to a charcoal artist on the opposite side of the room. "What'd you find?"

She sighed. "Beautiful pins, earrings, necklaces. Too many choices to pick just one."

He leaned over the tray and picked up a couple to scrutinize more carefully. "For you?"

"No. I'm looking for something to give Vanessa." She gave him a sly grin. "It is Christmas, after all."

"It's hard to remember in this gorgeous weather." He fingered each piece on the velvet lining, then looked up to find her watching him. "You're right, it's a hard decision. Vanessa has her own . . . style."

Karen smiled. "That's one way to put it. She's brassy and flamboyant."

And nothing like you, he thought.

"Uh-huh. What about this one?" he suggested, holding up a bright parrot pin with inlaid coral and semi-precious jewels.

"That one caught my eye, too," she agreed, taking it from his fingers.

His skin tingled where she'd just brushed his hand, sending a warm shiver through him. He cleared his throat and said, "That parrot just screams Vanessa's name, doesn't it?"

She chuckled. "That it does."

Karen took her selections to the cash register while Luke went back to where the artist was working. He watched as she supervised the wrapping. She picked out bright Hawaiian Christmas wrap for Vanessa's and sturdy boxes for the others. While Karen was busy, the artist slipped a sketch to Luke in a sturdy bag and gave him change.

"What'd you find?" she asked him when he returned to the counter a few minutes later.

"Now, now. People shouldn't ask so many questions when they see an unmarked bag." He flashed her a mischievous grin. "It is Christmas, after all."

Karen snapped her fingers. "My own words coming back to haunt me," she complained, but he noticed a pink flush on her cheeks.

"All set?" he asked, avoiding her questioning stare.

"Unfair!" She poked his arm. "I showed you my purchases, now you have to show me yours."

He turned to the sales clerk who seemed to be enjoying their banter. "Is that a rule?"

The woman's eyes widened in pretend innocence. "Not in Hawaii. Particularly not at Christmas."

Karen threw up her arms. "I give up." She gathered the handles of her shopping bag and started toward the door.

Her lips curled into a faint smile, beautiful, just like the rest of her. "All in good time," he said in a low voice, unsure if his words even reached Karen. It wasn't anything Luke could put his finger on, but he was attracted to this woman in a way he hadn't been before. She seemed different, more alive, more interesting. Or maybe, he was just ready now to accept someone new in his life, or at least to explore the possibilities.

The possibilities. His heart turned over at the mere prospect.

* * *

Luke spotted Karen at the railing as soon as he walked out onto the fantail. She was lovely in a pale blue sundress that showed off her shoulders and back. His pulse quickened as he joined her. "Hello," he said, feeling a little tongue-tied as he greeted Karen. They'd had such a great day, he worried that something would spoil it.

Karen swiveled around and gave him a welcoming smile. "Hi. Have you seen Herman?" she asked, tension evident in her question.

"No." Luke hesitated. "I don't think he's been back all day. How about Vanessa?"

"By the look of our room, she's been back. But I haven't seen her since we returned from the volcano. Herman's probably got her cornered somewhere."

He studied her a moment, then plunged ahead. "What is it you've got against Herman?"

Karen sighed. "It's not that I don't like Herman. Because I do. But Herman and Vanessa were together once and it didn't work very well," she pointed out to him. "It's hard to believe that it's going to be much better this time."

People deserve second chances, he thought. Look at us! His brow furrowed. "Who knows about those two? But I'm sure they'll be here before we set sail," he assured her, wishing he felt more secure himself. Knowing Herman, anything was possible. He could tell Karen was concerned, so he tried to take her mind off things. Abruptly, he asked, "You know what I miss the most?"

She stared at him with silent expectation. "About what?" Her voice was as distracted as her stance.

"Christmas." He leaned against the rail and stared into the distance, half looking for Vanessa and Herman, half enjoying Karen's closeness. She smelled wonderful, a mixture of soap and a floral perfume.

Karen turned away from the gangplank to face him. "No, what do you miss the most about Christmas?"

"Back at home bright, twinkling lights would be wrapped around all the houses in my neighborhood, and be tangled in trees and bushes. My neighbors hang lights anywhere an extension cord will reach." He chuckled, remembering the sight. "It's not the decorator showcase. Heck, it's even a little tacky, but I love it. How about you, Karen? What do you miss?"

She thought a second before answering. "I missed going to church services on Christmas Eve. My church had a live manger scene and we'd always sing Christmas hymns by candlelight." She had a wistful look on her face that spread into a tiny smile. "This year I spent most of Christmas

Eve on the airplane. But it was worth it to spend the holiday in Hawaii," she quickly added.

"It is beautiful here, isn't it?" he agreed. And so are you, he wanted to add.

"Hey, you two!" a familiar female voice drew their attention to the bottom of the gangplank. "We're back!" Vanessa shouted as she started up the steps.

"See, I knew they'd make it." His tone was confident, but deep down he was relieved to see them, too.

"Where have you guys been?" Luke asked when they reached the deck. "We were beginning to think you jumped ship."

"Nothing so mundane," Vanessa drawled. "My husband and I had better things to do."

Karen's breath caught as if the air had been knocked out of her. "Did you say husband?"

"Husband." Vanessa pronounced the word with obvious relish.

"Don't you mean fiancé?" Luke corrected with a sly smile directed Herman's way.

"No-o-o, husband." Beaming, Vanessa grinned and held up her hand. "See." She wiggled her third finger and flaunted a wide pink coral wedding band.

"Why you sly devil." Luke grabbed Herman's hand and pumped it vigorously while

Karen stood silent, shocked. "Why didn't you tell us, you old scoundrel?"

"We would have if we'd planned ahead two minutes before we took the plunge," Herman explained with a wicked look on his face. "We watched this young couple get married on one of those black sand beaches and the wedding bug bit us right then and there."

"Herman just walked right up to the minister and asked him if he would hitch us again and . . ." Vanessa held up her ring finger a second time. "We renewed our vows and the rest is history."

"There's a lot of this story that's being left out," Luke concluded. "But right now we have more pressing matters."

Speechless, Karen gave him a quizzical look.

"We have champagne to order and toasts to make," he finished with a grin. "Right after I kiss the bride." He leaned down and kissed Vanessa on the cheek. After that, everyone hugged and kissed and exchanged congratulations until Luke finally announced, "Follow me." Once again, he took charge and led the group to a table, gave their order to the waiter, then kept the conversation going until the bubbly arrived and was served.

"A toast," he announced, lifting his champagne goblet. "To the two most un-

predictable people in the world," he
started, trying to think of something pro-
found to say to commemorate the occasion.
"May the saddest day of your future be no
worse than the happiest days of your past."
They clinked their glasses together in the
center of the table. He took a long swallow
of the golden liquid.

"That's so sweet." Vanessa dabbed at her
eyes with a tissue from her pocket.

When Karen didn't readily speak up,
Luke turned to her and said, "That's the
best an almost-groomsman can do without
advance notice." He gave her a playful
wink. "How about the nearly-a-bridesmaid
doing the honors?"

"Of course. A toast." She lifted her glass
and graciously said, "To my oldest and
dearest friend Vanessa. May you be as
happy the rest of your life as you are right
at this moment." She looked to the groom.

"And to Herman," she continued. "May
you always be the husband Vanessa deserves
and forever share in her happiness."

"I love you," Vanessa told her as they
clinked their glasses again. "Honey bunch,"
she drawled out the word. "Why don't you
take our packages to my cabin so we don't
lose them?"

"But—" Herman protested.

"I'll help you old buddy." Luke volunteered, realizing that the women wanted a

few minutes alone for some "girl talk." He wouldn't mind a few minutes with Herman himself, to find out what they were going to do about sleeping arrangements for the rest of the cruise. This was one turn of events he hadn't counted on. "I've got something I want to get from the cabin, too."

"Oh, all right." Herman grudgingly rose from his seat. "But gab fast because we won't be gone long."

Vanessa reached out and ruffled what little hair Herman had on top of his head. "Now, you be a good boy. It's our wedding day. . . ."

Karen couldn't believe what was happening. She wanted to be angry at Vanessa for running off and eloping, but she couldn't. Her friend's happiness was more important to her than the little inconveniences she would have to endure, such as changing rooms. "Tell me all," she urged as soon as the men were out of earshot.

Vanessa leaned back in her chair and gave Karen a blushing grin. "I'm sorry you weren't there, honey, but the moment was right and it was so romantic." She downed the rest of her champagne. "This stuff is fine for starters, but I want something with a little more umpf." She waved a waiter down and ordered a couple of sloe gin fizzes. "I hope that was okay," she said, waiting until Karen nodded. "Now where were we? I hope you aren't too mad that we tied the knot without you."

"Van, hon, I do understand. Really." And she did, too. Heck, she was even a little envious. Vanessa was practically glowing she was so happy. "Don't misunderstand. I'm disappointed that I wasn't there, of course, but—" Karen took her friend's hand. "As long as you're happy, I'm happy."

"You are so damned perfect." Vanessa flung her hands into the air, then pressed one to her chest. "I run off and get married and don't even invite you and you're just so damned nice about it." She threw back her head and laughed. "My mama always said I was the devilish one and you were the angel."

Karen straightened, sighing loudly. "Look closely, Vanessa. There are no wings on my shoulders." She studied the mischievous look in her friend's eyes.

With a shrug, Vanessa added, "Hell, Karen, your sundress fits so perfectly that even the wings are tailormade."

Karen grimaced in amusement, but didn't say anything until the waiter served their drinks. She took a long swig, then said, "Vanessa, you're crazy."

"Maybe a little." Vanessa chuckled again, then grew serious. "I know you really disapprove of me and Herman remarrying the way we did." She paused to take a long draw on her drink. "But I'm not you, Karen. Never have been, never will be."

"Good." Karen felt a pang of regret that she might have unintentionally hurt her friend. Why hadn't she kept her feelings closer to the vest? She wasn't convinced Herman was husband material for anyone, much less Vanessa. But how could she tell her friend—Mrs. Herman Armstrong—that the man she had just remarried might be the biggest mistake of her life. She cleared her throat. "We're not really that different . . . are we?"

Vanessa clamped her hand on her forehead and closed her eyes. When she looked up with a disbelieving grin, she pointed to their drinks. "See that glass."

"Sure," Karen agreed with a nod.

"What do you see?" Vanessa prodded.

"What do you mean?" Karen knew that her friend was making a point. She had a habit of circumventing her elbow to get to her nose, but once there, the point was always crystal clear.

"Tell me what you see." Vanessa gave her a look of intractable determination and waited.

Karen stared at their drinks, then shrugged. "I see a couple of sloe gin fizzes."

Vanessa slid to the edge of her seat and picked up one of the drinks. "And?"

With a flip of her hand, Karen pressed, "And what?"

"Describe them to me." She held the glass up into the sunlight, the deep red of the sloe gin casting prisms of color on the white tablecloth.

"They're drinks, for gosh sakes." Karen picked up her own glass and twisted it in the bright rays causing a ruby pattern to dance between them. "It's just sloe gin. Red. I don't know, give me a hint, Van. What do you want? They're half empty. . . ."

"Ah-ha!" Vanessa slammed down her glass. The liquid sloshed to the brim but didn't spill over.

"Ah-ha?" she repeated.

"That proves my point. You see half empty." Vanessa excitedly waved her hands. "But I see half full. You'd clean up and empty them down the drain. I'd try to keep them filled to the rim."

Karen smiled. She imagined Vanessa with a pitcher of sloe gin filling the glasses after each swallow, only to be followed by Karen who would toss them out right behind her. It was a vicious cycle of fill and empty, fill and empty. She shook the ludicrous image out of her head. Maybe they didn't have much in common, but they brought out the best in each other. And that was enough for her, always had been.

Vanessa's voice clouded with emotion. "I've always wanted to be more like you. I'm Vanessa Jones Mullis Sutherland Armstrong. I'm a three-time loser who's trying it again with husband number three. I'm . . ." Her voice trailed off to a quiet whisper. "I'm the eternal optimist and you're the realistic one."

Surprised at her friend's sudden emotionally charged confession, Karen gave her hand a comforting pat. "Van, you don't need to be like me or anyone else. You're the best . . . one of a kind."

"Humph." Vanessa quickly waved aside the compliment. "I've got to tell you though—" she hesitated with a crooked smile. "My Herman is one of a kind, too. I know it's hard for you to believe, but he is. We made some mistakes the first time around. Hellfire, we both had a few wild oats to sow after our divorce, but I never, ever forgot him. Even with all of Herman's warts, he makes me happy, keeps a grin on my face, and . . . curls my toes, if you know what I mean. It was meant to be."

For her friend's sake, Karen pulled her mouth into a smile. She would willingly give her support and hope for the best. Inside, she still feared the worst. "So, you were born for each other?" Hopefully, her cheerful tone sounded better than it felt.

Vanessa burst out laughing. "Husbands aren't born, honey. The good ones have to be trained." Her lighthearted mood seemed to have returned. "And I'm a much better trainer than I was before. Age does have some advantages."

"Trained?" In spite of her concerns, Karen chuckled. "Vanessa Armstrong, you are wicked to the bone. I can't believe you said that." She shook her head. "I take that back, I can believe you'd do anything. Absolutely anything in the world."

Vanessa's head bobbed in agreement. "My naive, trusting friend. You certainly do have a lot to learn about men."

"Me?" Karen feigned shock. "I'm nearly fifty years old. If I don't know something by now—"

Vanessa interrupted with a wag of her finger. "You're never too old to learn. This old dog plans to keep learning new tricks until they put me six feet under."

Karen rolled her eyes. "What a lovely image!" she cried, good-naturedly.

"I'm available for consultations," she loudly whispered in a conspiratorial tone with an exaggerated wink.

Karen gave her a questioning look, afraid she didn't want to know what her friend was talking about. Sometimes it was better not to encourage Vanessa.

Without waiting for her to respond, Vanessa added, "—you know, for husband hunting."

"Don't you dare!" she threatened, knowing full well that Vanessa and Herman recently had stuck their noses in that barrel already. Luke Wendell wasn't here by accident. She would bet money on that fact, even if she couldn't prove it . . . yet.

Luke discretely gave the maitre d' a wrapped gift to hold for him at the reservations stand, then returned to the candlelit table draped with a white linen cloth . . . and Karen. "Where did our dinner partners disappear to?" He pointed at the empty chairs. "Or dare I ask?"

The corners of her mouth drew into a smile. "They ducked out between the salmon and sorbet, so to speak."

"Was I gone that long?" He pretended to be insulted that they'd left. "Or was it something I said?"

She leaned toward him and spoke in a low voice. "I think it was more what Vanessa whispered in Herman's ear—"

Luke covered his own ears. "That's more than I ever needed to know."

"Tell me about it," she conceded.

For a minute, Luke sat looking at Karen before he realized he was staring. Restlessly, he shifted in his seat, then offered, "What about some dessert?"

"Sounds lovely." With a lifted brow, she added, "Anything chocolate will do for me. It's my weakness."

"I'll remember that," he promised. "Rich and decadent are good choices, too," he added.

The waiter interrupted them to refill their coffee cups. "May I bring you the dessert menu?"

"No need." Luke waved his hand. "We already know what we want."

"Wonderful." The waiter held the coffee decanter, waiting for their order. "What may I bring you?"

Luke shared a glance with Karen. "Something chocolaty and rich and decadent," he ordered.

"I think we have just the thing to fit that bill," the waiter countered without hesitation. "The Chef's special and my personal favorite . . . two pieces of French silk pie coming right up. Or would you prefer one piece with two forks?"

Luke gestured to Karen. "It's your call."

"Better bring us two." She stifled a grin. "We wouldn't want to fight over dessert on Christmas."

The waiter nodded slightly. "Certainly, madame," he said, then left.

Immediately, Luke gave the maitre d' the signal to bring his package to the table.

"What's that?" Her lips parted in surprise as Luke slid the festive package in front of her wrapped in bright red paper tied with a white satin ribbon. "For me?"

Luke nodded, a tad embarrassed. Buying Karen a gift had been a spontaneous gesture that he'd wanted to do at the time, but had worried about ever since.

"You shouldn't have," she protested.

"It's just a little something I thought you might like." A tiny insecure voice inside made Luke wonder if he'd done the right thing. He could barely wait for her to open the gift so he could see her reaction.

"I feel so bad." Karen fingered the ribbon, but still didn't open it. "I'm embarrassed that I didn't get you anything," she apologized.

"Don't give it another thought." He felt an unwelcome warmth creep up his neck. "Aren't you going to open your gift?"

Karen picked up the package. "This is such beautiful wrapping. What a sweet thing to do, Luke."

His stomach nervously churned, but he kept his voice even. "You'd better wait and see if you like it," he teased.

She paused, her eyes bright with pleasure. "I know I'll like it because it's from you."

Luke gave her a thankful smile as he waited for her to open his gift.

"But you really shouldn't have." She untied the ribbon and ripped back the paper. Gingerly, she raised the lid and peeked inside. "Oh, Luke. It's beautiful!" She lifted a charcoal drawing out from the bed of tissue. "It's a sketch of us."

He felt as though he could breathe again because she seemed genuinely pleased with his gift. "The artist at the Volcano Gallery sketched us while we were shopping," he explained. "When I saw it, I had to have it."

"What a great idea!" She tilted it toward the light to better see the details. "It really looks like us."

"I thought so, too." Luke reached over and moved the sketch to see it more clearly, but accidentally brushed his fingers against hers. An immediate shiver of attraction coursed through him. "I wanted you to have it to remember today by."

Their desserts arrived, and Karen felt the conversation shift back to the newly married couple. She was delighted with Luke's gift, but needed some time to sort out her feelings about him. Everything was happening so quickly, she wanted to make sure she didn't blow it before they had a chance to get to know one another.

"Vanessa and Herman are missing out on a treat," she said after her first bite of the sinfully delicious concoction. Something told her the newlyweds were probably indulging in a few sinful delights of their own. By now, she hoped it was in their own cabin and not the one she and Vanessa were sharing. She caught herself frowning, then tried to hide it from Luke.

He placed his fork down on the plate and studied her as she jabbed at her dessert. His dark eyes were gentle, understanding. "You're really upset about this marriage, aren't you?"

Karen nodded, but didn't say anything. She was afraid if she started, she'd say too much about his buddy Herman.

"I know Herman pretty well." There was a soothing resonance in his tone. "If he made vows, then he's committed to them."

"Herman didn't do so well before," she reminded him. "If he really is big on commitment, then what happened the last time he took his marriage vows?"

Luke sat quietly for a moment. "I don't think he would deliberately hurt Vanessa." A note of sincerity rang in his voice. "Actually, I think he loves her in his own way."

"His way may not be enough," she said emphatically.

"Isn't that a moot point since they've already remarried?"

Karen was beginning to realize that Luke Wendell didn't pull any punches. His no-nonsense, straight-to-the-point approach was refreshing, but unsettling all at the same time. "I suppose it is," she said with a sigh. "I'm just worried about her. She *is* my oldest and dearest friend." A lump welled in her throat as she fought back the tears that misted her eyes.

Luke leaned close. "I understand."

"We leave them alone for two shakes of a lamb's tail and look what happens." From behind them, Herman's voice penetrated the noisy room.

With a sidelong glance, Karen turned and saw Herman and Vanessa. "Vanessa!" she cried, surprised to see her again tonight.

"I thought you newlyweds had, uh—" Luke waved them toward the empty chairs.

"Retired for the evening?" Karen suggested to help him out as they sat down.

"That's a good way to put it," Herman said with a slap on his thigh before sliding his chair under the table. "We've retired enough for the time being." He gave Vanessa a broad wink. "There's only so much retiring a man my age can handle at one time, right honey bunch?"

Vanessa leaned over and whispered something in Herman's ear.

"Why you little scamp." Herman gave her a kiss on the lips, then both of them burst out laughing.

"Private joke," Vanessa explained, practically glowing. She gave Herman some kind of a signal and waved her hand toward the bar. "Why don't you boys go and get us a nightcap?"

"But—" Luke started to protest, then stopped when Herman cocked his head toward the long walnut bar across the room.

"I think the women want a chance to chat." Herman loudly slid his chair back and stood up.

When the two men headed across the room, Vanessa reached into her purse and pulled out a small gaudily wrapped present. "For you," she said with a flourish. "Merry Christmas."

Karen chuckled and searched in her own bag slug across the back of her chair. "And for you." She placed a gift in front of Vanessa, then suggested, "Open yours first." She enjoyed watching Vanessa open gifts even more than she enjoyed receiving them herself. There was a childlike excitement that seemed to possess her when Vanessa ripped into packages.

"What a fantastic parrot!" she squealed. Vanessa held the colorful pin up to her shoulder, then grabbed Karen in an appreciative hug. "It's fabulous! Please pin it on me."

Karen carefully secured the parrot onto Vanessa's calf-length Aloha shift, brightly splashed with red and yellow flowers. "There you go."

"Thanks, Van. You're the greatest," she said, as Vanessa pushed the gift bag closer.

"Now you open yours," Vanessa directed, the excitement glittering in her eyes. "Herman and I did a little shopping today."

"I'm surprised you had time," Karen teased.

"Oh, you!" Vanessa blushed like a schoolgirl. "I hope you like it."

Karen separated the tissue and pulled a small white box out of the bag. When she lifted the lid, she gasped. "Van, you shouldn't have!"

"I hear no trip to Hawaii is complete without a little coral to take home," Vanessa said, her voice laden with emotion.

"They're lovely." Immediately, Karen replaced her gold shell earrings with the delicate black coral balls. She gently touched her friend's arm. "Thank you."

Vanessa lowered her lashes, then looked away.

In a serious tone, Karen asked, "Are you happy, Van? Really happy?"

"Unbearably," she answered with tears in

her eyes. "Herman and I still love each other."

"But it was so quick," Karen said, trying to keep the doubt from her tone.

"Sure, we acted impulsively, but—" she snickered. "For once in my life, I wanted something and just did it."

Karen's heart lurched. She didn't bother to correct Vanessa, but her friend had acted on impulse about most of life's big decisions, and this one was no different. "I do wish you all the happiness in the world," she told Vanessa, throwing both arms around her neck.

"We're back," Herman announced in his loud, gruff voice. "Did we give you ladies plenty of time?" he asked, setting a couple of brandies on the table.

Vanessa shook her head. "Almost, but I haven't told her about—"

"I've got some good news," Herman interrupted, "and some bad news. Which do you want first?"

Karen shrugged, a knot forming in the pit of her stomach. "Whatever."

"The bad news is there are absolutely no cabins left on this whole damned ship," Herman said, his words a bit slurred.

Karen's bad feeling was getting worse. She'd come here to relax, but she wasn't getting much of that tonight. "And the good news?" Good news would hit the spot right this moment.

"The good news is that we have our own white knight." He slapped Luke on the shoulder. "He's offered to give us his cabin for tonight."

"But where will Luke sleep?" Vanessa cried. "I thought you said there weren't any cabins left."

"I'll find a bed in the crew's quarters," Luke assured them. "Never let it be said I stood in the way of love."

Karen was impressed with Luke's graciousness about being ousted from his cabin.

"Honey bunch, I believe they are playing our song." Herman stood up and self-consciously bowed. "How about we dance the light fantastic, Mrs. Armstrong?"

"I'd love to take a spin around the floor with you, Mr. Armstrong." Vanessa took his offered arm with a big smile on her face. "We'll catch up to you guys later," she called over her shoulder to Karen.

"Make that tomorrow," Herman corrected with a wink.

"Those two are quite a pair," Luke said.

Karen watched the couple dancing cheek to cheek in the shadows of the dance floor. "I have to admit that they do look happy."

Luke glanced at his watch, then grinned. "We've got to go."

"Got an appointment?" she asked with a laugh.

"As a matter of fact, *we* do," Luke said, urging her toward the door.

"We do?" Karen grimaced in good humor. "Where?"

His mouth curved in a mischievous smile. "Up on the top deck." He reached out and took her hand. "Don't you remember?"

Karen felt the warmth of his hand spread throughout her body. Without giving him an answer, she laced her fingers more securely through his and eagerly followed across the room, down the corridor, and out onto the deck.

"I promised you a show," he told her with a sly smile as they moved out of the lighted area and up the stairs. "I'll bet you've never had a date take you to an active volcano before. After that, we can do whatever you like."

In the shrouded moonlight of the ship's deck, Karen could think of a few things she would like to do with Luke Wendell. She glanced over at him, but his face was barely visible in the dark.

Thank goodness, Luke can't read my mind.

"Here we are." Luke stopped next to the railing at the corner of the top deck in front of the ship's empty bridge.

As the ship rocked and swayed through the blackened sea, Karen could see isolated lights in the distant hills. The sky brimmed with stars that somehow seemed brighter as the lone ship sliced through the water with a swishing sound. A sliver of moon shone down on the wide expanse of watery darkness, barely illuminating the ocean with its light.

"What do you think?" His voice was husky and low.

"It's absolutely breathtaking." Karen did something spontaneous and out of character. Her pulse skittered as she stepped closer to Luke, her hand still linked with his. She tiptoed to reach him and gently kissed his strong, full mouth in a sweet, lingering kiss. Afterwards, Luke gathered her into his arms. With a sigh of pleasure, she pressed her head against his chest.

Luke whispered into her hair, "Now that was breathtaking."

"And I didn't even need mistletoe," she said, smiling. Her voice sounded loud in the quiet darkness.

Luke pulled something out of his pocket. "I had some just in case." He lifted a sprig of slightly wilted mistletoe to show her.

Karen laughed, feeling complimented that Luke had actually thought about kissing her again. "Hang onto that mistletoe for future reference." She snuggled back against his chest. "You know, this was such a good idea, I'll come up on deck with you anytime."

"I'm glad, Karen." Luke kissed the top of her head, then turned her to face the island, his arms still wrapped around her shoulders. "There it is!" His voice was filled with excitement. He pointed and cried, "Look! Over at the island."

"I can't see anything, can you?" Karen squinted at the darkened island to see what Luke was talking about.

"Magic," he whispered.

No, Luke, being here with you is magical.

"It's hard to believe that I'm actually standing here looking at lava. Real lava," he explained.

Her eyes focused on a bright red spot in the darkness. "Lava," she repeated, awed at the incredible sight. A tiny red line meandered to the land's edge and slowly descended into the sea, flooding the water with fiery streaks. As the lava hit the surface, steam sizzled and rose into the air.

"Scary, isn't it?" he asked. "Something that powerful is so close we can see it from the ship."

"Thanks." She turned to face him. "For everything; for sharing this extraordinary sight, the sketch—" she hesitated, "—for spending today with me."

"You don't need to thank me. You've made this a Christmas I'll never forget."

"I'll never forget, either." Karen stored away the memory of their perfect, sunny day together in paradise; the kind of perfection she had encountered rarely in her life.

Hand in hand, they leisurely strolled back to Karen's room. "Where *are* you gonna sleep?" she asked him when they reached her door.

"I'm not sure," he said, avoiding her gaze.

Karen touched his face to get his attention. "Luke, tell me the truth. There is no other available bed, is there?" she asked.

"Well . . ."

"It's okay. Your secret's safe with me," she assured him, the warm spot in her heart for him growing larger by the minute. "You just said that so Vanessa wouldn't feel bad about you having no place to sleep."

"I guess. But I'll be fine."

"You certainly will." Karen turned and unlocked her door. She shoved it open and waved a hand inside. "This is silly. There are two beds in my cabin . . ." Her face was blistering hot with embarrassment. "We're both adults," she stammered over the words.

"Thanks, but I couldn't," he protested, not following her when she entered the cabin. "I wouldn't want you to think that I'm taking advantage of you."

"I don't think that." She reached for his hand. "I trust you, Luke."

"Maybe you shouldn't," he teased.

"But I do," she insisted.

He paused. "Okay, then you've got yourself a roommate for tonight."

Karen self-consciously pulled the blanket up to her chin. Even in the semidarkness, she was embarrassed that all she had on was a satin nightie . . . and Luke was only a few feet away. Was he naked? she wondered. He must be, she thought, remembering that the porter had only delivered a shaving kit and nothing else.

"Karen?"

"Yes," she managed.

"I know I didn't make the best impression when we went out on our blind date."

Her heart hammered in her chest. "That was a long time ago—"

"I know, but first impressions last a long time." In the other bed, she saw him lean up on one elbow. "Let's wipe the slate clean and start over. What do you say?"

We already have. "Can you see me?" she asked, trying to ignore the fact that he was so close she could reach out to him.

"A little."

"Good." Karen looked to see that Luke was watching, then swung her hand back and forth in the air to erase an imaginary chalk board. "Consider it done," she said, smiling in the darkness. "Slate's clean as a whistle."

"I like your style, Karen Oliver," he told her.

She could feel a tangible bond growing between them. I like a lot of things about you, she thought to herself, keeping the words locked away as if saying them would scare him off.

"Merry Christmas." Luke settled back against his pillow. "And sweet dreams."

The very air around her seemed electrified. "Merry Christmas to you, too." Karen closed her eyes and started to drift off with images of Luke's sun-kissed face in her head.

"Karen?" Luke whispered from across the room. "Are you asleep?"

"Not yet." She held her breath, waiting for him to continue.

"Can we do this again?" he asked, his voice hopeful.

"How about tomorrow?" Her heart danced with anticipation as she waited for his answer.

"I'd like that very much."

"Me, too," she agreed, smiling in the darkness, images of mistletoe and magic and Luke Wendell in her head.

A Miracle in Miami
Stacey Dennis

"Honestly, Lil, you don't have to pretend with me. For heaven's sake, how long have we worked together? Ten years now? It's all right to let your hair down and admit that you're hurting. In fact, it's the healthy thing to do."

Lillian Wynnewood smiled at her friend and co-worker, Martha Smythe. Martha meant well, of course. That's why Lillian wasn't angry at Martha's insistent attempts to get her to admit that she was emotionally devastated by her recent divorce. And in all honesty, she had been, at first, when she and Andrew finally admitted that they shared nothing but a roof and the monthly bills. It had seemed like such a terrible failure, and all those wasted years! But no, most of them hadn't been wasted at all. She and Andrew had brought three healthy, beautiful children into the world, and the early years of their marriage had been good, busy, and filled with achievement, for them and their children. Only somehow, somewhere along the way, she and Andrew

had lost the magic. And by the time they
realized what had happened, it was simply
too late to recapture it.

So, the divorce was now final. Andrew
had resigned his position at Acto Produc-
tion Corp., and had moved to another state
to make a fresh start. After all the tears had
dried, they had parted as friends, and Lillian knew she would always care for the man
who had fathered her children and shared
the years of her youth and enthusiasm. But
it was over. A closed chapter, and now it
was time to move on.

"Martha, I'm fine, really. What can I do
or say to convince you? You know how many
tears I shed when Andrew and I decided to
split, but it's over. I'm over it. It's time for
me to get on with my life."

"Of course it is, and no one wants you
to do that more than me, but . . . well, it
just doesn't seem quite right for someone
to bounce back from a divorce as fast as you
have. Are you sure you won't have a delayed
reaction one of these days and end up . . ."

Lillian snorted and narrowed her eyes at
her friend. "Aha! Now I know why you and
the others have been watching me so warily.
You're afraid that one of these days I'll
snap . . . go off the deep end and shoot
this place up, right?" The idea was so ludicrous, so ridiculous that Lillian felt nearly
hysterical. Good grief! When would her

women friends let up on her? When would they start treating her in a normal way again?

"Now, Lillian, you know we're only concerned because we all care about you. Anyway, if you say you're fine, then I believe you. What are your plans for the holidays? Would you like to come and spend the Christmas weekend with me and Jim and the kids? Mark and Jessica and the baby will have the guest room, but Jim has a very comfortable sofa bed in his den and . . ."

"I'm going to Florida over Christmas," Lillian said, interrupting Martha's ramblings. "I already have my airline tickets."

"Florida? At Christmas?"

Martha looked like she had gone into shock, either that or Lillian was the one who had gone into shock and Martha was going to have to revive her. Her expression was so comical, Lillian couldn't repress a completely unprofessional giggle as she raked her french manicured acrylic nails through her cropped blond hair. "For heaven's sake, Martha, you make Florida sound like a third world country! It's warm and sunny and they celebrate Christmas there too, you know."

"I . . . well, of course. I'm sure they do, but . . . well how on earth can a person get into the holiday spirit when it's 90 degrees and humid? Really, Lill, it's un-American!"

"Maybe," Lillian said, closing and locking her desk and picking up her Fendi bag, "but I'm going anyway. I've spent every winter of my life up north shivering and braving ice and windstorms. This year I'm doing things differently."

"But what about the boys, and isn't Mandy due to have her baby soon?" Martha asked, hurrying as she fought to keep up with Lillian's lively pace on the way to the elevator.

"Mandy's baby isn't due until late February and both Eddie and John and their families are spending the holidays with their in-laws this year. That's how they do it, you know. They alternate years. Next year it will be my turn to entertain them, and since Mandy can't travel this year . . . well, it seemed like the perfect chance for me to do something a little different."

"Well, I suppose if that's really what you want . . ."

"It is, Martha, trust me," Lillian said. Impulsively, she gave her friend a quick hug, "but thanks for inviting me to join your family's festivities. I do appreciate it." She gave a brisk wave and sprinted towards the parking lot her firm maintained for its employees. And as she slid behind the wheel of her sleek silver Buick, she heaved a sigh of relief. One down and three to go, she thought, ticking off the names of her three closest friends before she closed her fingers around the steering wheel. Gail, Rose, and Paige. She still had to convince them that she hadn't lost every shred of her sanity when she signed the divorce decree. Once that was done, she'd get down to some serious packing. Miami, here I come, she thought, shifting into drive and pulling out onto the street that was rapidly filling with rush hour traffic.

"I really do love my job," Lillian explained to her cat, Liberace, as she opened a can of tuna treat an hour later, "and I really will miss you, but it's going to be great to forget about traffic jams and deadlines for a few days." She sat the dish of cat food on the floor and went to the sink to wash her hands. As she lathered and rinsed, she wondered why it was that none of her friends could understand that she was actually enjoying the freedom of living alone and having no one to account to after 28 years of marriage? Didn't they ever wish they didn't have to rush home from work and prepare a meal? Was the idea of spending nights alone with just a pet for company really that threatening to them?

But maybe she wasn't being fair. Everyone was different, and as she had told Martha and the others, she would always feel some regret that she and Andrew hadn't been able to maintain a warm, loving, fulfilling relationship. It would have been sweet to grow old together, to sit on the porch and rock as the sun went down, to see their grandbabies come into the world and grow up. Lillian shrugged. They would still do those things, just not together.

Carrying a plate of cheese and crackers and fruit into the living room, Lillian curled up in her favorite chair and picked up the remote that controlled her stereo. How wonderful it was to listen to her favorite piano classics as she ate instead of the drone of the television news shows Andrew had preferred. The news was always the same anyway, mainly depressing, but listening to soft, melodious tunes made her feel warm and mellow. Yes, there was definitely something to be said for the single life.

Ron Martin picked a towel up off the deck of his sailboat and mopped his brow. "Hot today," he muttered, straightening and massaging his back. "Any more of those cold beers, Willy?"

"Coming up," Willy Rodriguez said promptly, reaching for the cooler sitting on the dock.

When Willy handed Ron the icy can, Ron held it against his forehead a moment, then snapped the tab and took a long, grateful swallow. "Best thing ever invented," he said a moment later, grinning at Willy.

"Nah, women come in first in my book, old man. You've just forgotten what it's like to get all hot and bothered by a curvy chick."

"I've forgotten all right," Ron said, a mock growl in his voice as he turned to the younger man. "I've forgotten more than you'll ever know!"

"Prove it, oldtimer," Willy taunted good naturedly. "Come out with me and my buddies tonight and we'll scare up some action. Plenty of good-looking tourist ladies wandering around this time of year, you know?"

"Thanks, but no thanks, Willy, my man," Ron replied. "All I'm interested in right now is getting my boat ready to sail. I'm planning to cruise the Keys over Christmas." He gestured towards the golden Lab slumbering peacefully on the boat deck. "Me and Charlie have plans."

"Sounds good," Willy answered, finishing his beer and aiming the empty can towards a recycling barrel a few feet away. "I'd come with you, but me and Georgie got plans too, you know?"

"Yeah, I know. The eternal hunters. Well, good luck, buddy. You'll probably need it." He winked. "Or maybe it's the women who'll be needing the luck."

As he watched his young friend saunter

away, Ron grinned and shook his head. Maybe he was getting old, because the idea of cruising the streets of Miami, even the newly popular South Beach area that was drawing ever increasing crowds of the "rich and famous," or hitting the singles bars, simply did not appeal to him. No, he'd much rather curl up with a good book and listen to the classics on his stereo. For that matter, he thought, shaking his head again, listening to Charlie snore was more tempting than the sounds those singles bars gave off. Hard rock, disco. He'd never been able to "get with it," as his ex-wife, Clair, had so eloquently put it. And when he told Clair that he wanted to chuck his lucrative law practice and spend a couple of years sailing the warm Florida waters, well, for Clair that was the final straw.

So he'd joined the ranks of the newly divorced. Clair got the house in Atlanta, and a generous settlement, that should, if she wasn't too extravagant, keep her comfortably for many years. Oddly enough, the divorce was more of a relief than anything else. He and Clair had never had children. Pregnancy would have spoiled Clair's reed-slim figure, and running after "snotty-nosed brats," as Clair phrased it, was not the way she wanted to spend her days. So there really hadn't been much of a marriage to break up. It was more like two roommates, who had finally admitted that they weren't compatible, splitting up. And now, for the first time in years, Ron felt free. He no longer sat in his car fighting the early morning Atlanta traffic jams. He didn't carry a briefcase these days, nor did he wear the regulatory three-piece, pin-stripe suits and stiff collared white shirts. Instead, the uniform of the day was usually tennis shoes or docksiders with shorts and T-shirts. Smiling to himself, Ron looked down at his chest. The one he was presently wearing sported a colorful picture of Jaws's open mouth, and the words underneath proclaimed, "SEND MORE TOURISTS! THE LAST ONES WERE DELICIOUS!" Ron patted the shark's head companionably. Yeah, he knew. The height of "Tourist Tackiness." Clair would be appalled. But Clair wasn't here and he wore what he pleased these days, and besides, the idea, silly as it was, of Jaws systematically devouring tourists pleased him in a ridiculous way.

"Hell, not really," he spoke out loud. He wasn't that far gone, but sometimes he did wish that some of them would stay home. During "season," which seemed to be most of the year now, the entire state crawled with visitors. Camera-carrying, shorts-clad parents and their noisy, demanding kids. Senior citizens in wheelchairs and walking with canes. And the lovers, the young newly married or not, strolling the beach with their tight, hard bodies, arms clutching one another, their eyes glistening with hope and dreams. Ah, they were the ones that bothered him the most. Didn't they know that life never turned out the way you expected it to?

"I am getting old," Ron told himself. Because normally he was totally content with his life. It was only now and then that he thought about what he might have missed. Only occasionally that he felt a little lonely, and wondered what it would be like to have a good woman by his side at this stage of his life. He heaved his empty beer can towards the trash bin, and stood up. Back to work, if he ever expected to cruise the Keys.

"Well, you certainly have the right to spend Christmas any way you want," Paige Arther admitted grudgingly, "but I still think it's weird to be lying on a beach covered with suntan oil when all your nearest and dearest are baking gingerbread cookies and braving snow and sleet to find exactly the right present. Won't you miss all that?"

Lillian laughed and cocked her head to look at her friend as she carefully scrutinized her latest ad campaign for Super Crunch cereals. "Come on, Paige, what do you think? Be totally honest for once, okay?

Doesn't a relaxing few days sunning your buns sound like heaven? Especially when pitted against dealing with Steve's mother?"

"Ugh! Please! Don't remind me. Mother Arther is coming for two full weeks. Count 'em, that's fourteen long, miserable days and nights. No, scratch the nights. I'll go to bed at nine the whole time she's with us. Let Steve listen to her weep and wail. I swear, Lill, if she makes one more crack about my sausage stuffing . . ."

Lillian closed the folder she had been studying and smiled. "I rest my case," she said dramatically.

"Okay, I guess you've got a point," Paige admitted, shrugging, "but what choice do the 'good wives' like me have? I mean . . . oh hell, Lill, I didn't mean that the way it sounded. I know you were a good wife."

"Actually, I was," Lillian said, "but it still wasn't enough, so now I'm going to do exactly as I please."

"Amen to that, sister!" Rose Clemmins, a tall, gorgeously dressed and coiffed black woman, entered the room, a cardboard container of coffee and sandwiches in her hands. "Make room on the table," she instructed. "I've got roast beef, corned beef, and cheesecake for dessert, and I'm starved!"

"How does she do it?" Gail Carter and Martha said in unison, as they followed

Rose into the room. "If I ate like that my pantyhose would explode," Gail joked. "Tain't fair, Rose."

"Good African genes," Rose said, grinning and revealing pearl white, perfectly even teeth.

"And that's another thing. Those damn teeth. Good God! Do you have any idea what my dentist would charge for a set like that?" Martha complained.

"Do you have any idea what my plastic surgeon would charge for a set like that?" Gail asked, pointing at Rose's high, well rounded bosom.

"Ladies, ladies, please!" Paige chided. "This is our last chance to see Lillian before she flies off into the sunset, so let's dispense with the petty, juvenile jealousy, shall we?" Lowering her voice and cutting her eyes to the black woman, Paige leaned close and whispered. "What kind of hormones are you taking?"

Everyone laughed, then they all crowded around the display table that Lillian normally used to lay out her ads. At the moment it was covered with a plastic tablecloth adorned with gaudy palm trees and some long-necked white birds.

"What are those anyway?" Gail asked, pointing at the paper birds. "Anorexic swans or something?"

"Egrets, oh uneducated one," Rose said

regally, as she passed out sandwiches and containers of coffee. "And that," she said, pointing at an illustration that depicted an alligator that lay perilously close to Lillian's corned beef on rye, "is a man- or woman-eating, as the case may be, alligator, not to be confused with a crocodile which . . ."

"Stop it!" Lill pleaded. "I'm starving, but I can't eat and laugh at the same time. I say dig in and we'll chat later!"

"Amen!" Rose said again, reaching for a thick roast beef on pumpernickel. "Let's do it!"

A half hour later, when the food had been reduced to a disgracefully small pile of crumbs, Paige pushed back her chair with a groan. "Ten extra laps around the desk for me," she said. "That sandwich must have weighed at least a pound and a half."

"Did you bring the presents?" Gail asked Martha.

"Hey guys, what's with the presents? You didn't have to do that," Lillian protested. "I didn't get anything for any of you."

"No problem," Rose said, grinning. "We'll all get enough 'no-name' perfume to sink a battleship, not to mention the wrong size sweaters, funky animal-shaped bedroom slippers, and of course the obligatory electric can opener from our mothers-in-laws. No need for any more, girl."

"Rose, you are terrible. Who gives you no-name perfume anyway?" Lillian asked curiously.

"The grandkids. Who else? Trevor is following right along in his Daddy's footsteps. Allen always gave me a giant bottle of something called 'Evening Splendor' toilet water. Now I ask you, why would any woman of sound mind want to put water from the toilet on her bod?"

All four women laughed until their sides ached, then they sobered. "You all know I'm kidding," Rose said. "I wouldn't trade those precious gifts for all the diamonds in Africa . . . well, maybe . . ."

"All right, gals, it's present time. Here, Lill, open this one first. It's something I know you'll use," Martha said.

Lillian felt tears sting her eyes. These women, her friends and co-workers for more than ten years, were the sisters she had never had. Even though she was only going away for two weeks she would miss them. Her fingers felt clumsy as she struggled with the brightly colored wrapping paper. "It's a . . . oh gosh, it's a bikini! Do you have any idea how long it's been since I've worn one of these?"

"It's never too late," Gail reminded her, "especially when an old broad like you has a body that won't quit."

"Oh, I'm not so sure about that," Lillian

said, holding up the scraps of flowered material and eyeing them quizzically. "Do I dare?"

"Absolutely!" Paige said loudly. "You'll be letting all of us down if you don't."

"This goes with the bikini," Rose said, winking, "just in case you want to add a little mystery."

Getting into the spirit of things, Lillian opened the second package in record time and was soon holding up a length of wispy lace. "What," she demanded, pinning Rose with her eyes, "is this?"

"A cover-up, naturally," Rose said, trying to look innocent.

"What exactly do you expect it to cover?" Lillian asked, brows raised.

"Oh, Lill, get with it!" Paige said. "It's an illusion, a hint of mystery . . . a wisp of femininity . . . a . . ."

"Help! Someone stop her, please! She's in her advertising mode. Push a button! Pull a plug!" Gail cried.

"Will you all cut it out? I thought this was to be a serious, sentimental goodbye party for Lillian?"

All eyes focused on Martha. "Serious?" Paige asked. "Sentimental?" Rose murmured.

"All right, then laugh-in it is. But come on, let Lill open the rest of her gifts. Sooner or later we all have to get back to work."

When she left the office that night, after one last lingering look at the perfectly decorated, twinkling tree in the lobby, Lill felt tears sting her eyes. Maybe she was making a terrible mistake. Maybe she would have a horrible, miserable time. Maybe she'd miss all her friends so much she'd end up taking the first flight back up north. Maybe the sun would blister her skin, and the sand on the beach would make her itch, and maybe she wouldn't even like the Florida lobster she'd heard so much about.

"Get a grip, lady," she chided herself as she turned up her coat collar against the northern winds and hurried to the parking lot. "You made a decision and you're going to stick with it, and you'll have a good time if it kills you!"

The hotel was just as Lillian had pictured it. A large, pink stucco building that had once been glamorous, but now looked slightly tired and worn. But the rooms were clean and comfortable, the pool was heated, and best of all she could walk to the beach. Lillian had chosen this particular hotel over all the others because, despite what she'd told her friends, what she really wanted was a nice, quiet, relaxing few days in the sun. She wasn't interested in spending half her life savings, or hobnobbing with the "beautiful" people. All she really wanted was to relax and unwind from all the stresses of the past year. Her divorce, Mandy's near miscarriage, not to mention the daily strains of her job. Laughing lightly as the taxi driver unloaded her luggage and a uniformed porter came forward to take it, Lillian silently apologized to her yuppy daughter. Her position with Bradley Marketing, Inc., was not a "job." It was, as Mandy frequently reminded Lillian, a career, and a prestigious one at that. How many women achieved the degree of success in their chosen field that Lillian had? Well, she enjoyed it, of course, and she was proud of her small successes, but right now her position at Bradley's seemed like a job. Sorry, Mandy, Lillian said silently.

"Ma'am?" The porter was looking at Lillian expectantly and she quickly stepped forward. "I'm ready," she said.

Her room had an ocean view. It was the one thing she had insisted on. There was one queen-sized bed with a mattress that only sagged a little, a desk with a complimentary pad of writing paper and pen, a chipped and scratched dresser and a color television on a wall mount. But the bathroom was scrupulously clean, and there was a tub as well as a shower. Lillian closed her eyes and visualized herself soaking in floral scented bubble bath for a long, uninterrupted time. When had she last done that? After hanging her most wrinkle-prone outfits in the closet and settling her shorts and T-shirts in the dresser drawers, Lill put on khaki shorts and a plain white T-shirt. She slipped her feet into sandals and ran a comb through her fine, gray-streaked blond hair. Thank goodness she'd had a cut just a couple of weeks ago. Her hair was at the perfect length now. Short, but not severe, and it curled against her cheeks in soft wisps. Smart and sleek, but not old maidish, she thought, checking her appearance in the dresser mirror. Without pretense, she realized that Paige was right. Her body didn't seem to want to quit. Not movie star gorgeous, of course, but pretty decent for a fifty-year-old. Maybe she would wear that scandalous bikini after all.

Ron saw the woman and blinked. Great bod, he thought, but definitely not a kid. Fortyish, he decided, as he tossed a stick for Charlie to fetch, and damned attractive. But it wasn't just the woman's looks that appealed to him. There was something about the way she walked, slowly, as though she had plenty of time. Most of the female snow birds he saw acted as though they had a train to catch. Their movements were tense and jerky and their eyes darted constantly, as if at any moment they might hop up and flee, back to the corporate world he'd so recently escaped. Of course, he'd go back to his law career someday. He wasn't planning to be a beach bum forever. This was just a brief respite in time, a break from all the strain and stress.

"Hi," Lillian said, laughing as she approached and watched Charlie growl and snarl at the stick Ron had tossed him. "Is that your dog?"

"That's Charlie," Ron said. "He's my best buddy."

"Man's best friend, eh?" Lillian asked curiously.

Up close Ron could see that she was probably a little older than he'd originally thought, but definitely "well preserved," as Willy and his pals would often describe an attractive older woman.

"I'm Ron Martin," he said, holding out his hand, "and who are you?"

"Lillian Wynnewood," Lill said, placing her own untanned hand in Ron's weathered grip. Strong, she thought, when he gave a slight squeeze. Definitely a strong, confident man. She liked the way he smiled and interacted with his dog. Any man who was comfortable with animals was okay in her book.

"I just arrived," she said, "and I thought I'd take a little walk on the beach and explore. Are you . . . do you live here in Florida?"

Ron grinned. "What gave you the first clue?"

"Well, I suppose your tan could have been accomplished in a salon, but somehow you just look too comfortable to be a tourist."

"You're absolutely right. I am comfortable and the tan was achieved the old-fashioned way, by hours and hours spent in the sun. Charlie and I came to Florida last year. I'm working on a sailboat now and as soon as it's finished we'll be cruising the Keys. Ever been there?"

"The Keys? No. I'm afraid I never made it that far south. Actually, this is the first time I've been in Florida in years."

"Really? That's a shame. This is paradise, you know, or at least that's what the tourism ads proclaim."

"I know. I work at an advertising agency."

"Ah, the good old corporate conglomerate, and this is your brief respite?"

"Something like that," Lillian replied. Somehow they had fallen into step side by side, with Charlie dancing around them in the warm sand. Lillian had taken off her sandals and they dangled from her hand.

"Are you here alone?" Ron asked.

An alarm bell went off in Lillian's brain. Years of living and working in the big city had conditioned her. After all, she had no earthly idea who this man was. Just because he had kind gray eyes and a tan to die for didn't mean anything, nor did the fact that he had a good relationship with his dog. Hell, even serial killers had pets, she reminded herself.

"I'd better be getting back," she said, neatly sidestepping his question as she picked up her pace.

Later, after showering and napping for an hour, Lillian was back in front of the mirror. Was it silly to fuss so much with her appearance when there was no one to care how she looked? "I care," she reminded herself sternly. She had always been a touch vain, or at least that's what her ex had said. He hadn't minded, of course. In fact the time she spent in the bathroom and the cosmetics she collected had amused Andrew, at least in the early years. He had enjoyed showing off his nicely dressed, well made-up and perfumed wife. And Lillian had always taken pride in her appearance, hence the careful control of her diet and her continuous exercise routine. Aerobics three times a week and a half hour on her skier every evening. "I'll probably feel like a slug by the time I go home," she muttered to her mirrored reflection. Then she remembered that she had a heated pool just steps from her room, as well as a whole ocean to splash around in. Despite the fact that she was on vacation, she would exercise.

The hotel dining room, a large, plant-filled room was only half-full when Lillian entered. She stepped up to the hostess and requested a table.

"For one?" the woman asked, arching darkly penciled brows. "Or will you be meeting someone?"

"No, I'm not meeting anyone," Lillian said, trying to keep the irritation out of her voice. "I'll be dining alone."

"I hope not," a familiar, deep voice said from behind her.

Lillian turned and there he was. Her walking companion from the beach, only he was no longer wearing shorts and the Golden Lab was missing from his side.

"You," Lillian said. "Are you staying here, too?"

"Nope. I live on my sailboat, but the food here is decent so . . ."

"Will you two be dining together, sir?" the woman asked, her tone a shade more respectful than it had been when she addressed Lillian earlier.

"Would you mind?" Ron asked, smiling disarmingly. "I really do hate to eat alone."

Lillian nodded. "A table for two," she instructed the hostess. She smiled at Ron. "At home I dine with Liberace or Mantovani."

"Ah, a music lover," Ron said.

"That too, but Liberace is my cat, a silver-tipped Persian."

Ron laughed, lightly gripping Lillian's elbow as they moved to follow the hostess to their table. "I'm sure the real Liberace would have been thrilled to know there's a silver-tipped Persian named after him."

"Actually he was. I wrote and told him. I was a great fan of his and naming my cat after him was a sincere compliment. I'm pleased to say he took it as such."

"Will this be suitable?" the hostess asked, as she placed two menus on a small table next to the window.

"Perfect," Ron said, giving the woman a smile that made her thin cheeks flush. "Give us a few minutes before you send the waiter, all right?"

"Certainly. Enjoy your dinner."

"I think we just gave her something to talk about," Lillian said, as Ron held her chair. "I just finished telling her I was alone and then you show up out of thin air. She probably thinks I pick up men all the time."

"Do you?" Ron teased. "You handled yourself with perfect aplomb, as if you've had practice."

"Oh, absolutely. I live in Chicago and I dine with strange men every night. I also," Lillian joked, "walk alone on city streets and leave my handbag dangling on my shoulder and . . ."

"Ugh, it's that bad, is it? How quickly we forget."

"Come on," Lillian countered, "even Paradise here isn't free of serpents. There's been quite a bit of bad publicity about Miami and tourist crimes lately. Believe me, I thought about that when I made my airline and hotel reservations."

Ron handed Lillian a menu and shook out his napkin. "Unfortunately you're right. The worst part of all of it is that we haven't yet found ways to stop the violence."

Lillian nodded, agreeing, but she hadn't come to Miami to discuss crime or ways to stop it. "Could we discuss something else?" she asked. "I really do want to spend the next few days relaxing and unwinding."

"Sure," Ron said, bending his head to study the menu. "May I suggest the broiled yellow tail? That is if you're a fish lover?"

"I am, and I'll take your suggestion under consideration," Lillian replied, smiling, "but first I want to check out the desserts. I intend to pull out all the stops on this trip."

Did she mean it? Ron wondered. Or was he reading things into the lady's words that weren't there? He didn't know, but he was sure of one thing. He wanted to get to know this lovely woman better.

"So, when Mandy has her baby at the end of February, I'll be right there, playing the proud grandma for all it's worth. I'm hoping it's a little girl, but I didn't tell her that. Actually, the baby's sex doesn't matter as long as it's healthy."

Watching Lillian talk of her grown, married children gave Ron a pang he hadn't allowed himself to feel in years. Once he had dreamed of being a father. He'd imagined what it would be like to have a son or daughter, to cuddle and play with an adorable little baby and then watch it grow into a strong, capable adult. Lillian had done those things, and somehow it made him in awe of her.

"My ex-wife never wanted children," he said quietly, as the young waiter served them coffee and key lime pie. "I didn't think it was fair to force the issue."

"You missed a lot of joy," Lillian said, impulsively reaching out to cover Ron's deeply tanned hand with her long, slender fingers. "Not that there weren't also some hairy moments, like the time Eddie broke his arm playing hockey, or when John was expelled for printing cheat sheets in mass quantity and selling them for a dollar a piece."

Ron laughed, imagining the scene. Irate parents, defensive young boy. The anger and frustration, and then finally, when the situation was resolved, the pride in another hurdle cleared.

"Well, it's too late now," he said, shrugging and hoping he sounded nonchalant. The last thing he wanted from this lady sitting across from him was pity.

Sensing that they'd come a bit too close to a touchy subject, Lillian launched into a colorful recital of her last day at work, leaving out only the most provocative comments of her friends. By the time she finished their dessert plates were empty and Ron was begging her not to make him laugh anymore.

"I think a nice, long walk is in order," he said. "If I don't work off some of this food I'll never sleep." He fumbled for his wallet, but Lillian was already holding her credit card.

"Please," she insisted quietly. "Let me pay for my own meal. After all, this wasn't a date or anything."

Ron hesitated, then decided honesty really was the best policy. "That's funny," he said, "but I was thinking it felt very much like a date. I've enjoyed your company, Lillian. Please allow me to treat you to this dinner."

Lillian looked into Ron's eyes. They were a deep, gray-brown color, clear and honest looking. Would it really be so terrible to allow him to buy her dinner?

"Are you sure?" she asked, her hand hesitating over the Gold Card.

"Positive. It will be my pleasure. Now let's get the bill paying over with so we can take that walk."

They strolled along the street across from the beach. There were lots of other people walking and Lillian assessed them curiously. Mostly older couples, well dressed and obviously well heeled. "Snow birds," she murmured.

"Actually, the true snow birds don't arrive until after Christmas. Most people with families stay home until after the holidays, and then they arrive en masse." A sudden thought struck him and left him feeling curiously bereft. "You'll be gone by then."

"Yes." Lillian nodded. "I'll be hard at work creating ads for the new year and fighting the ice and snow and cold rains."

"Sounds deadly." Ron wasn't sure how Lillian would react, but he was suddenly compelled to reach out and grasp her hand. They swung hands like each had once done with teenage loves, and then they laughed.

"I feel sixteen again," Lillian admitted. Then she made the mistake of looking up into Ron's face. There was something there . . . a sweet warm longing . . . a need. Something she wasn't prepared to see or deal with. She shivered despite the warm, sultry air. "I'd better get back," she said. "It's been a long day."

Ron wanted to protest, but he'd felt her withdrawal, and he knew the fear of involvement all too well. "Whatever you say, lovely lady," he said. "Would you like to come and see my sailboat tomorrow? There's still quite a bit of work to be done on her, but she's coming along." He waited, and when Lillian didn't reply, added, "I'm really proud of her."

Lillian hesitated. Ron was nice. Maybe too nice, and she hadn't come to Florida for a wild romantic fling, or had she? Was this what had been in the back of her mind all along when she packed the backless black dress and the silky underthings? Would she dare wear the skimpy bikini in front of Ron?

"Where is your boat docked?" she asked. "I'm not making any promises, but . . ."

Ron grinned, feeling like a randy teen again. Maybe there was no promise in her words, but her eyes spoke volumes. Blue as a midnight sky, clear and sparkling with intelligence and humor. Yes, this was definitely a lady he wanted to know better. "I'll write the address down for you," he said happily, "and I'll make sure there's plenty of cold beer and lemonade in the cooler."

* * *

Lillian undressed slowly, letting the soft strains of the Christmas carols playing in the courtyard swirl around her. She felt strange, as if something very important was about to happen, and she wasn't sure how she felt about it. She reminded herself that she was free to do anything she wanted with these next few days, and if she did make any foolish mistakes . . . well, no one would ever have to know. She was a long way from Chicago.

After a breakfast of juice, coffee, and croissants on the terrace outside her room the next morning, Lillian showered and dressed in navy shorts and a red and white striped top. She slid her feet into red espadrilles and picked up her beach bag. In it was a beach towel, suntan lotion, her new bikini, and the lacy cover-up. Even though she'd never been a Girl Scout she believed in being prepared.

She found Ron easily. The yacht basin was just around the corner from her hotel. He was shirtless this morning and sweat glistened on his broad shoulders and still flat stomach. Lillian swallowed, stunned by the raw physical desire that streaked through her body. It left her hot and trembling and she started to turn away.

"Lillian! Hello. Over here!" Ron called, his smile wide and sun bright.

Swallowing and reminding herself that

she was probably just reacting to her surroundings, Lillian returned his smile and stepped gingerly out on the dock. Miami was a romantic place. Swaying palm trees, golden beaches, salt air, and waves crashing against the beach. It was a world away from Chicago, and she was simply reacting to the stimulus. Actually, it was a good sign. It proved she wasn't dead yet!

"Hey, don't you look nautical all done up in red, white, and navy," Ron observed, getting to his feet and wiping his hands on a rag. "Here, let me help you aboard."

"Maybe I shouldn't," Lillian said, looking uncertainly at the tools spread all over the deck of the sailboat. "I don't want to be in the way."

"Believe me, you won't be," Ron assured her. "Come on. Welcome aboard the Sea Dog."

She laughed. "Very original name. Did Charlie help you pick it?"

Hearing his name the big Lab raised his head and thumped his tail on the deck a couple of times, then he continued his nap as the sun and breeze tickled his golden fur.

"The picture of ambition, isn't he?" Ron asked. "But he's still good company."

Lillian stood on the boat deck looking around. It was a good-sized sloop, even to someone with her limited knowledge of sea-

faring vessels. Of course, if Ron really was
living aboard . . .

"Yes, I do live here, hard as that probably
is for you to imagine. Come on, follow me
down below and I'll show you my digs."

Lillian kept one hand on Ron's bare
shoulder as he led the way. How could a
man's skin be so warm and . . . okay, chill
out, Lill, old girl. Your replaced hormones
are getting out of line here!

"Oh Ron, this is . . . why I would never
have dreamed it could be so spacious and
comfortable!"

"It will be even better when I'm all finished, but I did start work on the inside
first," Ron explained, waving his hand and
pointing out the built-in conveniences of his
floating home.

"Come on, I'll show you the master suite.
I'm really proud of it."

Her breath coming faster than usual, Lillian followed where Ron led and then
gasped as she found herself staring at a
king-sized bed covered in a thickly quilted
floral spread. There were built-in night-
stands on either side of the bed and a beau-
tifully carved, built-in dresser with a large
mirror above it.

"Ron, it's wonderful! The height of lux-
ury. What more could you want?"

He grinned. "Maybe a refrigerator that
works and a functioning stove and oven. I

haven't replaced the kitchen appliances yet, which is why I end up eating all my meals out."

"This is wonderful," Lillian said honestly. "I think I could be quite comfortable in living quarters like these, although I'm not sure about Liberace."

"You'd be surprised," Ron said. "Most cats love living on or near the docks. All that fresh fish, you know?"

She laughed, and suddenly the last of her doubts slipped away. For better or worse, she was going to follow the path Ron was leading her down. She decided she needed this, the sun and warmth, the laughter and the touch of this man . . . the release of stress and tensions.

"I had my helper, Willy, buy us a picnic lunch. I was hoping I could persuade you to hang around while I work. See up there? It's a perfect spot for sunbathing. Is that your bathing suit?" Ron asked, pointing to the beach bag Lillian carried.

"Yes, but . . . I was really planning to spend a few hours on the beach."

"Change your plans, please," Ron wheedled boyishly. "There are lots of yummy things inside that basket," he said, pointing to the huge wicker hamper, "and I've got a great stereo system hooked up down below. I'll play all your favorites as you sunbathe."

"Well, when you put it that way . . ."

"Great! The head is that way. You can change there."

Lillian stripped off her clothes in the small, but well-equipped bathroom. *This was crazy! She was crazy!* But somehow all the reasons why she shouldn't be doing this had drifted out to sea when she put her hand on Ron's naked, sweaty shoulder. As she'd vehemently told Paige, she'd been the "good wife," and all her life she'd taken the conservative route. Now she felt like cutting loose . . . like following where her feelings led . . . like doing what felt good and damn the consequences! She held up the tiny bikini bottoms and grinned. Unless she missed her guess, Ron Martin was in for one hell of a surprise!

Fifteen minutes later, her earlier bravado almost deserting her, Lillian stepped up on the boat deck. She was wearing the bikini and the cover-up, which true to her initial assessment, covered nothing. The wispy lace only seemed to accentuate her near nakedness. Her breasts, still reasonably firm due to her diet and exercise regime, threatened to spill out of the tiny, flowered cups and her behind . . . well, most of it was there for all the world to see, the strips of fabric that passed for a bottom barely covering the most intimate parts of her body. *Crazy!* This whole thing was crazy. A fifty-year-old

woman, a soon-to-be grandmother, wearing
a scandalously skimpy bikini, planning a
tête-à-tête with a man she barely knew.
Whoops! There was that word again. She
couldn't seem to stop thinking naked and
bare. Ron was almost naked. She was nearly
bare . . .

"Lillian, is that really you?" Ron stood
on the deck, his mouth agape. "Wow!"

She laughed. It had been a long time
since a man had reacted to her in that way.
It felt good. "A present from my co-workers," she explained, indicating the bikini
and cover-up. "I promised to wear it, but I
feel like the Vice Squad is going to come
swooping down any minute and arrest me
for indecent exposure."

"If they do I'll bail you out," Ron promised. He grinned and made a pretense of
licking his lips and leering. "I always did
like little yellow flowers."

"Enough," Lillian said, laughing.
"Where can I stretch out and soak up some
of this gorgeous Florida sunshine?"

After spreading her towel and a small pillow for her head, Lillian slathered suntan
lotion on her arms and legs. Then she lay
down and closed her eyes. Ah. Heaven.
Pure heaven. The sun was warm and caressing on her flesh, but the soft breezes coming off the water kept it from being
oppressively hot. She felt herself begin to

relax, melt right into a puddle of warm softness.

The next thing she knew Ron was rudely shaking her awake. "My God, Lillian, are you crazy? Do you want to end up in the hospital with sun poisoning? Don't you know you can't fall asleep in this sun?"

"Wha-I didn't mean to fall asleep. . . ."

"Look, I'm sorry for yelling, but you already look like a broiled lobster. You'd better get inside out of this sun."

He helped her to her feet and for one dizzying moment, Lillian swayed perilously close to Ron's naked chest.

"Whoa," she said. "I feel a little wobbly."

"No wonder," Ron said. "This is all my fault. I should have warned you." He reached out and touched her shoulder. "You're too fair-skinned for a marathon tanning session."

"Ouch!" Lillian yelped. Her shoulders were tender and she was starting to feel very strange. "Maybe I better get inside," she mumbled, and then she swayed again.

The next thing she knew Ron had scooped her up in his arms and was carrying her down into the boat. His arms were warm and strong and Lillian rested her head against his shoulder gratefully. He even smelled good, she thought fuzzily. Like salt air and sunshine.

"Here you go," Ron said, depositing her

gently on his king-size bed. "Just relax while I get some cool water. You'll be feeling better in no time."

Lillian let herself drift. She was warm, too warm, but then she shivered as something cool and wet touched her flesh. She heard soft murmurings and the cool touch moved over her body slowly, sensuously. Her eyes closed and she slept.

When she woke she heard Christmas carols. She lay for a few minutes trying to get her bearings. She was in Ron's boat, she knew that, but how had she gotten into his bed? Good heavens!

"Well, sleeping beauty, how are you feeling?" Ron asked, sitting down on the side of the bed. "I was starting to wonder when you were going to join the land of the living."

"What time . . . is it late?"

"Depends on what you consider late," Ron hedged. "To some people 10 P.M. is the peak of their day."

"Ten o'clock? At night? But . . ."

"I'm afraid you slept through lunch and dinner too, but I kept the picnic hamper intact, because I knew you'd be ravenous when you woke up."

"Actually, I am hungry," Lillian admitted, pushing herself into a sitting position. "Uh, could you give me a few minutes to get dressed?"

"Sure. No problem, but I'd think about ditching that bra, at least for tonight," Ron said, pointing at her lacy underwire lying on top of her shorts and shirt.

"What?"

"The straps will kill your shoulders," Ron said casually. "Even though I've never worn a bra I'm sure it must be hell on a sunburn."

"Oh. Yes. I guess you're right." She waited and finally light dawned.

"Right," Ron said, nodding. "You want me to disappear while you get dressed. Okay. How about if I set out the food? You're ready to eat, aren't you?"

By the time Ron walked her back to her hotel it was after two in the morning. Lillian's shoulders stung even though she'd taken Ron's advice and left off her bra. She knew she'd be sore in the morning, and that she'd probably peel, but despite all that she felt more alive than she'd felt in years. While they inhaled the delicious picnic lunch, they had talked, about music and books. About animal rights. About her kids and his lack of kids, even about Mandy's coming blessed event. And Ron had seemed genuinely interested in everything Lillian had to say. Sure his eyes strayed to her unbound breasts from time to time, but she sensed he was sincerely interested in her as a person. She felt like he cared what she

felt and thought. It was something she had
sorely missed in the last, faltering years of
her marriage. She fell asleep easily and her
dreams were delicious.

"So, how about it?" Ron asked. Even
though his eyes were shadowed with disappointment, he was trying to make the best
of things. "I'm not going to have the boat
ready before the holidays. Hell, Christmas
Eve is only two days away. Even if the supplier sent my parts UPS it would be too late,
so I'm scrapping my plans to sail the Keys
over Christmas. However, that doesn't mean
you and I can't drive down there and enjoy
a real 'Island Christmas.' Come on, Lillian,
what do you say?"

"What will we do?" Lillian asked curiously, digging her fork into a tender slice
of avocado. "I mean, really, what does one
do on an island at Christmas?"

"Para-sail?" Ron suggested. "Have you
ever done it?"

"Come on. I told you I haven't been
south in years, and last time I looked para-
sailing wasn't a popular city sport. Is that
where people hang up in the sky and . . ."

Ron laughed and dabbed a napkin at the
corner of Lillian's mouth. They were having lunch on his boat, and he felt something
tighten in his gut. They'd shared a few

kisses so far, but he wanted more, and he sensed Lillian did, too. She was a warm, womanly woman, with hot, healthy blood flowing through her veins. Still, he sensed a reticence, a holding back, and he wasn't sure what she was afraid of.

"You don't exactly hang in the sky, honey," he said. "A boat pulls you, and you wear a parachute type thing that keeps you in the air. You really need to see it to understand what I mean, so how about it?"

Lillian considered for about thirty seconds. Hadn't she come to Florida for a different kind of Christmas? And wasn't she already having more fun than she'd had in ages?

"I'll do it," she said. "When do we leave, and how long will we be staying?"

"I thought we'd stay through Christmas, so you'll really have something to tell the folks back home. There are some really nice bed and breakfast places in Key West. I'm sure we can get a . . . couple of rooms."

But would they? Or would they end up sharing a room and a brief vacation romance? Lillian wasn't sure. She felt the sexual tension building between them, and they weren't children. They were mature, responsible adults. There was really no reason why they shouldn't enjoy a fulfilling sexual encounter.

"I want to call Mandy and the boys before

we leave," she said, before she could change
her mind.

Ron grinned. "They have telephones in
Key West," he said. "Even electricity."

Lillian swatted Ron playfully. "I know
that, wise guy. I just want to check in. The
kids worry about me, you know? The elderly mom on the loose in Florida . . ."

Ron studied Lillian silently for a moment.
With the sun glinting off her cropped
golden curls and her deep blue eyes sparkling with enjoyment, she sure didn't remind him of any elderly woman he'd ever
known. Of course, to a twenty- or thirty-
year-old he supposed the perception would
be different, and Lillian was their mother.
That put a whole different complexion on
things. No doubt about it, Lillian was a very
attractive female, but there was much more
to her than just her appearance. When he
watched her gently stroke Charlie's head
and scratch behind the big dog's ears, he
was filled with tenderness. And when she
spoke of her children, grown and married
now and no longer needing her as they did
as children, but nevertheless an important
part of her life, he almost wanted to weep
for what he and Clair had missed. He
hoped he would one day meet Lillian's children.

"Okay," he said, clearing his throat and
getting to his feet. "You pack and make

your calls and I'll see about a babysitter for
Charlie here. Unfortunately, we won't be
able to take him with us."

"Oh, I forgot all about Charlie. Are you
sure he'll be okay?"

"I wouldn't leave him if I wasn't," Ron
said quietly, his eyes sober.

And Lillian knew it was true. This was
the kind of man who treated his pet better
than many people treated their children.
Something warm and sweet blossomed in
her chest and she smiled. "Go," she said,
and then she dropped to her knees beside
the big dog, who appeared to be watching
the proceedings with interest. "We'll be
back, Charlie," she promised, laying her
cheek against the dog's head. "Don't
worry."

"Key West? You're going to Key West for
Christmas?" Mandy squealed. "Wow! Do
you know how much Bob and I want to go
there?"

Lillian smiled into the telephone. "Maybe
after you get that baby of yours safely into
the world, we can work something out. I
could babysit while you and Bob take a second honeymoon."

"The second honeymoon part sounds
wonderful, Mom, but I'm not sure I'll be

willing to leave my baby behind. Maybe the three of us will just pack up and take off."

"Whatever makes you happy, hon," Lillian said. "Did you get your famous pumpkin rolls baked?"

"We're all set, Mom. I'm sure it's going to be a great holiday, except that we'll all miss you. Dad is coming up for the day to have dinner with us, you know. I'll bet that even he misses you."

"If he does it will just be a bit of nostalgia, sweetheart. Please don't go weaving any dreams about me and your dad, okay? What we had is over and it's time for both of us to move on."

"Can I at least tell Dad you said 'Merry Christmas?' " Mandy wheedled.

"Of course, and give that handsome son-in-law of mine a big hug, will you? I'll call you on Christmas day."

After hanging up with her daughter, Lillian placed a call to her sons, but neither one was at home. She spoke to two answering machines, wished both young men and their pretty wives a happy holiday and signed off with a kissing noise.

She was smiling as she started packing the things she would take to Key West. No matter what else had gone on with her and Andrew, they'd done a good job with their children. Mandy was a confident, lovely young wife and soon-to-be mama, and the boys were doing well in their fledgling careers. Neither of them had children yet, but it probably wouldn't be long. They were enjoying their freedom at the moment, just as she was.

"All set?" Ron asked, as he loaded Lillian's suitcases into the back of his Blazer. "You packed your suntan oil and that sinful bikini, didn't you?"

"Aha! So you do think it's sinful. As the woman who wears it, what does that make me?"

"One incredibly sexy, terrific-looking grandma," Ron teased. "Did you also bring your dancing shoes?"

"I did," Lillian said. Unbidden her thoughts turned to the lacy, wispy lingerie she'd tucked between her shorts and T-shirts. Did Ron like a woman in black, she wondered, or would he prefer the peach gown with ecru lace? Would he be turned on by the garter belt she'd bought so impulsively, or would he think she was silly?

As if he read her thoughts, Ron's arm circled her waist and he pulled her close. "This is going to be a great trip," he said huskily. "Maybe even the best Christmas I've ever had."

Their eyes met and slowly, so slowly Lillian thought she would die of the waiting,

Ron lowered his mouth to hers. They had shared brief kisses before, but this was different. This kiss held the promise of untold physical and emotional delights. It was gentle, yet filled with excitement. Lillian shivered as her lips answered Ron's unspoken questions. Yes, this would be a wonderful Christmas.

The ride down the Keys was a revelation to Lillian. Water on both sides of them, the highway a narrow strip of black ribbon between gorgeous, crystal clear aqua waters. Small tourist shops dotted the highway, along with restaurants and marinas. People rode bicycles and walked along the side of the road, and signs in front of some of the motels proclaimed pre-season rates.

"So, it's really not full season until after Christmas?" Lillian asked. "I didn't realize."

"December 26th is the day," Ron said, laughing. "Especially here in the Keys. It's like someone pulled the plug. This highway is a solid stream of cars and campers."

"So we should enjoy the next couple of days of relative quiet, right?"

"Umm, you got it, pretty lady. Now, how about some lunch? Are you ready to sample some conch chowder and fritters?"

They ate at a small waterfront restaurant,

sitting on wooden stools at an outdoor bar, and Lillian couldn't remember when she'd last had such a delicious meal. The beer was icy cold, the fritters filled with delicious sauteed peppers and onions, and chopped conch meat, and the chowder was to die for. The sky was blue and clear, with great puffy clouds hanging overhead, and the radio behind the counter was playing Christmas carols. There was a huge pine cone decorated wreath hanging behind the bar and wooden cutouts of Santa and his reindeer dotted the lawn.

"See? I told you they celebrated Christmas here in the Keys," Ron teased, seeing Lillian's surprised look.

"It's just so different," she explained, chasing the last morsel of fritter around on her plate. "When I think of warmth and sunshine I think of summer, and when I think of Christmas, I think of cold and snow and . . ."

"Warmth is better," Ron whispered against her ear, his warm breath making her tingle. "It's what we both need right now."

Lillian nodded, afraid to even try and speak. At that moment she would have agreed to anything.

"If I ate like this for too long I'd have to throw that bikini away," she complained, when they headed back to the car.

"Don't do that, not yet anyway. I was too busy working on my boat to fully appreciate it the other day, but on this trip I promise to give it and you my full and complete attention."

Again Lillian tingled. Good grief! How long had it been since she'd experienced that particular sensation? Ten years? Fifteen? But it felt good. It made her realize that she still had a lot of living left to do, despite the fact that one important era of her life had ended.

"Okay, here we are. This is Key West, the last resort," Ron said, as they crossed a bridge and rounded a curve onto the famous island.

Lillian spotted a billboard that proclaimed, "Welcome to Paradise. Key West, the American Caribbean."

Palm trees lined the street and all the light posts were wrapped in red and white striped plastic and sported green leaves and red berries.

"Oh Ron, I love it!" Lillian said, sitting up straighter so she could see everything. "It really is Paradise, isn't it?"

"That's what we're going to find out on this trip," Ron promised, his voice soft and seductive. "I called ahead for reservations just to make sure we didn't have to sleep on the beach," Ron said. "The only thing is . . . well, I wasn't sure if . . ."

Lillian laughed softly. Ron was as transparent as plastic wrap. "One room will do fine," she said, meeting his eyes briefly.

Ron let his breath out in relief and took his hand off the wheel for a moment to lightly cup Lillian's knee. "That's what I was hoping you'd say," he admitted. "God, was I hoping!"

Their room was exquisite, large and airy with lacy curtains blowing gently against the open windows and an antique styled bed with a handmade patchwork comforter and tons of pillows. Huge ferns hung from baskets and the adjoining bath featured an old-fashioned claw foot tub as well as a thoroughly modern tiled shower.

"Think we can be comfortable here?" Ron asked softly, coming up behind Lillian and circling her waist with his arms. She was hard against him and her blood began to bubble in her veins.

"I'll bet we can muddle through," she teased, and then she twisted until she was facing Ron. Their bodies touched from breast and chest to his hard muscled thighs and her lean, long limbs. Excitement and anticipation charged the air around them and Lillian's blue eyes met Ron's heated, expectant gaze.

"Later, love," she promised gently, reaching up to touch the chiseled planes of his face. He would be a magnificent lover, she was sure, and when they finally came together it would be unforgettable, but not yet. She wanted to savor the longing, the long delicious looks, the touches that lighted little fires all over her body, and she wanted just a little more time to know the man, his thoughts and feelings, his dreams.

"Okay, then let's get out of here," Ron suggested. "Come on," he said, swinging Lillian's hand playfully. "There's something you have to see."

"Are we going shopping?" Lillian asked, as Ron pulled the Blazer into the parking lot in front of a strip of stores. "Did you forget to bring something?"

Ron grinned and hopped out of the car, coming around to offer Lillian his hand. "Come on, you won't want to miss this."

Lillian hurried along beside Ron, wondering what in the world could be so exciting about an ordinary shopping strip.

"Look," Ron said, pointing skyward, "here they come."

"Who? For heaven's sake, Ron! What is going on?" Then she noticed all the people crowding into the parking lot and she also noted that the center of the lot was clear of all vehicles.

"He's going to jump," Ron explained. "He does it every year around this time. Watch."

"Who is going to . . . oh my goodness! That's not . . . is it really Santa Claus?"

It was. A suntanned, shorts-clad, parachuted, well-padded Santa who landed with a thump in the middle of the parking plaza amid cheers and calls from all those gathered around.

"He . . . even has a pack on his back with toys . . ." Lillian murmured, shaking her head. "Santa Claus parachuting into a parking lot! Now I have seen everything!"

Ron grinned and hugged her, making her temporarily forget the red-suited fellow who was struggling to untangle himself from his parachute. Lord, but he felt good! Hard where a man should be hard, but with the softest, sweetest lips she'd ever kissed. Meeting Ron had definitely been a stroke of very good luck. Maybe it was her own special Christmas present.

"In Fort Lauderdale Santa sometimes arrives via a ski boat. He wears the regulation red, fur-trimmed hat and jacket, with red trunks, and he skis down the intercostal."

Lillian laughed and shook her head. "My kids would never believe this. I wish we'd gotten a picture of Santa as he was coming in for a landing."

"Next time," Ron promised, his lips dangerously close to Lillian's bare throat.

If this kept up they'd be back in their room before either of them could blink, Lillian thought, but what did Ron mean about next time? How could he know there would be a next time?

After the Santa caper, Ron suggested they rent scooters and tour the island.

"I've never ridden one of those things," Lillian said, eyeing the bright red and black scooters dubiously. "Is it safe?"

"We'll have to wear helmets, but if we're careful there shouldn't be any problems. The agent will give you a quick crash course . . . whoops, I didn't mean that the way it sounded. Look, if you'd rather not . . ."

"No. It looks like fun. Let's give it a try," Lillian said.

After being fitted with a bright red helmet, Lillian was shown how to operate the scooter and told to ride around the parking lot until she felt comfortable.

"Hey, this is easy," she called to Ron after circling the lot four or five times. "Let's go."

Ron laughed, pretended to rev up his scooter and headed out of the lot, knowing Lillian would be in hot pursuit. He was having fun, real honest to goodness fun for the first time in . . . he couldn't even remember the last time he'd laughed and played like this, and as he and Lillian toured the small, sun-drenched island, he felt young and free.

"Wow! That was incredible," Lillian said, when they stopped to rest and watch the sun set over the water. "Can we do this again tomorrow? I'm pretty good on this thing, aren't I?"

"You're great," Ron said. He slid off the scooter and draped his arm over Lillian's shoulder. "Look, the sun is dipping right down into the water."

After returning the scooters and picking up Ron's Blazer, they drove back to the bed and breakfast. "Are you up for some good, hearty Cuban food?" Ron asked. "It's a staple down here."

Lillian grinned. "Why not? This is a day of firsts for me. I may as well go all the way."

And she would, all the way to physical fulfillment with Ron, this man she'd known for such a short time, but who was already filling the huge hole her divorce had left in her life. Maybe she would never see him again after she went back home. She would regret that, but she knew she would always have the memories of these precious, sun-filled days.

She dressed casually in a sleeveless, cotton sundress, and as she applied make-up, Lillian laughed softly, thinking of her friends back home. They'd all be in the middle of dinner and kitchen cleanup about now, she knew. And then there would be presents to finish wrapping, maybe a hurried, last minute trip to the store to pick up something they'd forgotten. Paige would be trying to be civil to her abrasive mother-in-law, and Martha would be turning down the volume on the television as her husband dozed in his easy chair. All comfortable, familiar routines that Lillian herself had followed for years, but not this year. This year she was fulfilling a fantasy, living a dream, and she decided she deserved it!

They feasted on tender, succulent roast pork, Cuban black beans and yellow rice and sweetly delicious fried plantains. Once again, Lillian was groaning as she pushed her empty plate away. "That was sinful," she said. "Is all Cuban food this good?"

"Pretty much," Ron said, "at least what I've tasted is. We'll come back again before we go home."

"Home," Lillian repeated. It was like a dash of ice water in her face. Soon she would have to go home, but Ron would be staying here, in Paradise. It would be just him and Charlie again, the way it had been before she arrived.

"Don't think about it, not yet anyway," Ron said. "Tomorrow is Christmas Eve. We'll have to go shopping for presents for each other."

Lillian pretended to groan. "Can't I escape from shopping even here in Paradise?"

"You won't mind," Ron promised her. "We're going to be true-blue, die-hard tourists tomorrow. You'll love it."

And then they were walking along the moonlit beach. Was it really necessary to walk off all the food they'd consumed, Lillian wondered, or were they both worried about what was ahead?

Other than a high school romance, Lillian had never been with any man but her husband. In the early years, before they distanced themselves, their love life had been good, but then something had died, and they hadn't been able to recapture it. What if she wasn't able to satisfy Ron? What if they simply weren't physically compatible? Or what if she was just too old for romance?

But how could that be? Every time Ron touched her she tingled from the top of her head right down to her carefully lacquered toe nails. She grew breathless after a simple kiss, and even his laughter excited her. Oh, they were compatible, all right, and unless she'd lost all the womanly wiles she'd learned over the years, they'd both be satisfied before the night was over!

It was time to go back to their room. They could delay the inevitable no longer. Ron stopped walking and gently pulled Lillian into his arms.

"This is it, lovely Lill. Once we go into our room and close the door, there's no turning back. It's all the way, straight to the finish line. Any last minute doubts? If you want to bail out, now's the time."

Lillian thought about what Ron was saying for just a moment, but she knew that she'd played all the arguments against this over and over in her mind a dozen times during the last few days, and the doubts were gone. Somehow they'd been swallowed up in the warm, tropical sunshine and the fragrant, balmy sea air, and the smile of the handsome man holding her. She was ready. There would be no turning back.

She stood on tiptoe and kissed the cleft in Ron's chin. She inhaled his male scent and shivered. "Thank you for being so sweet and thoughtful," she whispered, unable to keep a slight tremor out of her voice, "but you don't have to worry." Now she grinned impishly. "I'll still respect you in the morning. I promise."

She could almost feel the tension drain out of Ron's body. His laughter rang out in the darkness, rich and warm. "Bless you, my sweet Lillian," he said. Then he bent and kissed her, lightly at first, then increasing the pressure as the fires within them ceased to smolder and burst into bright, hot flames. "We'd better hurry back," he murmured, releasing her. "I can't wait much longer."

Then they were hurrying up the stairs to their room, eager and impatient to give each other the pleasure they had been anticipating since the first time they met. It was inevitable, Lillian knew. The kind of meeting that was written in the stars, Preordained. She could no more have stopped herself from approaching Ron and Charlie on the beach that first day than she could control the rise of the sun each morning. And even then, watching him from a distance, she'd known that he would be more than a casual acquaintance.

Ron opened the door and flicked on the light switch.

Lillian stared, then gasped with pleasure. "Look, a miniature Christmas tree! Isn't it beautiful?"

Some time while they were out, the manager had apparently stolen into their room and set the tiny tree up on the nightstand beside the bed. Now, the tiny lights twinkled and the tinsel sparkled as Lillian's smile broadened. "Is this what Southerners consider extra amenities? Oh Ron, isn't it perfect?"

It was, and so was the woman beside him, Ron decided. Her pleasure was so pure and childlike, so genuine. It seemed to spill from her onto him, and his own joy intensified. Quietly, he slipped the lock on the door and reached to turn the room lights off so that the little tree glowed in the darkness.

He circled Lillian's slender waist with his arms and pulled her hard against him knowing she was sure to feel his arousal, knowing she was bound to absorb the desire running rampant through his body.

Slowly, Lillian turned until they were face to face, chest to breast, thigh to thigh. "You're a wonderful man, Ron Martin," she said softly, her fingertips lightly caressing his jawline. "I'm glad I met you."

Then words were suspended as feelings took over. The night was warm, and the windows were open to fresh air and the soft, familiar strains of Christmas music. Sight and sound and scent all blended together into one perfect, irresistible whole as Lillian surrendered to the feelings that were taking over her body. It had been a long, long time since she had felt so warm and wanted, so treasured. Even though Ron's hunger for her was evident, he took time and care as he wooed her, with soft, small kisses, tender touches, sweet, loving words.

Lillian forgot that she was fifty years old, that her youth had vanished into the past, that ahead of her were the "so-called" golden years. Pressing against Ron's masculine hardness, she was young and dewy again. She was hot and eager, and when Ron finally tumbled her to the wide, inviting bed she was ready.

"This is perfect. You are perfect," Ron murmured, his lips tantalizingly close to the tips of her breasts as he impatiently worked the straps of her sundress over her arms. "Tell me this is not a dream."

"If it is, I don't want to wake up," Lillian whispered, her hands smoothing the firm planes of Ron's back. He was steel and she was satin, and together they would forge a fire as bright and hot as any winter furnace. As the last of their restrictive clothing fell away and their bodies met, flesh to warm, eager flesh, Lillian's breath quickened and her movements became almost frantic.

"Easy, sweet," Ron murmured, his voice holding back a pleased chuckle. "We have all night and . . . forever."

Lillian heard the words, but feelings had taken over. She was alive, warm and womanly, giving and receiving pleasure as her body moved in tune with Ron's. It was glorious, a precious Christmas gift she would treasure for all eternity.

"Would you believe me if I told you that sex was never that good, not even in my wild, misspent youth?" Ron asked later, when they were cozily snuggled under a lightweight blanket. His fingers traced lazy circles on Lillian's bare shoulder, and despite her recent fulfillment, she felt her body stir.

"I was thinking the same thought, but I was afraid to say it," she said softly. She kissed Ron's chin and smiled. "We work well together, don't we? Especially for a couple of old folks."

"Hey! Watch it, lady! I'm barely into my prime, and judging from your recent performance, I'd say the same for you."

Lillian grinned. "Grow old with me, the best is yet to be . . . maybe it really is true."

"Umm, you're making a believer out of me, pretty lady."

Ron grew silent then, and a few minutes later, Lillian heard him snore softly. She smiled into the darkness, only the tiny twinkling tree lights illuminating the cozy room. What a wonderful Christmas this was going to be!

"I really didn't expect to be shopping today. I planned to spend the day on the beach sunning my buns," Lillian complained as Ron steered her towards Duval Street, the main drag in Key West.

"But what kind of Christmas would it be without presents?" Ron insisted. "And you haven't done Key West until you've toured the souvenir shops."

"Okay, I'm yours for the morning, but after lunch I'm putting on my bikini and hitting the beach."

"I'll help you," Ron said quickly, pretending to leer.

Lillian laughed and slapped at him playfully. It was Christmas Eve and she was strolling down the street on a tropical island in shorts and a t-shirt, peering into shop windows. The stores were decorated for the holiday season, but instead of stately pines and evergreens, all Lillian saw were swaying palm trees and heavily blooming hibiscus. There was a Santa on one of the corners, but he wore red shorts and sandals, and Lillian had to hold her hand over her mouth to stop giggling. "I love this," she said, waving her hands to encompass the entire island.

"It's definitely a break with tradition," Ron agreed, "at least for us Northerners."

"Will you ever go back?" Lillian asked, as a feeling of loss suddenly overwhelmed her. She kept forgetting that this was just temporary, that she and Ron were temporary, and when she remembered it was like a sharp knife stabbing at her.

"You mean back to the corporate rat race?" Ron asked. "Sure. Someday. I'm not ready to retire yet, and a guy can only stand so much decadent pleasure, you know."

"Decadent pleasure? Does that include

me?" Lillian asked, her brows arched quizzically.

"You're definitely part of the pleasure," Ron said huskily. "All right, you are the pleasure, but you'd better stop looking at me that way or you won't get any presents."

Lillian pressed close against Ron's side, letting her breasts brush his arm. "I can think of one present that won't cost you a dime," she whispered. She narrowed her eyes and lightly licked her lips, pleased at the flush that colored Ron's face and the way his jaw tightened.

"Later, shameless hussy," he growled. "Later."

"I absolutely have to have this shirt," Lillian said, holding the oversized T-shirt up in front of her. It was a pale pink shirt, handpainted with huge pink and red hibiscus blossoms. The local artist had even signed her name below the flowers.

"Wrap it up," Ron instructed the salesgirl. Then he turned to a rack of incredibly tacky, islandy earrings. "How about these?" he asked, pointing to a pair of painted pink flamingos. He cocked his head consideringly. "They look like you."

"Pulleeze!" Lillian cried, putting her hands over her eyes. "Not pink flamingos. I'd have nightmares."

"Personally I think flamingos are cute," Ron said, injecting a note of hurt into his voice, "but if you don't like . . ."

"So you like flamingos, do you? Then how about these?" Lillian barely held her laughter in check as she held up a pair of boxer shorts ablaze with brilliantly painted pink birds. "Now that I think about it, these are definitely your style." Grinning wickedly she let her eyes drop below Ron's waist.

"Cut that out, woman!" Ron commanded. He grabbed the shorts from her and shoved them under a pile of more conservative boxers. "Not on your life!" he muttered, dragging a laughing Lillian out onto the street.

They visited an art gallery next, where they enjoyed the work of local artists. Paintings and prints and sculptured birds and mammals, including one of a mama manatee and her baby on a coral rock. Lillian watched Ron's eyes roam over the costly piece hungrily, and suddenly she knew she had found the perfect gift for him. He could put it on the built in dresser in the bedroom of his boat, and maybe, after she was gone, it would remind him of their time together.

"I'm parched," she lied. "Would you be a sweetie and go next door and get something cold and wet?"

"Sure, but why don't we both go?" Ron

glanced at his watch. "It's almost time for lunch anyway. Aren't you getting hungry?"

Lillian shook her head. "Not yet. I'm just thirsty."

"Okay. Your wish is my command. I'll be back in a jiffy."

Lillian hurriedly had the clerk wrap the sculpture and whipped out her credit card to pay for it. By the time Ron returned the piece was safely hidden in her beach bag.

They wandered through a few more shops, then decided it was time to grab a bite to eat before hitting the beach. While they munched on seafood salads and drank tangy ice tea, Lillian tried not to think about how soon she would have to get ready to go home.

"What's wrong?" Ron demanded. "You're like a bottle of champagne that's lost all its fizzle. What happened to that smile I'm learning to love."

"I . . . that's it, I guess. I'm liking this too much, Ron, and in a few days it will be over. I'll go home and . . ."

"It doesn't have to be that way, Lillian," Ron said, leaning towards her earnestly. "I've been having those same thoughts myself. I know we don't have any commitment and we haven't made any promises to one another, but if we had more time who knows what could develop?"

"Time is just what we don't have, Ron.

We have totally different lifestyles. I know, you said you'll be going back to your law practice someday, but I have to go back to my work in a few days, and Chicago is a long way from here." She waved her arm and sadness shadowed her deep, blue eyes. "I wish there was more time too, but maybe it just wasn't meant to be."

"We can control our own destinies, Lillian. That's what I did when I made the decision to drop out of the 'real world' for a while. Believe me, it wasn't easy to make the jump, but I'm glad I did. I've experienced more life this past year than I ever did when I was dashing here and there and battling court cases every day. Watching the sun set with Charlie, taking a late night walk on the beach . . . feeding the lame egret that hangs around the dock. My career filled my bank account, Lillian, but this . . . this place, this lifestyle fills my soul."

Lillian had no answer to that, and they walked back to their room in silence. Once there Lillian disappeared into the bathroom to put on her bikini. She'd seen Ron wistfully eyeing the bed when they entered the room, but she couldn't make love to him now, not when she had so much to think about.

There were a few people on the beach, but as Ron had explained the bulk of the winter tourists would not arrive until after the holidays.

Lillian helped Ron spread the beach towels on the sand and then stripped off her cover-up, acutely conscious of the way Ron's warm, gray-brown eyes followed her movements.

"Here, let me," Ron said, taking the tube of sunscreen from her. "Lie down on your belly and I'll do your back."

He started with her shoulders and Lillian had never known that smoothing sunscreen could be so incredibly sensuous and arousing. She felt a quiver deep in her most private place, and found herself wishing she was back in the cozy room, with the door closed and the real world far, far away.

Then, as Ron's hands moved down her legs, smoothing gently, but thoroughly, she shuddered.

"Am I tickling you?" Ron asked innocently, his hands temporarily stilled.

"You know very well what you're doing, Ron Martin!" Lillian muttered, "and I think you better stop. I'm going to soak up some of this sunshine if it kills me."

Ron laughed and reluctantly relinquished the tube as Lillian sat up and reached out. "I'll do my front, thank you," she said firmly.

"Spoilsport," Ron chanted, pulling off

his shirt and exposing his broad chest and slender waist. "Do you want to do me?"

"Later," Lillian promised, flopping back down on her belly and determinedly closing her eyes, "now behave for a while, will you? How can I possibly go home without a suntan?"

It seemed like only minutes later that Ron was shaking her shoulder.

"Go away," Lillian muttered.

"No way. You're already plenty pink, and besides the parasail is here. Look."

Lillian sat up, grasping her top as it threatened to slip. She caught the twinkle in Ron's eyes and returned his leering smirk.

"Where is it?" she asked, shading her eyes and peering out over the water. Then she saw it, a large, bargelike float pulling a parachute clad person high above the water.

"Oh my gosh! That's what you expect me to do?"

"We could go up together," Ron coaxed, "they have a tandem harness, and it really is pretty safe. I know the guy who runs the boat. They check the equipment carefully every day. Besides, you know as well as I do that you could step out in front of a . . ."

"Mack truck and be flattened on the street on any given day. Or I could be mugged and shot on my way to work, or I could develop an incurable disease or . . ."

"Let's not get morbid," Ron said, laying a finger on her lips to halt the tirade. "Come on, Lillian, live a little. When will you get a chance to do something like this again?"

"We'll go together? One for all, and all for one?"

Ron laughed as he pulled Lillian to her feet. "Come on, the barge is heading for shore to pick up new passengers."

Lillian hung back as Ron talked to the man who ran the boat. What in the world would her friends say if they could see her now? For that matter, what would her very pregnant, slightly strait-laced daughter say? Or her two hip young sons? Even though they lived dangerously themselves, how would they feel about their mother doing it?

"Ready?" Ron asked, his hand at her back as if to prevent her from turning around and taking off. "Jack's getting the double harness. We'll be side by side. You'll love it, Lill. I promise."

Lillian shrugged. "What the hell?" she muttered under her breath. She would only live once, right? And it was Christmas Eve. What better way to celebrate than to soar across the sky like a bird, hovering over the warm, tropical waters of the Florida Keys?

Lillian felt herself tremble just a little as the workers adjusted the harness and explained what would happen when they took off. "You won't lift off into the air until the boat picks up some speed," the young man explained casually. "Then you'll go up, higher and higher as the boat speeds up. When you're ready to come down, the boat will gradually slow and you'll sink down. We'll be right there to pick you up."

The young man grinned at the pained expression on Lillian's face. "Having second thoughts? You don't have a weak heart, do you?"

"If I do, I guess we'll find out today," Lillian retorted, glaring at Ron. "Why did I ever let you talk me into this? I can see the headlines now. Middle-aged grandmother plunges to her . . ."

"Shush! That's not going to happen. This will be one of the most thrilling, titilating experiences of your life, if you let it. Just relax and enjoy. That's the trouble with you corporate types. You're all tense and strung out."

Lillian opened her mouth, then closed it without uttering a sound. Ron was right. She was tense and strung out, or at least she had been until a few days ago when she met Ron and Charlie on the beach. Now, although there were still remnants of the old Lillian, she could feel herself changing, opening up and softening. She grinned and raised her hands. "Let's do it!"

It was like a dream, yet at the same time it was the most incredible, real experience of Lillian's life. She was trembling as she and Ron waited to be lifted in the air, and then suddenly they were airborne, free and weightless. A feeling of freedom unlike anything she'd ever known washed over her, and she opened her mouth and laughed joyously. Beside her, Ron grinned and gave her thumbs up.

As she effortlessly floated through the air, the blue sky above and around her, the sparkling turquoise waters below her, there were no worries or cares, just a total, heavenly sense of freedom.

But it was over all too soon. Before she could fully absorb the intense pleasure, she and Ron were being helped out of their harnesses.

"Now, was that so bad?" Ron asked, grinning.

"It was wonderful. I just wish it had lasted longer."

"I don't want to completely spoil you," Ron answered, "and besides, tomorrow is Christmas Day. I have to save something special for that."

"What's left?" Lillian asked as they strolled back to their room.

"Let me worry about that," Ron said.

"For now, let's get showered and changed. No visit to Key West is complete without a trip to Mallory Square for sunset, and tonight it should be particularly festive."

Later, dressed in silk slacks and shirt, Lillian drank in the sights and sounds of sunset like a greedy child. From time to time she would touch Ron, or just turn to smile at him as if she feared he might disappear when she wasn't looking.

"This is great," she said, as they sampled conch fritters from a portable vendor. "Do they do this every night?"

"Every night. It's a tradition. Of course there are more vendors and performers during full season, but even at slow times there are always a few die hards up here, barring storms or hurricanes, of course. Look, see that guy over there with the cats? He's a real character. Want to watch?"

Finally, when the sun had gone down in a blaze of pink and gold glory, hunger drove them in search of sustenance.

"Seafood?" Ron asked.

"Perfect," Lillian replied, thinking that this whole trip had been perfect so far. She couldn't bear to think about when it would end.

That night, when she and Ron made love it was slow and sweet. Their hunger was just as intense as it had been earlier, but somehow, it was as if they wanted to prolong every single, perfect moment, as if they wanted to make the magic last forever. And it had been magical. Lillian tried to tell Ron before they fell asleep, but he pressed his fingers against her lips. To speak would break the spell.

"I can't believe it's Christmas morning," Lillian said when they woke the next morning. "I should be huddled in a warm robe and slippers waiting for things to warm up."

Ron eyed the sheer peach nightgown Lillian wore and grinned. "If you don't hurry up and get dressed, things will definitely heat up," he promised. "Go on, get decent. There's a special Christmas brunch waiting for us downstairs and I'm starved. Guess I worked up an appetite last night."

The main room of the inn was decorated with silk pine bows and red velvet bows. The scent of evergreens hung in the air and the huge spruce tree was trimmed with old-fashioned wooden ornaments and tons of tinsel.

"This is lovely. Now I feel like it really is Christmas," Lillian said, accepting a mug of eggnog from her host. There were trays of goodies everywhere and warming trays kept scrambled eggs and sausages warm.

"Glad you came?" Ron asked, hugging her.

"What do you think?" She wore the delicate gold conch shell earrings that Ron had surprised her with, and now she reached up and touched one with the tip of a finger. "I'll always treasure these," she said.

"Ditto the sculpture," Ron said. "I've been enthralled by the manatees ever since I learned that they're an endangered species. It would truly be a tragedy if those gentle creatures disappear."

Lillian nodded, but her mind wasn't on the manatees. Tomorrow was her last day. On December 27th, she was due to fly back home. She wouldn't return to work until the first of the year, but there were things at home she had to attend to. In a way she would be glad to get home. It would be good to be in familiar surroundings again, and crazy as it might seem, she'd missed Liberace, but how was she going to say goodbye to Ron?

"So, this is it, our last day," Ron said quietly. "We'll have to get an early start tomorrow morning to get you to the airport on time." They were on the beach back in Miami, lying side by side on their beach towels. They'd spent the last half hour just lying together holding hands, but now it was time. There were things to be said.

"It's been wonderful, Ron," Lillian said, not daring to meet his eyes. "Even the turkey dinner yesterday was great."

Ron laughed. "I can't believe we went all the way to Key West to eat turkey for Christmas dinner."

Lillian smiled. "Some traditions simply weren't meant to be broken." And it was true. Sometimes breaking old traditions and making new ones was good, but sometimes it was better to hold fast and true to beloved customs. Traditions were important; they made one feel warm and fuzzy, like the world would go on, no matter what.

"This," Lillian said, sweeping her arm to encompass the sun and sky and sparkling aqua waters, "and you," she added softly, reaching up to touch Ron's jaw. "It's been more wonderful than I can say. Just what the doctor ordered."

"Are you saying goodbye?" Ron asked. His eyes were dark and somber, and Lillian felt his tension. "Is this all there is?"

"Ron, we . . . we're different. Right now you're footloose and fancy free, as my mother used to say. I'm not. I have a career, and I worked long and hard to get where I am. And I have a family. Sure, the kids are on their own, but they still expect me to be around when they need a shoulder or some advice. I can't just chuck everything and sail off into the sunset with you, tempting as it is."

"Does it have to be either or?" Ron asked, tipping up Lillian's chin and forcing her to look at him. It was then he saw the sheen of tears in her lovely blue eyes. "Maybe it's too soon to say that we love each other," he admitted, "and maybe neither of us is ready to make a lifetime commitment, but there's no reason we can't stay in touch and give these feelings between us a chance, is there? Hell, I may take one trip on my sailboat and decide it's enough. I may end up in a building not far from yours toting my briefcase to court and back every day, or . . ." Ron paused and chuckled, "you, pretty lady, may decide it's time to give up the rat race and become a beach bum. You could do that and still be a mom and a grandma, you know. In fact, I think I like the idea of being a step-grandpa. And you can spend your vacations in Florida, can't you?"

Lillian was quiet, thinking. Maybe long distance relationships weren't ideal, but this was the nineties. Men weren't the only ones with important careers, and lifestyle changes weren't such an oddity anymore. Could it work? Wasn't it at least worth a try?

"You really want to give this . . . what-

ever it is between us, a try?" Lillian asked
softly.

"I do," Ron said. "You're a special
woman, Lillian, and I," he added, grinning,
"am a super guy. We're good together, and
life is short. Why throw away something that
could bring both of us joy and contentment
in this last half of our lives?" Ron cupped
a handful of sand and let it trickle slowly
over Lillian's toes.

Warm sand, brilliant sunshine, and then
from the picnic basket they'd brought with
them, Ron withdrew a sprig of mistletoe.
Smiling, he held it over Lillian's head as he
bent to press his lips against hers.

Just before contact was made, Lillian
sighed, with pleasure and anticipation. Was
she dreaming, or did she hear sleighbells
in the distance? This whole trip had been
a miracle, so why not? Her lips curved into
a smile under Ron's mouth. No matter what
the future brought, she would never forget
mistletoe in Miami.

Sun, Sand, and Santa
Phoebe Gallant

"So what do we do with this turkey carcass, Mom?" Natalie asked, holding up the denuded skeleton from which she'd just removed the last scraps of meat. "You certainly can't take it back to Edgeville on the plane."

"But I've always made Christmas soup with the Thanksgiving bird," Lucy said, eyeing the carcass thoughtfully. Natalie was right: how could she transport the smelly thing back home, and *then,* how could she make turkey soup in her tiny apartment kitchen? And once it was made, it wouldn't fit in her tiny freezer.

"Don't look at me," Debra said. "With a two-year-old and a baby on the way, I'm not up to making soup. And Hal can't do it . . ."

"What can't I do?" Hal asked, entering the kitchen with an empty ice-bucket, dumping it in the sink, upturning it on the drain board. "There's nothing I can't do."

"Here," Natalie said, swinging the turkey in an arc and nearly beaning Debra. "You wanna make the Christmas soup in your dorm room?"

"Seems I spoke too soon," Hal said. He crossed the kitchen to his mother and put his arm around her shoulder. "Hey, Mom," he said, into her ear, in a whisper. "We just finished Thanksgiving dinner. Do we really have to plan the Christmas Eve soup?"

"Of course we do," Debra said. "We *always* talk about the Christmas Eve soup on Thanksgiving. We put the bird in the freezer, so Mom can . . ."

Lucy felt tears beginning, way back behind her eyes. She'd never had Thanksgiving away from home before. But here she was, a guest in her daughter Natalie's Boston apartment, trying her best to make her family feel like a family.

But it wasn't a family anymore. Not without the house she'd just had to sell—the house she and Seth had lived in for thirty years. Not without Seth himself—the husband who had decamped with his young, beautiful law partner, leaving Lucy broke in both heart and pocketbook.

She felt Hal's strong arm around her shoulder, and spoke sternly to herself. He's a college freshman and he needs to feel secure. She reached out and patted his cheek. "I'll take the damn thing home on the airplane," she said. "Wrap it up good, in plas-

tic. Then in foil. We'll have our Christmas
Eve turkey soup."

Natalie and Debra wrapped the bird. Hal
filled the ice bucket and brought a pitcher
of water, ice, and glasses into the living
room. They *always* had big glasses of ice
water after Thanksgiving dinner. They always chewed the ice cubes afterwards, too.
Seth had maintained that it was an aid to
digestion.

They'd do it today, even though Seth
wasn't here to make his annual ice cube
speech. Then they'd go for their traditional
walk, though it would be very different
from the walk they always took at home.
They'd have to walk two by two to fit on
the sidewalk, and they wouldn't meet anyone they knew to exchange holiday greetings with.

Natalie had only lived here a year; *she*
didn't even know anyone. But they'd walk,
two abreast, up Commonwealth Avenue and
back, and then they'd return to Nat's apartment for the traditional tea and Lucy's
homemade gingerbread.

They sat in a circle in the living room,
sipping their water. Natalie got coasters; Debra left the room for a moment to check on
little Nate, who has having his nap. Debra's
husband, Dickon, looked like he wanted a
nap, too, Lucy thought. They'd all eaten too
much.

Damn you, Seth, she thought, draining her water glass. How am I ever going to do Christmas alone . . . in an *apartment*?

Hal interrupted her reverie. "Did you close the store for the whole weekend?" he asked.

"No way," Lucy said. Mention of her business made her brighten. She loved her needlework store, and she couldn't possibly close it for the whole Thanksgiving weekend; this was the busiest week of the year. Winters were long and cold in upstate New York, and a needlepoint project—particularly a custom-designed one—was the perfect Christmas present. She had orders backed up and many more to come.

"I'll be open Saturday," she said. "I did get someone to babysit the shop the two days before Christmas, when you'll all be home." *Home?*

She couldn't miss the look Debra gave to Natalie. *Help,* it said.

"Mom," Natalie said, "I can only get two days off. Do you think we could . . . cut back on some of the traditional stuff? Make it a simpler Christmas?"

"We could skip stockings," Debra said. "Nate is too young to know the difference, and I just don't have the energy . . ."

"And I don't have the time," Hal said. "Or the money."

Lucy stood and crossed her arms over her

chest. "What is this?" she asked. "A conspiracy?"

Natalie stepped up to her. "We think it's just too much this year, Mom," she said. "All these traditions. The stockings, the turkey soup. The decorations, the huge meal, the enormous breakfast, the big lunch, all the presents. It's too much. . . ."

"For you?" Lucy asked.

Her three children looked at each other, and then, "You've had a terrible year. You lost your house . . ."

"*We* lost *our* house," Lucy interrupted. "Even though you don't *live* there anymore, it was your home."

"And you lost Dad."

Lucy felt the tears start to sting again. What were her children up to?

"Look," she said, "I've got everything under control. I have reservations for all of you at the inn. The tree won't be as big as usual, but . . . there'll be a tree. We'll hang the stockings the way we always do."

"Are you sure?" Debra asked. Lucy could see the relief in her eyes; her younger daughter was excited about Christmas, the way she always had been. "Are you sure you can manage it all, Mom?"

"Of course," Lucy said. Now Hal's eyes lit up. Natalie's, too. They hadn't meant it about cutting Christmas to the bone. They were just trying to protect her. Well, she didn't need protection, thank you very much. She'd do just fine.

"Great," Hal said. "I'd hate to miss Christmas Eve church. And the high school reunion supper, and the caroling. . . ."

"We'll have the soup, too," Lucy said, and smiled, and hugged each of her children, and her son-in-law, and just then she heard Nate crying to be picked up from his nap. It was time to go for the traditional Thanksgiving after-dinner walk.

She'd do it, she vowed, and she'd do it well. She'd manage a traditional Allen family Christmas, even though she lived in a tiny efficiency apartment now, instead of a nice big Victorian house with fireplaces and high ceilings to hang mistletoe and a big oak door for the wreath. She'd manage. They were still a family, even without Seth. They'd make it.

"Let's get the baby and go," she said, putting her empty water glass down on the glass coffee table. The walk, the tea and gingerbread. Then it would be time for Hal to drive her to the airport.

Yes, they'd have their traditional Christmas.

But as she walked up Commonwealth Avenue, holding little Nate's hand and feeling the cold Boston wind tangling her newly set hair, a new and very radical plan began to manifest itself, at the back of her mind.

Home again in Edgeville, Lucy unpacked, checked her phone messages, and stuffed the turkey carcass into her icebox; she'd make the soup tomorrow, then ask one of her friends to keep it frozen for her.

She opened the store early on Saturday morning. The new shipment of yarn had arrived, and she unpacked the glowing skeins lovingly, hanging them on the hooks behind the counter. Two more orders for pillow kits had come in, both for college crests, one Cornell, the other Bard. Another order specified a pillow with the motto "The more I know about people, the better I like my cat." Lucy smiled; she'd stencilled a lot of those, sometimes with "dog," once even with "my Korean pot-bellied pig."

Business was brisk. Friends dropped in, too—her shop was across the street from the bank, next door to the diner, and catty-corner to the hardware store—to ask about her Thanksgiving. In their faces, she read concern: *How did you get through your first holiday alone?*

At lunchtime, she left the shop and walked to the travel agency where her friend Martha worked. The radical new idea that had come to her while she was being buffeted by the Boston wind had kept on tugging at her, and it was now or never. She feared it was never; it would be impossible, she was sure, to get reservations for a warm clime over Christmas.

"You're right," Martha said. "Everything's booked solid. Even the grungy parts of Florida."

"I didn't really want Florida," Lucy said. "What I hoped for was an island somewhere. A little house to rent. Right on the water. Even if it's expensive, I could swing it. Just this once."

Martha shook her head. "I'll check around, but even if I found you a paradise island, I'd never get you all those plane reservations. Where's Hal again?"

"Chicago," Lucy said. "Natalie and her new beau live in Boston, Deb and her family in Hartford . . ."

Martha groaned. "Impossible, Luce. You should have thought of this six months ago. That's how far in advance people book."

"Six months ago, if you recall . . . ," Lucy said. She couldn't go on.

"Oops. Sorry. So what do you hear from the bast—the ex?"

"Hear? I don't. He and his cookie are living in Poughkeepsie. I never go there anymore, even though I love the mall. I don't want to run into him. Them."

"You'll get over that. When you've been divorced as long as I have . . ."

"Martha," Lucy reminded her. "I'm not even divorced *yet.*"

Martha's phone rang, and she answered it. Lucy left, but not before entreating her friend to try—just try—to find her a tropical place to spend Christmas. Visions of little Nate digging in the sand, Natalie stretching out to get a tan, and Hal diving in the breakers made her smile.

Maybe though, she thought as she walked back to the shop, maybe it was a terrible idea. Maybe she should just do her best to replicate the family holiday they'd always had. The half-eaten Oreo cookies for Santa (where, with no fireplace?); the mimosas with Christmas breakfast, which *had* to include sausage and eggs with green and red peppers in them. The dreadful dessert, called Heavenly Bliss, that Seth's grandmother had made, and that never changed, though every ingredient in it was guaranteed to clog the arteries and put love handles on the hips.

By the end of the day, she was exhausted. Tomorrow, Sunday, she'd have to spend all day at the drawing board, planning and lettering the needlepoint projects that had been ordered. How had she even imagined she could make the Christmas soup tonight? She hadn't even allowed time for grocery shopping. It would just have to wait until Monday.

When she opened the refrigerator, the wrapped turkey carcass reproached her. "You," she said, poking it, "are a pain in the butt."

She made herself a Lean Cuisine, accompanied by a glass of chardonnay, and settled down to watch the evening news. Fatigue rolled over her. She stared around her small living room; the tree would go between the two front windows. The table, with the leaves added, would crowd the dining alcove, but that was O.K.; her family didn't mind playing kneesies under the table. Maybe it wouldn't be so bad. . . .

But when she imagined her three tall children, Debra's husband Dickon, Natalie's beau, and two-year-old Nate all crowded into this small but pleasant room, she groaned aloud. We will drive each other nuts, she thought.

She was just pulling her sweater over her head to get ready for bed when the phone rang.

"You're not going to believe this," Martha nearly shouted into the phone. "I've had an incredible cancellation. A family package. Four-bedroom condo, right on the beach. Plane reservations. Everything. Clients had a death in the family and canceled the whole thing. Lucy, it's got your name on it!"

Lucy sat down. "Tell," she said. "Can we afford it?"

"I think so," Martha said. "All the flights are from New York, though. Can you all get yourselves there? It's Kennedy."

Lucy thought of Debra, pregnant, and with a child. If she hired a limo to take her from Hartford . . . "Sure," she said. "But what day . . . ?"

"That's the problem," Martha said. "It's . . . for a week. Wednesday to Wednesday. One flight down is Wednesday, the others Thursday and Friday. Can you manage?"

"I'll have to make a few phone calls."

"Look, Luce," Martha said. "I love you dearly, but I can't keep this open forever. I've got several clients who'd kill for it. When can you let me know?"

"Tomorrow," Lucy said. "Morning."

She was about to hang up when she remembered to ask one more question. "Martha? Where is it?" She was hoping for an exotic small island she'd never heard of . . .

"Sanibel," Martha said. "You fly into Fort Myers."

"But that's Florida!"

"You'll love it. Come on over tomorrow and I'll show you the brochure. The living room is huge. Big terrace, hangs right out over the ocean. You have until noon tomorrow. . . ."

She was going to do it. A big living room meant a big tree. Maybe there'd be a big freezer for the turkey soup.

It wasn't as hard as she'd imagined. She called Dickon at his office; he'd fly down Friday evening with Debra and Nate. Natalie was delighted; she'd take the extra days off, fly down on Thursday and help get things ready. Her beau, it turned out, wouldn't be joining them for Christmas; he had to go home to Denver. She didn't sound very happy about *that*, Lucy noticed. And Hal, with a stroke of luck, got a connecting flight from Chicago on Thursday.

Armed with her credit card, Lucy walked to the travel agency and made the deal.

Then she went shopping for the ingredients of turkey soup. Somehow, she was going to get it to the airport. She'd make a smaller batch than usual, just enough for one meal.

Back in her small kitchen she retrieved the turkey from the fridge, set it to simmer in her largest pot, and began cutting up vegetables—white turnips, yellow turnips, new potatoes, carrots, yellow squash. She diced them fine, along with garlic, tiny white

onions, and a handful of parsley. She bagged
the chopped vegetables and put them in the
fridge; she'd add them in the morning; in
the meantime, the turkey would simmer in its
broth overnight.

But when she sat down to make a list, she
began to run into snags. How, without a car,
would she buy a tree and set it up? Did they
sell wreaths in Florida? What would she do
about candlesticks? They always had Christmas Eve dinner by candlelight.

Exhausted from so much decisionmaking,
she checked the flame under the soup,
turned out the lights, and went to bed.

But sleep wouldn't come. The Christmas
tree ornaments. The felt stockings (where
do you *hang* them in a Florida condo?). The
Oreos for Santa: did that make sense, without a fireplace? And how could she possibly
carry all the presents on the plane? How
would she get to New York, to the airport,
with all that stuff? Should she drive, leave
the car in long-term parking?

She tossed and she turned until she had
no more energy to toss and turn with.
Three weeks. That should be plenty of time
to solve all the problems. And the busier
she kept, the easier it would be to face her
first Christmas without Seth.

She hoped.

In the morning, things looked much better. List-making skills came back to her,

ideas flowed, and by ten o'clock, she'd made a deal with UPS to send two big cartons of Christmas presents and decorations to the Sanibel condo in time for her arrival. She'd reserved a limo to take her to the airport in New York; why spend time and energy agonizing over bad weather? She felt good.

Until Seth called. "Natalie tells me you're dragging everyone down to Florida," he said. "That's not fair. I can't believe you're doing this."

"Not fair to whom?"

"To them. To Barbara and me. We'd planned on seeing them over the holidays."

Lucy squared her shoulders, stood straighter, gripped the phone receiver more tightly, and took a deep breath. "I'm sorry, Seth," she said. "You'll have to make other plans. Ours are all made."

She hung up without waiting to hear his answer. The sound of his voice, even on the phone, was like needles in her skin. It hurt. It would hurt for a long time, but then one day—that's what she had been told, at least—it would stop hurting.

At lunchtime, she went home and added the veggies to the soup, sprinkled it with herbs, and left it simmering in the crockpot. On the way back to her office, she stopped off at the local department store to see if they had any bathing suits.

They did, and she bought two, and a terrycloth cover-up, two pairs of shorts, and a pink T-shirt.

A tropical Christmas would be fun. If she could pull it off.

The big storm hit two days before her flight. Lucy sat at her shop window, watching the big flakes fall, listening to the sound of the plow going up Congress Street every half hour or so, spreading sand, pushing the new snow out of the way. The temperature kept falling; so did the snow. The New York airports were closed for hours at a time; on television, she watched throngs of frustrated travelers lying on the floor of the airport, surrounded by bags and crying children.

Had she ruined her family's Christmas with her crazy scheme?

Well, it was too late to turn back. UPS had picked up her boxes; by now, they should be waiting for her in Florida. She'd bought so many last-minute presents that she'd still be laden like a packhorse when she went to check her baggage. What with the two containers of turkey soup, all her new clothes, and the dog—she'd completely forgotten about Cicero, until the last moment; he'd have to ride in the baggage compartment—she'd never arrive at the condo in one piece.

The snow kept falling. But, on Wednesday morning at six o'clock, the limo was waiting outside her door. Mercifully, there was a break in the weather just as she got to Kennedy. The plane took off only two hours late. By three in the afternoon, after a somewhat rocky flight, it touched down in Fort Myers.

The airport was chaos, but she found her way to the animal-claim after she'd retrieved her bags and left them with a porter. She stood in line with other animal owners, one a young woman with a screaming toddler. There was a bearded man waiting for a huge German Shepherd—his dog was brought out first—and a sublimely attractive man in jeans and a plaid shirt who couldn't seem to take his eyes off the book he was reading. She sneaked a peek: it was the "lost" Louisa May Alcott novel, published in the fall. She had read it and sent a copy to each of her children, all of whom had grown up, as she had, on *Little Women*. He had to be a nice man if he was reading that book and traveling with an animal. What strange criteria we have, Lucy thought with a smile, glancing at him again and wondering where he had come from, where he was going.

"Mr. Sands," the man behind the counter said, "your animal is ready."

That, Lucy decided, must be Mr. Sands. The woman with the screaming baby had already picked up her dog, and Cicero hadn't appeared yet. Lucy approached the man and tentatively touched him on the arm.

He jumped as if she'd shot him. "What the . . . ?"

"Are you waiting for a dog?" Lucy asked, looking up . . . up . . . up at him. He was enormously tall. She adored tall men. Seth was short, though she'd loved him in spite of it.

"Yes," he said, turning down the corner of the page of his book, "I am."

He stepped forward and signed for the cardboard crate which, Lucy could see, contained a large and very angry cat.

He turned to her then, bending down, and held out his hand. "I'm sorry," he said. "Cat, not dog. And thanks for your help."

The cat was meowing like crazy. Lucy peered in at it, and noticed that it had enormous gold eyes and the longest whiskers she'd ever seen. "He's beautiful," she said.

"Mrs. Allen? Mrs. Lucille Allen?" the voice shouted.

"That you?" the tall man asked.

Lucy stepped forward. The man handed her an animal container, from which came whimpers of distress. She took it and

dropped to the floor, peered inside. Cicero
was lying on his side, panting.

"Is he all right?" Mr. Sands asked.

"I don't know," Lucy said. "I . . ."

He folded himself down to her level and
peered in at Cicero. "Take him out," he
said. "See if he can walk around."

Lucy bent to release the clasp on the cage.
Cicero stood, on shaky legs, and pushed his
muzzle into Lucy's hand, still whining
softly. His nose was warm and he seemed
to be trembling.

"He's just scared," the man said. "Pet
him. Then take him out."

Cicero stepped out of the container, eyes
wide, and collapsed into Lucy's lap.

"Oh, dear," she said. When she looked
up, Mr. Sands had taken the container and
returned it to the airline official at the desk.
Then he reached into his own container,
removed his cat, and snapped a leash onto
its collar. The cat sat calmly at his feet.

"He walks on a leash?" Lucy asked.

"He does." The man smiled. "He's a vet-
eran traveler. Now then . . ."

He looked down at Cicero. "Is he better
now?"

Lucy snapped the leash on. "I think so,"
she said. "It's his first trip."

"What . . . sort of dog . . . ?"

"Heinz 57," Lucy said, smiling up at Mr.
Sands and noticing, for the first time, that

his thick gray hair fell over his eyebrows the same way Hal's did. Only Hal's was brown.

"Best breed in the world," the man said. "Meet Hoipolloi, my cat. Genuine Alley. Best cat in the world."

Lucy bent to pat Hoipolloi, who stuck his tail up straight and mewed happily. What a nice animal, she thought. *What a nice man.*

She looked around. The area seemed deserted except for his suitcase. Where had everyone gone?

She picked Cicero up in her arms and slung her carryall over her shoulder.

"I'll take that," Mr. Sands said, reaching for the carryall. "Why don't we see if he'll walk?"

We? "I'm not sure . . ." Lucy could feel Cicero trembling in her arms.

"Bet I know what's wrong," Mr. Sands said. "Come."

She followed him to the doors that led outside. Heat shimmered over the pavement, and she could see her porter, waiting for her beside a piled luggage cart. "That's my stuff," she said, hoisting a panting Cicero to her other shoulder.

Mr. Sands stepped up to the porter, spoke to him, then led Lucy outside. He steered her across the pavement and onto a small square of grass. "Put him down," he said. "I think you'll find . . ."

She found. Poor Cicero seemed literally

to sigh in relief as he answered a long-de-
layed call of nature. When he finished, he
looked up at Lucy and barked, then began
jumping around.

"Oh," Lucy said, grinning. Out of the
corner of her eye, she noticed Hoipolloi, at
the end of his leash, digging a neat hole.

"I . . . thank you," Lucy said. She
wrapped Cicero's leash around her hand
and reached for her carryall. "You've been
very kind."

But Mr. Sands was not about to be dis-
missed. He took her elbow and led her back
to the porter. "You have a great deal of luggage," he said. "Are you moving down here
permanently?"

"Just for a week," Lucy said. "Family
Christmas. I've rented . . ."

"Where?"

"Sanibel," she said. "A condo. I must
find a taxi . . ."

"May I drive you? I have a rental car waiting. And I happen to be going to Sanibel
myself."

"Oh, I couldn't . . ." She looked into his
eyes. They were almost too blue to be true.

"Please," he said. "I'd like the company."

She looked down at the two animals.
Hoipolloi sat at his master's feet, completely
unconcerned that a largish dog sat only a
few inches away from him. Cicero, too,
seemed unalarmed. Amazing, Lucy

thought, considering the way Cicero chased the neighborhood cats at home.

"I'll just run and pick up the car," Mr. Sands said. "Would you mind waiting here?"

Lucy smiled. No, she wouldn't mind. Before she had a chance to reach for her pocketbook to tip the porter, who very obviously didn't want to wait around any longer, her stranger had reached in his pocket and handed the man a folded bill. The porter grinned and began to unload the cart.

"Here," Mr. Sands said, handing Lucy the cat's leash. "I can sprint faster without him." And before she could answer, he had bounded away toward the car rental office.

Lucy stood on the hot sidewalk, a leash in each hand, one eye on her mountain of luggage. She felt a smile stretch her face, was aware of taking a deep, deep breath. Sun. How she loved it. Once she got settled in the condo, she had a whole day before the family began to arrive. Maybe she could sneak in a few swims and some suntanning between errands tomorrow. Once she got the tree up . . .

"I'm back." She heard his voice before she saw the car pull up. He hopped out, opened the hatchback, and began piling her things inside. Hoipolloi strained at his leash.

"Let him jump in," he said. "He loves to ride."

She released the cat, and he leapt into the back seat of the car. Cicero whined and tugged at his leash.

"Go ahead, let him jump in, too."

She did, and the two animals sat side by side, as if they'd known each other forever. Astonishing, Lucy thought, as Mr. Sands opened the passenger seat and motioned her in. "By the way," he said, "I'm Joshua Sands. Josh."

"Lucille Allen. Lucy. This is really awfully kind of you," she said. "I'm sure I'm taking you out of your way."

"Well, let's see," Josh said, heading for the bridge. Lucy couldn't help noticing his hand on the floor shift. It was corded, strong, with long slim fingers and perfectly groomed nails. Seth had had pudgy hands. "Where exactly are you staying?"

She told him, and he broke into a huge grin. "Amazing!" he said. "I'm practically next door. I rent this same condo every year. It's my reward for getting through the fall term."

So he was a teacher, or a professor. She wondered where, and of what. She waited for him to go on, but he didn't. He looked, suddenly, preoccupied and a little sad.

The silence was starting to become awkward. Well, Lucy thought, if he won't talk

I will. "This is an experiment for me," she said. "It's my first trip. My children are joining me for the holiday."

Josh perked up. "So that's what all the bags and boxes are for."

"And you wouldn't believe what's in here," Lucy said, pointing to her carryall, which she'd stored at her feet. "Two containers of turkey soup."

Josh glanced at her in disbelief. "You brought soup all the way from . . ."

"Upstate New York," she said. "It's a tradition. My family is very traditional."

"But they agreed to a change of venue."

"I insisted," Lucy said. "My . . . our . . ."

"Hey," Josh said, sensing her discomfort. "I didn't mean to be nosy."

"Oh, hell," Lucy said. "I'll tell you straight out. My husband left me for another woman, we had to sell the house, and I just couldn't imagine Christmas in my little hidey-hole. I have a grandchild, he's two, and everyone in my family is so . . . big."

Josh threw back his head and laughed, then grew serious again. "Funny," he said, "your situation is the opposite of mine almost. My two sons have always hated the holidays. Sometimes they don't even come home. But this year, I insisted." He paused. "It's my first Christmas alone, too."

"I'm so sorry," Lucy said.

"My wife died two years ago," he said. "Last Christmas my sister and her family came down here, to be with me, but it wasn't much fun. This year I put my foot down to the boys: come. Dad needs you. Now, though, I wonder if I made a mistake. If they come unwillingly . . ."

"How old are they?" Lucy asked.

"Reggie is thirty," Josh said. "Still unmarried. Adam is twenty-six."

"And unmarried, too?"

"Just divorced," Josh said. "And hurting. He's the one who made me promise an unChristmasy Christmas. His words. No decorations. No festivity. Lobsters for dinner."

"Oh, dear," Lucy said. "My kids would kill me if there wasn't a turkey. And all the right vegetables." She looked up and saw that they were crossing a long, low bridge. Beyond it, the island shimmered in the heat.

"How are you planning to get around?" Josh asked.

"Bikes," Lucy said. "They're already rented and should have been delivered. My real estate agent arranged it."

"Did anyone tell you," Josh asked, "how far it is from your condo to the grocery store?"

Lucy shook her head.

"You in as good shape as you look?" he asked.

Lucy felt her neck grow warm. How could he tell what shape she was in, under a raincoat?

Traffic had slowed to a crawl. The road was narrow, and on both sides, people on bicycles with little colored pennants on sticks behind them were pedaling along as if they owned the road. "It's awfully . . . built up," Lucy said. She had imagined a wild island paradise, stepping out onto that deck over the water, seeing only sand, palm trees, maybe one or two people walking on the beach.

"It's pretty honky-tonk," Josh said. "Until we get further out. Courage."

They rode in silence for a while.

"Look," Josh said finally, "I'm not expecting the boys till tomorrow. Would you have dinner with me tonight? There's a nice, simple little seafood place . . ."

"You don't have to . . . you've been so kind already. I . . ." *My God. This man is asking me for a date. No, he's not, he's just being kind, he's sorry for me, he's a Samaritan.* "I really shouldn't . . ."

"Please," he said. "Hey, I'll offer an added inducement. I'll drive you to the one place on the island where you can buy a Christmas tree. You certainly can't do that on a bicycle. . . ."

Josh hit the turn signal and pulled the car into an asphalt parking lot that led to a condo complex. "We're here. Say yes," he said.

Lucy looked up at the white stucco building. She could see a swimming pool surrounded with long chairs and umbrellas, a rack of bicycles, sand, palm trees, and, between two buildings, the ocean.

"Yes!" Lucy said. "I'd like to have dinner with you."

"I'll pick you up at 7:30," he said. "Give you time to get settled in."

He helped her unload, handed her Cicero's leash, and drove off, waving, after making sure she had help with her bags.

Lucy watched his car turn, visualizing her wardrobe and trying to decide what to wear.

She was going out to dinner with a man—for the first time in thirty years!

Lucy stood in the middle of the living room, looking out over the ocean. The sun was setting in a blaze of glory, tinting everything in the living room a warm pink. The furniture was pretty much what she'd expected—big, fat sofas upholstered in nubby tweed; glass tables; pictures of shells, a ceramic pelican. The kitchen was roomy and efficient, with a microwave and even a trash compactor. She'd explored the four bedrooms, mentally assigning them, taking the smallest for herself, leaving the nicest for De-

bra and Dickon, the next smallest for little
Nate. The crib, ordered ahead, was in place.
Natalie got the bedroom with a balcony; Lucy
knew how her daughter loved to sleep with
the windows open, the sounds of the sea coming in.

She unpacked, stored the turkey soup in
the freezer, and treated herself to a dip in
the pool, wearing her new bathing suit, before showering and dressing for dinner. She
chose a short, flowered cotton dress she'd
ordered from the Talbots catalogue and
beige strap sandals. She'd carry her nubby
red cotton cardigan.

At 7:00, she was ready. She stepped outside, onto the deck, and stood leaning on
the railing, staring out over the glistening,
silvery ocean. On the beach, a few people
walked, bent over, looking for shells. Beside
her, Cicero barked sharply; he'd spotted a
poodle running in the waves. Impulsively,
Lucy kicked off her sandals, grabbed
Cicero's leash, and walked down the outdoor steps to the sea. Cicero bounded toward the water, barked at the incoming
waves, barked again as the water receded.
Lucy watched him, a smile on her face, her
short, wash-and-wear brown hair blowing in
the breeze. So what if she'd just blow-dried
it with such care? She was outdoors, in the
middle of December, and she was warm,
and comfortable, and . . .

Happy. For the first time since Seth left her, she felt that lilting lift of happiness, of freshness, of delight that was all her own, that she hadn't felt for such a long time. Not the happiness, the joy, of having her children, her grandchild, her job, her friends. That was another kind. This was a happiness that was just hers, just for herself.

Was it because she was far away from home? Or was it because an attractive man had paid attention to her . . . had asked her out to dinner?

It didn't matter. It was a feeling to be cherished. Lucy cherished it . . . then turned to find Cicero, dripping wet and covered with sand, digging frantically. Her watch read 7:10. Heavens!

She was just toweling Cicero off when the doorbell rang.

A very different Josh Sands stood in the doorway.

"May I come in?" he asked, but he didn't smile.

She stood aside, motioned him into the living room. He didn't comment, didn't even look around. He stood with his hands in the pockets of a pair of very grungy khaki pants, his head down.

He certainly wasn't dressed for a date.

"I . . . ," he began to speak, but couldn't seem to go on. Something dreadful has happened, Lucy thought. She wished she

had something to offer him—a drink, a cup
of tea, anything—but the cupboard was still
bare. Maybe a glass of water?

"I have had some very unpleasant news,"
Josh said, his back to her. "I'm sure you
don't want to be burdened with . . ."

"Oh, but I do," Lucy said. She walked to
his side, stood just near enough to offer
support, not too near so as to startle him.
"I hope nothing serious . . ."

He sighed, turned to her, took one hand
from a pocket and raked it through his hair.
His uncombed hair, she couldn't help but
notice. "Serious? No. Nobody has died, nobody has been hurt, nobody has been diag-
nosed with a dread disease."

She waited.

"The boys . . . aren't coming."

She waited again. Finally, he went on.
"They were together when they called. Reggie has a business deal that can't wait. I find
that hard to believe, but that's what he said.
Adam has a new girl. She wants him to meet
her parents. Anyway, they're not coming.
After I . . ." He paused. "Reggie said I'd
bullied them into agreeing to come. *Bullied.*"

Lucy wasn't sure what to do next. If one
of her children had said something like that
to her, she would have . . . what? Cried?
What *do* you do when a family falls apart,
when the support isn't there, when your
kids put work and girlfriends ahead of you?

What you do, she realized suddenly, is to tell them just what you think, quickly and simply, and then go on and enjoy your holiday to the best of your abilities. But she couldn't say that to this man without sounding cold-hearted, to say nothing of sanctimonious. She wouldn't like it one bit, if someone were to lecture *her* like that.

"I have an idea," Lucy said, before she realized she'd had one. "Let's not go out to dinner. Let's just stay here and . . . and . . ."

Josh essayed a small smile. "And feel sorry for myself?"

"And bitch," Lucy said. "I've got plenty to bitch about. So have you."

"But what we don't have," Josh said, "is something to eat."

"Oh, but we do," Lucy said. She thought fast. A list formed in her head. "Could you perhaps take a short drive and pick up a jug of wine, a loaf of bread, and . . ."

"And thou?" he said, a smile finally breaking through. "But I'm too hungry for just bread and wine, lovely as you are, dear Lucy."

"I'll provide the rest," she said.

"But the tree . . . we were going to get the tree."

They went together. They bought the tree, then stopped in a small shopping center and bought crusty bread, a bottle of cha-

blis, a box of strawberries, and a container
of vanilla ice cream. At the last minute,
Lucy reached for an avocado, a head of en-
dive, and a bottle of Italian dressing. And,
finally, a small jar of instant, decaffeinated
coffee and a container of milk.

When they got back to the condo—it
wasn't too far to bicycle, Lucy noted with pleasure—she helped Josh drag the tree up the
steps and into her living room. They left it
lying on the deck, and she went to the kitchen,
fired up the microwave, and put a container
of her turkey soup inside. In the cabinets, she
found garlic salt for the bread, oregano for
the salad.

It was nearly nine o'clock when Josh
popped the cork on the bottle of wine and
the two of them sat down on the deck. The
sky was filled with stars; there was a light,
lovely breeze. It was like being in the middle
of nowhere.

For a while, they sat without speaking.
Josh put his feet up on the railing, cupped
his wine glass in both hands, and stared out
to sea. Lucy could see that he was wrestling
with his emotions, could imagine how embarrassed he was to have ruined their date.
She wished there were a way to tell him that
soup and salad on the deck was her idea of
heaven. She was too tired to go out to dinner. This was perfect. If only there were
some way to comfort him about his boys.

Finally, she broke the silence. "Shall we eat?" she said. "You sit there. I'll just be a minute. We'll bring trays out here."

Lucy ladled the Thanksgiving turkey soup into big ceramic bowls, took the bread out of the oven, and fixed two trays. Josh came and stood beside her.

She handed him one tray, took the other. "Candles?" he asked.

She smiled, pleased at his suggestion. There were two candlesticks on the dining table; she brought them to the terrace, hoping the breeze was not strong enough to blow the candles out.

Josh seated her, then sat, unfolded his napkin, and bowed his head. "Bless this food," he began, reaching for her hand, and she finished the blessing with him.

They devoured the soup, had seconds; one container was empty. *What will we do Christmas Eve?*

They polished off the wine, took Cicero for a run on the beach, then returned to the deck for strawberries and ice cream and coffee.

"I don't know when I've had such a pleasant evening," Josh said, rising to go. "You've been more than understanding. I don't usually lose my cool like that."

"And you," Lucy said, "have been delightful company, to say nothing of a godsend in the Christmas tree department.

You're right; I could never have brought that monster home on my bike."

"I'd like to help you set it up," Josh said. "I'll pick up a stand for you . . ."

"You've done enough," Lucy said. "And by the way, what will you do now? Stay out the week?"

Josh's dark frown returned. "I don't know. It's . . . Christmas is ruined for me. I'd be better off at home, in Boston, sitting by the fire . . ."

"Boston?" Lucy brightened. "My daughter lives there. I love Boston."

"Well," Josh said. "So do I. But I've paid for this condo, for the week. Maybe I should get myself a stack of good books and some suntan lotion and just forget it's Christmas."

"Do stay," Lucy said, before she had time to think about how forward it might sound. Her next words just tumbled out, unbidden. "I have a fine idea. You'll have Christmas with us. Share our traditions. You can laugh if you like, we are pretty funny. Say you will."

"How will your family feel," Josh asked, "about your inviting a perfect stranger into your midst . . . on the most important night of the year?"

"Say yes?" she urged.

Josh raked his hand through his hair.

"Only if I can help. Let me bring the wine, or the dessert, or . . ."

Lucy giggled. "You can't do that," she said. "Everything has to be exactly as it always is. Even the dessert, which you will hate and pretend to like. But I tell you what you can do. You can help pad out this soup for Christmas Eve. And you can help set up the tree, as you've offered. Fair?"

"More than fair," he said. He moved closer to her. "Are you some kind of guardian angel?" he whispered.

She drew back a little; she could feel the warmth of his breath on the top of her head. He was so tall that she had to crane her neck to look up at him.

"Hardly an angel," she said, feeling her cheeks go warm. He was bending closer to her. She studied the flecks of gold in his brown eyes, the bushy eyebrows, the long, straight nose, the sculpted cheekbones. He looked the way she had imagined, as a girl, that her ideal lover would look.

"Quite angelic, I'd say," he said softly, and reached out to cup her chin in his strong hand. He lifted her face closer to his. "You have helped," he said. "But that's not all. You . . ." He paused for a moment, then a broad grin spread across his face. "I like you," he said. "I just simply like you."

"That," Lucy said, "is the nicest thing anyone has said to me in a very long time."

He bent his head and touched his lips to her forehead, then to each sun-warmed cheek, then to the tip of her nose.

At his feet, Cicero set up a ferocious barking; the romantic mood was broken. But before Josh Sands drove away, he made a plan for the next morning: he'd bring a tree stand; he'd also bring brunch. Then they'd swim.

Lucy watched his car leave the parking lot, her hand wrapped around Cicero's leash. She felt a warm, wonderful glow; she had made a friend. She and Josh Sands had shared an evening.

As she walked back to her condo, she realized something very puzzling: she had never found out what it was exactly that he did. Nor had he asked her what *she* did. It was as if they had left their lives behind, in Edgeville and in Boston, and as if only what was happening here, in Sanibel, tonight, mattered.

Lucy looked up at the sky and whispered a small prayer to the heavens: make his boys call back, she prayed. At least call back. Better than that, please God . . . or Santa . . . let them surprise their father and appear in time for Christmas.

"Fat chance," Josh said as he flipped the hamburgers he'd brought. "I think they've put the whole subject behind them," he went on. He was much more cheerful this morning—better dressed, too, and his hair was combed. "Actually, I'll tell you a secret," he said, turning to Lucy who was sprawled on the chaise longue beside him, wearing her new bathing suit.

"I love secrets," Lucy said.

"OK, here goes. I'm somewhat . . . relieved. Once I got over being mad, or should I say once you *got* me over being mad, I started to think. Why did I—*bully* them into coming? I guess I was scared. Christmas alone sounds so . . . pathetic."

"Boy, do I ever know what you mean," Lucy said. She watched, admiring, as he deftly slid the burgers onto buns, added sliced onion rings, opened a bag of potato chips and put some on each plate. He set the plates on the glass table and gave her a hand; she rose to stand beside him. "It's scary as hell," she said, eyeing her hamburger with lust. "But now I'll tell *you* a secret. I'm enjoying myself completely. A part of me almost wishes my kids weren't coming . . . that I could just veg out for a week. All by myself."

"*All* by yourself?" Josh asked, putting his hands on her bare shoulders." I'd like to amend that slightly."

"Amend away," she said, sitting at the table, then jumping up again to get two Cokes from the refrigerator. "I feel like a teenager who's sneaked out the window to meet a forbidden date."

"You look like one, too," Josh said. Then he grabbed her hands again and said grace. She joined him. The sun beat down on her head; she felt warm all over, inside and out. The burgers were exactly as she liked them, red on the inside, dark outside, crispy, leaking juice. She devoured hers.

"Your brood," he said. "They're arriving when?"

"Two of them this afternoon," Lucy said. "Hal from Chicago, Natalie from New York via Boston. Their planes get in within half an hour of each other, so they'll share a cab out. They'll be here in time for supper."

"And the others?"

"Tomorrow. Why?"

"I . . . imagine you'll be too busy to . . ."

"Josh," Lucy said. "You're invited to Christmas Eve supper, that's the meal with the famous soup, and for dinner on Christmas day. Sunday. Between now and then, everyone's on his own. I know Hal will try to rent a sailboat; Natalie will sun herself till she fries to a crisp; Dickon and Deb will entertain Nate. I'll . . ."

"Can we sneak away?" he whispered.

"What did you have in mind?" she asked, astonished at the flirtatious tone she could hear in her own voice.

"Guess," Josh said. "No, seriously. I'd like to . . ."

"By the way," Lucy interrupted. "What do you teach? And where?"

"Economics," he said, obviously annoyed at the change of subject. "At Tufts."

Horrors. "How interesting."

"Back to the subject," Josh said, trailing Lucy to the kitchen where she put two mugs of instant coffee into the microwave. "I don't want to lose track of you."

She looked at her watch. "Mr. Sands," she said, "we have exactly—or should I say roughly—six hours before the thundering hordes descend. Do you have any suggestions as to how we might . . . spend those hours?"

Josh sipped his coffee and regarded her over the rim of his cup. He leaned against the kitchen counter, one long leg crossed over the other. "I'd like to extend an invitation," he said. "To you and Cicero."

At the sound of his name, the dog lifted his chin off his paws and trotted over to Lucy's feet, flopped down again.

"We'd love to hear it," Lucy said, calculating how many hours she could really spare. She had to go to the grocery store, plan the meals for the next three days, make sure she had everything Nate would need. Diapers. Milk. He adored mashed potatoes. Reality warred with fantasy as she dared to split her afternoon between the two. What had gotten into her?

"I propose a shopping expedition, first," Josh said. "Get you all ready for the on-slaught. That should take till about three. Then, Hoipolloi and I would like to invite you to our condo for . . . ," He paused, wiggled his eyebrows. "Afternoon tea."

"Yeah, sure," Lucy said, without think-ing, then felt herself blush crimson. That remark, she realized, had made her a party to his plan: I know what you're thinking; I didn't say no.

"Sure what?" he asked, assuming an in-nocent expression.

"Well . . ."

"A gentleman doesn't invite a lady's dog," he said, "to an assignation. Nor his own cat."

"Are you sure?"

"No." He gave her a quick hug and a pat on the fanny. She wondered, briefly, if hers was the last generation when a man could do that to a woman without getting a slap or a lecture.

Lucy knew exactly what was going to hap-pen at "tea." And she was looking forward to it. Nervously, perhaps . . . after all, it was her first time . . . but delightedly, too. After this week, she'd never see Josh Sands again. She was going to have a fling. A quick one, a matter of hours only. Her first ever, and probably her last. The thought made her heart race. Too bad they didn't have a couple more days together. Well, she'd just have to make the most of it. Tea, indeed.

She scooped up her grocery list, grabbed a sweater against the arctic chill of the Publix Market, and took Josh's arm.

"It's not every day," she said, "that Abelard takes Heloise to the grocery store."

"Ah," Josh Sands said, "but we accomplished seducers know that it's the surest way to a lady's heart."

"Are you sure it's my heart you're aiming for?" Lucy asked, hearing that flirtatious tone again.

"I'll tell you at the checkout counter," he whispered.

It was a day to remember. My fantasy, Lucy told herself as she showered and then slid the meatloaf Hal loved into the oven. He and Nat were due soon. The wine was chilling, and Hal's Coors, the salad was made, the groceries—she'd chopped for the whole week, taking advantage of Josh's car and his good nature—were all put away. They had savored every moment of their few hours alone together. What fascinated her most— surprised her most—was that the grocery shopping, the driving around, the cup of tea they actually got around to drinking . . . af-

terwards . . . were just as heady, just as intimate somehow, just as new and wonderful as
the hours they'd spent in Josh's bed. She'd
never known it was possible to *get along* so
well with someone, with so little effort. And
how wonderful it had been to feel like a
woman again—desirable, interesting, appealing.

Then, they had said goodbye—for two
whole days. Lucy wanted to devote every moment to her family, to make this Christmas
their very best ever. Wanted? Or felt she
should? She shook her head to clear it.
Wanted, of course. After all, she was their
mother, and Christmas was a family holiday.
She'd had her Christmas present. She didn't
need more.

Oh yeah?

She dragged the box of tree ornaments
and lights out on the deck, then flung herself down in the chaise. Maybe a quick
snooze before the kids arrive . . . or at least
a moment to close her eyes and remember
what it was like to feel Josh Sands's long
arms around her, his lips pressed against
her breast, or just to remember sitting on
the floor with him afterwards, drinking tea
and rolling a ball along the rug for Hoipolloi. Laughing together. Saying, both at the
same time, that the time had gone so
quickly. . . .

Merry Christmas, Lucille, Lucy said to

herself. You got yourself a present you never even dreamed of asking for.

Lucy could tell Natalie had been crying before she got up the wooden steps to the condo. Hal, behind her, looked strained and worried. Lucy opened her arms and Natalie dropped her suitcase on the landing and flung herself into her mother's embrace.

"There, there," Lucy said, looking over Natalie's shoulder at Hal, who flung up his hands, then made a throat-cutting motion across his Adam's apple.

"You broke up?" she whispered into Natalie's ear, pushing aside her heavy dark hair.

"I didn't," Natalie said. "He did."

"Creep," Hal whispered behind them. "Colorado creep."

Lucy held Natalie out in front of her and looked into her puffy eyes. "Is it final?" she asked. She had never met this beau; Natalie had been close-mouthed about him from the beginning, which was unlike her.

"Final," Natalie said. "He's found someone else. He said I'm too Eastern. As in never the twain shall meet."

"Which just proves that the mile-high city contains a few lowlifes," Hal said, dropping his bags and embracing his mother and his sister in one huge hug. "We don't need him."

"You don't look very happy yourself, Hal," Lucy said. "Anything wrong?"

"Bad exams," Hal said. "I may have flunked one, in which case my scholarship is out the window."

Lucy felt her well-being draining away. She helped the kids carry their stuff into their rooms; Natalie perked up a bit when she saw her balcony, but Hal was none too pleased to be sleeping on the living room couch. "Take Deb's room for tonight," Lucy said, patting him on the back.

She took drinks and snacks out of the refrigerator, turned on the lights, checked the meatloaf.

"The tree's awfully small," Natalie said, emerging from the bedroom, her hair combed but her eyes still puffy. "It seems weird to see a Christmas tree with the ocean in the background."

"Maybe when it's trimmed it'll look bigger," Hal said. He slumped in a big chair and hardly seemed to notice when Cicero jumped into his lap and began whining to be petted.

"I talked to Deb this morning," Natalie said. "She's not feeling very well and Nate has a cold. I just hope they get here."

Lucy's heart sank. Didn't *anybody* have anything *nice* to say?

Dinner was subdued. Hal complimented her on the meatloaf, the way he always did, but Natalie hardly touched her food. At nine, they turned on the TV, looking for a movie, but there was nothing worth watching. By ten, they were all in bed.

The phone startled Lucy as she was putting away the last of the dishes. She hesitated to answer it. Would it be Debra, saying they weren't coming? Then again, maybe it was Natalie's beau, having second thoughts.

"Ho ho ho," said Josh Sands. "Just called to say good night and I miss you."

"Who is it?" Natalie called from her room.

"Nobody," Lucy said, and Natalie shut her door. "Hello, nobody," she said. "Count your blessings. Enjoy your solitude."

"That bad?"

"Not really, nothing fatal, as you said yourself, nobody's died. Just . . . tense."

"What you need," Josh said, "is a nice cup of afternoon tea." Lucy could feel her face grow warm, her breath quicken.

They said good night, and Lucy stepped out on the deck for one last look at the sky. Tomorrow, she promised herself, she would lie on the beach, she would swim, she would have a glass of wine with lunch and then take a nap before the rest of the family arrived. *If* they arrived.

She shivered, remembering her afternoon in Josh Sands's arms. Already, only a few hours after their "afternoon tea" party, she could hardly believe it had really happened. The glow had begun to fade. She wanted it back.

She wished it could happen again.

The next day—Friday—it poured. Gray clouds hung low over the ocean, promising no relief from the dreary, heavy weather. Dickon called at noon; they were coming, even though Nate was still coughing and Debra was feeling exhausted. The sun, Dickon said, would do them all good. Lucy didn't mention the rain.

In the afternoon, she and Hal trimmed the tree while Natalie stayed in her room, curled up with a romance novel and a box of tissues. At four, the rain stopped, and there were a few breaks in the clouds. Lucy went for a walk on the beach—in the direction of Josh's condo. Before she reached it, she turned and began walking slowly back.

She hadn't told Natalie and Hal that he was coming to Christmas dinner; somehow, the moment just hadn't been right. She passed her condo, walked in the other direction for a half hour, then returned, called to check on Debra's plane. It had landed; she'd be home soon.

Hal had brightened considerably. He was

sitting on the floor in the middle of the living room, wrapping presents. "I'm giving this one to Nate ahead of time," he said, holding up a bright yellow dumptruck. "As a coming-to-Florida treat."

Lucy dropped to the rug and hugged him. "I should have thought of that," she said. "What a nice idea."

But when Debra and Dickon arrived, carrying a cranky Nate, more problems began to surface. Lucy had bought the wrong kind of diapers; the crib was too small; Debra was frazzled and exhausted. "I don't know why you did this," she said to Lucy. "I don't know why we didn't just have Christmas in Edgeville the way we always do." She sighed deeply and headed for the bedroom.

I don't know why, either, Lucy thought, but Dickon grinned and winked at her and produced a bottle of champagne from his suitcase. Nate smiled when he saw the truck and the batch of brownies Natalie had baked. And, just as the sun was due to go down, it peeked through the clouds, for a moment, and cast a shimmering silver brightness on the waves. "Sun tomorrow," Hal said, turning from the TV. "All is not lost. Sun and turkey soup."

Debra emerged from the bedroom, her lipstick refreshed, her mood a bit sunnier. "That's really what got me here," she said, trying for a smile. "Mom's turkey soup. I'm going to have seconds."

"Me, too," Natalie said, putting down her book and joining the group. "Imagine bringing soup a thousand miles on an airplane."

"Soup and the dog," Dickon said. "I sure did marry into a funny family."

"Funny ha-ha or funny peculiar?" Natalie asked.

"Both," Dickon said, pouring the champagne, which bubbled over the side of the glasses. He passed the jelly glasses around, and the family gathered into a circle. Lucy raised her glass. "To our first tropical Christmas," she said.

"To sunshine tomorrow," Natalie said.

"To us," Hal said, very seriously. "To our family. And to the new little one we'll have next Christmas."

Lucy watched the smile spread across Debra's face as she raised her glass—filled with Coke, not champagne—then touched it to her belly. Then she leaned down to Nate and gave him a sip.

Lucy's heart filled with love. They were trying, her kids. Each of them had a problem—a failed exam, a busted romance, a sick child—but they were all here, they were all smiling, and they would have Christmas together. Happily.

But unless she put her thinking cap on

and came up with a clever solution, they would not have seconds on turkey soup.

"You *what?*" Natalie asked, slamming down the bottle of sunscreen on the kitchen table. She'd been on the beach all day, and was on her way out again.

"I told you. I invited a man to share our Christmas," Lucy repeated. "He's alone, and he was very kind to me . . ."

"You picked up a man at the *airport* and invited him to Christmas dinner?"

Lucy stood, almost upsetting her coffee cup. "Picked up is not a very nice way to put it. We met at the airport. He helped me with Cicero. He helped with the tree. This is what Christmas is all about, isn't it, Natalie? Sharing?"

"Sharing with *each other,*" Natalie said. "Doesn't he have a family of his own?" Then she paused. "No. You're right. It's just . . . I'm tense. Hal's tense. Deb's tense. You're the only one who's not tense. This place sure seems to agree with you. You look about ten years younger."

"Thank you," Lucy said sweetly. "I'm as much of a sun worshipper as you are. It's nature's cosmetic, as my own mother used to say, before people started worrying about skin cancer. And it's lovely to have you all here."

"Have you told the others?" Natalie asked. "About the man? What's his name, anyway?"

"His name is Joshua Sands."

"Perfect. Mr. Sands of Sanibel. The Sands of destiny. The sands . . ."

"Just Sands. And yes, I've told Debra and Dickon. They just looked at each other and winked, and Nate thought I said the sandman was coming. Actually, they were very gracious about it. I had hoped for a more gracious response from you, as the eldest, but you're not doing too badly, dear. Considering."

"Hal will be delighted," Natalie said. "He loves strangers. He'll talk to anybody, listen to anybody's life story. I hope this guy has a sense of humor. And patience. This family can be somewhat . . . complex."

"He has a lovely sense of humor," Lucy said. "Mr. Sands has a cat with him. Hoipolloi. He walks on a leash. Maybe he'll bring him to dinner. Nate would adore him. He's a Maine coon."

"And Dickon would turn bright red and start wheezing. He's violently allergic. Your Mr. Beach . . ."

"Sands, dear."

"Sands had better not wear anything the cat has sat on. Dickon calls it dander."

"I'll mention it," Lucy said. Seth had been allergic to cats, too, but Lucy had always imagined that it was just an excuse not to have one. Seth was finicky. He never would have flung his jockey shorts across the room, carelessly aimed at a chair, before jumping into bed, the way Josh Sands did.

"You're right about Christmas, Mom," Natalie said, rubbing sunscreen on her midriff. "It's good to take in strays. I'm sorry I'm being such a beast."

"I've been a beast all year," Lucy said, picking up the sunscreen and rubbing it into Nat's shoulder blades. "It's no fun, is it, getting the green banana?"

Natalie leaned into the massage, then turned and gave her mother a quick kiss. "No fun at all," she said. "I really thought he was the one."

He. Natalie still hadn't mentioned the guy's name. Lucy didn't ask. After all, it was over.

"Have a nice swim, dear," she said, smiling at the memory of Josh's jockey shorts sailing through the air.

Natalie grabbed her towel, whistled for Cicero, and clattered down the wooden steps to the beach. Hal was still out in his rented sailfish, and Debra and Dickon had taken off on the bikes, with Nate, "to see the alligators." Lucy watched Natalie walk down the beach, Cicero at her heels. Suddenly, the condo was empty. And quiet. Everything was done; the big glass table was set for Christmas Eve supper. The turkey soup, secretly augmented with ingredients from the Publix, was simmering on the stove. The weather had been perfect all day. Nate's cold was almost gone, and Debra had reported feeling better than she had in months. Something about her sinuses opening up.

Still, Lucy felt uneasy, antsy. Josh Sands hadn't called since night before last. Was he regretting their tea party? Had he lost respect for her, as her mother had always told her a man would do if a girl was too "fast"? But I'm not a girl, Lucy thought, and this is 1995, and I'm not married anymore, except on paper, and . . .

Then why did she have to give herself this silly pep talk? Women her age had affairs all the time. There was no need to be ashamed about it. Nor to worry about what Josh Sands might think. As long as the kids didn't get wind of it . . .

Whoa, she stopped herself. Is *that* what I'm worried about? Remember your many lectures, she told herself, about being open about what you're doing. "If you're ashamed to have people know about it, don't do it." She should practice what she'd preached.

O.K., she admitted, cutting herself a little slack. It's not the smallest step I've ever taken. Actually, it's one of the biggest. Give yourself a break, Mother, she said aloud, stepping over to the mirror above the dining room table and smiling at her reflection. "It's O.K.," she said aloud. "You haven't done anything wrong. You've just had a little . . . interlude. With a nice man. Think how good it made *him* feel, just when he was lonely and sad about his sons. Think of it as a charitable gesture. A random act of kindness."

But she was still bothered. Maybe it was because she wanted it to happen again. And was afraid it wouldn't.

Why hadn't he called? How old do you have to be before you can stop asking that . . . forever?

In the end, she called him, ostensibly to tell him to leave Hoipolloi at home. He wasn't there. The condo switchboard took a message. Then she went out on the deck to take a breather for a few moments. Sermonizing to oneself was an exhausting business.

Lucy saw him first. Instead of driving, he had walked down the beach. His shoes were in his hand, and in the other hand, he carried a large, heavy-looking shopping bag. He was walking through the wavelets at the edge of the beach, kicking sand, heedless of the water that splattered his rolled-up pantlegs. Lucy smiled. Seth would never have waded in the ocean on his way to dinner. Seth didn't like the beach. Too much sand, he'd said. Lucy raised her hand to wave as Josh caught her eye.

She sensed someone behind her and looked down. Nate was pulling on her skirt. She lifted him up, pointed out Josh, waved again. Nate waved. "Is that the sandman?" he asked. "Is that Mr. Sandman?"

Lucy put the little boy down and led him down the steps. "Let's go meet him," she said.

They ran, hand in hand, at the edge of the water, waving and calling. As they got closer, Lucy saw two tall young men walking behind Josh. They, too, were barefoot, carrying their shoes, and splashing in the waves. One of them had white-blond hair, worn longish; the other was dark, with a big fuzzy beard. Both were smiling.

Josh put his bag down and raced up to Lucy. "Look," he said, pointing to the two young men. "They came!"

Lucy looked again. Both of the guys were smiling. As if on cue, each put down the shopping bag he was carrying and stepped forward, hand outstretched.

"Reggie Sands," said the tall, bearded one.

"Adam," said the blond. "And you're Mrs. Allen?"

"You're all Sandmans?" Nate asked, craning to look up at the three tall men. "I saw an allergator."

The soup, Lucy thought. It won't go around. But she was grinning so widely she could barely speak. The smile on Josh's face was positively beatific.

"Lobsters," he said, holding up the bag. "To pad out the soup."

"And a pot to boil them in," Reggie said, holding up his big bag.

"And lots of potato chips," Adam said. "And salsa."

"And beer," Josh said, "it's in the pot, with ice."

Reggie and Adam walked on, leaving Lucy and Josh standing in the waves; Nate had followed the two tall young men, and was splashing in the waves behind them.

"I just got your message," Josh said, putting the bag down and giving Lucy a hug. "I figured if I couldn't bring Hoipolloi I should bring a substitute. I hope nobody in your family is allergic to bullied sons."

"How . . . ?"

"Don't ask. They got here. They brought presents. They even brought a wreath for our door. I can't believe it, Lucy. My . . . heart is running over."

She could see that it was. He was beaming from ear to ear, his face flushed and rosy.

"I'm so happy for you," Lucy said, and

picked up the bag, but it was too heavy for her; he took it.

"Are you sure it isn't . . . too much? Having all of us?"

"I'm sure," Lucy said. "Come on."

It took forever to bring the water for the lobsters to a boil. Nate got fussy, and Deb gave him a peanut butter sandwich and put him down for a nap. The others sat on the deck, drinking beer, and talking. Dickon and Adam found lots to talk about, leaving Reggie to entertain Deb and Natalie. Within a half hour, Deb began to feel like a fifth wheel; she joined her mother in the kitchen.

But Lucy wasn't alone. She and Josh Sands stood, hands entwined, leaning against the kitchen counter, sharing a glass of white wine. Deb started to back out of the kitchen.

"Don't go, Deb," Lucy said. "Entertain Josh while I fix the garlic bread."

Deb sat; Josh sat beside her at the kitchen table. Within moments, they were deep in a discussion of the Louisa May Alcott novel. "It's like *The Bridges of Madison County*," Deb said. "A romance with a sad ending. A real . . ."

"Tearjerker?" Josh suggested. "Potboiler? Blockbuster?"

"More than that," Deb said. "I like sad books. Crying over a book or a movie sort of . . . cleans out my tear ducts. And my soul. I think it's my soul."

Josh threw his head back, as he had done in the car, coming over the bridge, and laughed. Lucy peeked over her shoulder to watch.

"I think it's my soul," Josh repeated. "That's one of the best pieces of literary analysis I hope to hear this year. And I agree with you. It made me cry, too, tough old bird that I am."

"The year's almost over," Deb said, getting up and approaching the stove where the turkey soup was simmering. "Hey Mom," she said, squeezing Lucy around the waist. "Merry Christmas Eve." Then she was gone; it was time to get Nate up for Christmas Eve supper. But Lucy knew her daughter well, and she knew that Deb's words had a subtext beneath them: "I see that you like this man, and I'm pleased for you." My lecture to myself paid off, Lucy thought. She smiled warmly at Josh, feeling that Christmas had truly come.

It was Hal who put a damper on the evening. Quiet, thoughtful Hal, who never made waves, wore a frown and sat in a dark cloud of silence. When he got up to help Lucy clear the table, he followed her into the kitchen and slowly, carefully, rinsed the plates and put them in the dishwasher before speaking. Lucy stood beside him, waiting, filled with apprehension. She knew her son; he would have trouble expressing himself; she would be patient. With luck, it would end in a hug.

Finally, he turned to her, reached over to close the kitchen door, took two steps away from her.

"They're very nice people," Hal said, crossing his arms over his chest.

"But?"

"But I don't like the looks between you and that man."

That man. Lucy waited for him to go on. Until he got the angry words out, there was no point in interrupting, or in reprimanding him.

"Do you know what I mean?" he asked, not waiting for an answer. "It just doesn't seem right. We all thought it was great that you invited him, that's not what I'm talking about, and he's a nice guy, and I like Reggie and Adam, but . . ."

Still, Lucy didn't interrupt.

"This is hard to say," Hal said. "It's . . . a man-woman thing. You two look like you were . . . like you were . . ."

"That's enough, Hal," Lucy said. "I don't want you to say anything you'll wish you hadn't said."

"Then . . . help me out."

Lucy shook her head.

Hal blundered on; it was too late to stop. "I just don't think it's cool that my mother is flirting with a man she just met right in front of her family and his. It's . . . I don't know how to act. I mean, I want you to have a life, you know that, but not . . ."

"Not in front of the children?"

"It isn't funny."

"I'm not laughing," Lucy said. "And you're not children anymore."

"You're still our mother. And you're *smiling.*"

"I'm hurting too, Hal," Lucy said. "You've always been encouraged to be up front. We don't have that 'not under my roof' thing some families have. You three never had to sneak around when you brought somebody home. Are you suggesting a double standard?"

"I knew you'd say that." Hal uncrossed his arms. "Look, I'm sorry. It just makes me uncomfortable. I just can't see you with . . . another man."

"Is this about your father?"

"He's different."

"Hal."

"I'm not very modern, Mom. I'm pretty old-fashioned."

"Until now," Lucy said, "I hadn't noticed."

"Not about myself. About . . ."

"About your mother."

"Yeah."

Lucy felt understanding come to her like one of those light bulbs over someone's head in a comic strip. Time marches on, but never very fast. Ideas don't catch up with each other in a neat, orderly fashion. Some things are slow to change. A boy's feeling about his mother seems to be one of them.

Lucy stepped closer to Hal, put a tentative hand on his shoulder. He flinched, but not much. "I see," she said softly.

"You do?"

"I said I see," she said, smiling but speaking firmly. "But I didn't say I like. Think about it, Hal. We'll talk again. But I do see."

His face relaxed. He reached behind him to open the kitchen door. But what he met beyond it was silence.

Lucy followed him to the dining room. The chairs were pushed back; nobody was there. She stepped out on the terrace. Moonlight flooded the ocean and the beach. The air was warm, limpid. From somewhere, the sounds of Christmas carols came, softly. Someone was playing a guitar.

Hal stepped up beside his mother. "Do you think they heard us?" he asked. "Having a fight in the kitchen?"

"It wasn't a fight," Lucy said. "And I don't care if they did. I'm glad you said it, Hal. I'm just sorry you feel it."

Hal turned to her, his face lit by a smile. What a beautiful smile, Lucy thought.

"I'll tell you a secret," Hal said. "I think maybe I don't really feel it. Even while I was saying it, something else was saying to me, 'you don't believe that.' I think sometimes we say stuff we think we ought to feel. Like mothers are supposed to be saints. Sexless saints."

Enough. Lucy gave him a hug. "If you want a saint in the family," she said, "pick on someone your own size." The tension broken, they laughed together.

"Look," Hal said, pointing. "There they are."

The little group was coming toward them. Dickon, with Nate on his shoulders, was wading in the water, holding Deb's hand. Adam had plunged all the way into the ocean, and was swimming, parallel to the beach. And, hand in hand, Natalie and Reggie were bounding in the waves, jeans rolled up above their knees. Cicero leaped among them. But where was Josh?

Lucy reached down and slipped off her good red sandals.

"Come on," she said. "Let's join the group."

Hal kicked off his sneakers, but before

Lucy could start down the steps, he took her elbow and stopped her. "Hey, thanks," he said. "For not getting mad."

"Count your blessings," Lucy said. "If it had been any night but Christmas Eve . . ."

She felt the tension whoosh out of her, the laughter bubble up inside as she raced down the beach. When Nate called out "Gamma!" from Dickon's shoulders, she shouted back, "Merry Christmas!"

And she spotted Josh. He was coming toward them, walking slowly, a small shape beside him. Lucy ran, splashing in the waves, until she caught up with him. Cicero, shaking himself, trotted along beside her. He had spotted Hoipolloi, on his leash, sitting catlike and quiet beside his master. Cicero barreled over to the cat and sat beside him.

"Having a little catwalk?" Lucy said, breathless from her run.

"Just a brief one. I knew Adam was going to swim, so I raced home to get this guy. He loves the beach. Adam can take him home . . . that is, if I'd be welcome for a while longer?"

"I think we can manage," Lucy said.

"He brought a present for his friend," Josh said, reaching into his pocket.

It was a Christmas collar, red and green braided leather with little brass star studs set into it. Josh showed it to Lucy, then knelt and put it on Cicero's neck. "See?" he said, looking up at Lucy, "Hoipolloi has one, too.

"I didn't get anything for you," Josh went on.

"You weren't supposed to," Lucy said, looking down at the two animals, who seemed almost to be communicating, as they sat quietly, side by side, in their new collars.

"Can I tell you something?" Josh said, putting a hand on her shoulder.

Lucy nodded. He looked very serious. Was he going to say *We shouldn't have? We never will again?*

"Adam got quite cross with me," Josh said. "He led me outside, while you were in the kitchen. . . ."

"Oh, no," Lucy said.

"He objected to the way you and I were behaving. He accused me of 'coming on to you.' He said it embarrassed him. I . . . blew up."

"I very nearly did the same thing," Lucy said. "With Hal. He said we were flirting."

"As indeed we were. I cooled down pretty quick, reminded him of how his mother and I had discreetly looked the other way when he brought a girl home and crept down the hallway in the middle of the night."

"Did the floorboards creak?" Lucy asked, taking his hand.

"How did you know?"

"Guess," she said. "So how did it end?"

"He apologized. He thinks you're terrific. I'm the one he was mad at. I think he saw me as a rank seducer. 'Right in front of her family,' he said."

"Those two guys should get together. Hal and I had a remarkably similar set-to."

"All better now?"

"All better. But if it was any night but Christmas . . ."

Josh laughed. "What about the others? Your girls?"

"No problems. And Reggie?"

"Look," Josh said, and pointed. A quarter of a mile down the beach, Reggie and Natalie were walking slowly through the waves. "They don't look very mad," he said.

Adam, his wet shorts and shirt flapping against his body, emerged from the ocean and approached his father. "Gimme the leash, quick," he said. "I'll run this cat home and then come back, okay?" In a moment he was gone. Cicero followed. "I'll bring him back," Adam called over his shoulder.

"All better," Josh said, pulling Lucy close to him. "We've survived our first crisis."

"This was the first time my kids have seen me with a . . . with a . . ."

"Is 'man' the word you're looking for?"

Lucy nodded.

"Me, too. With a woman, that is. I've been a hermit, me and Hoipolloi. Adam and Reggie have been after me for a year to start dating—boy, do I hate that word—but the moment I do, look what happened."

"It's an experience I wasn't prepared for."

"Nor I. But do you know what I think? I think Hal and Adam objected to our behavior out of love. Tough love, is that what they call it? They want us to be perfect. To stay on our pedestals."

"And we toppled."

"And it's okay. That's the best part."

Josh took her arm and they began walking back to the condo. "Can I tell you a secret?" Josh whispered into her hair.

"Shoot."

"I'd like to topple again. Soon. Often."

"I think," Lucy said, "that that could be arranged. I have a map at home that's marked with the shortest route from Edgeville to Boston. The trip takes about three hours. Think you could handle it?"

He stopped, gathered her into his arms, hugged her hard. "Does that mean we have to be good for the rest of . . ."

His pretty speech was interrupted by a wolf-call. Together, they looked up at the lighted deck. Hal, Deb, and Dickon stood there, side by side, beer bottles raised on high.

"Merry Christmas, rank seducer," Lucy whispered, wriggling out of his embrace and waving back.

"Merry Christmas, little flirt," he whispered.

Together, running in the waves, they raced home to their waiting children.

And On Christmas Morning . . .

Nate woke up very, very early. Lucy, curled into her pillow, heard Deb talking softly to him, shushing him when he made loud truck noises pushing Hal's yellow dumptruck down the hallway between the bedrooms.

Hal was up next, and Lucy heard him whispering to his sister, then leaving to take Nate for a walk on the beach. Lucy joined Deb in the kitchen.

Together, they started breakfast—the traditional one. Sausages. Scrambled eggs with little pieces of green and red peppers; biscuits made with Bisquick. Mimosas. By the time they had the peppers cut and the sausage worked into patties, Lucy heard the shower running. Soon, Natalie, already in her bathing suit and a long T-shirt, poked her head around the kitchen door.

"Ho ho ho," she said.

"Nat's got a boyfriend, Nat's got a boyfriend," Debra singsonged, as she had when she was twelve and Natalie was fourteen.

Natalie ignored her and hugged her mother. "Merry Christmas, Mom," she said, reaching behind Lucy to the cabinet where, she knew, the Oreos had been placed. "Who's going to take Santa's bite out of the Oreo?"

"You do it," Deb said. "I'll pour his juice."

"But there's no fireplace. Where . . . ?"

Dickon strode into the kitchen. "I've already figured that out," he said. He took the juice and cookies and stepped out on the deck. Deb followed him, dragging a huge suitcase she'd retrieved from the bedroom. "Everybody stay out of here," she said, indicating the deck. "If you peek, Santa Claus won't be able to land his surfboard."

Lucy smiled at Natalie. "I guess that leaves us to make the stuffing and get the bird ready," she said. "Unless you want a swim first."

"No way," Natalie said. "Now where are the chestnuts?"

Side by side, they began the dinner preparations, alternating with the breakfast ones. Giggling, Deb came in from the terrace, shut the door, and began setting the table.

Nate shrieked when he bounded up the

wooden steps, Hal close behind. "Santa Claus came!" he yelled, spotting the row of stuffed stockings hanging on hooks from the railing. "Mine!" he said, identifying his own.

"Hey, Nate," Hal said, "look at this. Santa ate his Oreos."

"He didn't *finish*," Nate said, then turned back to his stocking.

Lucy and Natalie joined them on the terrace. "But . . . ," Lucy said, seeing the row of bulging stockings, "I thought we weren't going to . . . that you didn't want . . ."

There were six stockings, plus a tiny one—one of Nate's socks—for Cicero, with a chewy bone sticking out of it.

"Oh, my," Lucy said, feeling the tears well up. Dickon had gone for the mimosas; Deb was on the floor beside Nate. Cicero, in his new collar, stood on his hind legs and snapped at his sock until he dislodged it, then retreated to a corner of the deck to chew his bone.

In a moment, the family was in a circle, glasses raised.

"To you, Mom," Natalie said, "for the best Christmas we've ever had."

"Hear, hear," said Dickon.

"To the strays," Hal said, "who made our Christmas even merrier." He paused for a moment, looked out over the sparkly ocean, took a sip of his mimosa. "You know," he

said, "we're all strays in one way or another."

Lucy was too overcome to speak. Finally,
she found her tongue to say, "I love you all.
I just love all of you."

"Gee, Mom," Natalie said, "no need to
get maudlin. And by the way, do you still
have that map you marked with the best
route from Edgeville to Boston?"

"I think I can find it," Lucy said. "But
why in the world do you ask? You know the
way." She winked at Natalie; Natalie winked
back.

Hal grabbed his sister and swung her
around so that her feet came off the floor.
"Don't do anything I wouldn't do," he singsonged, as he had when he was a little boy
and Natalie was dressing for a date.

Natalie smiled. "That's not very limit-
ing."

Lucy reached for Hal's hand, and for
Dickon's, and the family made a circle with
Nate on the floor in the center, pushing a
truck, and Cicero, chewing his bone, off to
one side.

Lucy bowed her head; they bowed theirs.
"Thank you, God," she said, as she had
said every Christmas of her life.

"Thank you, God," the others echoed,
squeezing hands, "and Merry Christmas to
all."

"And now," Hal said—his words another Allen family tradition, as invariable and predictable as all their traditions were—"let's eat."

A Picture of Love
Diane E. Lock

"Winter driving can be treacherous, dear, as you well know."

Linda struggled to keep the car under control on the icy road while her mother's voice clamored in her head.

"Must you use the back roads?"

"I'm a photographer, Ma. The best shots are not always on the interstate."

It was an argument they'd had often through the years. The last time had been two winters ago, when Linda had driven up into the White Mountains on the heels of a blizzard, hoping for a few good shots. She had spent four hours stranded in a snow-bank, a very expensive night in a ski lodge, and not one photograph was worth the effort.

Guess I'm a slow learner, Ma, she sighed, straining to see through the madly swirling snow, 'cause here I am again. Same road, different blizzard.

"I worry about you out there alone, Lin, ever since—"

"There you go, Ma, dragging things up that happened twenty years ago."

Nan Boyd had passed away in the spring,
and they'd never argue about that, or anything else, again, Linda realized with a jolt.

Winter driving was a fact of life in New
Hampshire, and Linda had overcome her
fear of hazardous conditions long ago.
Snow had been falling heavily all afternoon,
and the strong wind had blown and piled
it into drifts that stretched across the deserted highway. The plows hadn't passed in
hours, and for the last few miles she'd been
driving in the faint tire marks of the last
car to come this way.

I'll probably follow these tracks right up
to someone's door, she thought. Hope
they're having something good for dinner.
This morning's cheese sandwich hadn't
been meant to last all day, and Linda's
stomach growled. Her head ached from
staring into a curtain of driving snow, made
worse with the headlights on, and the con-
stant barrage of holiday cheer from the radio had grown stale.

A snow-crusted sign welcomed her to
Wolfeborough, New Hampshire, "America's
First Summer Resort," and she laughed out
loud, the sound hollow in the cavern of her
Suburban truck.

You spend too much time alone, her
mother's voice said.

Leave me alone, Ma.

A sigh of relief escaped when she rolled

into town a few minutes later. No matter what the roads were like, she'd be safe here. Cruising slowly along Main Street, Linda came to the white clapboard mass of the Wolfeboro Inn. Golden lamplight spilled from tiny-paned windows, welcoming travelers as it had for two hundred years. The swinging sign out front didn't say No Vacancy. There'd be dinner here and, with luck, a bed.

It was awkward with her cane, but Linda gathered up all of her bags and fought the howling wind across the parking lot, bursting into the lobby in a swirl of snow.

"Stop right there!"

Behind the booming voice came a tall, thin woman wearing delicate wire-rimmed spectacles, fluffy white hair, and a fluffy green angora sweater.

"What a mess," she scolded, eyeing the snow Linda had brought in. "And all these bags! You must be here for a week."

"Just the night," Linda said, handing over the lightest bag, "but I don't have a reservation."

"We'll find something for you. Can't send you back out in this weather. Wipe your feet and come with me."

"What a beautiful piece of work," she said, pointing to Linda's intricately carved black cane. "What's it made of?"

"This one is ebony."

"Have you had an accident?" The faded blue eyes were kind.

"No."

"But the cane."

"It's part of me."

"My brother-in-law has one leg shorter than the other, and he walks just like that. What's wrong with you?" The kindly blue eyes were direct.

"I was born with a dislocated hip." Linda braced herself for the pity that always sprang to their eyes. But not this time.

"My friend Millie's daughter was born with a rotated hip, but they got her fixed up when she was two. A pity your problem was never taken care of. Ah well, let's get you checked in. My, these bags are heavy. What have you got in here?"

"Cameras. Film. Lights, light meters. Stuff. Can't leave any equipment outside in this weather."

"You sound like a photographer. Welcome to the inn, dear. I'm Rose Barnes."

She was thin and bony, all sharp edges under the fluff, and her long strides led them across the wide pine boards to an antique rolltop. She set the cases down on the braided rug and turned to the modern computer hidden inside the desk.

"Your name, dear?"

"Werther." Linda said, dropping her

bags in an untidy heap. "Linda Werther. And yes, I'm a photographer."

"Well, you sure travel with a lot of equipment."

"This is nothing to what I have at home."

Linda had dozens of cameras, including her very first, a Kodak Instamatic, that Daddy bought her the Christmas she was ten. She remembered his proud grin, and her mother's tight-lipped disapproval.

"That's too expensive for a kid, Cyril. She'll break it, or leave it someplace."

Linda had clutched the bright yellow box, waiting anxiously for her mother to snatch the camera and put it safely out of reach on the top shelf of the closet with the other treasures waiting there until she was old enough.

"Aw, Nan, our Linnie'll take real good care of it, wontcha, hon?" Daddy hugged her. "You've seen how she hangs around my darkroom," he said over her head to his wife. "I think she's really interested."

"It's your money, I suppose," Nan Boyd said, dismissing his foolishness with a shrug. Cyril grinned and winked at his daughter. Linda released the breath she'd been holding and examined the precious gift.

"It's perfect, Daddy. Now I can take lots of pictures, just like you."

Thirty years ago. A long time.

Rose's gnarled fingers flew over the keyboard. "Have you stayed here before?"

"No, but my father used to come here often."

"What's his name? I might remember him."

"Cyril Boyd."

"You mean the photographer *Cyril Boyd?*" Her voice was reverent.

"Umhmm."

"I met him once, years ago. He used to stay here when the Hawkins family owned the Inn. He took the picture of old Dave Hawkins that hangs in the upstairs landing. It's so real, you can see the twinkle in his eyes."

"That's my dad." Cyril Boyd had been famous for his sensitive portraits of New England's most prominent people, but he loved the outdoors, and had taught Linda to appreciate the beauty of the world in detail. From him she learned to distill what she saw through her lens to its essence. A drop of dew glistening on a single blade of grass, the cool green aura of a woodland glade. Together they would trudge halfway around the lake out back of the house in Manchester to capture a snowdrift glittering like crystal in the sun, or a fat, furry squirrel, ready for the harsh New Hampshire winter.

Cyril died when Linda was eighteen, and she missed him still.

"I hear Fred Manning's oldest girl is getting married tomorrow night," Rose said. "You here for the wedding?"

"Nope. I don't do weddings or pictures of adorable babies. I photograph the great outdoors."

"Guess a mountain's less hassle than a nervous bride," Rose said.

"Or her mother," Linda said. They both laughed.

Some of Linda's photographs had been compared favorably to Ansel Adams and Eliot Porter, and her work brought high prices in galleries in Portsmouth, Boston, and New York.

"So you're on vacation?" The elderly woman held on to the room key, waiting for an answer.

Nosy, Linda thought, but essentially harmless.

"No, I'm working on a book of the seasons of New England, and winter's the last segment."

"Weather's perfect, then. It's supposed to clear up tomorrow."

"It looks like a movie set out there, with the snow thick as a blanket and the trees all lit up."

"Ah, those lights. Been lit up like a fairyland 'round here ever since Halloween. Got to attract the shoppers, they say. Well I say we've lost the meaning of Christmas. Anyway, I shop all year round, what with three married children and seven grandchildren, plus all the great-nieces and -nephews," she complained, with obvious pleasure, "but I'm ready. How 'bout you?"

"All done," Linda said, "at last." She had done all her Christmas shopping in ten minutes in August at a gift show. Geodes for her nephews, a jade clip for the string ties her brother Mike favored, a polished stone pendant for Sandy, his wife. Sent off weeks ago. Simple. Quick. Detached. Her parcel from Mike waited at home to be opened when she got back.

"I haven't eaten since breakfast. Is it too early for dinner?"

Rose consulted her watch, a plastic thing in psychedelic colors. "Dining room opened five minutes ago. Serve dinner from five-thirty to ten. Bar's open 'til one. Breakfast in the dining room from six to eleven, except for Sundays, when brunch goes 'til two. Try the clam chowder. It's great. Bon appetit!"

The only occupants of the dining room were an elderly couple who watched Linda make her way to her table with the look of sympathy mixed with guilt that she knew so well. A pity, but thank God it's you and not me, the eyes said.

Five foot two and trim, with curly blond hair piled on top of her head and sparkling blue eyes, Linda at forty-two still attracted attention when she entered a room. But she walked with a drunken, rolling motion, pitching her leg out and around with every step, and it seemed that all eyes quickly focused on her awkward gait, and she saw interest change to confusion and embarrassment.

The woman smiled, but Linda bent her head and studied her placemat. She learned that parts of the Inn dated from seventeen-fifty. The dining room had then been a tavern. The fireplace and the bar were original fixtures, as were the massive oak beams, hung for the holiday with ropes of greenery twisted with tiny white lights and red velvet ribbons. The scent of cloves and allspice filled the air, and it was easy to imagine how it looked over two hundred years ago. Lake Winnipesaukee was out there somewhere under the ice and snow. Must be a beautiful spot, she thought. In the summer.

The clam chowder was excellent, creamy and thick with clams and potatoes, and Linda finished it with regret. With her stuffed chicken breast she sipped mulled cider served directly from a copper kettle in

the hearth and debated having the grape-
nuts custard, a specialty of the house.

Outside she watched people battle the
drifting snow. It was good to be inside, with
good food and a warm fire at her back.

She ordered the custard, and studied a
pair of new arrivals over the rim of the
steaming mug of cider. Two men, one in
his seventies, the other fortyish, identical except for the difference in age. Both had
deep-set eyes and high foreheads with
prominent widow's peaks, one silver and the
other black. When their chowder came they
tested the hot soup in the same careful
manner, made identical gestures with their
hands as they talked, sent a falling shock of
hair in place with the same sideways toss of
the head. Father and son, she guessed, but
what a striking resemblance.

The younger man caught her staring, and
flashed her an engaging grin. He had a
photogenic face. Good bones, straight nose,
and full lips that curved up at the corners
in a permanent smile. Smoky gray eyes,
with dark, thick lashes. Nice.

"How's that chowdah, son?"

"Great, Dad." Confirming her guess.

"What're you going to have for dinner?"

"Don't know yet," he answered, eyes still
on Linda.

"Stew here's A-OK," his father said. "I've
had it before."

Realizing he didn't have his attention, he followed his son's gaze. Now two pair of smoky gray eyes held Linda enthralled. She watched a slow smile spread across his face, the same smile as his son's. What a portrait. If she did portraits.

The waitress came to the table, breaking the spell, and Linda noticed the room had filled with noisy groups of merrymakers and couples, faces radiant in the candle-light. A thin, pale young man began to play at a glossy black grand piano over by the bar.

"Chestnuts roasting on an open fire . . . ," his passable tenor lured half a dozen couples to the stamp-sized dance floor.

Linda signaled her waiter, a bored-look-ing young man with severe acne. "I've got an early start in the morning," she ex-plained as she signed the check. Like he cared.

Her clumsy walk attracted the usual at-tention, but she held her burning face high until she reached her room. Once there, she unpacked the small essentials kit she always carried, and turned on the TV.

Reception was bad. She had nothing to read, and seven-thirty was somewhat early for bed. Before the silence became oppres-sive, Linda bundled up in a down-filled coat and thick mittens and took herself out for a walk.

It was snowing lightly, and the whole town twinkled with myriad lights gleaming from wreaths and trees. Candles glowed in every window, and here and there Linda glimpsed people decorating Christmas trees. She imagined their conversations, the excited chatter of the children. Daddy had loved the holiday, she remembered. He spent hours choosing the perfect tree, draping the lead tinsel until the tree shimmered like a cascading silver waterfall, telling the same stories every year with every ornament he and mother hung. While he lived the entire house, inside and out, had been touched by the magic of Christmas.

After he died the spirit seemed to go out of her mother, and when Mike went away to college Nan stopped celebrating the holidays. She might have come around for Mike, but he met Sandy at Penn State.

She was from Arizona, used to the intense heat and delicate tan and lavender shades of the desert. The Northeast was too green, too cold, and too far away from home. They married right after graduation and moved to Scottsdale. Mike had been there fifteen years, and had twelve-year-old twin boys, Chris and Colin, whom Linda had met only twice.

Christmas was for families, Mother had always said, and too much work just for the two of them. Without Mike, all holiday traditions came to an end, including Christmas dinner.

"We'd have leftovers for weeks, Lin. A terrible waste," Nan would say, cutting a thick slice of the meatloaf they always ate on Thursdays.

And the tree.

"Trees make such a mess, dropping those sticky needles all over the house."

"Lots of people have artificial trees, Mother."

"Yes, and they're tacky. And we don't have Mike around to fetch things down from the attic."

So, no more huge evergreen in the living room, with branches dangerously laden with glass ornaments and showers of tinsel reflecting multi-colored lights. Remembering how the colors all ran together when you scrunched up your eyes, Linda stood in the street with her eyes screwed up tight and stared at a tree in someone's window. But they used those tiny white lights now, and colored lights worked better. Tucked away in the attic somewhere were lights that bubbled like a fountain when they heated up.

"Magic," Cyril used to whisper.

"Dangerous," Nan said.

Now that Mother had passed away, it seemed silly to get Dave Anderson over to drag the old decorations down from the at-

tic just for herself. Guess you know which
one you take after, Linda thought with a
wry grin. Things would have been different
if Mike were still here. Or Jerry.

After walking for an hour she went back
to the hotel bar to thaw by the fire with hot
buttered rum. The noise and laughter made
her feel melancholy, as if the merriment of
the holidays emphasized her isolation.

"You need a man, Lin," Nan used to
grumble. "Don't know how you expect to
meet anyone out by yourself in the wilds,
taking pictures of mountain streams."

"I had a man once, Ma, remember?
Guess I'm like you," she'd say, "we gals get
along just fine on our own." Mother had
been a trying woman, but at least she had
been company. Next Christmas Linda would
be sure to stay home.

By nine-thirty she lay in bed, watching
the snow drift slowly to the ground. Jerry
was on her mind, and on impulse she took
his picture out of her wallet. After nearly
twenty years the pain had faded, and she
looked at his picture fondly. Jerry gazed
back with the cocky expression he had, eyes
squinted against the smoke from the cigarette clenched in his teeth. Part of his tough
image, like the leather jacket and ripped
jeans, but Linda had known him well. His
long rust-colored hair was tied back in a
ponytail, and a thick curly beard covered

much of his face, like virtually every other
young man of the seventies. He leaned
against his bright red pickup. He'd been so
proud of that damned truck.

Jerry had been two years older than
Linda, her best friend Connie's brother. A
rough diamond, with a kind heart, Jerry
had dropped out of school to pump gas at
the Esso station in town. To pay for the
truck.

Linda fell madly in love with him at fifteen, when he kissed her during a game of
spin-the-bottle at Connie's "Sweet Sixteen"
party. "I think you're real pretty, Linny,"
he'd whispered in the dark, "bum leg and
all."

She was pretty, with those sparkling blue
eyes and a blond ponytail that showed off
her delicate features, but the leg thing made
her different. Only a very self-confident boy
would ignore the derision of his peers to
take her out. None did.

Jerry had a steady girlfriend, but he took
Linda to her Senior Prom. He asked her
the night Connie modeled her new formal,
a froth of peach-colored chiffon.

"It's perfect!" Linda breathed, "you look
like a princess!"

"Cute, sis," Jerry said, sticking his head

in his sister's bedroom door. "What color's yours?" With a curt nod at Linda.

"Don't have one."

"Aren't you going to the prom?"

"Waddayoucare!"

"Well excuuuuuse me for askin' a simple question."

"The answer is no. I can't dance, I have no dress, and no one asked me." The words bubbled out in a burst of tears, and she buried her head in Connie's pillow.

"I'll take you," he said softly, smoothing her golden hair with his grease-blackened mechanic's hand.

"I'm a real lousy dancer," he whispered in her ear as they awkwardly circled the room in a slow waltz. They both knew who was the lousy dancer, and Linda was grateful. "Let's get out of here."

Taking her arm, he swept her out to the brick patio, Linda radiant and fully aware of the other girls' surprise and envy. Jerry was an older man, good looking, and built like a linebacker. He dwarfed Linda, and her awkward deformity went almost unnoticed. In the soft summer night he kissed her, a tender, lingering pressure on her lips that thrilled her down to the pit of her stomach. "I like you a lot, Linda."

And later, up on Thompson's Hill, he

covered her with passionate kisses. "Feels right, bein' here with you. I want you to be my girl, Lin."

They'd been married a year when Jerry went hunting up in Maine. Linda, barely twenty and three months pregnant, had begged him not to go, but he won her over easily.

"Can't back out now, babe," he'd wheedled, coaxing a tearful smile. "Me'n the guys've been planning this trip forever—they'd laugh themselves silly!" He left her with a long, passionate kiss, and a fond pat on her rearend. "I'll be home 'fore you know I left."

But Jerry and his friends were killed in a blinding snowstorm on an icy road at Moosehead Lake. The state police found the truck crumpled against a huge oak tree, the engine rammed into the cab, two sad-eyed deer sprawled in the flatbed behind them. The police report said Jerry had been driving his shiny red pickup way too fast, and the autopsy showed that all three had been drinking heavily.

Numb with shock and grief, Linda lost the will to live, and lost the baby. Her mother nursed her back to health, and over time Jerry and the baby faded into memory like ripples on a lake. Once gone, it was like they had never been.

Linda considered herself lucky to have had Jerry, even for a short time, and she never looked for anyone else. Photography took up most of her time, and with work she loved, her mother's companionship, and the house, Linda had no complaints.

That night Linda dreamed of a big black bear, with smoky gray eyes and a fascinating smile. They were decorating a Christmas tree, on a beach, beside a sign that had "America's first summer resort" printed in mile high letters.

A glance out the window the next morning showed a different world. The snow had stopped, and breaks in the cloud cover gave glimpses of bright blue sky. On the ground a dozen birds twittered and chirped, pecking at bits of bread and seed scattered around the evergreens. One blue jay, bolder than the others, brazenly snatched a choice bit of toast from a pigeon's beak. A cardinal landed, adding a flash of color, and Linda reached for a camera. The red bird strutted through the flock and stopped beside two black-capped chickadees busily pecking in the snow.

Linda focused the camera. Framed in the viewfinder was a bough of snow-covered Scotch pine arched over the backs of the scarlet cardinal and two steel gray chickadees. She smiled as she squeezed the shutter. Taking two more shots for insurance, she dropped the camera into her handbag and went down to the dining room whistling the theme from "Palladin" between her teeth. That picture would be a terrific addition to the series of bird Christmas cards she planned for next year's collection. Linda often went for days without a shot like that. A day's work done by seven in the morning. The sun broke through the clouds as she crossed the lobby. This was going to be a great day.

The dining room was crowded.

"Got a single right over here," said the hostess cheerfully, "just follow me."

Right over here turned out to be the farthest corner of the room, and Linda felt every eye on her. In the hush of suspended conversation the tap-tap of her cane was loud and clear. Looking neither right nor left, Linda kept her eyes fixed on the young woman's softly rounded rump flicking sensually from side to side.

"Hello again," she heard as she settled into her seat. Sitting at the next table were the father and son from last night. Of course they'd been watching her, and she flushed, embarrassed, but the older man gave her a wink and a friendly nod.

"Good morning," said the son, with his charming smile. He flicked a shock of hair from his eyes with a toss of his head. "We met you in here last night."

"Yes, I think so," she said, flustered.

"Weather's improved, hasn't it?"

"It's lovely," she answered, realizing with a shock that he had the eyes of the bear in her dream.

"Great day for traveling," he said. "We're—"

"Let the girl have her breakfast," his father said, reclaiming his attention. "Y'know, Phil's really looking forward to seeing you," she heard him say. "Must be ten years since you saw him last."

"Not quite, Dad," the younger man answered. "Aunt Carrie died six years ago. Does he still live in that big house on the water?"

"Nope, Phil's in a retirement home now, still in Camden. He loved that place, but it was too much for him alone."

Linda thought he sounded just like her brother, Mike, the day of Mother's funeral.

"You can't stay here now, Linda. This place is too big for you."

Linda loved the house, a tall Victorian set on the banks of the Merrimack River in Manchester. Eleven rooms in all, with a walk-up attic that had been the envy of every kid in the neighborhood.

"Mike, Dad bought this house the year I was born. I've lived here all my life!"

"You need something easier to get around . . ." Anger flashed in her eyes, and he hugged her quickly. "Sorry, hon, you know I didn't mean anything, but how can you manage this huge place by yourself?"

"Do you think we've been doing it alone all these years? Dave Andersen from next door has been doing the mowing and plowing since you left, Mike. I'm sure I can rely on him. I'll keep the service Mother used for the heavy housework. There's no reason for me to leave this house. Besides, the real estate market in New Hampshire is really bad right now."

"Not for these big old Victorians, sis. The yuppies love 'em."

She thought about starting over somewhere else, with strangers who stared rudely or averted eyes filled with pity. Nosy people who *simply had* to know what was wrong with her leg.

"So do I, Mike. This is my home, and here I stay."

The two men left while Linda finished her breakfast, and by eight she was ready to leave.

"Told you the weather'd clear up, didn't I?" said Rose, the desk clerk, walking Linda to the door. "You'll get some lovely pictures today."

Sunlight glinted off the lake like firelight

on crystal. In the background, dark pines and snowy mountain peaks jutted into the bright blue sky.

"Have a happy Christmas," Linda said, turning to leave.

"You too, and be careful out there," the woman said, blocking the doorway. "The main roads're plowed, but I noticed on my way over here that there's still a skim of ice where the sun hasn't reached."

"I'm sure I'll be fine," Linda said, escaping at last. "My truck has four-wheel drive."

Listening to a Christmas tape by her favorite women's chorale, Linda rambled along back roads and byways for a while, frequently scrambling out of the truck for a picture. Finding a spot for the tripod in the drifted snow took time, and once she missed a terrific shot of a heavily antlered deer and his doe on the edge of the forest. But later, setting up beside a meadow where a creek meandered through the snow like a twisted ribbon, she caught a fox who had come out of the woods to drink.

If this weather continued, she'd have to stay another night in this area, Linda thought, happily shooting ice-coated branches gleaming against the blue sky, intricate shadow patterns on the snow, a hardy chipmunk perched on the limb of a pine tree piled high with soft mounds of white fluff.

She stopped for gas at a full-service station in what appeared to be the middle of nowhere. The attendant, a powerfully built man with a full red beard, reminded her of Jerry. She noticed his limp as he strode over to the truck wearing a broad smile.

"Lovely mornin', ain't it? Fillerup?"

"Yes, please."

"My pleasure." Another grin. They loved to see her pull in driving a vehicle with a thirsty forty gallon tank. He got the nozzle set up and came around to the window.

"Check your oil? Washer fluid?"

"All set, thanks. Where are we?"

"Tamworth. 'Nother fifteen miles or so to North Conway. Here for the skiin'?" His name was Jason, unless the badge on his shirt lied. Friendly enthusiasm shone in his eyes, and she had to smile.

"No. I'm a photographer," surprised into answering.

"You'll get some pretty pictures around here."

"Yes, I'm sure. Where do you keep the key . . . ?"

"No keys here, ma'am," he answered politely. "Facilities are inside, where it's wahm. Ladies' is the pink door."

She slid from the driver's seat and headed inside in her ungainly fashion. Her back prickled, expecting him to watch her, but he set the pump and limped inside with

her. She wondered what had happened to
his leg. Not in a million years would she
ask.

"Too cold to stand out here waiting for
this monster to drink its fill," he observed
with his big friendly grin.

The pink door was next to the blue men's
room door. Not very original, but it was
warm and clean.

"Are you close to a major route?" she
asked, wondering at the three repair bays
and well-stocked convenience store.

"No, ma'am. Unless you count the
Kankamangus Trail. 'Bout midway between
Laconia and Conway, but traffic's real good.
Lots of skiers this time of year, leaf peepers
in the fall, and all the summer people. Are
you up from Boston . . . ?"

His question hung in the air, inviting an
answer. Soon they'd be chatting away like
old friends, and eventually discuss their
handicaps. Linda scanned the loaded
shelves, pretending she hadn't heard.

"Yup, we're busy all year round," he continued, when she approached the register
with a pack of mints. "Great when it's your
own business."

"I thought these were all part of a
chain?" Drawn in at last by his friendliness.

"It's a franchise arrangement," he answered, with a proud grin. "And all mine

since last August—and the bank's, of course.
So far we're makin' out just fine."

They walked out to the truck, limping in
unison.

"Don't we make a fine pair," he said,
laughing.

Oh brother.

"Car slipped off the lift," he said, indicating his leg. "Hazards of the job, I guess."

Now she was supposed to tell him about
herself. In a pig's eye, buster. She clam-
bered into the truck and he shut the door
for her, big eager smile at eye level. He
looked like a big old St. Bernard, and she
couldn't resist those warm brown eyes.

"Dislocated hip," she explained, surprising herself again. "Birth defect," she
added, expecting pity, regretting her bitter-
ness when it didn't come.

His smile grew wider. "Could be a lot
worse, right? Stop in any time an' say
hello!" he shouted over the rumble of the
engine, patting the rear fender fondly as
she pulled away. She waved, and turned the
truck toward the road. Just a nice guy, like
Rose back at the Inn. She'd have to stop
looking for hidden traps behind every
smile.

"Well, Hogan, left or right?" she asked
the truck, named for the wrestler, at an in-
tersection. The vehicle seemed to pull left,
and she gave it free rein.

"The bear went over the mountain," she sang, "to see what he could see—" She had rounded a bend. The hills fell away, and she gazed at a valley holding a tiny gem of a village in its palm. It was exquisite!

"What a photo opportunity!" she breathed, pulling over to the shoulder of the road.

The scene looked like something out of a Little Golden Book, one of those miniature villages populated with bunnies.

She grabbed a camera and tripod and jumped out of the car.

The village of no more than a dozen houses nestled by a river in a crease of hills, the requisite tall white steeple rising from the center. In the foreground, a horsedrawn sleigh on runners moved slowly along the road toward a covered bridge. The four horses tossed their heads, breath puffing from their nostrils, their jingling bells clearly audible on the crisp cold air with every step.

She set up the tripod, hoping to catch them before they disappeared on the bridge. Plumes of white smoke hovered above chimneys in the stillness, and in the distance a few black and white Holsteins clustered in a pasture. The sun glancing off the snow made the whole scene glisten and sparkle like an old-fashioned Christmas card.

Half an hour later, thoroughly chilled but still enchanted, planning to cross the river into the village, she started across the deserted highway to the truck. Suddenly, out of nowhere, a gray sedan hurtled toward her on the narrow road. Swerving to miss her, the driver collided with the truck with a ringing metallic crunch. In slow motion, and in total silence, the car went into an agonizing spin on the icy surface, whirling slowly but surely towards the steep bank overlooking the river. Linda screamed, but one more miraculous spin sent it flying in the opposite direction. Horrified, she watched the gray sedan soar twenty feet into the air and land on its side in the ditch, half buried in the snow. Silence reigned. The sun shone, the snow sparkled, and two wheels spun slowly in the air. Linda heard herself moaning and clamped her mouth shut. She crossed the road on shaking legs and threw the camera equipment into the truck. Her cane proved useless in the deep soft snow, and she discarded it and ran awkwardly toward the disabled car, alternately cursing and praying.

As she came near the car, a man scrambled through the open window and rolled out into the snow.

"Thank God you're okay," she called out as she approached him. He turned at the sound and she recognized him as the father from the hotel dining room. His white hair was disheveled, gray eyes were unfocused, and a thin trickle of blood rolled down his cheek.

"We were trying to get to the Kankamangus . . . ," he said.

She wiped his face with the silk scarf around her neck, searching carefully for bits of glass.

"We have to get you to the nearest hospital," she said in a shaking voice, "but how?"

The impact had shoved her truck so deeply into the snowbank she thought it would take a crane to extricate it.

"A-Adam," the old man mumbled.

"What?"

"Adam . . . uh, Adam . . ." He waved his hand in the air.

"I suppose we must observe the formalities," she said, taking his outstretched hand. This guy must be some kind of kook. "Pleased to meet you, Adam. I'm Linda. Now, let's see about getting you out of here—"

"Adam is . . . in the car. My son . . ." He made another vague swipe at the open window beside him, but this time Linda got the message. Of course. The younger man, the handsome son, was still inside the half-buried car. She peered in cautiously, afraid of what she might find. It was dim inside the deathly silent car, but when her eyes adjusted, she saw him, slumped against the driver's door as though peacefully asleep. Please God, she prayed, it's Christmas. He can't be d-dead! Don't make me find a dead man in a car at Christmas! She stared at the still form, picturing the wonderful smile, the dusky gray eyes sparkling with life, now closed. Don't let him be dead! She climbed halfway into the car and clutched the shoulder of Adam's coat.

"Wake up, Adam, you've got to get out of here!"

The only sound was a loud moan from the old man out in the snow.

"Yo, Adam, time to go!"

Still nothing.

Oh God. I've got to find a phone, call the police, get an ambulance to take these men to a hospital. She glanced across the road at her car, rammed into the snowbank. I'm going to be sick, she thought.

"Is he okay, miss?" Blood trickled from under Adam's hair, and she mopped it with her hopelessly inadequate silk scarf. She pulled off her glove and held her bare hand under his nostrils.

"Is Adam alright?" The old man called in a querulous voice.

He was breathing.

"Miss?"

"He's, um, fine. I think." She backed out

of the window. "Look, I have to get help. You stay here with your son, and I'll walk to the village across—"

Her voice was drowned by the sudden squeal of brakes. A tow truck pulled up behind her Suburban, and a bearded young giant jumped out. It was Jason, from the garage. Thank you, God.

"Holy moly! What happened here?" he shouted as he loped through the deep snow. "Mornin' miss, didn't expect to see you again so soon!"

"Nor did I, but I'm sure glad you dropped by. What are you doing here?"

"Got a call to change a dead battery over in the village, but I guess it can wait."

"This man is hurt, and his son Adam is inside. Unconscious, I think."

"You people know each other?" Jason asked.

"No. It's a long story, and we haven't got the time."

"You got that right," said Jason, poking his head into the car. "You stay put. There's a radio in the wrecker. I'll have an ambulance here in just a few minutes."

Linda sank to her knees in the snow beside the old man.

"You've met Adam," he said. "My name's Vern, miss. Vern Fenwick. I'm sorry we almost hit you."

"Hi, Vern, I'm Linda. We met at the

Wolfeboro Inn last night. I shouldn't have
been in the road. I just hope your son is
okay. What are you doing here?"

"It's a pretty day, and Adam wanted to
enjoy the countryside. I warned him about
the secondary roads, but he wanted to get
off the interstate. He lives down south, and
he's forgotten about winter conditions.
What were you doing in the road?"

"Taking pictures of the village over there.
But I thought you were on your way to
Maine."

"We are. My brother-in-law lives in Camden. Ever been there?"

She shook her head. "Real pretty town
near the coast. He retired there with his wife
years ago. Phil's wife and my Irene were sisters, and we always spent Christmas together.
Beautiful girls they were, too. Irene passed
on nearly eight years ago, and Carrie, that's
Phil's wife, she's been gone five or six now.
Since I retired I go up every . . ."

Linda watched Jason come back carrying
an armload of what must be blankets.

". . . and Adam wanted to see him . . ."
The quavery voice droned on.

"He hasn't stopped talking," she said.

"Probably shock," Jason whispered, dropping one dingy colorless blanket over them.
He tossed the other one across the silent
young man in the car, and sat in the snow
to wait with them.

Fifteen minutes—an eternity—later, the shriek of sirens pierced the still cold air, and soon the ditch swarmed with activity. Two policemen asked questions and took notes. One of the ambulance attendants climbed into the car through the window to see to Adam, and the other looked Vern over quickly.

"Nothing broken, Pops. You're okay."

"We can move him," came a muffled voice from inside the car. "Let's right this thing and get him out of here."

The accident had attracted a few passing motorists, who left their cars and stood gawking at the roadside.

"There's a man inside the car," Jason called up to two brawny young men. "Can you give us a hand down here?"

Grunting with effort, the men set the car straight and helped maneuver Adam onto a stretcher. Vern squeezed his son's hand, and Adam's eyelids fluttered open. Tears sprang to the older man's eyes.

"Everything's A-okay, son, you're gonna be fine . . . he's fine, right doc?" he asked one of the young men carrying his son.

"Got to get him to the hospital, Pops. You, too. Walk in my tracks."

Linda helped the trembling old man into the waiting ambulance. "I'll see you at the hospital, Vern."

"You don't have to come, Miss . . . ah," he said. Don't leave me, his eyes pleaded.

"I'll be there," she said, as the attendant slammed the door. If she hadn't been in the road there wouldn't have been a collision. "For my own peace of mind, I have to be there," she whispered as the ambulance roared away.

As the sirens faded, she felt Jason, the mechanic, beside her.

"Oh Lord, I forgot to ask. Do you know where they'll go?"

"Down to Laconia's my guess. Biggest facility in these parts."

During the activity he had rescued her truck from the snowbank. Apart from a crumpled fender it appeared none the worse, and it stood ready and waiting. The only evidence left of the accident was the trampled snow in the ditch and a wild confusion of tire marks.

"Excuse me, Miss . . ."

"Werther. Linda Werther."

"Jason Porter." They shook hands, her tiny hand all but hidden in his big grease-covered paw.

"I can't leave the other car in the ditch, but I can tow it back to the garage."

"Great, Jason. I'll have Mr. Fenwick give you a call as soon as he can." They walked toward her truck.

"Are you okay to drive? You look kinda shaky to me," he said, concern in his eyes.

"No, I always walk this way." He looked

uncertain, and she laughed aloud. "I'm fine, really," she smiled, "and thanks for everything."

What a sweet guy, she thought, watching him wave goodbye through the rearview mirror. He made me laugh at myself. Maybe I am too suspicious of people.

The emergency waiting room was no more than a wide hallway, with seven mismatched vinyl chairs lined up against one wall. A huge television set blared from its perch high in a corner, and a reception desk took up most of the wall opposite. Droopy strings of silver stars tacked around the door frames made it Christmas. In the past hour and a half nine emergencies had come and gone, a gruesome parade of hastily bandaged cuts, mysterious fevers, sprained ankles, broken limbs, and screaming children.

Linda had exhausted the meager supply of magazines and stood to ease her cramped muscles, when a roar of applause from the TV overhead caught her attention.

A talk show had just started, and the hostess, a thin blonde wearing a berry red suit and a scarf covered in a holly design, leaned intimately into the camera. "Today we're discussing Wayward Husbands: Who They Are and Why They Wander." Hoots and more raucous applause from the audience. "Don't go 'way!" the blonde shouted over the din, "we'll be right back after this message!" The camera panned a studio full of angry-eyed women bursting to tell the world about their wandering mates.

Where did they find these people? Why would they want to discuss their private lives with millions watching? Linda crossed to the desk, waiting for the frizzy-haired woman at the desk to take her eyes off the computer screen. Though the room was overheated, she wore an oversized pink sweater slung over her snug white uniform. A badge pinned to the lapel said Pam Smith, and a plastic Santa with a lit red bulb for a nose hung drunkenly below it. Linda guessed the pin had ceased to amuse this harried-looking woman long ago.

Nurse Smith ignored Linda's polite cough.

"Excuse me, is there any news on Adam or Vern Fenwick? They were—"

"You know what I know," the woman answered, without raising her head.

Back in her seat, Linda considered leaving, knowing perfectly well she would stay until she knew they were okay. She didn't wonder what she'd do if they weren't.

The noise on TV had given her a headache. Six lucky women had been chosen to tell their stories, and they all shouted to be

heard over the whooping and applause
from the studio audience.

". . . started two months after the wedding—"

"He said he was fed up—"

"The bastard left me for—"

The volume was unbearable, and Linda
searched in vain for a knob or remote control device, then took her headache back to
the desk.

"How do I turn the volume down on the
TV?" she asked, raising her voice to be
heard.

"You don't." Nurse Pam's printer began
to chatter loudly, spewing out paper and
adding to the bedlam in the small space.

"The TV is here for everyone."

"But I'm alone—"

"Not for long."

"It sounds like the Friday night fights."

"It takes people's minds off—"

"Mozart would do it better."

"The TV stays on."

Bitch.

"It shouldn't be long now." She actually
bared her teeth in a smile, and her voice
held a hint of kindness.

Stressed out, Linda decided. Overworked.
She forced a smile and went back to her
seat.

Half an hour later, the older Mr. Fenwick

walked unsteadily through the double swing doors, buttoning his shirt.

"You're still here?" he caught her hand and held it as he lowered himself into a chair.

"I couldn't leave without knowing how you were."

"Well, they tried hard, but there isn't a darned thing wrong with me, Miss . . . ah. Got a burn across my chest from the seat-belt, but otherwise, I'm A-OK!"

"Did they check this lump?" she asked, pointing to the purple swelling visible through his sparse white hair.

"Bumped my head on the window, I guess. Got a slight concussion, but other-wise, I'm A—"

"And your son?"

"Nothing yet . . ." The twinkle in his eyes died, and he slumped back in the chair.

She wouldn't be leaving soon.

"Mr. Fenwick, I bet you're hungry. Why don't we get a sandwich?"

"No, thanks. But you go, Miss . . . ah."

"Call me Linda. How about a cup of cof-fee? I've had two, and they weren't bad."

"I should stay here."

"Coffee shop's just down the hall. We'll be back in five minutes."

"Well, maybe I could stand a bite of something."

She left him at a table and picked up coffee and a couple of ham sandwiches. Linda demolished half in three bites, but after a bite Vern's face became still and grave.

"I'm sorry, Linda. Guess I'm not hungry after all. I have to be there if Adam needs me. You know how it is when you have kids."

She didn't, but he was gone before she had a chance to say so, and she followed him back to the waiting room. There was still no news when they checked at the nurses' station, and they settled side by side into two surprisingly comfortable blue chairs.

The shrieking women on TV had been replaced by a depressing, but quiet, soap opera, and Nurse Smith's eyes were glued to the screen. Linda flipped through a magazine she'd scanned earlier, not seeing a single word.

"It's snowing again," Vern said, coming back into the windowless room from the door. She remembered it was Christmas Eve. Sitting next to her, the old man sniffled, coughed, and blew his nose.

"Are you okay?"

"I was remembering the first time Adam was in the hospital. He was just a little tyke, maybe seven or eight. Broke his leg falling from a tree his mother'd forbidden him to climb, and he tried to pretend it didn't hurt. Poor little guy, more scared of his mother than any old hospital." He sighed.

"Adam's nearly forty-two, but he's still my baby. It's tough when your child is hurt and you can't do a damn thing to help. You know how it is."

"No, I don't, Vern."

"No kids?"

"None."

"Married?"

"I was, once."

"Divorced, I suppose?"

"No. My husband died."

"Oh. I, um. Korea? Vietnam?"

"Neither. Jerry was killed in a car accident up in Maine."

He looked uncomfortable. "I'm sorry."

"It was twenty years ago, Vern, and we were only married a year." As if that explained anything.

"My Adam's a college professor. Teaches art appreciation or some such down in Pennsylvania. Not married, never has been. He's on sabbatical. Going to Italy for a year. Or he was, but now . . ."

Linda had chewed another nail down to the quick when a doctor finally came towards them through the swing doors. They jumped from their seats together, but she reached the doctor first. "Mrs. Fenwick?"

"Oh no. Just a . . . a friend." She turned to her companion. "This is Adam's father."

"Mr. Fenwick, Doctor Kemp." The men shook hands. "Your son is doing very well.

We've put him through a battery of tests, and the first X-rays are back from Radiology. The right femur is broken—an easy repair," he added, when a look of horror crossed Vern's face. "There's been some damage to the hip, but we don't know the extent as yet. I've given him something for pain. He's groggy, but conscious, if you want to see him."

A tinny female voice suddenly crackled from the intercom over their heads. "Doctor Kemp. Please report to ER immediately. Doctor Kemp."

The old man sagged visibly. "Adam?"

"No sir, this is a new emergency. Your son's up on six." He nodded curtly and rushed off, his mind apparently on the next crisis.

Vern raced ahead to the elevators, foot tapping with impatience when forced to wait for a car. His fingers drummed on the elevator wall during the slow trip to the sixth floor. He rushed down the corridor and halted abruptly at the door to his son's room. Stood and stared at the inert shape on the bed.

"Oh my God, how pathetic he looks." His voice cracked. Taking a deep breath, he crept slowly into the room, but Linda hung back at the door. *What am I doing here? I don't even know these people.* Vern had reached the bed and took Adam's limp hand in his own.

"Hi, son." The old man's voice boomed in the humming silence. Adam's eyelids fluttered. "It's Dad."

The younger man's eyes flew open, and his face lit up.

"Dad," he croaked. "I'm thirsty."

"Thank you, God," Vern whispered. Linda saw his shoulders begin to heave, and she rushed to his side, holding him while tears ran unchecked down his cheeks.

"I see you found yourself a cute one, Dad."

"This is Miss . . . ah. My friend, Linda."

"Has your friend got a sister?"

"Hi, Adam," Linda said. "It was my truck you hit this morning."

Adam's eyes looked puzzled. "Haven't we met somewhere . . . ?"

"At the Inn in Wolfeboro. Last night, at dinner."

"I remember now!" The cloudy gray eyes softened. "You sat next to us at breakfast. Was it only this morning? I hoped we'd meet again."

"So we did. This morning, on the highway."

His lopsided grin tugged at her heart.

"Linda's been a great help and support today," Vern said.

"After what happened, I could hardly go on about my business."

"I might have hit you."

"But you didn't. I got away with a crumpled fender."

"How about my car?"

"I don't know. It was towed away."

"Linda will take me back to get it later," Vern said.

Adam looked at his father, then turned back to Linda.

"Will you look after my dad?"

How could she refuse. "Sure, I'll take care of him."

The gray eyes filled, and he turned his head away. "Thanks, Linda. This old guy means a lot to me." His eyes slowly closed.

Half an hour later Linda heard him mumbling. Vern had fallen asleep in his chair, and she moved closer to the bed.

"So thirsty," she made out.

There was a cup with a straw on the nightstand and Linda held it to Adam's lips. He drank half the water, then sank back against the pillows.

"I feel wiped out," he confided, "and I hurt in places I didn't know were there."

"You were in an automobile accident, remember?"

"I don't even know what's wrong with me."

"The doctor told your dad you have a broken leg, but they haven't got all the X-rays back. There may be some damage to your hip."

"So I'm stuck here."

"For a while, I guess. Tomorrow is Christmas Day, and I'm sure they'll have only a skeleton staff."

They both found that funny, and their laughter roused Vern from his nap. He joined them with a pleased grin.

"You like my friend, Adam?"

"Just remember who saw her first."

"Excuse me, gentlemen, don't I have any say?"

"I'll share," grinned Vern.

"Dad, does Uncle Phil know what happened?"

"No, I forgot to call him. Hell, we should have been there by now. He'll be worried sick."

"I'll make sure he phones, Adam."

"You're an angel." The gray eyes fixed on hers were like banks of clouds, mysterious and intriguing.

"An angel? Not yet. No thanks to you."

"Not funny, Linda. You gave me the scare of my life. We had just passed through the most wonderful little village. It reminded me of a Currier and Ives scene. We rounded a bend and there you were, in the middle of the road. Next thing I knew we were skidding madly, and you saw the rest. What were you doing?"

"Photographing the same little village," she said.

"I should have been paying closer attention to the road," he answered, his voice edged with tension.

"Don't beat yourself up over this, Adam. You're the one in the hospital."

"Luckily, we're all here to talk about it."

He flashed his captivating smile. You'd never tire of that face, she thought. His mouth tilted up at the corners, and lights twinkling in the depths of his eyes gave him a mischievous air. Good thing his nose is crooked, otherwise I'd really be in trouble here.

"I'm too dopey to argue," Adam said, breaking the spell. "But when I'm feeling better . . ." His eyes closed, and for Linda the room dimmed.

While she got more coffee, Vern called Phil in Camden. Adam was barely awake when they returned.

"Your uncle's happy that you're all right," Vern said, his voice husky with emotion, "and so am I."

Adam had fallen back to sleep.

"That sedative's a strong one," said the nurse, coming in to check on him. "He'll sleep all night. A good time for you to get some rest."

Vern wanted to stay, but she strongly urged a good night's sleep in a real bed.

"Your son will be well taken care of here, Mr. Fenwick, but all we have for you is a

hard vinyl couch. You've been injured yourself, and by morning you'll be bruised and
sore. I prescribe a good dinner and a comfortable bed."

"But I don't have a place to stay, and I
don't even drive anymore. Which reminds
me, where is Adam's car?"

"It's been towed to a garage in Tamworth,
Vern," Linda answered.

He seemed very tired and confused.
When he had trouble shrugging into his
coat, Linda straightened the collar, tucking
his scarf snugly around his neck.

"You can check on it after the holiday.
I'll be happy to drop you somewhere on my
way home."

"Thank you, my dear." His smile reminded her of Adam's, and must have
warmed many hearts in its day. She tucked
her arm in his and they left the hospital.

It was three-thirty and almost dark in Laconia. Shops had closed early for the holiday, and traffic was sparse. Snowflakes
sparkled in the glow of street lamps, and
lights twinkled from wreaths and windows.
The town seemed like a stage set the moment before the show begins.

When Vern spoke, his words echoed her
thoughts.

"Ever notice how Christmas Eve is different from every other night? Quiet and
peaceful and . . . waiting?"

"Mmmm."

They drove a few silent blocks.

"I've been thinking, Vern. I feel terrible just dropping you off at a hotel. My place is only an hour away. I've got plenty of room, and I'll get you back here as early as you like in the morning."

"Thanks, Linda, but I'd rather be close by, just in case. Anyplace here in town will be fine. Can you stick around while I check in? I'm taking advantage, I know . . ."

"Not at all. I'm pleased to help out." And happy to be needed.

"I'll be back for you around noon," she said when the clerk gave Vern his key.

He looked grateful, and very tired. She kissed his grizzled cheek, and he rubbed his face.

"I don't have my shaving kit? And where's my luggage?"

"All in Adam's car, but we can't get your stuff tonight. Will you settle for emergency supplies from the nearest drugstore?"

"I couldn't put you to any more trouble," he said, halfway back to the door.

"Think I'll pick up a crossword puzzle magazine," he yawned, "in case I can't get to sleep."

"I don't think you'll have any trouble in that department. Make sure you order something to eat from room service."

"Care to join an old man for dinner?"

Again the smile, charming and heartwarming.

"Thanks, but I'll take a raincheck. I want to get the drive home behind me, and get to bed early. I'm exhausted. Will you be all right?"

"I'm A-OK. Thanks for everything." This time Vern kissed her cheek.

The clouds had disappeared, the highways were dry, and the dark sky was studded with stars. Linda drove swiftly, listening with half an ear to Christmas carols. Her thoughts flitted from Bethlehem, to Santa Claus, to Adam Fenwick's fascinating gray eyes.

The long driveway had been cleared, and she blessed Dave Anderson for plowing it as she drove between tall columns of leafless poplars, rolling to a crunching stop at the front entrance of the darkened house.

The enormous Victorian, gingerbreaded, turreted, and gabled, had been built by the founder of a New England chain of defunct supermarkets, a man with delusions of grandeur. Spacious rooms with ten-foot ceilings, a beautiful view, and a heating bill fit for a king. Unwilling to waste oil heating up the whole house, and too tired to light a fire in the woodstove, Linda threw an old comforter over her shoulders and brewed a pot of peppermint tea. With a grilled cheese sandwich it was dinner.

She flipped through the mail and checked her answering machine. Connie's cheerful voice wished her a Merry Christmas, and Linda eagerly returned the call, but had to settle for wishing Connie's machine a happy holiday. She wandered from room to room, followed by the irregular echo of her footsteps. For the first time since Mother died the house seemed empty. Mike's advice had probably been wise. Much as she loved the house, it was awfully big for one woman, a handicapped woman at that.

It had been a long day, and around nine-thirty Linda took another pot of peppermint tea up to her bedroom, intending to climb into bed and read. She shivered into her nightgown and snuggled under the cozy duvet. But the book lay unopened on her chest while she thought about Adam. Why, after all these years, would she feel a spark of romantic interest in a man? Why this particular man?

She saw his face, the fine gray eyes and sweetly uptilted smile. Surely she'd met men with nice eyes over the last twenty years, but not the smile. That was unique to Adam.

Maybe it was because he didn't make her feel self-conscious about herself. Not once since she'd met him or his father had she felt uncomfortable or awkward.

Suddenly Linda remembered Vern telling

her in the hospital that Adam planned to
live in Italy for a while. Romantic, and possibly part of his attraction. Interesting, but
unattainable. Alas. Linda laughed and
pushed the thought from her mind.

Did he plan to live in Rome, she wondered, or Venice? That would be romantic,
and quite exciting. What a shame if this
morning's unfortunate collision prevented
him from going.

Not a shame, her mother's voice whispered. An omen.

Christmas morning Linda woke early to
a room full of brilliant sunshine. Frost had
etched intricate ferns on her windows, and
she opened one to have a look outside.

A noisy flock of chickadees gossiped
around the feeders hung in the trees, and
the muffled sound of children's voices rose
from a skating party down the lake. She
watched them glide smoothly, effortlessly,
and remembered the little girl who had
gazed wistfully at other skaters. . . . Shivering in her warm terry robe, Linda shut the
window and went downstairs for breakfast.

In the front hall she nearly tripped over
a large package. Mike and Sandy's Christmas gift, forgotten until now. With a flutter
of excitement, she ripped open the expensive foil wrap. Inside were a white ruffled

blouse, a science fiction novel, and a box of nuts. Generic gifts for a woman they didn't know. Carrying the bundle of torn paper into the kitchen, Linda wondered if her gifts were creating the same disappointment in Scottsdale.

While coffee brewed, she called the hospital. An efficient female voice informed her that Mr. Fenwick had passed a comfortable night, and had eaten a light breakfast.

She was relieved and delighted, and realized how much she wanted to see Adam again.

"Can he have visitors?"

"Certainly. I'll put you through to his line."

"Oh, no, please don't disturb—" Too late. He was on the line.

"H-hi, Adam. This is Linda W—"

"Werther. I knew it would be you."

A warm glow filled in her chest.

"Since I've already heard from Dad, who else could it be?"

The glow died.

"I'm really glad you called, Linda. Dad didn't know where you lived, and I had no idea how to get in touch with you. I hoped to see you again."

"I told your dad I'd take him over today."

"Do you live in Laconia?"

"Not right in town, no. Just a few minutes

down I-93." So it was a lie. He'd never find out.

"Joy to the World," Linda sang, paying closer attention than usual to her make-up. She made the drive to Laconia in forty-five minutes, hoping the traffic cops had better things to do on Christmas morning.

"Let me put it this way, Mr. Fenwick. It'll be some time before you run the Boston marathon."

Perched on the edge of Adam's bed, Dr. Stevenson, the orthopedic surgeon, delivered his verdict in a soft voice. Vern sat like a stone in the green vinyl chair beside the bed. Linda stood beside the bed, watching Adam's mobile face grow still.

During the last ten days she had come to know this man well. He spoke intelligently, and had faced the surgery with stoic good humor. In the intimacy of a hospital room they shared dreams and disappointments, condensing a lifetime into a few hours, like people do when they will never meet again. He talked of his dream to live and work in Italy, and she fell in love with him. Now he seemed impossibly calm.

"Will I walk again?"

Adam's right femur had been shattered by the impact, and his leg was encased in plaster. A worse injury was the fractured hip, and a few days after Christmas Dr. Stevenson had inserted a steel pin into the joint.

"The surgery is healing well. Looks like you've accepted the pin. As you know, it will be part of you for about two years."

"Will I ever walk again, Doctor?"

"Of course you will. You're a healthy young man." To the three pairs of eyes locked on his face, the doctor's smile seemed forced.

"You'll have to use a cane," he said, gazing at a point somewhere behind Adam's head, "at least for a while. There may be a residual weakness in the socket, which could affect your gait. It's hard to tell with this kind of thing."

"When will you know?" Adam's voice shook, and Linda took his hand.

"Let's take this one step at a time," the doctor said cheerfully, "if you'll pardon the pun." He snickered. "In a week or so you'll go home to your lovely wife." He raised his eyes to Linda. No one corrected his mistake. "TLC alone works wonders. Then physical therapy for about six weeks. We'll have a better idea in about three months."

"Three months? My God, what am I going to do for three months? Where am I going to live?"

"Have I missed something?" Dr. Stevenson seemed perplexed.

"We're not married, Doctor," Linda explained. "I'm a friend."

"I'm supposed to be in Italy in a few days."

"You won't be leaving the country for a while."

"I sublet my apartment."

"Can your father help?" He turned to Vern. "You are his father," he asked.

"Dad lives in a retirement home."

"Now, son, this isn't the doctor's problem. I'm sure we'll manage. Look how kind Linda's been the past few weeks."

Vern had accepted Linda's invitation to stay with her. He insisted on paying his share, and she let him help out with the food, though the man ate like a bird.

"Well I guess I'll just move in on Linda, too. C'mon, Dad, get serious."

Linda had been thinking. "Why not?" she said. "There's plenty of room, and I'm sure you'll be comfortable for the duration."

"Aren't you carrying this guilt thing a little far?"

The words stung. Guilt? Her feelings for Adam had nothing to do with guilt, and it seemed she had misread his.

"I've come to think of you and your father as my friends, Adam, and I'm offering you a way out of this dilemma. You can get physical therapy in Manchester, I'm sure, and the house is big enough, as your dad will tell you. We won't get in each other's way, and you can leave as soon as you're able."

"I'm sorry, Linda. You've been so kind. I'm an ungrateful boor. If you and Dad think it's a good idea, we'll give it a try."

Dave Anderson helped Linda move her mother's fourposter down to the first floor library so Adam wouldn't have to deal with the stairs. A small table and reading lamp beside the bed and a comfortable wing chair by the fireplace made the large space cozy, but Linda was nervous.

"Suppose he hates it, Connie?" she asked her friend. "What if we don't get along?"

"Good heavens, Linda, stop worrying. If they don't like it they can go to a hotel. If you want my opinion, you've done more than enough for these people. What do you have to feel guilty about?"

"I don't feel guilty. I wish everyone would stop saying that. I'm just trying to help out an old man. And his son."

The day they brought Adam home Linda rushed into the library, fluffing pillows and poking at the already blazing fire.

"How's that for a view, son?" Vern asked, wheeling Adam into the room.

The deep bay windows looked out on a forest of evergreens and birches. Through the trees the windswept lake gleamed, and beyond that the White Mountains rose in the distance.

"This is a lovely room, Linda," said Vern, glancing around the book-lined walls, the walnut panelling, the fieldstone fireplace. "I'm sure Adam will be very comfortable here. Right, son?"

Adam slouched in the wheelchair and said nothing.

"Imagine having a library. Did your father build the house?" Vern asked, filling the silence.

"No, it was built in the twenties by a man who owned a couple of grocery stores around Manchester. After he died his two sons added a second kitchen and a bathroom on this floor and turned it into a two-family. This was used as a dining room. When he bought it, my dad turned one of the kitchens into a darkroom," she said, the words coming too fast. "The bathroom is right through here." Linda awkwardly crossed the parquet floor to the bathroom.

"Your own private suite, son," said Vern. "It's perfect."

"Right, Dad. Perfect for a cripple," Adam said, in a voice filled with self-pity. The harsh words brought Linda to an abrupt halt.

"You're tired, Adam," his father said

quickly. "He's very tired," Vern said again, to Linda.

Two bright red spots stained her cheeks. What have I let myself in for? she wondered.

"I made soup for lunch. There'll be a tray in the kitchen for your son."

Adam gazed out the window, apparently unaware of the discomfort in the room. Vern followed her down the hall, still apologizing.

A few days later Linda helped Adam into the car for his first appointment with the physical therapist.

Adam seemed pleased to be out in the fresh air. Linda was pleasant and remote. She had herself under strict control, and under no circumstances would Adam ever find out how she felt.

It had been a record year for snow, and huge banks lined the streets to the hospital, creating a tunnel. It was cold, with temperatures well below freezing.

"I've never seen so much snow. Some of these banks must be three feet high."

"We get lots of snow."

From the corner of her eye Linda saw him looking at her, but she stared straight out the window.

"Cold up here in the Northeast," Adam said.

"Mmhmm."

"Cold outside, too," he quipped.

"Oh look, they're sledding on Thompson's Hill. We used to go there when I was a kid. I couldn't skate like other kids, but a cripple can fall off a toboggan just as well as the next guy."

"Linda, I . . . I want to apologize for what I said the other day."

"No need, Adam."

"It was a careless remark."

"Nothing I haven't heard before."

"But I wasn't referring to you."

"So your father said, but as my mother used to say, 'If the shoe fits, you wear it.' "

"I was feeling sorry for myself, and I didn't think—"

"Didn't think what, Adam? That I'd get hurt? At least you've made your feelings clear."

"But I'm not hiding anything. We're in the same boat, you and me, and I understand how you feel . . ."

"Oh no you don't!" she shouted, pounding the steering wheel with her clenched fist. "Don't ever think that walking a mile in my shoes makes us the same. For a few weeks out of your life you'll be confined to a wheelchair, walk with a cane. But you're the victim of an accident, not a freak. People will sympathize, rush to help. Me? I'm an embarrassment." She was dangerously close to tears. "Let me tell you the worst thing about being handicapped. It isn't physical, at least not for me. Many people are worse off, and you've seen for yourself that I get around perfectly well. The hardest part is the p-pity, the aversion, in people's faces. . . ."

Tears spilled over. Dammit, she thought, I always cry at the wrong time. She sniffed and fumbled in her pocket for a tissue. "Guess I'm having a bad day."

"Linda, please . . . don't." His hand covered hers, and she snatched it away. "Why don't you pull over."

"Adam, you couldn't possibly understand. Three, four months from now this will be no more than a bad memory for you, an annoying interruption on your way to Rome, or Venice."

"You don't want me to go."

"I don't care if you go or not. I'm just saying that I live every day with this ugly . . . deformity!"

"Ugly? Linda, I think you're a very beautiful woman."

The warmth in his voice made her heart lurch, but she wouldn't be taken in by glib words.

"Sure you do. Look, Adam, I don't need empty compliments."

"But you are beautiful. You're a coura-
geous woman, Linda, and I think I'm in
love with you."

"Words to warm my heart when you're
gone."

"If I didn't have a job waiting . . ."

They had reached the parking lot. Linda
shot into a space, snatched the keys and
slammed the door. She had hoped for too
much, and made a fool of herself. She blew
her nose, collected the wheelchair, and went
to help Adam out of the truck.

"We're here."

"Sorry, I can't get out without help." His
voice was tender, and she kept her eyes on
his jacket.

He dropped his arm across her shoulders,
but made no effort to move, and she forced
herself to look up. His face showed strain,
but his velvety gray eyes gleamed with
laughter. Quickly he leaned forward and
brushed her lips tenderly.

"I guess you didn't hear me. I think I'm
in love with you."

"Adam, we don't have time for this." She
shook her head to shut out his voice.

"Please Linda, hear me out."

"We're late for your appointment," she
said, tugging at his waist. "Let's get you inside."

"We'll talk later."

"No, Adam, there's nothing else to say.

You have plans that don't include me, and I have to get on with my life."

Settling him roughly in the wheelchair, she marched into the hospital.

As the weeks passed they settled into a routine. Linda made sure she was never alone with Adam. While he had physical therapy three mornings a week, she and Vern ran errands or stopped for coffee at the new café on Main Street, where they met Connie one morning. Vern was at his charming best, and an hour passed quickly.

"Gotta run, Lin," Connie said. She smiled at Vern. "I hope your son's all right."

"His leg's coming along just fine, but his spirits are low." He gave Linda a speculative look. "I think the boy could use some perking up."

"Vern's a great cook, Connie. Why don't you and Steve come for dinner on Saturday?"

The evening was delightful, with good food and conversation flowing as freely as wine. Steve taught math at the high school in Concord, and he and Adam hit it off well, entertaining them with anecdotes from school. At the first opportunity Connie cornered Linda in the kitchen.

"You let me think you were helping out

an old man and his son! How altruistic of you. Have you snagged him yet?"

"Don't be silly, Connie. Adam's not interested in me."

"Really! Any fool can see he's nuts about you."

"He's got places to go."

"So you change his mind, honey."

Connie asked about Adam's trip.

"I've been wanting to do this for twenty years," he said, his eyes alive with anticipation, "and it's finally come together. I got a contract to teach for a year at one of the American schools in Florence. If it works out, I'll stay on." Then, with a sidelong glance at Linda, he added, "At least, that was the plan."

She couldn't stay away from him. Working together on a jigsaw puzzle, he'd touch her hand and she'd let it linger a moment before slowly pulling away. Arm in arm they'd walk around the garden, laughing because their uneven steps matched.

"We're made for each other, Linda."

"For the moment."

"Suppose I canceled my plans."

"You'd never forgive me."

"Come with me then."

"I can't. I have my work."

His eyes met hers in a look she trembled

to define. If he cancels his trip, she thought, I'll know.

"How come Adam never married, Vern?"

"Guess he never found the right girl, but you and I know he's found the right woman."

"He's got plans, Vern, and they don't include me."

"You're not smarting from one careless remark?"

"Not at all."

"Hiding inside your shell, then."

Adam did not cancel his plans. Instead, Vern decided to go with him.

"Adam will need some help, and I've always wanted to see that part of the world. We'll travel around together, and when the school assignment starts in June, I'll come home."

"When will you leave?"

"Sometime in April."

By mid-March Adam was walking alone. He used a cane, but had discarded the walker, whose rubber-tipped feet had pounded the floors for weeks. Now he moved silently.

Early one morning, fresh from the shower, Linda threw on a kimono and went down to start coffee for breakfast. Passing Adam's empty room, she went in to strip the bed. Turning to leave, she was shocked to see him behind her.

"Oh, my, I didn't hear you come in."

A smile spread slowly over his face, reminding her of a spider and his web, and she regretted her impulse to come into his bedroom.

"I'll just take your sheets," she murmured, picking up the bundle. She turned quickly, catching the delicate silk on a chair. It parted, exposing firm breasts with rosy nipples, hardening as he gazed. Embarrassed, she tried to hide behind the bundle of linens, but he moved toward her, and Linda suddenly remembered the sweetness of his mouth on hers.

"You're quite beautiful, you know."

She shrugged, and her hair fell across her face like a damp curtain. Adam parted her hair and raised her chin tenderly in his warm hand, forcing her to meet his eyes. In their smoky depths Linda saw his desire, and she shivered, imagining the feel of his hands on her body. Instead, he took the ends of the silk ties hanging useless at her sides and closed the robe, an innocent gesture until he encircled her waist. She squirmed, but he held her firmly.

His hands slid to her hips, and she tried to wrench away.

"Don't be embarrassed. You're a beautiful woman, Linda, all of you. Stay with me," he said more softly, "please."

Her stomach fluttered, her throat closed, and she stood still, trembling and speechless.

"I'll take that as a resounding yes," he said, with a smile in his voice.

He buried his face in her hair. "You smell so good," he whispered, his voice hoarse. Slowly his hands moved upwards, gazing steadily into her eyes as he tenderly brushed her stiffened nipples through the delicate fabric. He pulled her to him, and she felt herself melt against his firmness. A perfect fit, she thought, with a sigh.

His lips sought hers and covered her mouth in a hungry kiss.

"Adam," she whispered, "I don't know what to say."

"Say nothing, love," he said softly, covering her lips with his long fingers. "Just feel. Enjoy what's happening to us."

He tugged the tie of her robe, parting the silk, and kissed each taut nipple. Placing her gently on the bed, he stretched out beside her, touching her with the length of his lean body, and gazed at her with an impish grin.

"You look mighty pleased with yourself."

"This is better than my wildest dreams," he murmured, with a wicked laugh, kissing her parted lips, the hollow of her throat. "I'm going to make love to you," he said, caressing her thigh. She flinched and clutched the robe when he grazed her hip, but his hands moved gently and firmly under the robe.

"This is your number one erogenous zone," he whispered, bending to kiss it, "and when we're done you will believe that every inch of your body is beautiful to me."

She didn't notice the robe slip from her shoulders and land in a shimmering heap on the floor.

It was impossible to settle into the old routine, unthinkable to pretend nothing had happened between them. Linda had made love with a man who found her beautiful, who said he loved her, and everything was different. Adam's eyes, his mouth, his hands . . . had invaded her world and made it his. Now, surely, he would stay.

On her knees in the garden Linda watched Adam cross the lawn, and her eyes filled with pride. He walked with a slight limp, and needed the help of her exquisitely carved ebony cane. He had healed well, and soon he would go, leaving the house, and her life, empty again.

"These are lovely," he said, bending to sniff the first hyacinths. "And they smell heavenly. This whole bed is beautiful."

"My mother laid it out many years ago. I kept them up, for her in the beginning, but I've grown to really enjoy gardening."

"Linda," he said, settling himself on a nearby bench with a sigh.

She threw herself into the weeding.

"Linda." His tone arrested her, and she leaned back on her heels, waiting.

"My dad and I have really appreciated what you've done for us—"

"My God, Adam. Don't. We're beyond polite guest speeches. When are you leaving?"

"On the first."

The first of April. A week away.

"I have to go. Please try to understand."

She had known this moment was coming, he had never pretended otherwise, but surely in the last couple of weeks since they made love he had had second thoughts? Tears stole down her cheeks and she brushed them away with her work gloves. Tenderly Adam wiped the streaks of dirt from her face.

"If it weren't for the job, Linda, you know I'd stay, but they're counting on me."

"So go."

"I'll write."

"Don't bother."

He stretched out his hand, but she had ducked her head to hide fresh tears and didn't see it. After a while he left her and went back to the house.

As suddenly as he came into her life, Adam was gone, and Linda seethed with anger, mostly at herself. After all these years of being afraid to trust anyone she had fallen for a man who took what he wanted and ran away. I'm such a fool, she thought, as she cried herself to sleep at night.

A postcard came from Rome. "Good flight. Beautiful country. Miss you. Adam and Vern." Linda tore it up and went on a shopping spree.

With the spring came new work, and she threw herself into it. Her agent wanted a dozen picturesque New England doors to be used for note cards, and she went away for a week. When she came home there was a letter from Vern crowded onto a single sheet of flaky blue airmail paper.

They were having amusing problems with language. Adam's Italian was rusty, and Vern's nonexistent. They had rented a tiny Fiat to go from Rome to Naples, and his comic description of the drive had her in stitches. "There we were on a ten-lane *autostrada* in a torrential downpour when the ONLY wiper blade flew off the car, and we drove ten kilometers to the nearest town with our heads stuck out the windows, yelling to each other.

"Adam sends his love," he wrote in the last paragraph. Sure he does, she thought, but her heart leaped with joy and she had to wait 'til it stopped pounding to read the rest. "He hasn't been himself since we left, Linda. The life has gone out of the boy, and it's all your doing, my dear."

Lovely words, but they hadn't come from Adam.

Her life crawled along in the same old way, though she seemed amazingly lonely for a woman who had spent most of her life alone. The realization made her angrier still.

In addition to the doors, Linda photographed a series of windows and sent them off to be turned into note cards and stationery. When she wasn't working she puttered around the house or read voraciously.

Connie's daughter got married in May, and Linda allowed herself to be persuaded to do the pictures. It wasn't a bad experience, and she accepted a few other weddings, just to keep her mind occupied.

In June, she went on a weeklong publicity shoot for New Hampshire Magazine. When she wasn't working, Linda tended the gardens she had come to love, dividing perennials and tending vegetables.

Notes and letters came faithfully every two or three weeks from Vern. Always signed Vern and Adam. Never Adam. They had crossed the Appenines and followed the Adriatic coast to Venice, "the most romantic city I've ever seen."

The streets are narrow lanes that open up suddenly into tiny piazzas, with restaurants and pensione tucked away behind secretive grilles or shutters. The canals are dirty, but who notices! Bridges everywhere, no two alike, and all are beautiful, from the simplest to exquisitely carved lacy marble humpback bridges. Scented flowers bloom everywhere, musicians stroll, and of course the gondolas are filled with lovers, and singing gondoliers. The aquamarine Adriatic Sea surrounds us on all sides.

Adam contacted the school and they've delayed the start of his term until September to give him time to recover fully. Their kindness gives us the opportunity to visit Milan

*and Siena. I'll come home when Adam set-
tles in Florence.*

Mike had been right. It was time for her
to move on, maybe to one of those condo
complexes she'd seen in Nashua, where
she'd meet other single men and women.
If not New Hampshire, an apartment in
Boston, or New York would be exciting, or
she could move to Arizona, warm and tran-
quil, near Mike and Sandy. She might get
a cat or a bird. At forty-two even a footloose,
fancy-free woman needed someone, or
something, to love.

Linda often dreamed of Adam's return.
It would be morning . . . she'd be sitting
by the lake . . . he'd stride toward her
through a film of mist across the emerald
green lawns, while autumn leaves drifted
slowly in a swirl of dazzling color, and the
golden ball of sun rose over the sparkling,
azure blue lake. . . . She'd turn in surprise
and run swiftly and smoothly into his waiting arms. . . .

Or it might be night . . . she'd answer
the door in a low-cut flowing velvet gown
of deep forest green, her best color, and
there he'd be, his face lit softly by the lamplight from the sconces beside the front door,
the dazzle of love bright in his eyes. . . .

Silly, romantic fantasies that embarrassed her when she woke and remembered.

It was sundown when he actually came, on a sweltering hot day late in August. Dressed for cleaning out the cellar, Linda had her hair pulled back in a ponytail, her face bare of makeup and streaked with dust, wearing an old flannel shirt whose original colors were a memory.

"Hi."

She nearly jumped out of her skin, but her heart knew Adam's voice, and leaped, threatening to burst from her chest at the sound. She turned and walked into a vast cobweb.

"Pffffftt!"

"I'm happy to see you, too." The smoky gray eyes that filled her dreams sparkled with infectious mirth, and she laughed with him. More than anything she wanted him to take her in his arms and tell her how he'd missed her, how much he loved her.

"What on earth are you doing?"

It was difficult to talk around the swelling in her chest.

"Mucking out the cellar. I have to get rid of this old stuff if I'm going to sell the house."

"Sell it? But you love this place."

"Yes, I do. But it's too b—I want to try something else."

"Like . . . ?"

"New York. Boston. Phoenix. It doesn't matter, really. I haven't decided yet."

"Oh." His face fell.

And what's it to you? she wondered.

"Whenever I think of you I picture you in this house, or down by the lake."

"Everything changes, Adam."

"Yes. That's why I'm back. I've done a lot of thinking—"

"You must be hungry. Let's get out of this musty basement. I'll make you a sandwich—"

"Can we talk?"

"Of course, but there's iced tea in the fridge—"

"Linda. I've got things to say, things I've stored up for months."

She led him outside to a bench in the cool dark shade of a chestnut tree.

"You never wrote."

"No. I didn't know what to say."

"Really."

"Linda, I hope you can forgive me. I've been a bachelor all my life. That's no excuse for my behavior, I know, but I've never taken the time before to get to know a woman, to fall in love with someone. Or maybe I've never known anyone like you before. As a young man I was too busy with school. I've taught Art Appreciation from Maine to California, and by the time I settled in Philadelphia with a job that paid real money I was thirty-six years old and had stopped looking. I've been to Italy twice in the past ten years, and when I was offered this position teaching American students the wonders of Italian Renaissance art I thought I'd died and gone to heaven. Everything had come together for me. I had the experience, the opportunity, the job. Then fate stepped in, and dropped you into my life. But it was the wrong time, and I tried to fight against it. I went to Italy, and tried to put you out of my mind, but the longer I was away from you the more I missed you. Ask Dad, I nearly drove him nuts! I realized that I don't want to live without you."

He had been gazing earnestly into her eyes, but now he looked towards the lake glimmering through the fringe of trees. When the leaves began to shimmer and swim, Linda realized her eyes had filled, and when he looked back at her, the tears spilled over.

"I'm sorry, I always cry at the wrong time."

"Oh, sweetheart . . ." He pulled her into his arms, and she nestled against his shoulder, with the feeling that she'd come home.

"What about Florence?"

"Some other lonely bachelor can have it," he said against her lips. "How would you like a honeymoon in Venice?"

His lips touched hers in a tender kiss full of love and promise.

"Your job?"

"Can we enjoy the moment?"

"But it's important."

"I have several options up my sleeve."

"Do they include me?"

"How swiftly she drops her maidenly reticence . . ."

She stopped his laughter with a kiss.

"I have a position in Florence beginning next June, if I want it. I'm expected back in Pennsylvania next August, unless I give notice. I can see neither of these makes you giddy with joy."

She answered reluctantly. "In my line of work I can set up shop anywhere, and I was thinking of selling anyway—"

"There's one more possibility. The night Connie and Steve came for dinner, he said there were several colleges in this area. Seems there's an opening in the Arts Department at a college here in Manchester."

Her face lit up. "We'd stay here?"

"Thought that might please you. We buy your brother out and stay here. On one condition."

She smiled. "Your father is part of the deal."

"Would that be a problem?"

"Silly. I fell in love with Vern before I ever knew you."

For the first Christmas in years candles glowed in every window, and fresh greenery garlanded the banisters and every chandelier. All day Vern had directed Mike's sons in the fine art of trimming a Christmas tree, and now it stood, breathless with anticipation. Lights glowed softly throughout the house, and the woodsy scent of pine and juniper mingled with the smells of food. The Andersons were in the kitchen supervising the buffet that Sandy and Linda had prepared over the last few days.

In her bedroom, Linda smoothed the fabric of the seafoam crepe creation that she and Connie had found at Jordan Marsh. The fabric draped softly, softening all movement, giving her a sense of grace, and the tiny seed pearls that draped the bodice sparkled and glowed with every breath.

Muted sounds filled the big house. A shower hissed, glasses and china clicked as the caterers set up the buffet downstairs, high heels clicked across the parquet floor. Down the hall a door opened, and the splendid ba-

roque music of Mannheim Steamroller
spilled out. When she heard Adam whistling
in the next room Linda's heart filled with
joy. *"This is the moment, I've waited for . . ."*
"The Hawaiian Wedding Song." She had
waited a lifetime for this moment, and she
was ready. As she slipped the diaphanous
dress over her head someone planted a noisy
kiss on the back of her neck.

"Oh my, whoever can it be?"

"A vagrant, ma'am, passing through,"
Adam's voice whispered into her hair.

"You'll compromise my innocence, sir.
Suppose someone comes in— "

"I'll have to make an honest woman out
of you." He nibbled her ear, and she
turned to kiss him, catching their reflection
in the mirror. Over Adam's shoulder Linda
saw a handsome man in a black tuxedo and
a woman in seafoam green. She grew still,
and Adam's eyes, glowing with love, met
hers in the mirror.

"Don't we look a picture," she murmured.

"Yes we do," he whispered, "a picture of
love."

Suddenly the doorbell chimed through
the house, and Linda heard the minister's
booming voice in the foyer. "We're here for
a wedding. Where is everybody?"

Adam bent to kiss her. "Ready?"

Linda sighed with happiness. "Ready."

Arm in arm they went down the stairs together, the long wait over at last.

Let Nothing You Dismay

Linda Swift

"My turn already?" Kala Vandergriff pressed closer to the high counter so that Sandy Hodge could squeeze past her.

"You're on." Sandy inclined her head toward the crowded hallway and continued in an undertone, "And watch out for the slugger in the Brave's baseball cap. He was putting pennies in the candy machine when I came by. Lord only knows what he'll do when he gets to the Barkley room."

"Not to worry," Kala shrugged into her jacket and squared her shoulders, adding a whispered aside, "I'll fix him with my mother-of-three-boys stare and he'll shrink into submission."

"Pardon me for mentioning it, but your three boys are men now and kids don't shrink much anymore." Sandy turned to the man on the opposite side of the counter who was studying an outspread map. "Have you found what you're looking for, sir?"

"I'm still not sure whether to take the Bluegrass Parkway or I-65 from Elizabethtown . . . ," his voice trailed off and he glanced up, his eyes shifting between the two

women with a puzzled frown. "But this lady
was—"

"I have to leave now," Kala smiled and
stepped around the counter. "Have a good
trip."

As she made her way toward the noisy
crowd outside the door, she could hear
Sandy question the tourist. "Have you ever
seen Shakertown? If you haven't, I'd like to
suggest . . ."

Kala cleared her throat and raised her
voice to be heard above the din. "May I
have your attention, please? The next tour
will begin now if you'll all step this way, as
close together as possible." She waited
while people shifted positions, then began
her practiced monologue.

"Welcome to Whitehaven. My name is
Kala Vandergriff and I will be your tour
guide today. In 1860 this was the back outside wall of the house," she pointed to the
brick wall that separated the enclosed
area—with its benches, vending machines,
and elevators—from the original structure,
"and the kitchen was in a separate building."
Kala had said the words so many times in the
eight months since she began working at the
Welcome Center that it was no longer necessary to consciously think about them. The
speech had become like a cassette which she
could play while her thoughts were elsewhere,
and right now she was thinking of her three

grown sons and that reminded her of Sandy's warning. She spotted the little guy in back of the others, turning the water fountain on and off, sticking first one hand and then the other under the spray, wiping both on his jeans afterward. At least he'll not leave dirty fingerprints on anything. "Before we enter the house, I'd like to ask that we all stay together as a group so I can tell you a little about each room as we go along." *And so I can keep an eye on a certain member of the group who can't be trusted not to swing from the chandeliers.*

As Kala led the crowd into the wide hallway, she continued, "The house was started in 1860 but wasn't completed until 1866 because of the Civil War." The words flowed effortlessly as her eyes swept over the rooms which already bore the beginnings of the annual Christmas decorations done by area garden clubs and her mind wandered back to her children and the coming holidays.

Will had been gone almost eleven months now, she never used the term "dead" because it seemed so final, and the season loomed ahead like her own private Mount Everest which she somehow must get through, around, or over for the sake of the family. Thanksgiving last weekend had been easy because they all gathered at Trey's farm. She was grateful her eldest son had exercised his prerogative to begin a new tradition. But no one had issued invitations for Christmas; probably they assumed she would insist on her usual Hallmark Holiday extravaganza.

She entered the music room, waited for the others to crowd in beside her and fall silent. Just as she said "The rosewood piano you see is 118 years old," the little boy grabbed the velvet rope separating observers from the observed and slid under it, then banged a hasty rendition of "Chopsticks" on the yellowed keys before his mother could reach him.

"Kevinnn, I don't think the lady wants you to play her piano," the woman said and gave a slight shrug as though Kala should know that boys will be boys.

Hastily concluding her remarks about the other instruments, Kala led the way up the polished oak stairs, pointing out the facing hallway mirrors that infinitely multiplied reflections like some house of horrors attraction. She fervently hoped that Kevin would be so fascinated with the image of so many more little Kevins that he would miss the rest of the upstairs tour.

She got through the master bedroom and sitting room and was well into her detailed explanation of the former vice-president's memorabilia before Kevin's attention was diverted to the Veep's assorted collection of walking canes. Grabbing the closest one, he pointed it at the group and began making machine gun noises. Kala tugged at the cane while Kevin's mother pulled at him and the two were finally parted. Quickly stashing the cane, Kala ushered the crowd back downstairs, watching out of the corner of her eye as Kevin threw a leg over the banister and his mother dragged him back. She summoned a weak smile. "We're very proud to be Kentucky's only welcome center located in an antebellum mansion. Thank you for taking our tour and have a safe and pleasant trip to your destinations." And for one member of the group, the sooner the better.

Weaving her way through the people in the hallway and around the information counter, she rejoined Sandy, mumbled under her breath. "Now I know why God gave children to young people. If that kid were mine, I'd throttle him."

Handing two maps to a tourist, Sandy smiled sympathetically. "That bad, huh? But I'm sure you were better equipped to handle all that energy in motion than I would have been. At least you've got grand-children."

"Sure, but the only ones I ever see are practically adults now. The youngest are so far away I hardly know them."

"Will they be here for Christmas?"

"Owen's family won't make it. It's their

year to spend the holidays with his wife's parents who live near them on the West Coast, but Shane and his gang are driving up from Georgia, and Trey and family will come." She stopped, then added, "And of course, Leslie."

"Pardon me, are there any motels near the interstate?"

"Yes, sir, but you'll have to go to the next exit to find them." Sandy stepped around the counter to pull brochures from a rack beside the doorway. "Why don't you get a cup of coffee and start on the daily count?" she said to Kala. "The crowd is thinning out now, I can handle things till closing."

Kala took the register from the counter and went out to the small office and poured herself a cup of coffee. Shedding her jacket and shoes, she got comfortable and began counting. Finished with both count and coffee, she closed the book and sighed. She liked her job here at the Welcome Center but after Christmas she really must start seriously looking for something else. The salary was average for part-time work, but it wasn't going to pay the medical bills left by her husband's long illness. And with winter just beginning, she was facing huge utility bills for several months, too. At least, it hadn't been necessary to buy any clothes for this job and she had adequate transportation.

"Let's call it a day." Sandy came into the office, hung up her jacket, and pulled on an all-weather coat. "Temp's dropping out there. Think I'll make a pot of chili tonight."

Kala put on her own wool coat and followed Sandy outside. A sharp wind made her turn the collar up to shield her face. "It seems awfully dark for six o'clock, doesn't it?"

"Sure does. Have a nice weekend." The two women said good night and Kala unlocked her car, her cold fingers fumbling awkwardly with the keys. She let the engine warm up before she left the parking lot, watching Sandy drive away in her jaunty little Toyota. When she pulled onto the access road the motor coughed and jerked. Probably still cold, she rationalized. Just as she turned onto Alben Barkley Drive, the car shuddered and stopped completely. Damn. I can't be out of gas. A quick check showed half a tank. She pumped the accelerator, tried the ignition again. Then again. The lights beamed brightly on the dark street. Not the battery. Putting on the emergency blinker, Kala locked the door and started walking back toward the Welcome Center where she was certain of a phone and a safe, warm place to wait for towing service. She sighed, heading into the wind. So much for her adequate transportation.

* * *

"Mrs. Vandergriff?"

The man in the white coat stood at the door of the brightly lit waiting room reminding Kala of the surgeon at the hospital who had come to tell her that the operation was over and Will's condition was terminal. Somehow from his expression she felt the outlook for her '89 Buick might be the same.

"Yes?" She stood and walked toward him, praying her intuition was wrong.

He shook his head and intoned solemnly, "It's the transmission."

"Transmission?" she repeated blankly.

"Yes, the mechanism that controls the shifting of your car's gears."

"I know what a transmission *does*," she said impatiently. "What's wrong with it?"

"Well, from just a quick look, it's hard to say. If you want to leave it overnight, I could pull the pan in the morning and check the filter. That will give some indication if the stalling is serious. If I find metal shavings, it will mean the problem is in the internal system and," he shook his head apologetically, "that could mean a new transmission."

"But the car isn't all that old, and we've never had any trouble with it before—"

"I checked the fluid level and it was two

quarts low. When was the last time you changed or added fluid?"

"Oh, dear, I don't know." Kala looked distracted. "My husband always took care of that and he . . . I'm a widow now."

The man looked at her with a mixture of pity and irritation. "Cars need more than gas in the tank and air in the tires to run properly. You do check the tires, don't you?"

Kala felt her face flush at his condescending question. "No, I—well, they haven't looked low . . . I don't think," she finished lamely.

"Never mind. But I would *strongly* suggest, if you are going to drive a car, that you learn to take care of it. There are classes that teach you how, you know."

"You mean at the college?"

"No, the vocational school offers short courses for general car maintenance from time to time. In fact, I think I saw an ad in the paper just last week. Anyway, the immediate concern is the stalling. Do you want me to check it out for you in the morning?"

"I suppose . . . yes." Kala cleared her throat. "And if it does happen to be a . . . worst case scenario? How much will it cost?"

The car doctor knitted his brows together. "For a rebuilt transmission, about a thousand. For a factory guaranteed job, about twice that amount."

Kala made a concerted effort to control her shock. But if she didn't get out of there in a hurry she was going to cry and she wasn't about to give this male chauvinist another reason to lecture her. She'd already filled out an admittance form for the patient so all she had to do was get a cab and go home.

"Call me when you know what the problem is, please. I'll be at my home number tomorrow."

"Sure will, Mrs. Vandergriff. Do you have a way home?"

She nodded. "I just need to use your phone."

"Over there." He motioned to a counter near the door. "And we'll be closing in ten minutes."

"No problem. I'll be out of here." She turned her back to make the call and when she finished, she was alone in the waiting room. A thousand dollars, at the very least. And all because she had stupidly assumed her car would take care of itself. As a Yellow cab pulled up to the entrance, she fought back the tears that were threatening to overflow. Oh, Will, why did you have to leave me? When am I ever going to learn to cope alone?

Kala paid the driver and hurried up the walk, crunching brittle dead leaves underfoot. She hadn't been able to keep up with the daily deluge from the tall oaks that surrounded the house and hiring a yardman was out of the question so she'd spend the weekend raking and bagging.

Inside, she switched on a lamp in the entrance hall and went toward the kitchen. She heated a can of soup, made a cheese sandwich—she'd found herself doing that a lot lately—and checked last week's newspapers while she ate. Her subscription expired at the end of the year and after that she would read the complimentary copy left at the Welcome Center, if she was still there.

The ad was so unobtrusive she almost missed it. A small insert announcing a class on car maintenance for adults, six evening sessions to be offered by the vocational school, beginning December 4th. The fee was fifty dollars and preregistration was requested. Kala tore out the page and carried it upstairs with her.

After a warm shower, she pulled on a flannel gown and crawled into the large four poster bed to read. On the days she worked, Kala had begun leaving the thermostat set low to conserve fuel. Even with all the insulation added when she and Will had remodeled, the cavernous rooms of the three-story house were exorbitantly expensive to heat. She had considered sleeping in the den downstairs but it reminded her too painfully of Will's last days at home and besides, there was no way to close off the open stairs. And since heat rises, I may as well follow it, she reasoned.

It felt good to relax and lose herself in the pages of her book and soon the words began to blur and she felt herself nodding. Just before she turned out the light, Kala looked again at the scrap of newsprint on the bedside table. It wasn't something she wanted to do but she really had no choice. She would call Monday and sign up if the class wasn't filled. At least with it starting that night she wouldn't have time to lose her nerve before it began.

"Why me?" Rex Ruffner scowled at his boyhood friend who sat across the desk from him.

"Because it's the end of the semester and the full-time staff is covered up with exams and recording grades, not to mention the holiday hoopla." Tom Allen tented his hands and rested his chin on them.

"Then why not wait till January?"

"Can't. The funding has to come out of this year's budget. Anyway, the community has been asking for this since September so it's long overdue."

"When I signed on for a few classes, I

didn't envision any sessions with a bunch of powder puff mechanics."

Tom's eyes widened with alarm. "Don't use those words, man, you'll get us both hanged. Doesn't the term equal opportunity mean anything to you?"

"Yeah, what's mine is yours," Rex spat out the words, "and what's yours is yours."

"We're talking about teaching a class, not settling a divorce," Tom answered mildly. "It's all set up. Mondays and Thursdays, beginning next week, will take care of six sessions before we break for the holidays. And look, Rex, I'm sorry to do this to you; I thought I had it covered but MacFarland just got married and he begged off at the last minute. I couldn't expect him to leave his new bride two nights a week, could I?"

"God forbid. And I have nothing better to do than enlighten a bunch of . . . airheads on what's under the hood of a car, have I?" Rex hunched his shoulders in resignation. "So do you have a curriculum I can use or do I have to come up with one?"

Tom's face brightened as he pulled a folder from his desk drawer. "Here's some old material, but I expect a GM exec like you will be able to come up with something better."

"Just ex." Rex took the folder and stood. "Any regs on division of time?"

Tom shook his head. "Divide the lecture

and shop time to suit yourself and the needs of the class. And Rex," he paused and looked up at the man who towered above him, "there is still a good possibility the class won't make. We've had only five sign up so far and we need six minimum. But I have to be ready in case it does. So thanks."

"Don't mention it," Rex said flatly as he turned toward the door.

Dodging students in the hallway, Rex made his way out of the building. He'd behaved like an ass in there and Tom Allen hadn't deserved it. He ought to be grateful that Tom had called him when he'd heard he was back in Paducah. And even more grateful for the offer of a job. He hated to think what his mental state would have been by now just sitting in that apartment hotel all day long. Maybe it hadn't been a good idea to come back to his hometown after all. But it had been the only thing he could think of at the time. And it was only temporary—until he could decide what to do with the rest of his life.

The wind was sharp for early December and he zipped up his jacket as he crossed the parking lot to his car. It was already a lot colder than this in Michigan; but he wasn't *in* Michigan anymore, he reminded himself bitterly. The Corvette's well-tuned engine purred as he pulled onto the highway and headed for someplace to eat. Later tonight he'd have to start thinking about the class he'd agreed to teach. The first session was only a weekend away. But maybe . . . no, he'd prepare for the worst. With his luck, it was bound to happen.

Rex glanced at the list one more time before he left his office. Damn. If only the Vandergriff woman hadn't signed up at the last minute he'd be off the hook. He put on his coat and straightened his tie, then headed down the hall. He couldn't say why he'd dressed more formally tonight unless it was the idea of standing before a group of females.

He paused for a moment in the doorway, counted six heads, and walked to the desk. "Good evening."

The quiet conversations stopped, all eyes faced the front, and he cleared his throat, suddenly self-conscious under such expectant scrutiny. "I'm Rex Ruffner and I'll be your instructor." There was a collective sigh from the group which made him even more uncomfortable. "Before we begin, I'd like to call roll and have each of you tell me why you're taking the course. Knowing what you want to get out of these sessions will help me know what and how much to present. Okay," he glanced at the list he held, "Virginia Elrod."

A blonde in the middle row raised her hand and gave him a friendly smile. "Virgie. I just got my first car and, you know, I need to learn what's under the hood."

He nodded. "Phyllis Greene." A striking redhead, obviously aided by Clairol, wiggled her fingers at him from the front row. "Hi, I'm here to find out all I can about cars. I'm," she paused and looked at him flirtatiously, "divorced and I have to take care of things myself now."

Nodding again, Rex felt himself flushing and loosened his tie as he studied the list. "Kim Irvin.

"Here." The deep voice from beside Virgie Elrod caused him to look up quickly. The name, the long hair, the earrings, the jeans, there was no way to tell anymore except . . . and a sloppy shirt hid that vital part of anatomy. "First car and my old m— my dad made me take the course."

Satisfied Kim was indeed male Rex moved on. "Shelly Norris."

The overly endowed late fortyish woman beside Phyllis Greene said smartly, "I'm a widow and I don't want anyone taking advantage of me because I'm dumb about cars."

Rex couldn't imagine anyone taking advantage of that one but he acknowledged her remark and moved on. "Lynn Quintana. Did I get that right?"

"Yeah." Part of the youthful trio in the center, she gestured toward the other two. "Same as them."

"Kala Vandergriff." The other member of the class sat alone near the door, wearing an expression that made him wonder if she was contemplating escape. It was hard to guess her age since the lighter streaks in her wheat-colored hair could be natural or otherwise.

"I want to learn what a car needs and take care of as much of it as I can."

Her voice was low and well-modulated and it matched her well. She didn't meet his eyes, though he waited a minute longer just to see if she would before he continued. "Now I'll give you just a brief summary of the parts of a car that we will cover in these sessions and then we'll take a few minutes to talk about each one. I have some handouts before we begin," he looked toward Kim but the redhead was already on her feet, reaching for them.

In the silence while Phyllis Greene distributed the handouts, Kala surreptitiously studied the instructor. She hadn't expected him to be so . . . old. His black hair had definite streaks of silver at the temples and there were traces of silver in his moustache, too. She hadn't expected him to be so . . .

handsome, either. But the combination of his classic features and tall, lean frame were almost movie star perfect. A sort of cross between Clark Gable and Tom Selleck with maybe a little Burt Reynolds thrown in for good measure. Suddenly aware that she had been so busy admiring the instructor she'd missed what he was saying, Kala sat up straighter and made a determined effort to listen. This was going to be hard enough with her undivided attention.

They were given a brief break before going into the shop and Kala, with a stop at the water fountain, followed the others to the restrooms. When she entered, Shelly was saying, "Omigod, what a gorgeous hunk. Where did *he* come from?"

"Heaven." Phyllis stood at the lavatory, repairing her already-flawless makeup.

"I think he's new this semester," Virgie volunteered. "My boyfriend takes auto mechanics here and he teaches the class part of the time. He says *Ruffner* is a good name for him."

"Yeah." Phyllis smiled slyly and Kala felt sure she was not thinking of rough the same way Virgie's boyfriend had been.

"Eyes to die for," Shelly gushed. "I've always been a sucker for blue, blue eyes."

"How long have you been a widow?" Phyllis asked pointedly, as she closed her purse.

Shelly sighed and answered as they went out the door. "Long enough, honey, long enough."

Kala stood looking after them, asking silently, How long is long enough?

"And that pretty well covers our overview." Rex straightened up and wiped his hands on the cloth he'd left lying on the bumper and closed the hood with a decisive thud. He glanced at his watch before he spoke again. "There won't be time for any questions tonight but make a note of anything you want to ask and we'll deal with it next time. So that's all, except bring old clothes for shop next week because you'll be getting dirty. See you Thursday, same place, same time."

Kim, Virgie, and Lynn made a dash for the door as Kala gathered her notes and put on her coat. Phyllis and Shelly were unabashedly staring at Rex as he removed his long tan coveralls and reached for his tweed coat.

"There is one thing I'd like to ask you before I go," Phyllis was saying in a very seductive voice as Kala left the shop.

Yeah. Like do you make house calls, handsome? Kala supplied the words silently as she walked down the hallway and out into the chilly night. She saw the three young people roar out of the parking lot as if they were heading around the Indianapolis Speedway and wondered again at the wisdom of giving wheels to anybody under twenty-one.

She tapped the accelerator and turned the switch. The engine didn't start. Damn, it had been doing fine since she'd gotten it back from the garage. This was a great time to get temperamental on her again. She waited a minute, repeated the procedure and the engine choked, caught, and she put the Buick in reverse and began backing out. When she shifted into drive, it stalled again. Double-damn. What am I going to do now? she moaned silently.

The knock on her window startled her. Rex Ruffner stood beside the car, bending down to speak to her and she lowered the window to hear what he was saying.

"Having trouble?"

"Yes, I . . . I have a stalling problem. It's happened before."

"Any idea why?"

"Well, yes," she hesitated, then went on. "The garage said it was probably the transmission. But it was running okay again until just now."

"Mind if I try to start it?" He opened the door as he spoke and Kala moved over to the passenger space without answering.

Rex slid into the seat, his knees almost

bumping the steering wheel. He made several abortive attempts to bring the engine to life, but there was only the labored effort of the switch trying unsuccessfully to make a connection. He sighed. "I'm afraid it's a lost cause. Any more and it will run your battery down. Let's get this contrary baby back in a parking space and I'll take you home."

"But how—"

"Simple. I'll push, you guide."

"But—"

"Leave it in neutral and guide me in."

He was out of the car and had his hands placed on the trunk before Kala could protest further. She glanced at his long arms, muscles tensed to lean against the car, and gave an involuntary shiver that had nothing to do with the cold coming through the open window. The car began to move slowly forward and she concentrated on turning the wheel. When she looked back again, Rex was still straining to push the heavy machine forward and he was beginning to win the battle against inertia.

"That's got it," he called. "Put it in park."

Kala hastily did as told, rolled up the glass, and gathered her things. Rex opened the door for her, puffing from his effort.

"Okay, leave the keys with me and I'll see about it in the morning."

"But I—"

"I'll be here around seven and I'll take a look at it and call you to report. Who knows, it may be running by then."

"I hope," she added fervently, as she tried to match his long gait across the parking lot.

He headed to a low slung sports car that looked expensive and opened the door for Kala. Getting behind the wheel, he looked at her and asked, "Where to?"

"Fountain Avenue. Do you know—"

"I know." He turned the ignition and the powerful machine roared into action. As he turned onto the highway, she said in an apologetic voice, "I hope this won't be out of your way."

"No problem. I live at the Ritz."

Kala knew the old hotel, elegant in its day, had been converted into small apartments, but she was surprised to know that Rex Ruffner lived there. Maybe he and his wife were still looking for a place to buy. If he had a wife. For the first time the question occurred to Kala with a sudden jolt.

They rode in silence for a few minutes, then Rex asked, "Lived in Paducah long?"

"All my life. In fact, the house I live in now belonged to my parents and I was born there. What about you?"

"Grew up in this town but I haven't lived here since college—until a few months ago."

He didn't elaborate and Kala didn't pry. The silence lengthened as they drove down Jefferson Street but there was a sense of intimacy in the warm car that made her acutely aware of Rex Ruffner's presence close beside her, his hands so steady on the wheel. He turned onto Fountain Avenue and she told him which house was hers; then he swung the car to the curb and was out and around opening her door before she could protest.

"Thank you for the ride." She turned toward the house but his longer stride brought him ahead of her before she reached the steps.

"Your house is dark. I'll see you in."

"Oh, no, that's not necessary." Did he expect her to invite him inside? She certainly had no intention of it.

He waited silently while she unlocked the door. Then she turned to him and the faint scent of his aftershave caused a catch in her voice as she spoke. "Well, thanks again. Good night."

"Why don't you turn on the light? I'd really feel better about leaving you alone then."

With a sigh of resignation, Kala crossed to the hurricane lamp beside the stairway, flooding the entrance hall with a mellow glow.

Rex, standing in the door, looked appreciatively about the room with its elegant Victorian furniture and commented, "Nice place."

"Thank you." She took a step toward the door.

"So, good night." He took a step backward, still looking at her, then as an afterthought asked, "Uh, where can I reach you tomorrow—about your car?"

"I'll be at the Welcome Center all day. That's where I work."

"But how will you get there in the morning?"

"Oh, I'll call one of my co-workers."

"Why don't I come by for you? It's not out of my way, and we can check out your car. Unless you don't go in so early?"

He'd mentioned seven and she *didn't* go in that early but she found herself saying, "Fine. I'll be ready." Watching him drive away, Kala felt the stirring of something unfamiliar and just a little frightening. And for some inexplicable reason the question flashed in her mind again. *How long is long enough?*

Rex thought about Kala Vandergriff as he drove the short distance to her house on Tuesday morning. Appearing aloof and somehow vulnerable at the same time, she was an enigma to him. Her obviously well-appointed house indicated above average income, yet she drove a six-year-old car that needed repairs she chose to delay and she had a job that he'd guess was minimum wage. She wore rings on the third finger of her left hand but appeared to live alone. And what the hell was any of that to him? She was a student in a class he was less than enthusiastic about teaching and he was doing her a favor. Period. End of subject. So why did he feel a rush of pleasure when she hurried out to meet him as he pulled to the curb?

"Good morning."

Rex glanced at Kala and returned her greeting, then concentrated on the street although traffic was minimal. He was conscious of her light perfume, the damp tendrils that escaped from hair pulled back and fastened with a gold barrette, the soft wool skirt draped enticingly over her shapely leg only inches from his hand on the gear shift. She was even prettier in the light of day than she'd been last night and because of that his tone was curt when he spoke again.

"If your car starts, I'd like to take it for a short drive."

"All right."

They rode in silence until Kala asked, "Did you play basketball in high school?"

"Yeah. And a little football, too."

"Then I should remember your name but I can't seem to."

"Cheerleader?" He asked and she nodded. "But not Kala Vandergriff then?"

"Kala West."

Rex shook his head. "Sorry, me either." After a moment he asked, "Class of '63?"

Kala drew a quick breath. "No, ah, a little before that." *Twelve years to be exact.*

They were turning into the vocational school drive and Rex was saved from finding a way out of his faux pas. Damn, who would have thought she was ahead of him in school?

A thorough attempt to start the Buick proved futile and Rex returned to his own car where Kala waited. "Let me get you to work and then I'll have a look at it," he told her as he headed for the Welcome Center. "If it is the transmission, were you thinking of a new one?"

"No, rebuilt."

There was no doubt about it. The lady was in a financial bind and he saw a solution for part of the problem. "Would you consider allowing us to rebuild it? I have a student—Tyler Smith—who is an excellent mechanic. Of course, I'd oversee the work myself." When she still looked undecided, he played his ace. "The only charge would be for parts, no labor."

"How . . . long would it take?"

"A couple of days—a week max. And I'd be happy to continue our carpool arrangement, if you like?"

"Oh, I couldn't—"

They were in front of the antebellum mansion which had been converted into an interstate rest stop. Rex reached across her to open the door and his hand accidentally brushed her knee. Her instant knee-jerk reaction made it evident there was nothing wrong with her reflexes. Their eyes met for one brief second and Rex looked away first as he mumbled, "Sorry." As she got out of the car, he spoke again. "I'll call you. And you can be thinking about what I said."

Just as Kala thanked Rex for the ride, Sandy Hodge parked beside the Corvette, looking at them with frank interest. The two women exchanged greetings and walked together toward the side door.

"Hummm, nice car. Nice-looking fella, too," Sandy remarked. "Old friend?"

"Oh, no. He's the instructor of my class," Kala said quickly. She was aware that Rex Ruffner had looked even more ruggedly handsome in his navy turtleneck sweater than he had in a sport coat and her coworker's appreciation confirmed it.

"Well," Sandy looked amused, "nice going."

"But," Kala began, stopped, took a

breath, went on, "it's not . . . my car stalled again and he, well, he's going to look at it."

"Sounds good to me." Sandy smiled broadly at Kala's discomfiture. "It's about time you got on with your life."

There it was again. That reference to time. Was there an invisible calendar that marked the stages of widowhood?

"It's beginning to look a lot like Christmas," Sandy sang softly as she lugged a heavy cardboard box up the stairs.

"And none too soon, I might add, with the candlelight tours starting tomorrow." Kala sat on the floor trying to untangle the strings of tree lights spread in front of her.

"I'll go back down and lock up and get the pot of fresh coffee I made, then we'll get busy on this."

Sandy disappeared before Kala could answer. She looked at her watch. Four-thirty. And she had class at seven. Rex had promised that her car would be ready this afternoon and she wondered why he hadn't shown up yet. Just thinking about him increased her pulse rate and she made a conscious effort to take deep breaths. Ever since she'd learned how much younger he was, Kala had told herself to stop responding to his attention like a silly ingenue. Bringing her to work the past three days he had volunteered nothing about his personal life except that he lived alone at the Ritz. She sensed that he was lonely but just because he'd been kind enough to do her a favor didn't mean he was attracted to her, for heaven's sake.

"Kala, here's someone to see you." Sandy's voice broke into her reverie as she appeared at the top of the steps, followed by Rex and an unfamiliar younger man. "I invited them to come on up and have a cup of coffee with us."

Kala felt her face grow hot when the object of her thoughts suddenly materialized but she managed to exchange a nonchalant greeting with Rex before he made the introduction. "This is Tyler Smith, the guy who is responsible for making your transmission as good as new."

"I'm so glad to meet you and have an opportunity to thank you in person," Kala said sincerely.

Tyler seemed embarrassed and Rex cut in smoothly, "We thought you might want to give it a test drive with the mechanic to make sure you're satisfied with it."

"Of course." Kala started to rise but Rex motioned her to wait.

"After we have coffee." He looked at the confusion of wires that surrounded her. "Looks like you have a mess here. Need some help separating the sets?"

Kala shrugged. "Sure."

Rex knelt and began methodically unwinding the wires. When his hand accidentally brushed hers, their eyes met in surprise at the current that arced between them, and Kala quickly looked away. "You make it seem so easy," she said softly.

"Practice," he answered.

Sandy, passing styrofoam cups of coffee, seized the opening. "Spoken like a true family man, Mister Ruffner. Husbands always get that tree trimming job, don't they?"

"Rex." He took the cup of coffee from her and set it on the floor beside him. "And I'm divorced."

"Oh, sorry," Sandy said softly, but she didn't look the least bit sorry, Kala observed out of the corner of her eye. Sandy picked up one end of tinsel roping and spoke to Tyler. "As long as we have someone young and agile here, we may as well ask for your help, too. I'll bet you could manage the ladder to fasten this to the upper tree branches better than I."

"Sure." Tyler repositioned the stepladder, took the tinsel, and gave his attention to the task.

"Our annual candlelight tours begin tomorrow and we've got to get these decorations done tonight. You guys showing up was the answer to a prayer."

"But they—," Kala started to protest and Rex interrupted.

"We'll be glad to help. Just keep the coffee hot and tell us what to do."

It was six o'clock when Kala mounted the ladder, held steady by Rex, to attach a porcelain angel on top of the decorated tree.

"Perfect." Sandy beamed at the two helpers at floor level. "And finished in record time, thanks to you two."

"Why don't we go to Burger King and celebrate a job well done?" Rex asked. "My treat."

"Sorry, I have to get home," Sandy said reluctantly. "But don't let that stop the rest of you."

Kala backed down the ladder and right into Rex who was still standing, arms bracing its sides. "Thanks, but I—" Feeling the warmth of his closeness, she momentarily lost her train of thought.

Finally backing away, he said, "You have to eat somewhere. And afterward, Tyler can accompany you on that test drive to the school and pick up his truck."

When he put it that way, Kala felt she didn't have any other choice. She began gathering their cups. "I'll get my coat."

"Fine." Rex folded the ladder as Sandy and Tyler picked up empty boxes.

Kala glanced at Sandy as she reached for the coffee pot and was rewarded with a smug smile and a wink. With an innocent look, she turned and went downstairs.

As she came out of the office a few minutes later, Rex was waiting for her in the hallway. "I sent Tyler on ahead in your car to get a table for us." He took her coat, held it. Kala nodded, putting her arms into the coat sleeves.

As they went down the steps, Rex placed a hand under her elbow, his light touch making her very much aware of the subtle tension between them. What is it about this man that makes me feel so . . . unsettled? she asked herself.

Rex helped her into his car, then as he fitted his long frame behind the wheel, she asked, "Will it be all right for me to give Tyler a small check, just to show my appreciation for his work?"

He hesitated. "It's not school policy, though some people do. But sure, Tyler can put it to good use." As they left the circular drive, he added, "He wanted to go to Auburn, get an engineering degree, but his family lives on a small farm out near Wickliffe and there just wasn't money for anything like that."

"What a shame. He's such a nice young man."

"Yeah, maybe next year. I'm working on it."

Ahead the lights of the fast food restaurant glowed in the darkness. Suddenly Kala was seized with an irrational fear. What if someone she knew saw her with Rex Ruffner? What would they think? Then she remembered they were meeting Tyler and relaxed somewhat. After all the years with Will, it was hard to realize that she was no longer married to him, free to be seen with other men. But was it too soon for that? Her husband's illness had ended their physical relationship long before it took his life, but that didn't change the fact that she had been widowed not quite a year. Not long enough, her conscience said, but her heart told her otherwise.

"First you take the dip stick," Rex removed the flexible rod from its position under the hood and wiped it clean, "and put it in the oil pan and then you slide it out and check the level of the oil."

The class crowded nearer to see the demonstration in progress. Kala watched his graceful hands and his words faded from her mind. His fingers were long, tapered, and she imagined the feel of them tracing the curves of her body.

Rex wiped the excess oil from the stick again, then held it out to her. Startled, she took a step backward.

"Here, Kala, you try it now." Gingerly she took the stick and plunged it in. "Easy. This isn't a sword fight. Now, bring it out carefully. No, don't bend it, keep it straight and clean. Okay, what do you think?"

She tried to concentrate on what Rex had told them about determining the level but her mind went blank. She would hazard a guess. "It's low."

"How low?" He looked at her intently, calling her bluff.

"A quart?"

"Not bad for a wild guess but I'd like an accurate reading." He looked at the dripping stick she held and shoved a roll of paper towels toward her. "Wipe it off, please, and somebody else can try it."

"I will," Phyllis volunteered quickly and snatched the stick from Kala, slinging drops of oil onto Rex's immaculate coveralls. "Ooooh, I'm so sorry," she said sweetly. "Here, let me just wipe that off."

Kala stepped back, feeling flustered and embarrassed at her failure to take a simple dip stick reading. Why hadn't she been paying attention? Now Rex would think *she* was dippy and she suspected he did not suffer fools gladly.

The remainder of the shop time passed without further mishap and Kala removed Will's oversized faded shirt and gathered her things. Before she left, she'd wanted to tell Rex how pleased she was with the work on her car but Phyllis Greene was still fawning over him offering to take his coveralls home to launder so she headed for the door.

Getting into her cold car, Kala clamped her chattering teeth together and gave herself a good scolding. So you've got a crush on the teacher, Kala Vandergriff. You and everyone else in class except Kim Irvin and for all you know he may, too. So what if Rex bought you supper at the Burger King? And helped you decorate a Christmas tree. Sandy had practically drafted him to do that, and the supper invitation had been for everyone involved. Get a grip on yourself, Kala. With a femme fatale like Phyllis Greene attaching herself to him like Elmer's glue, he isn't going to waste time with you.

As she drove home, Kala reminded herself of all the reasons she should put Rex Ruffner out of her mind. He was a lot younger than she was. But he doesn't look it. He already had one failed marriage. Maybe it isn't his fault. She needed to be thinking about finding a job. Why not have a little fun for a change? She didn't need any complications in her life right now. So if that little voice in her head would just stop bugging her she might be able to concentrate on dip sticks and get her money's worth out of the course she'd paid for.

"God rest ye merry gentlemen, let nothing you dismay . . ." Kala absently hummed the words as the sounds from the stringed instruments in the music room echoed throughout the Welcome Center.

"So why are *you* looking so dismayed right now?" Sandy asked as she joined Kala behind the information desk.

Kala looked up from the brochures she had been sorting. "Does it show?" She gave Sandy a wry smile. "I guess I was feeling a little depressed. Shane called last night to say they won't be coming for Christmas after all. Deborah is in her seventh month and the doctor thinks it best that she doesn't make the trip."

"But you still have your son in Kentucky, and your daughter coming from New York, don't you?"

Kala sighed, thinking of the Tennessee ham she'd bought, the barbecued pork shoulder she'd ordered, the turkey in her freezer. "Yes, but instead of the twenty we had last year, there'll be only seven, and none of the little ones will be here."

Sandy looked sympathetic. "Maybe you should call it off, take a trip or something."

"Oh, no, I couldn't." Kala forced an optimistic smile. "Well, here goes. The natives appear to be getting restless out there." She nodded toward the entrance which was crowded with people waiting for the last candlelight tour. "Jolly ho, ho, ho."

Kala's next words were spoken more loudly. "Good evening, welcome to Whitehaven's Candlelight tour. I'm . . . ," her breath caught on the words as she recognized Rex Ruffner standing at the back of the group, looking at her with expectation. Damn. What was he doing here? Wasn't it enough that she'd thought about him all day without him showing up to make her stammer through her presentation?

Rex stayed near the back of the crowd that followed Kala through the downstairs rooms, resplendent in their festive decorations. Only in the upper hallway when the authentically costumed Santa and Mrs. Claus were greeting the guests did he get close enough for her to ask. "What brings you here?"

Rex shrugged self-consciously under her scrutiny. "I just thought I'd see how our handiwork looked by candlelight. Pretty impressive, huh?"

Kala nodded, went to the nearest door, and continued her memorized speech. "If you will step this way, please." She paused, waited for the people to assemble behind the velvet ropes. "This area was used as a sitting room. The blue settee and chest of drawers were at one time in the Governor's mansion." She spoke the words smoothly while her thoughts were a jumble of confusion. He had come to take the tour, nothing more. So why was she feeling so disappointed?

Finished, she led the group downstairs, wished them happy holidays and started toward the office. Rex closed the distance between them with one giant step and touched her arm.

"Kala?"

She turned back, warily hesitant. "Yes?"

"I was wondering . . . well, if you're finished here I thought maybe you'd have dinner with me?" He grinned at her, then added, "Prime rib, not hamburger."

"Thank you but I—"

"I owe you an apology, Kala. For last night."

Perhaps it was the way the candlelight shadowed his handsome features or the way his dark eyes reflected tiny points of fire but suddenly Kala couldn't think of any reason not to say yes. Because of today's occasion Kala wore her best forest green wool, and Sandy had worn a vibrant red, so Kala felt dressed for whatever Rex had in mind.

"I thought Executive Inn, if that's okay?"

"Fine," Kala smiled, noticing for the first time that he wore a dark sports jacket and tie. "I'll get my coat."

They made small talk on the way downtown, and ordering and consuming a hearty dinner occupied their attention until the waitress had removed their plates and they were left with only refilled coffee cups.

"Will you be leaving town for Christmas?" Kala asked.

He shook his head. "Will you?"

"No, I always do Christmas for my children." Her face fell, remembering. "But there'll only be two of the four this year."

"Fifty percent isn't bad." Rex toyed with his cup. "I'm batting zero myself. Both my girls will be in Michigan with . . . their mother."

"Have you been," Kala hesitated over the word for a moment, "divorced long?"

"Since soon after I was phased out of my job with GM last year." He took a quick drink of coffee and set his cup back in the saucer with a loud clink. "And the two events were not just coincidental."

"I'm sorry," Kala said softly, fighting the urge to reach out and touch his hand that gripped the cup so tightly.

"You may as well hear the whole sordid

mess. I had an executive position, a nice home, a perfect family, the coveted American dream. Then they let me go; we had to sell the house to keep Janine in design school—she's at Chicago Art Academy—and Laura was set to enroll at Mount Holyoke last fall." His words were coming faster now. "My wife couldn't take it, the cutting back on our lifestyle, dropping our country club membership. So she split, and six months later she married my ex-boss, a widower who had been my friend since right after college when I'd gone to work for him. Naturally, since he is paying my daughters' tuition now, they'll be spending Christmas with him and my wife, getting acquainted with their new stepfamily." He gave her a stricken look, then shrugged. "So there you have it, the sad saga of Rex Ruffner who came back home to lick his wounds and figure out what to do with the rest of his sorry life."

"Grief takes time," Kala said slowly. "I guess it's the same, no matter how you lose persons or possessions you treasure. My husband was ill for a very long time and I've lost everything, too, except the house. And if I don't figure out a way to meet all the debts I'm left with, I won't be able to keep it much longer."

"And I thought I had major problems." Rex looked at her with sympathy. "At least I have an adequate pension—for a scaled-down standard of living, anyway." He was silent a moment, considering his next words. "Will your children be . . . able to help you with this . . . situation?"

"I haven't discussed it with them. They have families of their own." She lifted her chin determinedly. "I'm looking for another job and if it doesn't work out, I'll just sell the house and get an apartment."

"But you were born in that house. And it's filled with all those wonderful antiques."

"Yes, they should be worth quite a bit." She forced herself to smile. "And maybe it's time I lived someplace else instead of rattling around in that old mausoleum."

Rex didn't look convinced by her show of bravado but he averted further discussion with an unexpected suggestion. "Say, why don't we adjourn this meeting to the Silver Saddle? They have a live band tonight and I hear they do a lot of Elvis tunes."

"Oh, I—" Kala once more started to protest, then remembering the lost way Rex had looked when he'd told her about his family, she again put her reluctance aside. "Why not?"

The lounge adjacent to the motel dining room was dim and crowded and the noise level made conversation impossible as they sat down at a small table near the door. The waitress took their drink orders and Kala quickly looked around the smoke-filled room, feeling relieved when she didn't recognize anyone. The band segued into a slow song and Rex leaned forward to speak close to her ear. "Come dance this one with me?"

Taking the hand he offered, Kala followed him to the small dance floor in front of the makeshift stage. He'd never held her before and when he put his arm around her and began moving, she felt as if she'd had too many drinks instead of none at all. She missed a step and he pulled her closer so that his breath was warm against her cheek. She felt herself growing warmer and she was torn between a desire to press herself even more tightly against his lean frame or to break away and run for the nearest exit.

It's only a dance, Kala, she cautioned herself silently. Don't make a big deal out of it. Just move with the music and enjoy the moment. She closed her eyes. How long had it been since she had danced? Even this simple pleasure had been missing from her life for such a long time, ever since Will. . . . She opened her eyes just then and found herself staring into the interested faces of a couple she and her husband had known for years. She nodded a greeting to them and missed another step as Rex watched her with concern. "I—I'd like to sit down if you don't mind," she told him quietly.

As they sipped their drinks in silence, she chided herself. *It doesn't matter. I have every right to be here. I'm not doing anything wrong.*

After a moment, Rex said softly, "This is a small town. It's bound to happen, you know. But you have to get on with your life."

"I know." Kala gave him an apologetic smile. "But I just don't know when or how."

He reached for her hand. "Come on, I'll take you home."

As she followed him down the deserted stairs and to the parking lot, Kala wondered if she had offended the only man who had treated her like a woman since Will. . . . She left the thought unfinished wondering if maybe it was time she got used to that word—died—and that would make what happened final to her.

On her dark front porch, Kala unlocked the door and turned back to Rex. "Thanks for dinner and . . . everything. I enjoyed it very much."

He took her coat collar in both hands, turned it up to touch her cheeks, then slowly bent until his lips brushed her upturned mouth. It was a gentle kiss and when it ended he still held her face cradled as he said softly. "So did I. And thanks for listening."

Kala closed the door behind her and

leaned against it in the darkness. Tonight Rex had not suggested following her inside to turn on lights. Perhaps he'd been as distracted by their kiss as she had. She touched her mouth with trembling fingertips, awed by the depth of feeling such a casual goodight kiss had evoked. No, she corrected herself, there had been nothing casual about it—not for her.

Rex sat in the car forcing himself to take slow, deep breaths. Hell, he'd been so preoccupied with kissing Kala he had forgotten to see her in. Maybe it was just as well since he wasn't sure he would have wanted to leave. He hadn't meant to kiss her but it happened anyway. She'd made him forget for a minute that he didn't intend to be seriously involved with any woman ever again. He watched the dark house until the lights went on, then regretfully drove away.

Kala glanced out the window with a worried frown. It was snowing harder now, and the traffic on I-24 had slowed to a crawl. The Welcome Center had been crowded all day with travelers going home for the holidays which was only three days away. She sighed. Ever since Leslie called last week to say she was taking a Caribbean Holiday Cruise, Kala wondered if she'd made a mistake not accepting her daughter's invitation to go along. Only Trey and Caroline and their three grownup children would be coming for Christmas now but she stubbornly refused to cancel her plans for a family gathering. After all, this might be the last year . . . she left the depressing thought unfinished.

She had considered inviting Rex Ruffner to share the holiday festivities but decided it would take too much explaining and asked him to share Christmas Eve alone with her instead. It had been two weeks since the night he first took her to dinner and dancing. And because she had two season tickets to the symphony it seemed only gracious to return the favor by inviting him to the Christmas concert. He'd taken her to the town's nicest restaurant before the performance that evening but when he took her home, there had been no goodnight kiss.

In the interim between the kiss and chaste handshake, she had completed the last four sessions at the vocational school and could now change oil, spark plugs, and a flat tire with equal skill and felt right at home under the hood of her Buick jump starting the battery. So Rex was no longer her instructor and she hadn't decided exactly what his new role in her life was now or even what she wanted it to be.

"Excuse me?" Kala looked up, startled to

see the woman on the other side of the counter. "Could I get change for a dollar, please? The change machine isn't working."

"I'll take care of it." Kala took a key from under the counter and followed the woman toward the vending machines where two small children waited for her. They were wearing only sweat suits and their tennis shoes were wet with snow. As she unlocked the machine and reached for a handful of quarters, Kala glanced at the mother, noting her open sandals and a light sweater over faded jeans. "You must have come from someplace warm today."

"Florida," the woman answered, as she fed quarters into the coffee machine and took a steaming cup.

"Momma, can I have a soda?" the little boy asked.

"May I," she automatically corrected him. "How about hot chocolate, to warm you up?"

"I want chocklet, too," the smaller child, a frail blond-haired girl chimed in.

The woman hesitated, put in three more quarters. "Just one, Heather. You can share." She held the cup in front of her daughter. "Take a sip, but don't burn your tongue. Then I'll let David hold it."

She's traveling with little money, Kala told herself and felt her voice choke up as she asked, "Do you have far to go?"

"St. Louis, if the wea—"

"Oh, Momma, look at the Christmas tree." David, who had stepped into the hallway, turned back with his wide brown eyes shining.

Heather stood entranced, still staring at the tree.

"Can we go see it better, Momma?" The little boy took his mother's hand hopefully.

She glanced at the wall clock. "I don't think—"

The door behind her opened and a large patrolman and a gust of frigid air entered.

"Hi, Kala. Got any hot coffee in here?"

"Sure, Jim. The usual?" When he nodded, Kala went toward the office to fill the mug she kept for his frequent stops.

"It's a skating rink out there, and getting worse." He took off his gloves and noticed the children for the first time. "Why, hello there."

"What's the weather like north of here?" the woman asked as Kala gave the steaming mug to Jim.

"Latest report is I-55 closed from Metropolis on up."

"What about southbound?" a man asked as he followed Sandy—and a woman Kala took to be his wife—in from the hallway, the sole participants in the day's last tour.

"Already closed from Sikeston to Memphis. Ice and snow are moving across from the west in a line all the way from Iowa to Texas."

"Oh, dear, what are we going to do?" The older woman looked tearful and her husband put a reassuring arm around her.

"Don't get upset, honey. We'll just get a motel and wait it out."

"Not around here, you won't." Jim shook his head. "I'm afraid all the motels in this town have been full since early afternoon."

"But what will we—?"

Kala made an impulsive decision. "You can come home with me." She looked at the younger woman and added, "All of you." At Sandy's startled glance, she smiled reassuringly. "I have a very large old house and I live alone. I'll be happy to have you stay."

"That's very kind, but we hate to—" the man began but his wife interrupted.

"Well, only for the night. We're on our way to Houston to spend Christmas with our son and his family."

"We're going to my grandma's house," David, who hadn't missed a word, offered now. "Our daddy left us and we have to find a new place to live."

In the brief silence that followed, Jim cleared his throat. "Well, you'd better lead them on into town, Kala, before the Blandville Road gets impassable. This thing's moving fast."

"Yes, do go on," Sandy urged. "Oscar is coming for me in the four-wheeler so I'll stay here and lock up."

Kala got her coat and ushered the tourists outside. Jim and the man brushed snow from her Buick and the younger woman's station wagon which had clearly seen better days, then took care of their own vehicles.

"Y'all drive carefully now." The patrolman smiled and waved toward the group. "Let's get rolling, folks."

Kala and her small caravan followed the patrol car to the access road that paralleled the interstate. Driving was already getting hazardous and she concentrated on staying in the slushy ruts that were near to becoming ice. She glanced in the rear view mirror and realized suddenly that she had invited five strangers to come home with her and, except for the children, she didn't even know their names.

Kala unlocked the door and waited while her guests stomped snow off their shoes and assembled in the pine-scented entrance hall.

"What beautiful antiques." The older woman looked around appreciatively. "That petticoat table is one of the most unique I've seen."

"Thank you, it was my great-grandmother's." Kala walked to the mahogany hall tree whose seat held a large poinsettia. "You can leave your coats here if you like, and I'll show you to your rooms. But first, I think we should introduce ourselves. I'm Kala Vandergriff."

"And we're Preston and Frances Young of Syracuse." The older man said.

"I'm Brenda Johnson, and this is David and Heather."

"I'm five," David announced importantly.

"And I'm this many." Heather held up three fingers.

"I'm going to put you and the children in the upstairs sun room," Kala told Brenda. "My three boys used to sleep there so it has three single beds." She looked at the Youngs. "And you two can take my room, it has a double bed."

"Oh, but we don't want—"

"I'll be very comfortable in my daughter's old room." She led the way up the stairs which were draped with pine garlands. "There are two baths up here, and a half bath downstairs. I'll get fresh linens while you get your luggage and settle in and then I'll begin dinner."

"Allow me to make the beds, please," Frances insisted.

"I'll help in the kitchen," Brenda said, "as soon as I take my children to the bathroom."

After moving a few personal things to the smaller bedroom, Kala went back downstairs. Deep in thought about what to serve for dinner, she was startled by the ringing of the phone. *Now who . . . ?* "Hello?"

"Kala?" At the sound of Rex Ruffner's voice she was instantly alert. "Glad to know you made it home all right. This is a snowstorm worthy of Michigan."

"Yes, I can't ever remember seeing snow this deep here before."

"Listen, I have a favor to ask of you. I know this is presumptuous but you have that big house and . . ."

"What is it, Rex?" *Could his daughters possibly be— ?*

"Well, you remember Tyler Smith? He's gotten stuck in town and I'd keep him but I have only one bed and the sofa is not long enough for—"

"I'd be glad to have Tyler stay here, Rex." She would put him in the other upstairs room that Will had used as a study. It contained a comfortable daybed. "Where is he now?"

"Here with me. We'll have dinner in the restaurant downstairs and then he'll be along. And Kala, thanks."

"Glad to help," Kala said sincerely as she replaced the receiver. She would make spaghetti. There were plenty of vegetables for salad and homemade bread and pies in the freezer. And for breakfast she'd have country ham and biscuits with a grits and egg casserole. Then if her guests were still here at noon, she'd serve the assorted quiche she'd made ahead for the holidays. Hurrying down the basement steps to raid the freezer, Kala smiled to herself. It was beginning to feel a lot like Christmas, even if her house was filled with people she didn't know.

Tyler arrived in time to share dessert with them. After the last piece of pumpkin pie was devoured, he and Preston brought in wood and built fires in the adjoining corner fireplaces in the living and dining rooms, the heat increasing the pungent scent of their pine-decorated mantels. Brenda cleared the table and Frances loaded the dishwasher while Kala foraged in the third-floor playroom for games to entertain the two children.

"What a beautiful old organ." Frances crossed the living room for a closer inspection, then looked toward Kala who was arranging pieces of a simple puzzle on the dining table. "Do you play?"

"No, it was my mother's. I had lessons, but unfortunately was never musical."

"Play something for us, Frannie," Preston

said to his wife as he settled into a Windsor chair beside the fire.

"Yes, do," Kala added.

Frances sat down on the velvet padded stool and tentatively touched the keys. "Lovely tone." She played a hymn and then switched to Christmas carols and before long Brenda and the children were singing and the others joined in. Kala thought of Rex alone at the Ritz and wished she had invited him to be with them, but then he hadn't known about the others and would probably have insisted on different arrangements for Tyler if he had.

The songfest over, Tyler lay sprawled on the floor beside Heather, coaching her on what card to play against her big brother in a game of Old Maids. His family may not have been able to provide him with financial help but they gave him other qualities to compensate, Kala thought before she asked aloud, "How about some popcorn?" Her suggestion was met with approving nods all around. "And soda." She met David's eyes and winked.

"I'll help." Brenda followed her to the kitchen and filled glasses while Kala prepared the corn popper for the open fire. The children were enthralled with the novelty of actually watching the kernels pop, and took turns helping Tyler and Preston with the task.

"Takes me back to my boyhood," Preston said as he settled back into his chair with a generous bowl of corn. "We've gotten away from too many of the simple pleasures in life."

"Things that cost almost nothing to do," Frances added.

Heather had forsaken the refreshments to curl against her mother's knee and Brenda scooped her up and touched David's arm. "Come on, son." She looked at Kala. "It's time I put these two in bed; we've had a long day. Good night, and thanks for taking us in."

"It has been my pleasure," Kala said, then asked. "Need any help?"

"I'll get this fella." Tyler tucked David under his arm and started toward the steps. "Think I'll turn in, too."

"What sweet children," Frances said in a low voice. "I can't imagine any father leaving a family like that."

"It's past my bedtime, also." Preston yawned and patted his ample midsection. "Thank you for all the food and fellowship. Don't know when I've enjoyed myself as much."

Preston banked the fires while his wife and their hostess gathered up the dishes. Kala stayed behind to set the dining table for breakfast. She was not a morning person and anything she could do ahead of time to make feeding half a dozen people an easier task would be helpful.

Just as she turned out the kitchen light, the doorbell rang and she hurried to answer it before the noise disturbed her guests. Who on earth could be out in this storm, unless Rex— "Megan, what on earth are you do—?"

"Gram, just let me get inside, please, before I freeze my a—tail off out here."

Kala stepped aside as her granddaughter, nineteen-year-old Megan swept in, stamping snow onto the Persian rug without seeming to notice.

"Jeez, what a bummer. The interstate's closed and I had to take the lake road. Slid into a ditch and some old guy had to pull me out with a tractor."

"You came from Murray?"

"Yeah, I stayed an extra day to—anyway, it started snowing and I thought, you know, I'm outta here. No way am I gonna spend Christmas in a creepy deserted dorm." She shrugged out of her short coat, leaving a long sweater that reached almost to her knees. "I figured I could get to good ole Gram's and the rest of the guys would show up tomorrow, right?"

"I hope so, Megan. Do your parents know where you are?"

The girl tossed her long blond mane. "I thought I'd call them from here, okay?"

"It's probably just as well; they'd have been worried to death knowing you were on the road tonight." Kala shook her head despairingly. "So call them now and I'll make some hot cocoa." She cast an apprehensive look at the puddles on the carpet but decided they could wait. "And it would be a good idea to call from the kitchen because we have people sleeping upstairs."

Megan looked surprised. "But I thought you said—"

"It's not family. Some tourists who got stranded traveling are spending the night."

"Cool." Megan's stomach growled. "Do you have any food around here, Gram? I didn't take time to eat before I left."

"How about a sandwich? *After* you make that call," Kala promised and led the way to the kitchen.

As she heated milk and toasted bread, Kala breathed a grateful sigh that her impulsive eldest grandchild had made it safely through the storm. She'd put Megan in the other twin bed in her room. That should keep her out of trouble for the rest of the night at least. It was amazing how much more this girl was like her Aunt Leslie than her own father Trey. There seemed to be no accounting for how genes got jumbled from one generation to the next.

* * *

Preston Young returned to the dining room where the others still lingered over breakfast and shook his head at his wife's questioning look. "Not a chance of making it. Interstate's still closed." He sat down and reached for his coffee cup. "I called Charles and Verna. It's bad in Houston, too. We've got a real blizzard out there."

"So I guess we should try to find a . . ." Frances began but Kala quickly interrupted.

"Then you'll all stay here. My son who was coming called from Smithland this morning and they're snowed in and anyway he needs to keep an eye on his livestock with this bad weather." Kala smiled at them. "There's plenty of room and lots of food and—"

"We'll be happy to pay you, of course," Frances cut in. "Preston and I were saying last night this is nicer than any bed and breakfast inn we've ever seen and we've stayed at several. Have you ever considered converting it to one?"

Kala laughed. "Not since the children left. But we *are* zoned for it now so I suppose I could."

"Mrs. Vandergriff, if you have a shovel, I'll clean your walks," Tyler offered.

"In the garage," Kala told him, "but with the snow still falling I'm not sure it will matter."

"I'll join you," Preston added, following

Tyler. "I need to work off a few calories and we can make a path to the street at least."

"Can we play in the snow, Momma?" David asked hopefully.

Brenda shook her head. "No, David, you don't have any boots to wear."

Kala hesitated a moment as Frances rose and carried plates to the kitchen, then said in a low voice, "I just thought of something . . . our church has a supply of winter clothes, all sizes, for . . . times like when a family gets burned out. It's just in the next block and I'm on the distribution committee so I have a key to the supply room, if you . . . ?"

Brenda took a deep breath. "Sure, why not?"

"You can wear a coat and a pair of my boots over there." Kala stood up. "Come on upstairs and we'll see what we can find."

Tyler, bending to the task of lifting shovels of snow from the walk, didn't see the girl until she spoke. "May I get by?"

Jerking his head up at the sound of the sharp voice, he saw the snow angel standing close enough to touch. "Who are you?"

"I might ask you the same thing." She tossed her blond hair, "But I suppose *you're* one of Gram's refugees."

"Yeah, you could say that." Blue eyes met

brown with a level gaze and Megan looked away first.

"Oh, there you are, Megan." Kala and Brenda came down the steps behind her. "I see you've met Tyler already. And this is Brenda Johnson." Kala glanced toward Megan's bright red Mazda. "My word, child, why are you taking such a car full home for two weeks?"

"I'm not going back, Gram," Megan said matter-of-factly, then added, "and don't call me child."

"Not going back?" Kala repeated, dumb-founded.

Megan shrugged. "You got it."

"Does . . . your dad know about this?"

"Not yet." Megan looked defiant. "But there's nothing he can do to stop me any-way."

Realizing they had an audience, Kala pulled herself together. "We'll talk about this later. Right now, I have another matter to take care of."

As the two women walked away, Tyler asked softly, "You're quitting college? Why?"

"That's none of *your* business." She made a move to step around him and slipped on a patch of ice and he grabbed her and held on until she got her balance. Brushing off her long white sweater where his hands had touched her, she added over her shoulder

as she headed for her car, "School is boring."

"Only for people too stupid to learn," Tyler said heatedly as he turned his attention
back to the shovel.

It was snowing harder when they returned from the church and Kala didn't notice three people shoveling snow until she
almost collided with Rex.

"Why, hello." Her face lighted up at the
sight of him. "Did you get drafted?"

"Your phone's down so I came over to
check on you and Tyler, discovered the
house party going on, and decided to vol-
unteer."

She introduced Rex to Brenda who hurried on inside to dress her children for outdoor play, then continued, "Speaking of
volunteers, there's a roomful of Christmas
baskets for needy families at the church and
no one to deliver them. The minister is
frantic. Do you suppose . . . ?"

"My car wouldn't make these streets—I
walked over today—but Tyler could take his
truck and Preston Young has the van."

"Great. I'll call and—no, go back and tell
the minister we can help."

"Let me do it." Rex grinned. "I need a
break from all this exercise."

"Okay, I'll start lunch preparations. You're invited to stay."

"Deal," Rex called as he strode toward the church.

Brenda and two wide-eyed children met Kala at the steps.

"Wow." David reached down, grabbed a handful of snow, and slung it haphazardly.

Heather giggled and waded into the closest snow drift.

"They've never seen snow like this before." Brenda smiled, watching them.

"Neither have I," Kala said ruefully as she went inside.

When she returned to the porch a while later to announce lunch, Kala paused for a minute watching Rex playing with the two children. He had fashioned a makeshift sled from a sturdy cardboard box and David and Heather were taking turns sliding down the yard's gentle slope to the sidewalk. What a wonderful grandfather he would make, she thought suddenly.

During lunch, it was decided that Rex would accompany Preston in the van and Tyler would take his truck alone. As Kala, Frances, and Brenda started the cleanup, Kala said, "I think I'll bake the ham and turkey now. With all this snow still falling, the power could go off any time and we might be stuck with cheese and crackers for Christmas dinner."

"I'll help," Frances told her. "I make a great stuffing, if I do say so."

"I can do something," Brenda glanced at her sleepy children, then at Megan, "if someone will put these two down for a nap."

Megan stood quickly. "I thought I'd go along for the delivery." She looked at Tyler. "You can use help with the baskets, can't you?"

He nodded and went to get his coat.

Tyler was warming the sluggish engine when Megan climbed into the truck and settled herself on the tattered seat. "Now don't get any ideas," she said. "It isn't that I wanted to do this so much, I just preferred it to taking care of those little brats." She sighed dramatically. "I thought with all my bratty cousins not coming, Gram's house would be peaceful this year."

"Tell me something," Tyler looked at her grimly. "How did a nice lady like your grandmother get stuck with a *brat* like you?"

Megan opened her mouth to reply but Tyler roared away toward the church, slipping and sliding in the slush, and her angry words were left unspoken as she held on for dear life.

* * *

It was almost dark and still snowing when Megan and the men returned. While they removed their coats and warmed themselves in front of the open fires, Kala served them mugs of steaming cranberry punch, redolent with the scent of cinnamon. Brenda brought a plate of assorted cookies, basking in the praise of her culinary efforts that followed the sampling.

"Where is Frannie?" Preston asked.

"Helping David and Heather make gingerbread men," Kala told him, then looked at Rex. "We're having chili and hot tamales later on, and then we'll trim the tree. You'll stay the night, won't you? The family room sofa makes a hide-a-bed."

Rex hesitated a moment before he answered. "Thanks, but I've trimmed my quota of trees for the season so I'll be going. I'm, uh, expecting a call anyway."

His daughters, Kala concluded, and didn't press the invitation.

Refusing the offer of a ride back to his hotel, Rex put on his coat and Kala walked with him to the front door and stepped out onto the dark porch, already white again with blowing snow. "Come for pancakes and sausage in the morning," she shivered in spite of her bulky knit sweater, "about eight or anytime after."

Without premeditation, Rex opened his jacket and wrapped her close; instinctively

Kala lifted her face and his mouth covered hers. It began as a friendly goodbye kiss but took on momentum and deepened into a hungry tangling of tongues that left them both breathless when they finally pulled apart.

"Maybe," Rex whispered before he plunged into the drifts and disappeared in darkness.

Kala stood for a moment, unconsciously touching her lips, wanting to call after him. Don't go. I need you. I love you. *Love?* Stunned by the unexpected realization, she hurried inside. She had guests to feed. She would have to deal with this later.

His feet numb with cold, Rex plowed doggedly toward his destination wishing his mind had as little feeling as his limbs. He could have stayed so why had he invented an excuse not to? Because being with Kala Vandergriff—even with a houseful of people—was too tempting. She made him lose control of his resolve, like kissing her just now. He wanted her, he admitted, in a way he never intended to want anyone again, and it scared the hell out of him. She was not a woman to have a casual fling with and he wasn't sure he was willing to offer her anything more. He saw the lights of the Ritz ahead and quickened his pace. He'd make a stiff drink and deal with it later.

* * *

"Right there, honey, that's perfect," Kala said as Heather, held tightly by Tyler, set the glittering star atop the tall tree. "Now the lights, Megan." Her granddaughter had been unusually subdued since the basket delivery and Kala supposed the exposure to the harsh reality of poverty had been a shock to her.

A chorus of ooohs and aaahs followed as Megan plugged them in and soft color reflected off the gold tinsel.

"Just beautiful," Frances said. "I never see lights like those anymore."

Kala laughed. "They're antiques, too. We've had them since the children were small and every year we think next time we'll buy new ones but we don't."

"Momma," David sat cross-legged beside the tree, still putting icicles on the lowest limbs, "do you think Santa Claus will find us?"

"I don't know, David." Brenda touched the top of his head. "But you've been a good boy so I'm sure he'll try."

"But he thinks we're gonna be at Granny Barlow's house."

"Are you nearly finished?" Brenda took Heather's hand. "Time for bed now. Tomorrow there'll be deeper snow to play in."

As Brenda led the children upstairs, Kala said softly, "I wish there were toys for them, but with everything closed down shopping is impossible." She looked thoughtful. "There is a sled in the basement somewhere. It isn't new but . . ."

"If you have some paint, I could make it *look* new," Tyler offered.

"There's the dark green enamel I used for wrought-iron porch furniture last summer."

"Perfect," Preston said. "Come on, Tyler. Let's get to work on a first coat tonight."

"Gram," Megan said slowly, "remember that Chatty Cathy doll of Aunt Leslie's? She gave it to me and I left it here to play with. I'm sure it's still in the playroom somewhere."

"For Heather?" Megan nodded. "But it won't be dressed—"

"I can stitch up something by tomorrow night if you have a few scraps of material," Frances told them. "I've made lots of doll clothes for my girls."

A little later as Kala and Megan crept down from the unheated third floor with the doll and a small cradle in tow, Kala seized the opportunity to ask, "Now what about school, Meggie? Why do you want to drop out?"

Megan entered Leslie's bedroom and flopped onto one of the ruffled twin beds before answering. "I want to get on with my life, Gram. Like Aunt Leslie, you know, live someplace exciting and travel around the world and . . . have fun."

Kala sat down on the opposite bed, weighing her words carefully before she spoke. "I think I can understand that, Megan. I rushed into marriage with your grandfather when I was about your age, because I thought life was passing me by, too." She smiled and shook her head. "But there was plenty of time if I had only been able to see that. Soon I had your father to take care of, and then the other three, and I missed a lot of the carefree days that were there for the taking, before I made a commitment."

"You're not sorry you married Grandad, are you?" Megan asked with a suspicious frown.

"No, of course not," Kala assured her. "But I *am* sorry I didn't stay in school and prepare myself for a secure job first. It would be so much easier now, with your grandfather gone. And your Aunt Leslie got a degree in marketing that enabled her to find an exciting job as a buyer for Saks and live in New York City, you know." She reached for her granddaughter's hand. "You have enough time for all of it, Megan. College, a career, falling in love, marriage. Don't hurry. Enjoy every moment."

Megan stood up quickly. "I'll think about it, Gram." She picked up the cradle. "I have to take this to the basement and see if there's any paint left for it." At the door, she stopped, turned back. "Gram? That Rex Ruffner? Do you, like, date him or something?"

"We're just friends, Megan. Why do you ask?"

"Oh, just a feeling I got." She looked smug. "Quite a hunk, Gram. And I think he's got the hots for you if you know what I mean." She was out the door and halfway down the stairs before Kala recovered herself enough to muster a protest.

It was after midnight when the power went off, and Megan found and lit a candle so Tyler could finish painting the cradle. At almost two, they reluctantly ended their deep philosophical discussion, climbed the basement stairs, and opened the door to a kitchen filled with smoke. "Get down, cover your face," Tyler commanded as he grabbed her hand and pulled her through the room. "Stay down, and crawl to the front door. I'm going up after the others."

"No!" Megan coughed. "I'm going, too." She pushed his hand away.

Tyler didn't take time to argue. Feeling his way toward the lavatory in the small powder room under the stairs, he wet towels and gave one to Megan. "Come on, the back room first. You carry Heather and I'll get David. We'll try to wake the others without scaring them, then lead them out. Keep down now."

Crouching, they made their way up the dark steps. Megan hesitated at her grandmother's door but Tyler jerked her forward. "The kids first," he said in a tone that booked no resistance.

As they struggled with the children, wrapping them in blankets, Tyler called urgently to Brenda. "Wake up, we have to get outside."

"Huh? What are you—?"

"Hurry, Brenda. Get a blanket and follow us."

"What is it? What's happening?" She reached for Heather. "Give me my baby."

"Do what she says," Tyler told Megan. "Go on and wake the others. I'll get these three out."

The smoke was noticeable in the upstairs hallway now and Megan hurriedly woke her grandmother, then the Youngs, as she pulled her toward the stairs.

"The children?" Kala stopped, tried to go back.

"No, Gram!" Megan shouted. "Tyler's got them." She urged the three people down the steps and out the front door, with Tyler and the others following close behind. David and Heather were awake and crying now which only added to the confusion.

"Get them in the cab of my truck," Tyler yelled.

"We can use my car," Kala, coming fully awake, ran toward the street. "I've got keys taped under the hood."

Tyler shoved David into Megan's arms. "Take care of him," he said and ran back up the steps.

"Tyler, where are you going? Come back," Megan shouted but he was already inside the house before she finished. "Hush, David." She struggled to hold the wriggling child as she carried him toward the car. "It's okay now."

"I've got to call the . . ." the words froze on Kala's cold lips as she remembered the phones were down. With shaking hands, she started the motor. She had to keep the children—and all of them—warm. Only Megan had on shoes.

After what seemed an eternity, Tyler emerged from the house and sat down on the steps, coughing and gulping deep breaths of the frigid air. Megan ran to him, took his arm, urging him up. "Come to the car, Tyler. It's warm in the car."

"Warm enough here." He inhaled and coughed again. "Let me get my wind—then help me open—windows. Fire's out."

"Out?" Megan asked uncertainly.

"Yeah. Tree was on fire. I got it outside."

"Oh, no." Kala had come to stand quietly

behind Megan. "The lights must have shorted out." She shivered violently. "We could have died." Suddenly she had a terrible need to share this awful disaster with Rex, to feel his arms around her. But he wasn't here, by choice, so she had to take charge of things and get the house aired out and warmed again. At least the commotion had not awakened the neighbors. Perhaps it was just as well they hadn't been able to call the fire department. She became aware of the darkness and turned to Megan. "Did the fire cause a breaker—?"

"No, Gram. The power's been off since midnight."

This was even worse than she thought. They'd have to use all the fireplaces when the smoke cleared. Thankfully, Trey had insisted on bringing her a winter's supply of wood which he'd stacked in the garage, well protected from the storm. And she'd dig out the old percolator and make coffee on the Franklin stove in the family room. But first she would find warm socks and shoes for her numb feet.

Creaking sounds from the water pipes overhead alerted Kala that the people upstairs were beginning to revive after the night's excitement. Unable to sleep, she had spent the past few hours curled up in a chair beside the fire, making some important decisions. Decisions that would involve asking Leslie to co-sign a large loan for her, but she knew her successful single daughter could well afford it. Untangling herself from the afghan that covered her, she put another log on the fire and went to the kitchen to start breakfast.

"What can I do to help?" Frances asked from the doorway.

"Watch the sausage on the stove while I mix pancake batter," Kala told her as she took a large bowl from the cabinet. "I thought I'd make blueberry."

"Sounds delicious," Frances took the fork and began turning sausage patties in the heavy iron skillet, then said in a low voice. "Don't worry about the little ones not having presents, Kala. Preston and I talked it over last night and we've decided to give them all the gifts we brought along for our three small grandchildren in Houston. There's toys and clothes and most of it will be suitable, I think."

"That's very generous of you but won't your gr—"

"They get so much for Christmas, they'll never miss it," Frances said emphatically. "Besides, we can shop for more on the way down, *if* we get down."

"If is right," Preston added as he entered the kitchen. "I've just been listening to the van's radio and they're calling it the blizzard of the century. Interstates closed all across the midwest and South to the Georgia-Florida line, people stranded everywhere." He smiled at Kala as he poured a cup of coffee from the percolator. "We're very fortunate that you took us in."

"Well, it's good practice." Kala returned his smile. "I'm seriously considering the bed and breakfast idea that your wife suggested. There's the annual week-long quilt show and dogwood festival, and Paducah's antique shops and quilt museum attract hundreds of visitors all year. So I think I could make a go of it. And since you've had a lot of experience as guests, I wonder if we could talk about that after breakfast, Frances?"

"I'd love to." Frances beamed. "This place would be just fabulous. We'd recommend it to all our friends."

"Need any more help?" Brenda asked as she joined them.

"The table should be set," Kala said. "I'm starting pancakes now, but with only a stovetop skillet it will take a while."

"Sit down and enjoy your coffee before the children wake, dear." Frances poured a cup and put it on the kitchen snack bar. "Preston and I will take care of it."

After the Youngs went into the dining

room, Kala asked, "Brenda, what will you do in St. Louis?"

Brenda sank onto a cushioned stool, picked up her cup. "Look for a job. You see, Rick—he's my husband—was laid off and we got evicted, so he's gone to Oregon where one of his buddies from Nam is working. And we thought it would be best if I took the kids to my mom's house for a while, though her place is already crowded with my younger brothers and sisters."

"How would you like to stay here and work for me?" Kala asked. "You're good in the kitchen and if I get the project going that I have in mind, I'll need some help."

"Do you mean it? Right away?"

Kala nodded. "I couldn't pay much. But you'd have room and board free for you and the children."

"Just that would be enough for me," Brenda slid off the stool. "And speaking of my kids, I'd better go wake them for breakfast."

"We'll talk details later," Kala promised, wondering if she'd been premature hiring help with such nebulous plans. I have to start somewhere, she said silently and smiled to herself, feeling more optimistic about the future than she had since Will died.

* * *

Heather and David had been so disappointed by the loss of the tree that as soon as breakfast was finished, Tyler and Preston left in the truck for Kroger's with hopes of finding another. Frances, humming happily, had disappeared into her bedroom with Kala's sewing basket and several scraps of material. Brenda had taken her children upstairs for sponge baths while there was still warm water in the tank and so with Megan still asleep, Kala was once more alone in the kitchen. She put a kettle on the stove to heat water for washing dishes and made more coffee.

She hadn't really expected Rex to come for breakfast so why was she this disappointed? She'd thought a lot about *him* in the long hours before daylight, too. Rex Ruffner absolutely oozed sex appeal from the top of his well-barbered head to the toes of his polished shoes. Any woman would be attracted to him. And maybe—just maybe—he was attracted to her, but she was certain he wasn't looking for another wife. She wasn't ready to think about a husband either and when she did, a May-December marriage held no appeal for her, especially if she was the latter. So to continue seeing Rex was risky, just like starting her business would be. Maybe one risk at a time was enough.

There was a noise at the front door and she went to see if she could help with the tree. But Rex stood on the porch, hand raised to knock again. "Oh, I was about ready to throw a snowball at the window to get your attention. Am I too late for breakfast?"

Kala smiled, feeling warm in spite of the sharp wind that gusted in the open door. "Come in, you must be freezing. The others have eaten, all but Megan, but there's plenty left and a pot of fresh coffee."

Rex stopped suddenly in the entrance hall. "Do I smell—?"

"Smoke." She finished the word with him, nodded, and told him quickly all that had happened since he left.

He reached for her, gripped her shoulders. "You could have been dead now—all of you." Rex shook his head. "I should have stayed. I wanted to, but . . ." He pulled her into his arms and tilted her chin, then bent to meet her lips with his own. The kiss was hard and passionate, saying what he had been unable to verbalize.

"Gram?" They broke away from each other to look at Megan standing halfway down the stairs.

"Meggie, I—" Kala tried frantically to think of some plausible excuse for being caught in Rex Ruffner's embrace.

"Good morning, Megan," Rex reached a hand toward her as though kissing her grandmother was a mundane happening, "I just heard about the fire. And since you and I are the only late sleepers around, do you think we could persuade a certain person to serve us some of those leftover pancakes?"

Taking her cue from Rex, Kala said brightly, "Pancakes coming up," and exited toward the kitchen without meeting Megan's knowing smile.

By the time they finished eating, the incident in the hallway seemed to be forgotten and Kala's face had returned to its normal color. They had talked about the presents for the children—both recycled and new—and the plans for another tree. And a discussion of Kala's bed and breakfast idea had been enthusiastically approved.

"I think I'll take a shower, Gram, and then I'll help Heather and David make some ornaments for the new tree."

"I'll do the dishes," Rex offered and Kala nodded and looked for an apron to cover his dark wool slacks.

Moments later, Megan returned wearing a plush pink robe, her long hair pinned atop her head. "Gram, there's no water."

"But I told you the water heater is off and—"

"No, I don't mean *hot* water, I mean no water at all."

"What—?" Kala began, as Rex dried his hands and gave her shoulder a reassuring pat.

"I'll check on it."

After a look upstairs, Rex returned and asked directions to the water heater. "In the basement," Kala told him and led the way to the door on the back porch opening to the lower floor. She had forgotten there were no lights and by the time she found a flashlight and returned, Rex was already halfway down the steps.

"I think I've found the problem," he said grimly as he took the light. One sweep of its bright beam confirmed his fears as they saw the murky water covering the floor and pouring from a frozen pipe along the wall.

"Oh, no, what else can happen?" Kala wailed, then quickly went into action. "The shut-off valve is out front. We need a wrench, don't we?"

"Right, a T-handle. Where are your tools?"

Kala looked apologetic. "Over there, the workbench by the furnace."

Rex sat down and began removing his shoes and socks, then rolled up his trousers. "Nothing like a cold dip on a snowy morning to—"

"You can't wade through that ice water," Kala protested.

"Got any better ideas?" he asked with a grin, and stepped into the frigid water.

"Oweeee, if it was any colder, I could skate across," he mumbled through chattering teeth. Grabbing the toolbox, he heaved it onto the steps and took the towel Kala had run to get from the downstairs bath. Walking barefoot up the stairs, he sat for a moment warming his soles. "Can you find the valve?" he asked Kala.

"I think so."

"It may take a bit of digging because of the snow."

"I'll get the shovel while you put on your shoes," she told him.

Together they poked in the deep drifts until a sharp sound of metal on metal told them they had hit the target. "Pay dirt!" Rex dropped the shovel. "Hand me that wrench, lady, we're home free."

Kala gave him the tool and sighed with relief when he finally was able to turn the valve. At least they wouldn't be flooded. But with no power and no water they were a long way from home free.

Kala's Christmas Eve dinner was a huge success, served by candlelight in a dining room warmed by an open fire. From the freezer in the basement whose temperature equaled the frozen food, she had gathered yeast rolls, corn on the cob, and broccoli casserole to supplement the baked ham and stovetop candied yams.

"Don't know how I can make room for dessert," Preston sighed contentedly, "after that pancake breakfast and two bowls of beef stew for lunch and now this feast."

"You don't want to miss Gram's fresh coconut cake," Megan said as she served generous slices around the table.

"But save room for turkey and stuffing and cranberry salad and pecan pie tomorrow," Brenda warned him as she poured coffee.

Preston groaned and Frances shook her head. "It's a good thing it has stopped snowing and the interstate will be open by day after tomorrow or we might be too fat to fit in the van."

Kala, radiant in her holiday green dress, glanced around the crowded table with a feeling of accomplishment. In spite of foul weather, fire, and flood she had managed to provide a happy holiday for eight people so why couldn't she make a successful business of being a hostess?

Heather and David excused themselves from the table and went to admire the new tree, resplendent in its ropes of popcorn which they had spent the afternoon stringing under Megan's supervision. The extra gingerbread men from the previous day's baking also hung from several branches as

well as colorful satin bows filched from
Kala's packages designated for people who
were not going to be there.

It had been impossible to get any plumb-
ing supplies today but Rex was hopeful of
repairing the busted pipe by Tuesday. They
had taken turns during the afternoon going
to Rex's apartment to freshen up, first
Brenda and the children, the Youngs next,
then Kala and Megan, and finally Tyler and
Rex. Perhaps it was the spirit of Christmas
that had made everyone take the inconve-
nience with such good humor.

"Momma," David asked with obvious
concern, "do you think Santa Claus knows
we're here yet?"

"Don't worry, son, he'll find a good boy
like you. And your little sister, too." Preston
assured him.

"Yes," Kala agreed. "Santa checks here
every year because we always have children
visiting and he doesn't want to overlook
anyone."

Brenda stood. "Come on David, Heather.
Santa only stops when boys and girls are
asleep."

As they said good night and started upstairs, Kala hugged each child in turn, then
touched Brenda's shoulder and said softly,
"Santa *will* be here. Sleep well."

A flurry of activity began as soon as the
Johnson family was out of sight. The

Youngs made a trip to their van and returned, arms laden with packages. Tyler and Rex brought the sled and cradle from the basement while Megan carefully dressed the doll in the lace-trimmed outfit Frances had sewed.

Frances played carols and Kala served egg nog with just a dollop of Will's good Kentucky bourbon. Somehow the thought of her absent husband brought only a feeling of acceptance on this night of miracles.

"Time we senior citizens were in bed." Preston stood, and reached a hand toward his wife. He guided her to the archway between living and dining rooms, stopped. "But first, a Merry Christmas kiss."

"What—?" Frances got no further before she was soundly kissed.

Releasing her, Preston pointed to the sprig of mistletoe hanging above them. "Tyler and I sneaked this in from Kroger's. And they didn't even notice, did they?" He winked at Tyler. "So I guess you should try your luck next, eh?"

Tyler pulled Megan to the spot vacated by the Youngs. "Merry Christmas." He shyly bent to brush her lips and she flung her arms around his neck and returned the kiss eagerly.

Her face still suffused with color, Megan next embraced Rex, then her grandmother. "Gram," she said in a low voice as she walked with her toward the stairs. "I'd like to spend the rest of the holidays with you, okay? Even when the roads to Smithland are clear? Tyler's asked me to the Silver Saddle New Year's dance. And," she took a deep breath, "I've changed my mind. I won't be leaving school right now."

Kala nodded and kissed her granddaughter's cheek. "I'm so glad. Merry Christmas, Meggie."

"And one more thing, Gram," she nodded toward Rex and then looked up at the mistletoe, "go for it."

When the footsteps faded on the stairway, Kala looked at Rex and smiled. She reckoned she just might take some good advice as well as give it. "Well?"

He stepped directly under the archway. "Would you do me the honor?" He pulled her to him and his arms enveloped her with a feeling of belonging there. She lifted her face and he met her lips with a tentative kiss that deepened as he sensed her answering response.

When they finally broke apart, flushed and flustered, she whispered, "I'm glad you decided to stay the night. I've put the linens on the hide-a-bed."

"Kala," he took her face in his hands, lifted it so that she met his eyes, "I've fallen in love with you. I couldn't admit it until I realized this morning that I'd almost lost

you. Maybe it's too soon but I want us to
be together, always."

Without hesitation, Kala answered, "I
love you, too, Rex. And I think the time is
right for us—now." Suddenly May and December didn't seem so far apart and she wondered if maybe the contrast could bring out
the best in both.

"Tom Allen offered me a full-time job—a
newly married instructor is leaving next semester—and I haven't given him my answer
but I know what I want to do."

"I was planning to offer you room and
board to help out with my B&B venture."
Kala smiled at him. "I could use an on-site
plumber, especially one who is also good
with cars."

"No problem. There's always time to
moonlight," he assured her as he led her
to the family room where a single candle
burned beside the sofa bed. With slow de-
liberation, each removed the other's clothing until they were clad only in the warmth
of the Franklin stove. Then with soft kisses
and caresses, they gave themselves to each
other in the greatest gift of love.

About the Authors

Thelma Alexander, who lives in Houston, Texas, is the author of *True Texas Love,* August, 1994. She also writes contemporary romances for another publisher.

Betty Cothran lives and works in Flowery Branch, Georgia, on the shores of Lake Lanier. *Over the Moon,* her first novel, was published in June, 1994.

Stacey Dennis recently moved from Key West, Florida, to her new home in Rio Grande, New Jersey. She has written three To Love Again novels: *Full Bloom,* December, 1994, *Sealed with a Kiss,* September, 1993, and *Remember Love,* December, 1992.

Phoebe Gallant lives in New York City and Millbrook, New York. When not writing, she enjoys playing with her two Jack Russell terriers and her cat, Riffraff. She has written two To Love Again novels—*The*

Best Man, August, 1995 and *With Someone Like You,* July, 1994.

Diane E. Lock, the mother of three children, resides with her husband of 27 years in Ashland, Massachusetts. She is the author of *True Love,* the only book in the To Love Again series to be written in first person point-of-view.

Linda Swift lives in Bradenton, Florida, and in Paducah, Kentucky. She is the author of *That Special Summer* which was published in February, 1994.

Taylor—made Romance From Zebra Books

WHISPERED KISSES (3830, $4.99/5.99)
Beautiful Texas heiress Laura Leigh Webster never imagined that her biggest worry on her African safari would be the handsome Jace Elliot, her tour guide. Laura's guardian, Lord Chadwick Hamilton, warns her of Jace's dangerous past; she simply cannot resist the lure of his strong arms and the passion of his *Whispered Kisses*.

KISS OF THE NIGHT WIND (3831, $4.99/$5.99)
Carrie Sue Strover thought she was leaving trouble behind her when she deserted her brother's outlaw gang to live her life as schoolmarm Carolyn Starns. On her journey, her stagecoach was attacked and she was rescued by handsome T.J. Rogue. T.J. plots to have Carrie lead him to her brother's cohorts who murdered his family. T.J., however, soon succumbs to the beautiful runaway's charms and loving caresses.

FORTUNE'S FLAMES (3825, $4.99/$5.99)
Impatient to begin her journey back home to New Orleans, beautiful Maren James was furious when Captain Hawk delayed the voyage by searching for stowaways. Impatience gave way to uncontrollable desire once the handsome captain searched *her* cabin. He was looking for illegal passengers; what he found was wild passion with a woman he knew was unlike all those he had known before!

PASSIONS WILD AND FREE (3828, $4.99/$5.99)
After seeing her family and home destroyed by the cruel and hateful Epson gang, Randee Hollis swore revenge. She knew she found the perfect man to help her — gunslinger Marsh Logan. Not only strong and brave, Marsh had the ebony hair and light blue eyes to make Randee forget her hate and seek the love and passion that only he could give her.

Available wherever paperbacks are sold, or order direct from the Publisher. Send cover price plus 50¢ per copy for mailing and handling to Penguin USA, P.O. Box 999, c/o Dept. 17109, Bergenfield, NJ 07621. Residents of New York and Tennessee must include sales tax. DO NOT SEND CASH.